HIDDEN CHILDREN

C. S. Magnuson

you're experiencing them. You're Mercy and Jaelynn. You're Minerva and Jodie. You're feeling the energy from the cave, being submerged in the water. You see *Her*...just out of view but never gone. You keep going back. If you're a reader, like me, who hears body horror, small-town folklore-driven horror, or mountain/woods-based horror and feel immediately prepared to add to your TBR, then this one is for you. *Hidden Children* is here to lure you into the cave with its saccharine siren song...but will you get back out again? Only one way to find out..."

ARC Team Review

"In my view, the masterful writing, the vivid mountain town atmosphere, the locally inflected dialogue, and the fantastic twists, make this a flawless, immersive, though very dark and triggering, horror novel. It's the work of a hugely talented author that no horror fan can miss. I cannot recommend it enough!"

ARC Team Review

ALSO BY C. S. MAGNUSON

Dark Things Crawl Out
A Light on the Bayou

ALSO BY HORRORSMITH PUBLISHING

The Devil Came Down the Mountain
Still, Dark Places
Dark Things Crawl Out
What We Do in Secret
Lake of Secrets
Haint Blue
The Taste of Tiny Bones
A Light on the Bayou
Haunted Halls
Their Hearses
Three Garden Village
Hidden Children

HIDDEN CHILDREN

A Dark, Small-Town Horror

C. S. MAGNUSON

HORRORSMITH PUBLISHING

An Imprint of Horrorsmith Publishing

Cover Design by The Cover Collection
Editing by Lyndsey Smith, Horrorsmith Editing
Interior Illustrations by Amanda Bergloff and Lyndsey Smith
Interior Formatting by Lyndsey Smith

ISBN 978-1-967163-90-8

For Grant, Gemma, and Stellan, who keep me going always.

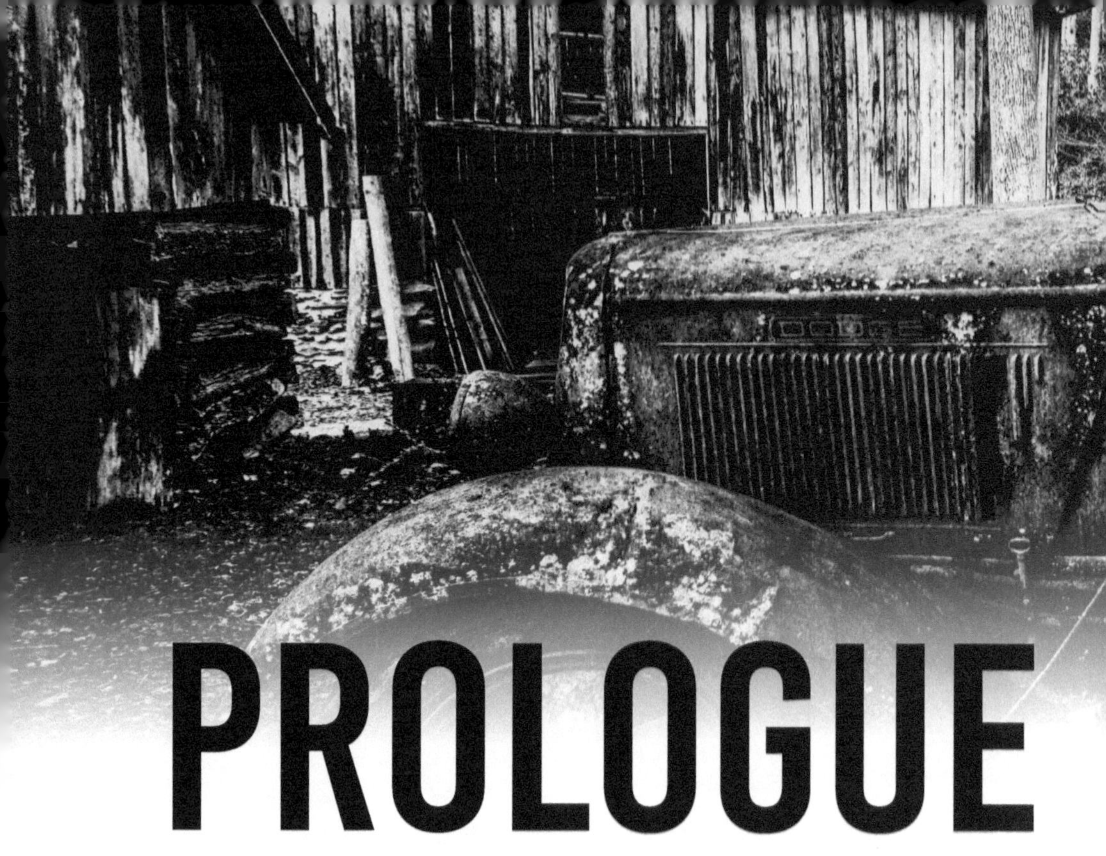
PROLOGUE

Oracle Springs, Arkansas 1977

Mercy Burden, fifteen and half-feral in appearance, shook her hair from her face and planted her feet in the dirt. She craned her head back, like a coyote about to howl, and aimed a revolver at the moon. The gun felt strange in her hand—very unlike the long shotgun her mama kept by the front door and had taught her to use when she was nine. If not for the weight, the .38 special might have been a toy.

Its owner, the man watching Mercy from the shadowy edge of the forest clearing, had worn it strapped to his calf in the jungles of Vietnam during the war that took both his left hand and a good part of his soul.

"Take your aim now, girl. Careful." The man could see Mercy easily, bathed in moonlight as she was, but all she could make out of him was the red cherry glow of his cigarette. "Be sure you don't shoot straight up but at an angle-like."

"How many times I gotta shoot the poor ol' man in the moon?" She dropped the revolver to her side.

"Only one bullet in the gun and it'll do." The bullet was new and made of the shiniest silver; Mercy's target was old and pale as milk. "All you have to do is fire at the moon for the ritual to work. No need to blast away like a brainless fool."

Mercy took aim once more and squeezed the trigger. The gun belched out a spurt of light and an explosive bark. The night air filled with the smell of black powder, and the gun's recoil jerked Mercy's thin arm back. It pained her, but she shrieked in excitement.

The man flicked his cigarette away. It went sailing into the dark in a sputtering red arc while he approached her. "Do you remember what I told you? Do you recall the story?"

"Tell me again." She allowed him to take the gun from her.

"How many times I got to recite it, Mercy Burden?"

"I like to hear you tell it, is all. Tell it to me just one more time."

Her pleading tone stirred something inside him, and he ran the back of his calloused hand—his only hand—over the rib-knobbed expanse of her chest. His knuckles were rough, but the gun he held was smooth against her young skin and still warm from firing.

"One more time, but that's it, y'hear?"

Mercy nodded in the dark and stepped closer to listen.

The man began in a low voice. "Once, a long time ago, God came knocking on the house of a woman who had twelve children."

"Was it *the* God that came knocking or just *a* god?"

"Hush now. Let me finish. The woman's children were dirty, and she'd been washing them in a tub near the stove in the center of her cabin when she heard God approach."

Mercy pictured the woman bathing her children right there in the middle of the living room, their slippery little bodies writhing and splashing in the sudsy water. *Imagine, God coming up the walk like the Fuller Brush man, only to find bath time playing out on the good rug for all to see.* She giggled at the thought, but the man's body, so near to hers, stiffened. Mercy smothered her laughter.

"Go on," she said, trying her best to sound somber.

"God came knocking. *Rap. Rap. Rap.*" The man tapped his fist against Mercy's chest, and her heart lost its own rhythm for a moment, syncing with the pace of the man's touch. "And the fear of God filled the woman, and she was sorely ashamed. The Lord Almighty stood at her door, and only half her babies were clean and worthy of presenting. So, what did she do? She hid the dirty ones—buried them in hay, tucked one or two away beneath loose floorboards. She popped one in the well out back and even stowed one in the ash bucket. Yes, ma'am. She nipped 'em out of view best she knew how, hopin' God wouldn't see their filthy nakedness."

"But he found 'em anyhow."

"Hold your horses. We ain't there yet, but yes. You can't hide nothin' from God, Mercy Burden. He and his hosts see all, and what they miss, the Devil himself gon' work out. When God come inside the house in all his thunderin' glory, he demanded to see the children, and the woman brought out the few clean ones. Well, God knew at a glance that the half of 'em weren't all there was, and the woman had to bring forth the hidden ones."

"And the Lord blessed the clean ones," Mercy recited in her best Sunday school voice. "They'd walk in the light and know his favor their whole lives. But the other'ns—the filthy ones—he cursed."

"That's right. Since their mother had seen fit to hide 'em, they'd be forever hidden. Cloaked in her shame, bound to live in shadow, locked away in rocks and streams, in caves and in trees—tied to forbidden places and the haunted corners of this here world."

"Demons and shadow-folk." All laughter was gone from her voice. Mercy nodded her understanding.

"Yep, demons and the like. They are the hidden children, the forsaken ones." The man stepped back and tucked the gun into the waistband of his jeans before pulling a cigarette from the pocket of his worn field jacket. He let the cigarette dangle loosely from his lips while he lit it.

The spark from his Zippo cast enough light for Mercy to catch a glimpse of her companion's eyes—eyes almost black in color. "Too black to bewitch," he had told her once. Those dark eyes, at odds with his ruddy complexion, were a sign of what he was: a witchmaster. Just like the golden flecks in Mercy's brown eyes were a sign of what she was and what her companion had said she would become when their rituals—like shooting a bullet of the purest silver at the moon— were complete. A real and true witch.

"Have you seen one of these hidden children?" she asked, breathless.

He took a drag of his cigarette before answering. "Nearest I got to one was during the war. In Vietnam, the locals called 'em *Ho ly Tihn*. A local witch got the idea to raise one up to fight the Viet Cong. She freed it—thought she was helping her village—but she lost control. I didn't see it myself, but I heard the stories. Thing took out friend and enemy alike, left a trail of rotting flesh through the jungle. Official report was that it must have been some kind of chemical attack—napalm or something like that. I saw it for what it was, though—the work of a demon. They're the worst kind of trouble. Regular folks'd do well to keep away. There's only a few who know how to control 'em."

"Witchmasters." Mercy's eyes gleamed. "Someone like you."

"That's right."

"Why would you want to, though? Control 'em, I mean? Wouldn't it be safer to kill 'em?"

"Knowledge, Mercy," the man said, growing impatient. "Killin' them, if you could even figure out how, is a waste. Used the right way, creatures like that can tell us things. Time doesn't mean to them what it does to us. All we can see is the exact moment we're standing in. Right here. Right now. These creatures, they see it all. Time is webbed to them with everything—the past, present, and future—connected but shooting off in different directions. They sit in the center like a big ol' spider and can look in any which way."

"So?"

"So, they know the future, Mercy. The goddamn *future*. They know all kinds of shit we don't. The trick is getting them to share what they know. They won't, or maybe can't, tell any old person directly. That's why there has to be a witch."

"Why?"

"We've been over this a thousand times, Mercy. I told you, it's a like how a radio works. There's radio waves flyin' through the air all the time, but they don't do you any good unless you got some sort of receiver to catch hold of 'em and turn 'em into something you can make sense of. That's what the witch does. The witch is the receiver—what my grandpappy called *the doorway*."

"And you think that's what I am? A receiver for the stuff these hidden children see and know?"

"You've got the gift. It's in your blood for sure."

The man knew more about Mercy's blood than she did. His kind watched her kind—studied them, even—had done so for generations in that part of the country, keeping a record of conjure folk and seers, people who had what they called in states east of there the *gris gris*. His family had a ledger, a leather-bound tome thick as any phone book—Mercy had seen it. He had showed it to her, pointing out her name and her mother's and her grandmother's, all the way back to her great-grandfather, Linus Burden. It was all part and parcel of him being a witchmaster.

There was another part too, a darker one, which no one dared put down in writing. That part involved keeping wayward witches in line. When cows gave bloody milk and folks discovered curse crowns—strange little knots of tangled feathers—in their pillows, it was a sure sign someone was throwing spells. Frightened townsfolk might then call in a witchmaster to identify the witch behind it all and to put her down if needed.

"I can already tell the future some," Mercy said, a small measure of pride creeping into her soft voice. "I get feelings—like a shiver inside my belly—and that's when I know things are gonna happen. I know'd that Hank Fenny was gonna lose his leg after he got bit by that moccasin, and I can tell a storm comin' more regular than any weatherman."

"Those're little things, Mercy." Her companion dismissed her with a wave of his hand and a puff of invisible but pungent cigarette smoke. "How'd you like to know big things—*powerful* things? The kind of things that could change the world?"

"Dunno. Maybe I like the world how it is. Got everything I want right here, don't I?" She rested her hand on the burgeoning bump underneath her shabby floral dress. "Did I tell you I dreamt there were two babies—a boy and a girl?"

"Mmm."

"I'm gonna name the girl Minerva. I heard that name once on the radio. It's pretty, ain't it? Don't know what to call the boy. We could name him after your side if you like. Maybe after your grand-pappy, Joseph."

"We ain't calling him after my granddad. Think, Mercy. How's that gonna look to folks?"

"I'd call him Jodie for short, then, and no one'd know you were his daddy until we was ready to tell."

The man had stopped listening. The glowing cherry of his cig-arette moved away through the dark until Mercy could no longer smell the smoke. The moon half hid behind a cloud bank, and she struggled to make out where her companion had gone until he opened the car door and a watery yellow light seeped from the interior onto the surrounding grass. The man reached into the back seat and pulled out a paper sack from which he produced a dark-feathered fowl. He gestured for Mercy to come and take the dead bird from him.

"It's a hen, Mercy—the blackest I could find." He shoved it into her hand. "The final step in the ritual. Bury it under a bush outside your house before dawn today, and then it's done. The pact will be complete, and you'll be a full-blown witch—the most powerful I ever seen, I reckon. Powerful enough to tempt the creature from its hiding place, at least."

The bird was cold and stiff in her hand, but its feathers ruffled softly in the night breeze and tickled Mercy's wrist. Hope flirted with the edges of her impatient heart.

"And then you'll leave your wife like you promised? I'll be your woman, and we'll be together, Pyron?" She said his name shyly. He was twice her age, and though she had already given herself to him, body and soul, the informality of first names still felt odd. "Then I'll belong to you?"

"To no other." His voice was suddenly as rough as his second-day stubble.

"You'll show me what I have to do to be the doorway and let this thing talk through me?"

"Surely as I showed you all them other things." He pulled her to him and began to lift the hem of her thin cotton dress.

CHAPTER

ONE

Tight as a drum. The phrase rattled through Tyler's head every time he looked at the girl's tan thighs and her high, rounded apple-cheeks. What was her name again? Madison? Mackenzie? It didn't matter. Tyler had taken one look at her striding across the gas station parking lot in a barely there tank top and short shorts, looking fit for a mudflap, and instantly forgot what Mitchell had said to call her. Whatever name she went by—Melissa or Marjorie, Miss Northwest Arkansas, even—she was there for him. That was all Tyler needed to know.

He opened the truck door and pulled the front seat forward so she could climb in, savoring her scent when she brushed past. Mitch had told him the girl was "so fresh outta school, you can still smell the textbooks," but Mitch was wrong. It wasn't the smell of textbooks wafting off her but the sweet tang of early morning, post-shower sweat and cloying drugstore perfume. The mosquitos were going to love her. Tyler, on the other hand, only planned to screw her.

"We got one more in the back, so you're gonna have to scootch."

The girl nodded and slid over to the farthest corner of the bench seat, where she would be catty-corner to Tyler in the front and he would be able to look at her with a slight turn of his head.

"Little help, maybe?" Althea, Mitch's girlfriend, lurched across the parking lot. She was carrying a couple of heavy plastic sacks of ice, one in each hand, with her arms raised to keep the frosty bags from hitting her bare legs. She reached a patch of mottled shade and nearly disappeared for a second in her camo shirt, green cargo shorts, and hiking boots.

Tyler pulled a wad of mucus up into his sinuses with a gagging snort and spat it onto the ground, all the while congratulating himself for leaving his own woman at home. Not that Jaelynn had needed much convincing on that front. She never went further south than Neosho.

"You got this," Tyler said to Althea, making no move to assist.

Althea reached the vehicle and tossed the ice up to Mitch, who stood in the truck bed, straddling a large cooler box. He ripped open the bags and let the contents shower like hail stones over an army of beer bottles, then he replaced the cooler lid and hopped down. Mitch gave the quad trailer's hitch a reassuring kick and yanked the straps on the dirt bike once before climbing in behind the steering wheel. The truck peeled out of the parking lot in a storm of pea gravel and dust.

Tyler twisted around in his seat to grin at the girl. She returned the smile, revealing—dear Lord—dimples and Granny Smith-green eyes.

"Thanks for lettin' me tag along."

"You get out into the woods often?" Tyler asked, shouting to make himself heard over the road noise coming in through the four open windows.

"It gets old 'round here when you're local," the girl yelled back. "You seen one tree and a couple of show-caves crammed with tourists, and you seen enough. You guys come down outta Kansas City or St. Louis? Your profile didn't say where you're from."

"Bolivar," Mitchell replied.

"Oh, sure." The girl's pretty smile sagged. "That ain't so far, then." She stared out the window, fiddling with a heart-shaped charm hanging on a slim metal chain around her neck. It had begun to turn green where her fingers played over the gold finish. She crossed her long legs, bumping her shin against the center console inches from where Tyler's elbow rested.

Tight as a drum, he thought, glancing down at the bronzed swell of her calf.

Mitchell nudged him.

In the back seat, directly behind Tyler, Althea leaned to the side, trying to make out Mitch's face. Wrinkles high on his cheekbones—faint crow's feet—he was grinning behind his wraparound shades, enjoying his friend's potential conquest—enjoying it a mite too much maybe. They had left the stench of Missouri's turkey farms and industrial hog lots behind an hour or so earlier, and the air was fresh and clean, albeit thin with a sour, metallic taste.

"Jaelynn have to work this weekend?" Althea asked Tyler.

"Something like that," Tyler mumbled, staring hard at the road ahead. "Camping's not her thing, and she hates riding bitch on the quad."

"Didn't she grow up around here, though? Like, exactly 'round here?" Althea stretched her leg to the base of Tyler's seat and pressed her boot against his seatbelt.

The strap pulled tighter against his neck, and Tyler shifted uncomfortably.

"Seems weird she wouldn't want to swing on by for a visit if she still has people down this way," she continued.

"You get a job I don't know about, Thea? You with fuckin' CNN now? Put away the goddamn waterboard!" Mitchell glared at her in the rearview mirror. "I think we need some tunes to get this party started."

The truck swerved toward the center of the road while Mitch examined his phone, searching his playlists for the right song and finding it seconds before the last tire exited their lane. He righted the car and thumped the steering wheel with the meaty part of his palm when a guitar began to wail and Axl Rose welcomed them all to the jungle, promising them fun and games.

"We're in the jungle now, baby," Mitch crowed, taking a hard right off the cracked black asphalt of the main highway and onto a narrow dirt road which dropped into the dense foliage of the mountainside. "Back to nature. Howl with me," he instructed Tyler before letting out a long, ululating cry.

"Dumb ass." Tyler shook his head. "This song is older than your mother."

The young girl laughed and undid her ponytail, freeing her long blond hair. It whipped around her face and caught in her heavily mascaraed eyelashes. Even Althea pulled her foot back from under Tyler's seat and relaxed.

A bead of condensation slid down the slender neck of Tyler's beer bottle. He caught it on his tongue and licked it off, then finished the beer in one final swig, flinging the bottle away. It hit the trunk of a tree and shattered with a sharp crash. Across from him, her narrow rear perched on the seat of Tyler's ATV, the girl grinned and tossed her own bottle in the same direction. It fell short and landed with a soft thud in a clump of moss.

"You wanna look for the others now?" she asked.

"Naw." Tyler shook his head. His brain rotated a dizzy half-turn in his skull.

They had lost Mitch halfway along the trail, when he shot upward on a path too narrow for the quad. Tyler had been forced to head down, following switchback after switchback until he and his companion reached the very bottom of the gorge. Now they were alone in the hollow of the mountain, a deep cradle sunk in the center of the hill.

Jutting stone cliffs rose above them on four sides, and all around, emerald foliage heaved in the afternoon heat. Plant-life burgeoned from the forest floor, like green lava streaming out of a volcanic cauldron, and surged upward to form a canopy, trapping the warmth and turning the basin into a stifling, tropical pot. The sultry atmosphere made Tyler's head spin and set his ears ringing. There was tangible electricity in the air, and not all of it was emanating off Madison...McKenzie...whoever-she-was sitting across from him.

"Hear that?" he asked, leaning forward suddenly and throwing his body off-balance. Tyler caught himself with an elbow on his knee.

"Hear what? The bike? It's your friend's, I think. It was up there across from us maybe fifteen minutes ago. That way." The girl pointed over Tyler's shoulder to a high tree-lined ridge, then frowned, unsure. "Maybe it's over there?" She pointed at a second ridge which ran perpendicular to the first.

A hawk screamed, its shrill cry ricocheting at them from multiple directions.

"I can't tell." Defeat crept into the girl's voice. "Everything gets mixed up out here, with the cliffs and all. That's why I don't come here. I hate these woods. Something about 'em feels like they want to swallow you up."

"I didn't mean the bike," Tyler snapped. "I meant the buzzing." A cloud of irritation settled over him, making him forget the girl's apple-green eyes and the smell of her smooth skin.

The girl shook her head. "You sure the buzz ain't from that six pack you just sucked down?"

Tyler held up his hand. "Shut up and listen."

High-pitched enough to set it apart from the quad's motor, a whirring hum had followed him and the girl ever since they split off from Mitchell and Althea, but Tyler couldn't determine its source. There were no power lines nearby. No cell towers. The place was a wasteland.

The closest town was a two-bit hole at the top of the mountain called Oracle Springs, where they had stopped for ice and beer and to pick up the girl. It was the town where Tyler's girlfriend, Jaelynn, had been born, and she had told Tyler a few stories about growing up all the way out there in Nothingsville, AR. No streetlamps. No radio signal. TV reception so bad you couldn't even get a single network station without connecting to cable. It sounded like hell on earth to Tyler.

"C'mon." Tyler staggered to his feet and gestured for the girl to follow. They left the quad behind and, for thirty minutes—maybe more—tramped through the forest.

Years of fallen, decaying leaves slid over one another like dull satin under the pair's feet and gave off the stodgy, throat-tickling scent of autumn, even though spring wasn't half burned through yet. The couple ducked and dodged low-hanging tree limbs and thick spiderwebs and swatted at clouds of insects congregating in the shade. They plodded through marshy creek beds.

Tyler took the lead, determined to find the source of the noise, and the confused girl scurried behind to keep up. They stopped only when they ran smack into a sheer wall of rock on the far edge of a deep pond.

"End of the road, seems like." The girl giggled nervously. "Should we head back?"

Tyler craned his head up to where the towering rock met the sky and vines snaked down over the top, forming an uneven fringe. Pale, mint-colored moss clung to the underside of minor outcroppings, but the cliff was mostly a smooth plane of honed, gray granite which reflected darkly in the water before it. A narrow crevice ran down the center of the vertical rock exposure, widening at the bottom to form a slender, pyramid-shaped doorway into the mountain. It looked like the opening to an ancient temple hidden in a jungle.

"Let's check it out." Tyler grabbed the girl's hand and pulled her toward the opening.

"I don't know." She hung back, resisting Tyler's dogged attempts to drag her forward. "Some caves around here are no good. Folks go missing in 'em, they say."

"*Who* says?"

"Old-timers."

"Do I look like an old-timer to you?" Tyler scowled, and the girl wilted under the weight of his glare. "Don't be stupid. You got me with you, so there's nothing to worry about." He held out his hand, and the girl took it, finally allowing him to lead her through the angular opening.

A robust thermal weight struck the pair when they stepped inside. Before them was an undulating, ribbon-like path of slippery, sweating rock leading into a deep, tunnel-like cave. A sheet of light cut through the gloom from a gash in the rock overhead, illuminating the tapered corridor as far as the eye could see, which wasn't that far at all. The stone walls of the cave had formed in waves and hair pin turns and, every five to ten feet, turned back on themselves, rendering a full assessment of the cave's depth impossible.

"How deep into the hill d'you think it goes?" the girl asked in a whisper.

"Don't know," Tyler said.

"What if we get lost?"

"Nowhere to get lost. It's a single path. C'mon."

Tyler pulled her deeper into the conch-like cave, tugging her along when her pace slackened. Humidity formed clouds of fat water molecules which caught the light streaming down onto the couple's shoulders. Despite all the moisture, however, little to no moss or algae grew on the walls. They glistened, slick and barren, fading from deep charcoal to the color of warm sand and then to that of a ripe peach as the trail wound on.

"We been walkin' for ages," the girl said after a while. Her small voice still managed to echo in the hard space. "Let's head back."

"Not yet. I think we're close to it."

"Close to *what*?"

"The goddamn buzz! It's coming from down here."

Down here. They were headed down, descending while they made their way toward whatever lay ahead.

At the entrance of the cave, the path had been level and, for the first few hundred meters, possessed the merest intimation of grade. But as it progressed, the path grew steeper, and each step had carried the pair lower. The roof of the cave yawned away, and the sunlight receded. No longer cascading down in a brilliant sheet, it trickled over them in unreliable glints and flickering patches until it finally abandoned them altogether.

Undeterred by the darkness, Tyler unhooked a small flashlight from his belt.

"I want to head back," the girl said. "I wanna go *now*."

Tyler's light moved around the cavern. The warm sunset oranges and terra cotta tones of the stone had deepened further and were now rich and rusty, the color of raw flesh. In the wavering light, they throbbed like something living. The space had the air of something soft and yielding. Like an organ. Like a beating heart or a womb.

The flashlight died.

It went out without so much as a blink. Tyler and the girl were alone in the dark. Their ragged breath beat against the walls—those deep red, living walls, invisible now in the gloom—and the girl tugged at his hand.

"Let's go. We can find our way back, even without the light. Sure we could." Her voice was hoarse and tremulous. "Like you said, it's one path. Only one way back."

"No." Tyler's reply was a Neanderthal's grunt made less abrupt by a slight echo. He shook off the girl's hand and took a step further down the path, remarkably sure of himself in the darkness.

One step, then another, and a light appeared around a bend. Tyler moved toward the glow, and the girl followed. The narrow passage took one final twist before ending in a wide-open inner chamber. Tyler stumbled out of the dark and was momentarily blinded.

High above the floor, in the stone roof of the cave, was a skylight—a grass-rimmed oculus large enough to light the chamber and set the ruddy walls aglow. It illuminated a pool of Aegean blue at the far end of the stone rotunda. A slope, like the funnel of a spiral wishing well, led to a deep central point in the water which peered up at them like a black pupil within a bright blue iris.

Tyler approached the pool and leaned over to assess its depth. Close up, the water was so clear that the trough appeared to be filled with nothing at all. Staring into it gave him vertigo.

"What's wrong with those fish?" The girl leaned over Tyler's shoulder, breathing into his ear, her smell no longer sweet to his senses. A school of silvery white minnows swam toward them, rushing this way and that in blind unison. Where they should have had eyes, there was nothing but pale scales, smooth and undisturbed from nose to gill. "Where're their eyeballs at?"

"Animals living in pure darkness don't need eyes," Tyler answered. If the girl had known him better, she might have wondered at the unnatural evenness of his voice.

"But it ain't dark in here." She pointed to the hole in the ceiling while still watching the fish in horrified fascination.

"No, it ain't," Tyler agreed, looking around the cave.

A few feet away, on the lip of a stone outcropping, a white salamander perched, motionless. It, too, lacked eyes. A membrane of thin bluish skin stretched taut over the round organs, which twitched and quivered underneath.

Tight as a drum.

Someone—or some*thing*—repeated Tyler's words to him. The buzzing noise grew louder, and a ripple formed on the surface of the water. A small V-like wake which matched the shape of the cave's entrance grew wider as it cut through the water. It raced toward Tyler and the girl.

The buzzing in Tyler's head stopped, and for a moment, he thought he heard someone laugh. Tyler laughed too, and he kept on laughing even when the girl, Madison...or McKenzie, or whatever... began to scream.

CHAPTER

TWO

Out in the wasted, chicken-scratch no-man's land between two boxy duplexes, an ancient dog basked in the sun. She lay on the hard earth, absorbing its heat like a lizard or some other cold-blooded thing. Her wooly coat, once tan and black, had long since faded to straw and ash, and her ears were tattered from fly-strike. All in all, she appeared molded from the same matter as her worn and weathered surroundings.

A young woman stepped out of one of the duplexes onto the back porch. A hot breeze swept between the houses and wrapped around her, making her dark hair shiver. It blew her gauzy skirt out behind her like a billowing sail and wafted her scent toward the dog, who inhaled and knew the human was there without opening her eyes.

Jaelynn clicked her tongue to catch the dog's attention. The roar of a semi-truck thundering down a lonely Missouri highway alongside the housing complex threatened to drown her out, but the shepherd's maimed ears pricked uncannily and swiveled a few degrees toward the sound.

"What good are you, Miss Mouse, if you don't keep track of your flock?" Jaelynn's voice was soft. and the dog, associating the tone with belly rubs and gentle pats, yawned. "You're s'posed to watch him for me, and now he's nowhere in sight."

The canine, detecting a hint of reproach, raised her heavy head off her paws and pointed her muzzle indifferently into the distance. There, an abandoned propane tank as big as a midsize sedan sat rusting, flaking apart, in a patch of scrabbly weeds that had once been a lawn. The same feather-light wind that ruffled the woman's skirt stirred the long grasses, making them whisper when they brushed the sides of the metal cannister. Dried dock and bull thistle danced in soft waves under the afternoon sun, but the ribby dog sat still and as unreadable as a sphinx.

"Not gonna tell me where he's gone then, huh? Stubborn old thing." Jaelynn scanned the edges of the complex one more time, then closed her eyes and tilted her chin toward the heavens. Images formed behind her eyelids: narrow strips of hazy blue hyaline and clouds, as well as her own slender outline, reddish black against the sky. When she smelled musty earth and moss, she looked down between the deck boards beneath her feet. "I know you're under there, little man. Come on out."

There was a scuffling sound, and a small, dark head emerged from beneath the edge of the porch. A slender boy waggled side to side on his back in the tight space until he had rocked his body clear of the decking. Jaelynn hauled her son to his feet and administered several light clouts to his back and sides, which served the dual purpose of admonishing the child and brushing the dirt from his clothes.

"You'll get snake-bit under there, Benji," the young mother said with a frown. Although she was barely into her twenties and still more girl than woman, there was a deep groove between Jaelynn's eyebrows and a papery slackness around her tired mouth.

"Didn't see no snakes," said Benji.

"Not this time, but there's other creepy-crawlies under there that are near as bad."

Jaelynn shuffled her son into the duplex, pausing to see if the dog had a mind to follow. Miss Mouse heaved herself to her feet and slowly brought up the rear with an arthritic swagger. Once indoors, the old beast turned a circle or two before lying down on the kitchen floor beneath a flimsy dinette table.

Hidden Children

Benji peered into the living room, where a large pile of camping and fishing gear had appeared. "Ty's back?

"Yep. Mitchell brought him back not twenty minutes ago. He's sleeping, though, so you missed your chance to say hello. Lord, you're a mess." The boy's shirt had dirt and grass stains up the back, and he smelled like moss and sweat. Jaelynn turned the child around to face her and realized he was still wearing his pajamas. "I guess you were gonna have to put on regular clothes anyhow."

A plastic basket with a mountain of laundry sat atop the kitchen table, ready to collapse in an avalanche of unfolded T-shirts, towels, and underthings. Jaelynn didn't have to dig too far before pulling out a pair of knit shorts and a faded Ninja Turtles T-shirt.

"These work for you?"

"I didn't want to say hi to Ty," Benji said. There was defiance in his golden-brown eyes, and he was giving off a wave of something fiery. "He didn't take me with, so I hid on porpoise."

"Arms up. Shirt off. And you hid on *purpose*, not on *porpoise*." Jaelynn bugged her eyes at the boy and wagged her head. "Ty didn't take me with him neither, but you don't see me gettin' my panties in a wad."

"Why didn't he take us?"

"Wasn't that kind of trip."

"What kind of trip was it?"

The crease between Jaelynn's brows deepened. What kind of trip, indeed? Tyler had called it "guy time"—*just him and Mitchell and the hog suckers*. But Jaelynn had noticed Mitchel's fiancé, Althea, in the back seat of the truck when Mitch had come to collect Tyler a few days back. It had been an awkward party of three that headed out that afternoon but a party of three which was guaranteed to have become four at some point between home and the campsite in the mountains.

She swallowed a sigh before it could escape and reminded herself that having a boyfriend who cheated didn't mean the end of the world. There were worse things men could do, and she had seen them all done at one time or another. Besides, even if Ty *had* asked her to come along, there was no way she would have said yes. She would rather boil her head than return to the hills she had once called home.

That could have been Ty's game all along, though Jaelynn wasn't sure she gave him that much credit. In the end, it didn't matter. The important thing was, he had not cut and run and stuck her with the entire rent and whatever other bills he had run up in her name.

Benji's eyes played over his mother's face like searchlights. A shadow had fallen over his own pale countenance, and it lent a grimness and a gravity to his small features, making made him appear fifty, not five. Jaelynn caught the worried gleam in his eye and smiled broadly for his benefit.

"It's nothing personal, little man. Guys like Ty gotta get out on their own every now and then, burn off some steam. He's back now, though. That's what matters. Stick 'em up!"

Benji raised his arms, and Jaelynn pulled his pajama top over his head, catching his hands before he could lower them and giving his armpits and torso a onceover for ticks.

"You're clear. No bloodsuckers today."

Benji dropped his arms to his sides. "What if there were ticks that, when they bit you, gave you superpowers?"

Jaelynn rocked back on her haunches and leveled a serious gaze at her son. "What kind of powers are we talkin' about?"

"The kind you use to get prevenge on bad guys."

"To get *revenge* on bad guys," Jaelynn corrected. "No such luck, bud. All we got are plain-o, boring ticks. They'll suck your blood and make you sick, so stay out from under the porch, 'kay?" She handed him his shorts and T-shirt. "Come on now. Get your clothes on. I need to get you 'cross the way to Auntie Donna's before too long."

"Why can't Ty watch me?" Benji slid the T-shirt over his arms and head.

"'Cause he's restin' up. He had a long weekend, and he's tired."

Benji pursed his lips and closed his thoughtful eyes a moment. "He come back mad?"

"Seemed like he was in an okay enough mood to me. Just tired." Tired and a tad feverish. Jaelynn had felt the heat coming off his body when she helped him bring the camping gear inside. He had caught a cold or something like it. *Who* he had caught it from was the million-dollar question.

"Can I take my crayons and paper to Auntie Donna's?"

"Sure. Take your new markers too, but don't get any on Auntie Donna's couch."

"How come we call her *auntie* if she ain't family?"

"Just a thing folks do."

"Do I have an aunt? A real one?"

"You have a lot of questions." Jaelynn watched Benji warily while he wobbled first on one leg and then the other to climb into his shorts. She could tell him *no*, that he hadn't any family, but there was little point in lying to Benji—*never* any point in lying to him. He would read the fib in her eyes before the words left her mouth, so she came clean. "You've got a grandpa named Jodie and a great-aunt called Min, but I haven't seen them since you were born."

"What are they like?"

Jaelynn shrugged. "Regular folks."

"But what do they look like?"

"Kinda like me and you. Papaw Jodie is my daddy, and Aunt Min is his sister. They're twins."

"Where are they?"

"They live back where I grew up, where Ty just come from, or at least I *think* they do. I don't know anymore. They mighta moved."

"Does Aunt Min smell like cat piss like Auntie Donna?"

"Benjamin Joseph Burden, why would you say that?" Jaelynn didn't have to ask. Behind Benji's cruel words lurked Tyler and his smart mouth. "Don't talk like that, baby. Be my sweet boy. I need you on your best behavior over at Auntie Donna's tonight, or else she won't watch you no more."

"And then you can't work?"

Jaelynn nodded. "And then I can't work, and I need to work."

"You hate it." He looked up at her with a scowl and lips pursed, like a disapproving schoolteacher.

"Sometimes. Sometimes it makes me feel—" She struggled to think how best to explain it to the child, how to tell him what she did. Palm readings in a cheesy strip mall storefront, right between a dollar store and a bail bonds office. Most days, it felt like a harmless party trick, but she had the uncanny habit of hitting the nail on the head, and it made her nervous. She was playing with people's lives, and even the accuracy of her predictions didn't stop her from feeling like a fraud or a con. "Sometimes, I just feel like—"

"A lyin' whore."

It took Jaelynn a moment to realize the words had come from Benji's mouth. If he hadn't been looking at her so expectantly, like he was waiting for a response, she might never have believed it and swung her hand out to slap him.

Her palm struck the boy's soft cheek and made a jarring crack in the quiet apartment, loud enough that Miss Mouse picked up her sleepy head and emitted a throaty rumble of disapproval. Jaelynn stared, aghast, as Benji's face crumpled and his eyes teared up.

"Oh, baby!" Jaelynn gathered her son up into a tight hug. "I'm sorry. I'm so sorry, Benji. I didn't mean it."

A raspberry welt was spreading over his cheek, and his lips were clamped shut in a tight line across his pale face. The slap mark stood out like a stain, but the child appeared more afraid than pained—afraid something else might escape his lips if he failed to keep them closed.

This time, it had not been Tyler's voice in the boy's mouth. It was Jaelynn's own. These were her words tearing back at her, like tiny daggers or rampaging bees. That exact insult and worse played over in her mind—a continuous internal rumble of past accusations and epithets which sounded like thunder before a storm. And there *had* been a storm, a hell of a big one that had driven her from her home and made her vow she would never go back, not even if the devil showed up and tried to drag her there.

"You're okay, baby boy. You're okay. *We're* okay." She snuffled wetly and tried to smile. "I know what. How'd you like to watch your cartoons? That sound good? You can have some cereal and watch your show while I take a shower."

Benji, still tight-lipped, nodded, and Jaelynn hauled herself to her feet, rising slowly under the weight of her guilt.

She retrieved a box of Cap'n Crunch from the pantry cupboard, switched on the TV, and selected one of Benji's favorite shows. "Keep the volume down so you don't wake Ty. And try to keep Ms. Mouse away from the door. I don't want her barking at him like before. Don't know what got into her, but if Ty's in a mood, like you say, we don't need the dog makin' it worse."

The boy nodded, but his eyes were already pulling magnetically to the screen. Jaelynn slipped quietly out of the room.

Hidden Children

Benji waited until the shower began running in the next room before he climbed onto the sofa and began to bounce. His cereal rattled while it rose and fell inside the package, and he reached his small, grubby hand into the box, pulling out a fistful of the tiny barrel-shaped biscuits and shoving them eagerly into his mouth. The hard bits tore at his gums and fell from his lips, but he munched and jumped higher. Between bites, he began to mumble, keeping his voice low so it wouldn't reach his mother in the other room, so she wouldn't hear the words that popped out of his mouth, along with bits of cereal.

"Dumb bitch."

Benji's head was full of dark, grown-up words. These ugly morsels of loathing and hate floated around in other people's minds, and he collected them, not intentionally, but like a staticky blanket picks up socks as it comes out of the dryer. When people touched him or got too close, the words leapt out of them and into him. He tried to keep his distance so he wouldn't collect too many and fill up with all the nastiness with which most people were brimming, but his mother was a different story.

Her words hurt her, and so he took as many of them from her as he could. Although, it had occurred to him on more than one occasion that they were endless. No matter how many he took, she still had more, and when he had taken too many, they found ways of escaping. Now, jumping up and down on the couch, with his mother in the other room, he spit them out like men spit out black-brown juice from their chewing tobacco.

"Fuckin' tramp." A spring inside the sofa punctuated his landing with a metal twang. "Slut." *Boing.* "Dirty cunt." *Sproing.* He was growing lighter now, ridding himself of the vilest of these words. "Dumbass hick." He jumped again, higher than before.

The altitude surprised him, and he felt a hot moment of alarm when he rose, the sofa and coffee table now too far below for comfort. Panic surged. His arms jerked and spasmed, and for one frightening yet glorious moment, he found himself aloft in a sugary-sweet cloud of cereal with the feeling that he was flying. Then he came crashing down onto the arm of the sofa, bits of Cap'n Crunch raining over him while he gasped for air. The remaining cereal spilled out of the box onto the floor.

Miss Mouse hauled herself to her feet quicker than seemed possible, considering her age, and trotted over to the mess. She began hoovering it up, flicking the cereal bits into her mouth with an agile tongue, hardly bothering to chew. Benji caught his breath and leaned over the arm of the sofa to survey the damage and give the dog a pat, but he drew his hand back as though it had been burned.

Near Miss Mouse's feet, where the cereal had landed, lay a human body.

Benji blinked, hoping it would disappear, but the corpse's blue-white skin, pale like paper, stood out blindingly against the dingy carpet. Its hair was dark and long and fell in ropey, wet squiggles around its shoulders. Though it lay chest down on the floor, its head was turned toward Benji. Where there should have been a face, there was nothing.

Nothing but a red, pulpy ruin.

Blood soaked the carpet around the body, turning the nylon fibers black and spreading outward to form an oblong pool. There was something strange about the blood, the way it moved and how it seemed to glisten and shimmer.

Curiosity forced Benji to lean forward for a closer look, and there, writhing within the plasma, were thousands of small black worms. The stain spreading out over the carpet was not seeping, but crawling. The creatures worked their way in steady streams away from the body—away from the void that had once been a face.

In the midst of it all, Miss Mouse stood, unbothered. She hunted through the mess for cereal bits, unaware of the tiny creatures wriggling beneath her wide, padded paws. Benji, however, scuttled backward, as far from the waves of crawling things as he could get. On the far side of the couch, he tucked his knees to his chest and closed his eyes. His breath came in uncontrolled, hiccoughing gulps.

It was just a picture, like something from a movie.

It's not real. It's not real. Not. Real, he chanted silently, holding his breath and waiting for the urge to vomit to pass.

Once his heart seemed to start beating again, he hazarded a second peek over the sofa arm and found the floor bare and clean. The body was gone, as were the worms. There was nothing but the box Benji had dropped, along with a scattering of linty cereal. And soon that was gone too, devoured by Miss Mouse.

CHAPTER

THREE

J odie Burden was already halfway down the hall to the kitchen when his phone rang on the counter next to the stove. It startled him out of some sort of fog. Last thing he remembered, he had been sitting in his reclining chair, mindlessly picking at the frayed armrest, a full can of Coors and a bowl of chips on the table next to him. He had been waiting for the Cardinals to take the field, but something had propelled him out of the chair and down the corridor even before the phone began to chime.

The dry, nylon carpet of his double-wide trailer was scratchy underfoot, but indecision rooted Jodie to the spot. A cheer went up from the crowd on the television in the living room while a few feet away, the phone rang insistently. Whoever was trying to reach him wasn't going away, so Jodie trundled down to the kitchen to answer the call.

"Yeah?" he barked into the receiver.

"Daddy?"

The word seemed to hang in the air, suspended in the swirl of whatever digital magic had carried it there. A wintery chill blasted through Jodie's body, numbing his hands and feet and driving a spear of frost deep into his core. If someone had plunged him headlong into a tub of ice water, he couldn't have felt more shocked.

"Daddy? Are you there?"

"Jaelynn? Goddamn, baby girl, is that really you?" Jodie tried not to drop the phone. "I can't believe it. Goddamn," he said again. "How'd you get this number? No, forget that—it's not important. I'm just glad you called—real glad, baby girl. You had me worried sick all these years. Your aunt Min too. How you been, baby? You been good? Everything all right? How's little Benjamin? You still callin' him Benji?"

Too many questions. He was asking too many questions and running the risk of losing his daughter all over again. If he didn't slow down, he would spook the girl, and she would hang up. Jodie wasn't sure if he could stand that, so he took a deep breath to slow his racing mind.

"Can't tell you how good it is to hear from you, Jaelynn."

"Daddy, I'm real sorry."

"No, baby girl. You don't gotta apologize for—"

"I shot him, Daddy."

"What're you sayin'?" Jodie wheezed. "I don't...You're not coming in real clear."

"I killed Tyler." Jaelynn was coming in clear enough. She sounded calm.

No, not calm—she sounded empty, and Jodie's mind emptied as well. Seconds earlier, he couldn't stop talking, but right then, he couldn't think of anything to say.

On the other end of the line, Jaelynn waited. "Are you still there?"

"I don't understand, Jaelynn. Who's Tyler? Is he your boyfriend or something?"

"He is...*was*. But he wasn't himself."

"Say again."

"It wasn't him. When he came back a couple days ago, he was... He wasn't *him*."

Jodie scratched his gaunt face. He had never managed to grow more than a scant hint of a beard, and he wasn't given to five o'clock shadow, but right then, his stubble was itching like crazy. Jodie felt like he had stumbled into a bumper patch of poison oak. His whole body was on fire.

"I'm tryin' to follow you here, Jaelynn-girl, but you gotta tell me straight.”

“I want to, Daddy, but...”

“But nothing, darlin’. You gotta tell me, or I can’t help you,” he urged. “Whatever you done, we’ll work it out.”

“But you won’t believe me. No one’s gonna believe me. They’ll send me to jail, and I can’t go to jail.” Hysteria had finally broken through the flat surface of her voice. It rose an octave when she spoke. “I can’t go where I can’t see Benji. I can’t lose him. Oh god, it feels like I’m losin’ him already.”

“I’m afraid I don’t follow, baby girl. Please tell me what happened.” Jodie was close to begging, desperate to piece together the puzzle. “This Tyler fella, was he tryin’ to hurt you?”

“It wasn’t him, I told you. His eyes were wrong. I’ve never been so scared, Daddy, never in my whole life. Not even back at the mill when—”

“Well, that’s it, baby girl,” Jodie interrupted, not daring to let her finish speaking. “You call the cops, and you tell them that. You tell them he was tryin’ to hurt you and it was self-defense. Happens all the time. This Tyler hit you before? If he did and you told someone, then you got a witness. You got a *pattern*. Now tell me where you’re at, and I’ll be there soon’s I can. We’ll work it out, I promise.”

“Bolivar. I’m in Bolivar. A complex called The Elms.”

“Hell, that ain’t far. I can be there in little over an hour. I’m in Cassville now. You hold on, and together, we’ll work this out with the cops.” Jodie scanned the countertop for his car keys.

“Tyler never hit me, Daddy. He was a cheat, and he could be mean, but he wasn’t like that. Somethin’ happened. He went away, and when he came back, he wasn’t the same.” She took a shuddering breath. “He was cold...*weird* and cold, and he looked all wrong. I couldn’t understand it at first, but...I think Benji did. That’s why I did it. There was something *in* him. I heard it calling, even after he died. It’s in the blood.” Her voice dropped to a whisper. “I think it wants me...*She* wants me.”

“You’re not makin’ any sense, Jaelynn. I need you to listen to me. You tell the cops that he was tryin’ to hurt you. Don’t say nothin’ else. He was threatenin’ to kill you, and you done him first in self-defense. It’ll all work out, I swear.”

“Like before, Daddy? Like how it all worked out back then? You said it’d be fine as long as I told them everything that happened.

But it *wasn't* fine. They didn't believe me. No one did. Maybe not even you." And like that, she plunged him right back into that icy tub.

Jodie gripped the countertop with calloused fingers. His skin made like it would crawl right off his body and down the sink drain.

"But you believe me this time, Daddy, don't you?"

"I believe you saw a side to this Tyler you'd never seen before. I think you—"

"I saw what I saw! I'm not lyin'!" Anger rose out of her, and her rage turned to static over the line.

Jodie pulled the crackling phone away from his ear.

"Something's here. It came back from the mountain with Ty. He didn't come back alone. I need you to believe me. This time, you have to. Because if I can't make you believe, what chance do I have of makin' them believe?"

"You're a good girl, Jaelynn. I believe that." Jodie nodded solemnly to the empty kitchen. "I'll tell them you're a good girl. I'll tell them—" He stopped because he thought she had hung up.

There was silence on the other end of the line. It swallowed his words and made him feel their uselessness. Static fizzed, and the line crackled once more. Something popped. She was still there.

"It won't be enough, Daddy. It wasn't back then, and it won't be now. I can't listen to them say nasty things again—call me a liar and all those other ugly words. Everything that happened will come out, and it'll be like it's happening all over again. I couldn't take that."

"No, Jaelynn," Jodie whispered. "You're strong—the strongest girl I know. You hold on. You got your boy to think of."

"That's who I *am* thinking of—Benji. If whatever it is wants me... then it's for the best. You gotta promise me you'll love him, though. Swear you will. If I'm gone, then maybe it will go too."

"Jaelynn, what're y—"

"It's here now. Don't you hear it? It hums."

"What hums?"

"Swear you'll take care of him."

She didn't wait for his reply, didn't give him a chance to make the vows she had demanded of him.

The sound of the gunshot which followed her final words would have dropped him to the floor if he hadn't already been there. Jodie pulled his knees to his chest. He gripped the cabinet door with one hand to keep himself from washing away on the tidal wave of misery rushing out between the cracks in his broken heart.

Jaelynn was gone. He didn't need to hear the blast of the gun to know it. Jodie had felt her go with a wrenching sensation, like his guts were being pulled out through his mouth.

His eyes burned, and his hand shook, but he clutched the phone to his ear while the quiet pushed through the receiver, throwing his ragged breathing back at him like a cruel and hollow echo.

CHAPTER

FOUR

It was some time after the gun went off that Jodie managed to pick himself up from the kitchen floor. He gathered his wits as best he could and climbed into his car.

Jodie had some vague picture in his mind of flashing lights in the distance when he came tearing down the offramp toward a little housing complex on the outskirts of Bolivar. Although he couldn't have told anyone what exit he had taken to arrive at his destination, those lights—the way they grew brighter and broader as he approached—were burned into the backs of his eyeballs. He would likely see those lights dancing behind his eyelids for the rest of his life.

Police were crawling over the place like ants when Jodie pulled into The Elms. He left his car at the end of a long line of cruisers and emergency vehicles and staggered on bandy, quivering legs toward the sad, ivory-colored cluster of duplexes scattered like corn for hogs over the dismal landscape. Jodie ducked his way under a string of police tape unnoticed and made it all the way to the front porch before he was intercepted by two bullish officers.

They grabbed him by each arm and tried to haul him back out onto the lawn. He wouldn't go. Despite the size of the officers holding him, Jodie put up a good a fight. He was screaming her name when he broke free and charged through the front door.

Jodie noticed Benji first, asleep on the sofa and looking so much like Jaelynn that Jodie almost broke down right there. Jaelynn had a complexion like milk and cocoa—white skin and soft brown hair. It ran in the family. She bore a likeness to Jodie's own mama, Mercy Burden, who he had only ever seen in pictures, and to his sister, Minerva. It was uncanny, the way certain traits presented so strong in the family, reaching down through the generations, all the way to the grandson Jodie hadn't seen in nearly five years.

The child was curled around himself like a dry leaf. He seemed so small lying there—all spare ribs and no meat. Beside the boy sat a pile of paper towels he had used to try to wipe up his mother's blood.

More than anything, Jodie wanted to stop there, to stay with the sleeping child who somehow managed to look peaceful in his slumber despite the things he must have seen that night and the blood covering him head to toe. Beyond the couch, however, lay Jaelynn, and Jodie forced himself to see her. He owed it to his daughter to look and to finally believe.

The floor was covered in crimson. It formed scallops and swirls which decorated the kitchen vinyl like the prim scrolls on an old lady's floral drapes. Spread out for what seemed like miles to Jodie, its gory pattern was broken up only by paw marks here and there and Benji's small footprints. In the center of all that mess, was Jaelynn, lifeless and still.

A second body—a man's—rested just beyond hers. They were a matching pair, with feet pointed toward the living room and heads angled to the back door. There was an intimacy in the way they lay, so closely aligned with one another. Jodie might have blushed if he had found them situated like that while they were still alive. In death, the lovers faced each other...

Or would have if either of them had had faces.

Bile rose into Jodie's mouth, burning the back of his throat. The policemen whose clutches he had managed to escape earlier caught up with him then and took him by his arms once more. They let go, however, when a wail like that of a wounded animal came out of him with no warning.

Hidden Children

Without their support, he dropped to the floor, crouched into a tight ball with his elbows on his knees, and wretched and dry-heaved. Something hard and sharp in the carpet pressed into his shin, and he picked it up.

It was a tooth, blown clear out of the kitchen and into the living room.

Between the two corpses, the floor was littered with bits of skull and teeth. The pieces gleamed, white and shiny like peppermint hard candy, amidst twisted strands of bloody-black hair and brain—all of it mixed on the kitchen floor. All of it "excepting the boyfriend's brain," a third officer shared with the coroner across the room. "His gray stuff got ate up by the dog 'fore we got here. Right out of his skull, like Alpo from a tin."

"Jeez. Look at all them insects. Never seen anything like it. It's only been a couple hours."

"Must have had a window open somewhere—only way to account for all these goddamn flies." Unable to help himself, the officer nudged a nearby clump of pink issue with the toe of his boot, sending up a burst of black flies.

It was more than Jodie could bear. His lunch—a grilled cheese sandwich and pickles, well on their way to being completely digested—slid up his throat and past his teeth. With a silent heave, he deposited the gooey remains onto the rug, just missing his knees.

CHAPTER

FIVE

Minerva Burden leaned back against the porch steps of the old cabin and stretched out her legs. Her feet disappeared into the shadows at the far edge of a square of light shining from the open front door. Oak, walnut, and cottonwood trees stood as blackened silhouettes in a jagged ring against a sky easing its way from nighttime's deep navy to early morning's faded indigo.

Funny old mountains, Minerva thought. *Crazy old hills.*

Although it was still late summer and the day was likely to be a scorcher, there was a chill, pre-dawn dampness to the air, and Min wrapped her hands around her coffee mug for warmth. She fingered the chipped rim and marveled at the reflective mood which had come over her that morning. Philosophical deliberation was out of character, but it was easy enough to explain.

Jodie was back.

That had to be the reason for her introspection. The prodigal son, her wayward twin, had returned, and he had brought with him a bit of the outside world—not just a tangible souvenir in the form of an orphaned grandson, but an elusive tang of *somewhere else*, a heady whiff of *yonder*. He had brought the trace odor of *out there* into Min's little corner of the world and forced her to consider *in here*.

That was Jodie's best magic trick—disappearing when it suited him, leaving everyone else to pick up the pieces. He would take off and then swan back in, upsetting the apple cart all over again. It was a trick Min had never mastered for herself, not in all her forty-two years of life. She couldn't imagine flitting from one place to another like her brother did, coming and going like a rolling stone.

The two might have been twins and looked it one hundred percent, but the mountains had a hold on Min alone, like a magnet. Those craggy surroundings had worked their way into her soul and into her blood and infected her until she no longer knew who she would be without them or outside of them. They were home, family, and friends all rolled into one. They knew her secrets, and she knew theirs.

Min had a theory, one she kept to herself so as not to be accused of whimsy, that the mountains—desirous of isolation and wanting to be left the hell alone—disguised themselves. They presented as meek and banal, not worth exploring, to throw strangers off and keep the outside world at bay, something Min could understand well enough.

Visitors came, of course. They wandered into the area, en route to Bentonville or Hot Springs, and stayed a day or two. In the summer, they came for the bed and breakfasts lining the main streets. In the fall, they showed up for ghost tours and UFO conventions, but none of them ventured far beyond the cracked cobblestones of downtown Oracle Springs.

They never saw the wooded coulees and gulches where ginseng grew wild in clumps bigger than a fist. They never smelled the air in the dells, sweet and musky with the scent of rotting crocus and snakeroot blooms. The tourists were oblivious to the streams and creeks—too numerous to name—which cascaded down the mountainside one waterfall at a time, like a Slinky toy rolling down a flight of stairs. Min was sure this was by design—backwoods trickery of the purest sort.

It was the same deceit the mountains used to seemingly blind visitors' eyes to the alien rock formations and rugged precipices where the locals' houses perched. These homes balanced wherever they would fit, hanging onto the narrow rock benches for dear life, appearing to defy gravity while they overlooked a roiling green abyss. It was like a stadium, only in this case, the nosebleed seats were the ones you wanted. The higher the house, the better the vantage point to watch the poorer and more destitute squirm and twist in misery below.

Haves at the top. *Haven'ts* at the bottom: Same as it had been for centuries the world over.

Min was a *haven't,* and down in the depths of the basin—at the bottom of the barrel—where she lived, there was *less.* Less money. Less hope. Even less daylight as the sun rose later in the bottomlands, putting its arrival off until the very last minute like an onerous chore. Min sat on the porch steps of her sunk-down cabin less than a hundred feet above the basin floor and raised her hand toward the brightening sky, where a thin ribbon of pale gold smoke hovered—like so many other things, out of reach.

The gesture was futile. She balled her hand into a fist and pulled it back protectively. Around there, if you stuck out a hand too far, someone was likely to come along and cut it off out of spite. Unlike money or hope, spite was one of the few things you didn't have to look too far to find in Oracle Springs.

Min ran her fingers over the deck post next to her and the cool metal embedded there—a spray of bullets and buckshot planted in the wood. Some of it was new and some of it old. All of it was rusting away to nothing, even though the animosity which had propelled it there was still fresh and shiny. Grudges were another thing common as crows in Min's world, and they lived a hell of a lot longer.

She wiped the powdery dust from the bullets off her fingers onto her jeans before taking a swig of coffee. Drinking the black liquid was like swallowing bitter tar. Once again, she had made it too strong. Now she could look forward to Jodie's complaints. He was always bitching that she had made it wrong, though how he could taste it with all that cream and sugar was beyond her.

Well, if he wanted weaker coffee, he could just—

"Make it his own damn self," said a small voice.

Min turned her head. A tendon crimped at the back of her neck. "Mornin', Benji," she said. Min pressed her thumb into the sore spot, trying to appease the angry muscle.

Benji—slender, moonlight-pale, and wearing a Spiderman pajama top with Batman bottoms—hovered in the doorway. He was alone, no dog at his side. Without the great brown and black beast next to him to lend him some bulk, Benji seemed small and lost in the emptiness of the doorway. He appeared so tiny and solitary that the icicles along Min's spine—the ones which grew in prickling corkscrews whenever Benji performed that neat but terrifying trick of completing a sentence Min hadn't even begun to speak aloud—started to melt.

"You ready for breakfast, lil man?"

A nod.

"You want Eggos?"

A shake this time.

"Cap'n Crunch again?"

Another nod.

In her mind, Min counted the words the boy had spoken to her. *Make it his own damn self.* Six. Not bad. Then again, they hadn't been his words; they were hers, stolen right off her tongue, and it was possible that was all anyone was going to get from the child that day. Min wouldn't be surprised if he didn't speak again before dinner.

She hauled herself to her feet. "Let's see if we can roust your grandpappy before he makes us all late for creation."

Min steered Benji toward the kitchen, shepherding without touching him. "He don't like to be handled much" had been the first thing Jodie had told her about the boy when the two of them appeared on her doorstep a few weeks earlier. That was understandable, considering what he had been through, seeing things no kid needed to witness. Nothing explained why Jodie hadn't felt the need to call first and let Min know he was coming, though.

She pulled a dining chair out for Benji and pushed it back in once he had sat down, then poured him some cereal. Benji didn't wait for her to fetch the milk before he dug in.

"Careful. Don't want to get your pictures all crumby." Min gathered up a scattering of drawing papers and moved them out of the way of Benji's breakfast. The boy might not have been all-in for chitchat, but he did love to draw and burned through paper at an alarming rate. "Maybe you could draw on the backs too, huh? Fill 'em up a bit more?"

Min eyed several sheets which had nothing more than a large black triangle drawn on them and a couple more with a single red circle with a line through it. She made a mental note to sneak some paper later that day from the printer at the store where she worked.

"You do this one last night?" Min held up a sheet on which Benji had at least taken the time to draw two stick figures.

One figure was small—Benji, Min guessed, from the brown hair and the size. The other was taller, with two empty Os for eyes and a wide, straight line for a mouth. Although he had drawn clothes on himself—blue shorts and a red T-shirt—he hadn't added many details to the other figure. No clothes. No hair. Just black crayon.

"Let me guess. This is your Papaw Jodie?"

Benji shook his head.

Min squinted at the picture. "Well, if it's me, you forgot my hair. I look bald." She tossed her long brown hair, but again, Benji shook his head. "Not me, huh? Is it—?" Min stopped herself.

The two figures were holding hands. Of course. The child had drawn his dead mother, Min's niece, Jaelynn.

"It's real pretty, lil' man," Min said quickly. "How 'bout I put it on the fridge?"

Benji went back to staring at his cereal while Min pinned the drawing to the fridge door.

The wall behind it shook.

Pipes vibrated inside the thin wood-paneled walls as water—hot water, and maybe all of it—flowed into the shower on the other side. Min pounded on the wood hard enough to rattle her grandmother's ceramic trivets hanging above the stove next to the fridge.

"If you ain't drowned in there, why don't you come'n join us?" she shouted, recalling with great appreciation her days alone in the cabin before Jodie had shown up.

It wasn't that she begrudged Jodie his return—he had as much right to the family cabin as she had—but they weren't exactly getting lost in the tiny place, and Jodie hadn't yet said how long he planned to stay.

The water continued to run, and Min tried to reconcile herself to the idea of a cold shower. As usual, less for Minerva, more for Jodie. Jodie-boy. St. Joseph. The firstborn who had come out like quicksilver and left Min squirming alone in the womb. While she strangled in the twists of the umbilical cord, he had enjoyed the light of their young mother's exclusive adoration for a few inequitable moments.

How Min had resented him for those moments later, after their mother had run off and it became clear that whatever time they'd had with her back then was all they were going to get. No,

Min could never forgive Jodie for being first, for having more, for leaving her behind, and then for coming back.

"Benji, I ever tell you that I'm a woman with a fondness for solitude?"

The boy looked up at his great aunt with wide brown eyes but said nothing—showed nothing on his passive cherub's face.

"Present company excluded, of course."

CHAPTER

SIX

A delicate bead of water formed on one dog-eared corner of wallpaper above the shower. It grew fatter and heavier until the shower wall shook and caused it to plummet. A pounding noise made Jodie jump near out of his skin. His sister, Min, yelled something through the wall about him being drowned in the shower. But he wasn't in the shower. He was sitting on the toilet seat with a soggy towel clutched to his chest. And he wasn't drowned either, even though his lungs felt full and his chest heavy.

Jodie had been struggling to breathe since waking up. He'd had the dream again—the one which made his flesh crawl and his heart race. It must have been a dozen times or more since Jaelynn died that he had woken up gasping, feeling like there were flies crawling over his skin and a heaviness in his gut working its way up into his lungs.

It was always the same. In his dream, Jodie had been filled with a powerful thirst. It wasn't a regular thirst, like the yen for water on a hot day or after a hard catch of labor, though it was that too. This was a pining for blood and sex and power and all the things in life a man could want mixed together in a way Jodie had never felt in his waking hours. The aching need this thirst created in him was stronger than any desire he had ever known, and it made him nauseous. He yearned to climb inside someone, push his way into their body—their soul—and rip them apart while he came and watched his seed mingle with their blood.

The viciousness of the thought shamed him upon waking, but in his dream, the urge had filled him with desperation and forced him through a dense fog to a riverbed. With parched lips and spasms in his muscles, he fell forward into the sand, sinking into a million hot grains of glass. Water so clear he could barely see it had been just out of reach.

The thirst was killing him, and the last thing he saw before he died was a creature—an eyeless woman, almost as canine as she was human, with a wide, carnivorous mouth and legs that bent like a dog's haunches. The last thing he heard was a buzz or a hum which became the sad dead-inside-drone of Jaelynn when she sat on the couch all those years back and begged him to believe her.

And so, Jodie had awakened that morning as he always did, with a start of panic and a layer of sweat covering his body. His bed sheets were soaked with perspiration. Jodie was gut-punched, sucked dry, and to make matters worse, there was the dog, Miss Mouse, staring at him, watching him while he had slept. He didn't know which was worse: the dream or waking up to that dog giving him the eye. Jodie swung his legs out of bed, kicking them at the canine to shoo her away.

When he flipped the sheet off his lap, he noticed the dark circle spread out across his shorts. It occurred to him he had cum in his sleep, like some fucking teenage boy, but it was worse than that—he had pissed his pants like a young child.

Nausea had propelled him toward the bathroom, where he turned on the shower tap. Water ran, condensation collected, and Jodie sat, his bare ass plonked down on the pink plastic toilet seat while he tried to forget the dream. He went on ignoring his sister's pounding in the other room and tried his best to make his mind blank.

CHAPTER

SEVEN

Rain from an overnight storm had puddled in front of the Burdens' little cabin. It filled the deep ruts made by Min's pickup and drew the attention of Benji and Miss Mouse. The latter drank from the muddy troughs while the former crouched beside the biggest one and scratched a long-limbed stick figure into the soft dirt with a cottonwood switch. Min watched the boy warily and opened the truck door.

"Give me a minute to make a space, and don't get dirty before school."

An assortment of trash had accumulated on the vehicle's floor. Min shoved food wrappers, receipts, and soda cans into a plastic convenience store bag. When she leaned over the console and reached under the driver's seat, she pulled up an empty beer bottle.

Jodie! Drinking while driving her truck, even after she had expressly told him not to.

Min shoved the bottle into the bag, sensing herself being scrutinized. She turned around. Her eyes fell upon her great-nephew. "Anyone ever tell you it ain't polite to stare?" Benji looked crestfallen, and Min felt a pang of guilt. "I'm sorry. You can't help that you come from a family of barbarians."

"Bar-burans another way of sayin' Burdens?" Benji asked, startling Min, who hadn't expected a response, especially not such a long-winded one.

"One's about the same as the other, I guess," she said, considering—and not for the first time—the possibility the boy didn't speak because he didn't care to rather than because he couldn't. That's when she noticed the mud coating his hands and arms. It formed a reddish clay glaze all the way up to his elbows. Min sighed irritably. "What in God's name, child? I told you to stay out of the puddles."

She dropped beside her great-nephew, spinning him around to check his clothing. Min pushed his short sleeves up to his shoulder to keep the cuffs away from the mess.

"This is going to be hell to get out if it gets on your shirt."

"Just like blood?" the boy asked, inspecting his hands.

"Hush," Min snapped. "All I asked was for you to stay clean. Was that too much?" Her spine prickled while she spoke, and there was an odd pulling sensation in her brain which brought to mind a tooth extraction under anesthetic.

Benji was staring at her with an odd intensity she couldn't read. He leaned close and whispered something, and for a second, Min thought she must have misheard.

"What did you say?"

"Dike," the child answered, his voice low. Benji's eyes were wide and wondering.

"Where did you...Why the hell would you say somethin' like that?"

"It's like socks," came the befuddling reply. "The words stick."

"Well, unstick 'em, or I'll wash your mouth out." Min scowled at her great-nephew, who appeared unperturbed. "What's gotten into you, boy?"

"Mama had words in her head too. I couldn't take them all, so she had to shoot them out." He smiled sheepishly up at Min, who was suddenly dizzy.

"Jodie! You need to look to your grandson right about now."

Jodie had stepped out of the cabin onto the front porch, all slouch and string-bean body. He scratched at a patch of curly, gray chest hair sprouting over his T-shirt's frayed neckline and looked up from his milky coffee to where Min and Benji stood together across the drive, near the truck.

"What for?" he asked, before noticing the thick sludge coating Benji's small hands and arms.

There were flecks on the boy's shirt, as well as a dime-sized splat on his cheek. From a distance, the mud—rusty old Arkansas clay—looked like blood—like *her* blood. Hot coffee sloshed over Jodie's wrist when his hands began to shake. His vision blurred. His knees trembled, and he was back in Bolivar—The Elms, Unit 4A—with memories flying at him in bits and pieces, like shattered bone or scattered buckshot.

"Jesus, Jodie. Hurry up already!" Min snapped.

Jodie blinked. "And do what?"

"Get me a towel outta the kitchen to clean up this mess. You gone stupid or somethin'?"

Jodie set his coffee mug down with a sigh and trudged back inside. He returned with a damp dish towel, which he tossed at Min. She caught it at the bottom of the steps.

"Anything else you need from me, ma'am?"

"Since you're asking, yeah." She placed her foot on the last porch step and leaned closer, lowering her voice. "You can stop lookin' at the kid like that."

"Like what?"

"Like he's a gall-dang goose turd or something'." Min stalked back to Benji and began swiping roughly at the child's hands and face with the towel. "Come on. Hold still so I can clean you up."

She was seething. Jodie could tell by the way she had almost taken Benji's head off with the towel when she wiped the mud from his cheek. With that in mind, Jodie's heart rate slowed, and a warmth crept into his soul. The dream he'd had the night before had left him out of sorts, and there was nothing his misery craved more than company.

He waited until his sister had helped Benji into the truck and shut the door before tightening the screw further. "I nearly forgot.

Don't worry about the meeting at school next week. I figured, since my schedule is clear, it makes sense for me to go to the school alone."

"*You*? You're gonna meet Benji's teacher and the nurse?" Min froze, her eyebrows arched in a mix of suspicion and astonishment.

"Why not? He's my grandson, isn't he?"

Min narrowed her eyes. "If I recall, I'm the one had to go down and get him enrolled. I take him every day. You even know where the school is?

"I do. His mama went there. Just figured it might be best if I took care of the meeting is all." Jodie kicked the porch post.

Min's mouth torqued off to one side of her face in a lopsided frown. Jodie had succeeded in getting under her skin.

"It's not a problem," she said. "I can get time off at the store. Paula ain't goin' to give me any shit for it."

"Maybe not, but that isn't the only reason it might be better if I go." Jodie took a swig of his coffee and swilled it around in his mouth before swallowing. "Might surprise you to hear it, but I'm not so dumb that I don't know folks got a problem with me and him coming back. The only Burden they ain't got in their sights right now is you, but that could change easy enough. I don't want to make things worse is all."

"Real considerate of you, Jodie, but I don't follow." Min crossed her arms over her chest. "Clearly, you got somethin' to say, so go on and spit it out. How's me going to the school gonna make things worse?"

"There's folks don't want him here. They think I came back to town to rub it in and cast shame over some people. They think I'm flauntin' him. Now, if you start flauntin' *your* thing, you know, by makin' a point to go down and see that pretty nurse at the school, well, could be more trouble maybe."

"My thing? Trust me, there's no *thing*—not with Nurse Hardesty or anybody else, for that matter." Min shot her brother a poisonous look. "And if there's so much trouble brewin' and you're so concerned, why bring him here at all, huh? You could have stayed in Cassville and avoided it altogether. Why come back to Oracle Springs?"

Jodie smirked. He leaned casually and comfortably against the porch post. "I had to come back, Min. You're all I got."

"Don't I know it." She climbed inside the truck and slammed her door shut, but as soon she had started the engine, she rolled

down the window so she could stick her arm out and raise her middle finger—a parting salute to her ornery brother.

Min backed into the road with tires spinning, kicking up a cloud of dust before tearing up the hill toward the highway. She swerved around a young man out walking, and Benji turned around in his seat to wave. The pedestrian returned the gesture before continuing down the roadside toward the cabin.

"Apologies for my sister, Lucas," Jodie called out from the porch. "She's somewhat tetchous today."

"No harm done, Mr. Burden." Lucas Tanner stopped in the road at the end of the dirt driveway. He pushed his long, lank hair away from his eyes and adjusted the strap of the leather satchel he carried so it sat higher on his shoulder. "How're things? How's Benji?"

Jodie worked a troublesome coffee ground around in his mouth until he had it on the tip of his tongue, then spat it out into the yard. "'Bout as good as he can be. You done with school now?" Jodie tried to do the math. Had Lucas been a year ahead or a year behind Jaelynn in school?

"Classes start next week. I got another two years before I have my degree."

A degree. Jodie wasn't going to try to fool himself into thinking Jaelynn would have gone away to college and gotten one of those. That sort of thing wouldn't have been in the cards for a daughter of Jodie Burden, no way, no how, but it went without saying she had deserved better than what she got. Jodie took another sip of coffee and scowled. It was bitter as shit.

"Still up in KC?"

Lucas nodded. "Yeah. Thinking about changing my major, though, to art." He swung his satchel forward so Jodie could see the large sketch book sticking out the top.

"Art, huh? What's your pop say about that?"

Jodie didn't have a problem with the Tanner kid. Never had. But even so, the way the young man's face fell at the mention of his father brought Jodie some petty satisfaction. Lucas's pristine white sneakers—brand new out of the box, most likely—and his fancy leather bag, probably engraved with his name or something, hadn't escaped Jodie's attention. Lucas and Jaelynn had been friends throughout childhood, inseparable at times, but now Jaelynn was rotting in a pine box, and Lucas was playing Picasso at his fancy school up north.

"Dad's not happy, but we're working towards a compromise," Lucas explained. His voice faded in and out of Jodie's hearing, like the shifting hum of a jarfly. "I think if I present my case and—"

"You hikin' down to the big pool today to do some drawing?"

The big pool lay at the bottom of the hillside, half a mile or so below the Burden's cabin. It was a slippery trek over rough, rocky terrain to reach the gully where the water collected between the steep incline of the mountain and a sheer slab of rock. It acted as an unforgiving backstop to anything rolling downhill.

On summer nights, when the temperatures rose and wouldn't seem to break, even after the sun set, a person could smell the water from the cabin door despite the distance and inhale the odor of the things growing on its oily surface—warm lake weed, algae, and rotting lily pads.

"No." Lucas appeared relieved that Jodie had changed the subject. "I won't be going that far down."

"Maybe you want to try the mill instead, then," Jodie said. He knew his suggestion had hit the right mark when Lucas blanched.

"No, sir." Lucas shook his head. "I don't go to the mill much at all, not since...Well, I just don't."

"No," Jodie said, drinking the last of his coffee in one long gulp. "I don't suppose you would. Don't let me keep you, then." He turned away before Lucas could offer up a hesitant wave.

CHAPTER

EIGHT

A soft mildewed scent tickled the back of Lucas Tanner's nose, and an industrial hum—not the usual whisper of wasps or bees, but a unique thrumming—met him when he stepped off the road and into the woods. The noise invigorated him, as did the light filtering through the dense foliage. The sun's rays cast rich, contrasting shadows on the dirt path before breaking through the canopy of a clearing where a great elm had fallen.

Most of the tree's boughs had broken off and rotted away, but the gnarled roots remained, upended, extending in a tentacular snarl. Lucas sat down on the rotting log and thought about what he had said to Jodie Burden moments earlier, about hoping to major in art. Despite what he had told that sad rail of a man with a dead wife and daughter about reaching a compromise with his father, things were nowhere near settled. No matter how erudite his argument, Holt Tanner was not going to give Lucas his blessing on a switch from pre-law to art—not on his dime anyway.

A branch snapped nearby, and birds that had been calling back and forth to each other in the cottonwood fell silent. Something had disturbed them.

Lucas forgot about his father and looked to the trailhead from which he had just emerged, listening for approaching footsteps. A tatty dog shambled into view and limped toward him, panting in the intensifying heat. It was the Burden's dog—Jaelynn's dog, Lucas had gathered—which had arrived with the boy and went everywhere with him when he was not in school.

Lucas slapped the top of his thigh, and the creature cocked her wedge-shaped head at him. "Hey, old girl. Did you come to keep me company?"

The dog's collar jangled while she hobbled to him. The sound was bell-like, metallic, and somewhat alien in the natural surroundings. Lucas kneaded his fingers into the thick ruff of fur around the dog's neck, giving her a scratch before rotating her collar to read her name tag.

"*Mauser*. Like the rifle?" Lucas couldn't imagine his childhood friend, Jaelynn, naming a pet something like that. The dog was probably a rescue, he decided, already christened with the moniker before being adopted.

Despite never having been much of an animal person, Lucas worked his fingers into the dog's coat, then leaned over and pressed his face into her furry neck. He inhaled her scent. She smelled dry but musty too, like old crackers or stale tortilla chips. Lucas found it an odd but reassuring odor.

"Do you miss her?" he whispered. The dog nuzzled into Lucas's neck, and he stroked her muzzle. "Did you try to protect her? Did you try to stop her?"

She gave his hand a quick lick. Her tongue was dry and scratchy, a bit like sandpaper, and her teeth grazed Lucas's knuckle.

"Because I didn't. I didn't do enough to stop what happened. Maybe my father is right about artists. Maybe we are all useless."

Lucas breathed in the dog's dull odor once more before bestowing a final pat on her head and pulling his sketchbook and pencil case out of his leather bag. He selected a Blackwing Pearl pencil, gave it a quick turn in a sharpener, and settled back against a bowed branch of the log, scanning his surroundings for a desirable subject. The dog settled in too, turning around a couple of times before dropping in the sun-warmed dirt. Lucas zeroed in on a large black oak with a full, umbrella-like spread of foliage and began setting the tree down on paper.

Hidden Children

After half an hour or so of sketching, he held the drawing up at arm's length to inspect it and scowled at the result. Something wasn't right.

He had sketched the tree and the surrounding bracken exactly as he saw them, but things were off in a way he couldn't quite put his finger on. It wasn't that the sketch was bad or poorly done. No, everything that should have been there was and perfectly to scale. Lucas had captured the shadows and the light correctly and had worked with care to create a fair rendering of the space, yet something about it wasn't entirely realistic.

The sketch possessed a level of detail and accuracy which went beyond realism—beyond hyper-realism, even. If pressed, the only way Lucas could have described it would be to say he had drawn the tree not as it was, but how it was then and would be in the future, all at the same time—an intricate impossibility. The tree's entire existence unfolded on the paper in front of Lucas. Life marched toward death between the simple pencil lines, and nihilism lurked in the soft graphite shading.

What have I drawn? he wondered. The picture had become something dark and unnatural, something hopeless, and it matched the feeling growing inside him.

Stranger still was the fact that Lucas appeared to have drawn a figure in the picture. Without intending to, he had sketched a strange sliver of a shadow onto the page, as if someone had been standing behind the tree, barely visible. It was only an extra line or two within the existing shading, but the effect was so realistic.

Lucas looked up, expecting another person to be across the clearing, watching him while he worked. There was no one there, but the figure he had drawn, vague as it was, made him certain someone had been there and that he had known it subconsciously. The thought made his stomach knot and soured his mood further.

Lucas tossed the sketchbook away. It landed a few feet from him in a heap of dried leaves and mast not far from the Burden's dog, disrupting a cluster of insects. Lucas's eyes settled on the creature, and he was stung with bitterness. Ever since the canine had shown up, there had been a pall over the morning. Lucas had been prepared to forget about his father and their disagreements, but then she had appeared and brought a melancholy into the clearing. She had winced in with stiffened gait, carrying the stench of stale urine and rotting breath, along with memories which tugged at Lucas's heart.

The dog was an ugly old thing. Her long coat and the fur on her muzzle were stiff and bristly, like sandy-gray wire. Her eyes were clouded and blue, like frosted sea glass, and when the light hit them, they appeared pupil-less and opaque—milky and dull—reflecting nothing in their flat surface but a flickering reminder of age and inevitable decay.

Now that he stopped to consider it, Lucas was suddenly aware of the decay all around him. As pronounced as if they were boring into his own ear canal, termites tunneled into the rotting tree upon which he sat, and worms gnawed through dead matter deep within the earth. Bark fell from trees, crashing like falling timber. Petals dropped like wet blankets onto the ground. Nature broke apart at a molecular level, fracturing and failing, and Lucas heard it all as clearly as shattering glass. Worst of all, he could sense his own body breaking apart.

He looked at his hand and, like the picture he had drawn, knew it was his yet hardly recognized it. Without actually changing, it shriveled and gnarled, withering arthritically before his eyes. Lucas was young but dying even still. Locked in a simulcast of age and youth, he watched his own inevitable and miserable demise play out before him. He would die without ever fulfilling his dreams, crushed under the heaviness of his father's expectations.

The forest, with its low hum and sickly scent of rot, told him this. All around him was a symphony of death, and it was the dog, with its foul odor and ragged breathing, who had sounded the first note.

A fly landed on his face. Its miniscule legs tickled the corner of Lucas's mouth.

"What good are you, Miss Mouse," he hissed, "if you don't keep track of your flock?"

CHAPTER

NINE

Benji hugged his knees to his chest, rubbing his skin where it had erupted in goosepimples along his shins. The vinyl cot in the nurse's office at Oracle Springs Elementary was stiff and cold against his bare arms and legs. He had been sweating when the playground monitor brought him into the office, but after a few minutes lying there, with the air-conditioning blasting from a vent above him, his perspiration had turned to ice water and now he shivered.

During first recess, Benji had hidden beneath the playground slide. Under the spiraling green plastic, there was a trough where the creosote bark chips had been pushed aside and the dirt was worn away, creating a nest his size. The playground monitors couldn't see him, and most of his classmates—even the ones who went out of their way to torment him—were too busy swinging, climbing, or playing tag to pay any attention to where he had gone.

Beneath the slide, it was cool and dark, and Benji imagined he was hiding under the porch back home in Bolivar. He pictured his mama somewhere close by, hanging laundry on the fraying clothesline or pulling up the poke weed which grew heavy along the side of the house. It dropped poison berries that popped and squished when folks stepped on them.

Just as his mama's face hovered into view in his daydream—*Peek-a-boo. I found you. Lord, you're gonna get snakebit one of these days*—a strange thing happened. With a jerk and a spasm, Benji's small body went solid as stone. His mother's, looking down on him, began to change.

Within seconds, she was no longer Benji's mother. She was *something-else*, the monster he saw in his dreams, the one Tyler had brought back from the mountains—a thing not quite human but trying to be, with eyes as white and round as snakes' eggs in a face spliced in half by a too-wide grin.

That grin.

It was less a smile than a knife's slash in white clay.

Benji knew her every feature. He had drawn her a thousand times with his crayons since she first appeared to him. Since she first showed up, unwelcomed, riding inside Tyler, like a hitchhiker where only Benji could see her—*truly* see her. Once, Benji had drawn a bird, a blue jay. He had been proud of the drawing, enough so that he showed it to Auntie Donna, the woman who lived across the way and watched him while his mother worked. She said he had captured the bird perfectly.

At the time, it had worried him because he hadn't wanted to capture the bird or trap it in any way. When Aunt Donna wasn't looking, Benji ripped up the drawing, hoping it would be enough to free the bird from its papery prison. But that was why everything had to be perfect when it came to drawing this creature, even if it meant drawing her a million times. If he could capture her just right, then maybe he could save himself. Save Papaw Jodie and Aunt Min.

The creature continued to reach out to Benji while he trembled and shook beneath the slide. She moved closer, a breath away now, and her impossibly long, white fingers wriggled over his arms. They tickled their way up to his shoulders and just beneath his ears.

Go away, Benji thought, as hard as he could.

The creature cupped his face in those spidery hands.

Never, she whispered, her wide grin unmoving.

Benji didn't have his crayons or his papers with him. All he could do was lie beneath the slide—prey frozen in a predator's hungry stare. All he could think was, *I hate you*, while the pale creature's eyes flashed and her inhuman face contorted. She slid her hands over his small chest and pressed hard against his ribs. Benji gasped when she wrapped her cold, clammy fingers around his heart.

She had done this before, so often in fact since his mother died that Benji was sure his heart must be scarred from her touch. It grew a little harder every time the monster gripped it, but she hadn't managed to crush it yet, hadn't managed to squeeze all the feeling out of it. Benji could still care. He loved Papaw Jodie and Aunt Min. They were his family. He had to protect them.

I'm family too, the creature said. *I am of your blood and in your blood, and you must choose.*

This game again.

Make your choice and we will be together. Even in his head, the voice was an unpleasant hiss.

The creature's body was slender and white, snake-like until it wasn't. It twisted and lost shape, like a stream of spilled milk, shifting into something which looked almost like Jaelynn before spreading out so far and wide that it was no longer something else, but altogether nothing.

Mother, mother, mother, the white thing moaned. *I have been called the pale mother, and I will be yours.*

The light went out of Benji's world, and a heavy weight settled over him. If he had known the word, he might have described the feeling as despair. How could he ever capture this creature when she could turn into nothing so readily? You can't capture *nothing*. He could no more draw her whip-thin, lizard-like body, the way it hunched like a dog about to pounce, than he could draw her scent— sour and metallic—or the way it lingered after she had gone.

Benji's body had begun to twitch, then jerked uncontrollably in the dirt. His arms, which had been reaching out toward his mother, now pulled back into his chest all by themselves until he guessed they must have looked like claws. He bit his tongue and tasted blood.

There were footsteps in the bark chips. The others had discovered his hiding place. Children crowded around, screaming and laughing.

The recess monitor had found him under the slide, where his classmates had left him at the sound of the bell. She brought him inside, covered in his own vomit and the spittle a few of the older children had hocked onto him.

In her office, Nurse Hardesty had wiped his face with a wet paper towel and asked the monitor to hunt down some clean clothes for him to wear.

"Stick out your tongue," she ordered, kneeling in front of him.

Benji stuck his tongue out at her shyly.

The nurse, using a flat wooden stick, pressed his tongue one way and then another. "I see teeth marks, but the bite didn't go all the way through." She smiled and stood up.

Benji pulled his sore tongue back in his mouth.

The recess monitor returned with a new shirt from the giveaway closet, which was where Aunt Min had gotten Benji's shirt in the first place.

Benji didn't mind wearing hand-me-downs from the closet. They smelled nice, all perfumed and chemical-fresh, like his clothes used to after his mama did the laundry. Not like they did after Jodie and Min finished the washing, which was like nothing or sometimes mildew if they both forgot the laundry too long in the machine.

The nurse had left him then, presumably to make notes in his file, which was already growing fat after only a couple of months of school being in session.

"Did you say something in there?" Nurse Hardesty peeked in the doorway from her office.

Benji shook his head.

"All right. Well, I think you're going to make it, kiddo. Still, I'm going to have to give your granddad a call." Nurse Hardesty lifted a telephone from its cradle on the wall and dialed nine.

"Why?"

The nurse froze with the phone halfway to her ear. People at the school did that sometimes. They stopped moving and stared when Benji spoke, like they couldn't quite believe it had happened.

"*Why?*" she repeated after a moment or two. "So you can go home is why. You threw up, and someone has to come pick you up now, Benji. It's school policy. Don't you want to go home?"

"Can't go home, not ever."

Nurse Hardesty's sweet smile disappeared. A line formed between her eyebrows, and she gave a faint nod.

"Right. To Min's house, then, your great-aunt's place," she said, correcting herself. "Go ahead and lie down again while I see if I can reach your granddad." She hovered in the doorway a minute longer, regarding him with a curious look.

Hidden Children

When she finally left, Benji lay down on the little cot and waited in the cold, listening to the sounds of children he couldn't see and the filtration system of a small aquarium on a table across the room. He curled up into a ball on his side and tucked his knees to his chest again to get warm.

The wall opposite him was the color of green pudding, the kind Papaw Jodie called *moustachio*. Nurse Hardesty was dialing Papaw Jodie right then, but Benji knew he wouldn't answer. His phone, which was *out-of-credit*, was on the table beside his bed, and Papaw Jodie had left. There was no one at Aunt Min's house.

Benji could sense its emptiness, and he knew no one was home, same as he knew that, not far from there, something bad had happened to his friend Lucas. He didn't want to be near whatever that was.

"No answer," Nurse Hardesty said upon her return from the outer office. "We'll try again in a minute or two." She picked up a thermometer and walked over to the cot. "No fever. That's good."

While she tried Papaw Jodie's phone a second time, Benji focused on the aquarium and the fish inside. Their vivid crayon-colored scales flashed brightly while they darted about, zipping here and there spastically. One little fish thrashed in the pebbles at the very bottom, wriggling his nose into the rocks and stirring up a cloud of stringy gray fish feces and algae. Benji decided he would call that one Lemon Freckle, for its yellow scales and the small black dots along its sides.

The nurse pressed her finger against the disconnect button in the phone's cradle, then released it and dialed the phone again. The key tones sounded out a different melody this time.

"Min, sorry to bother you. I know you're probably busy at the store. It's Sheila over at the school," Nurse Hardesty said after a few moments. "I've been trying to get a hold of your brother, but he's not answering. I'm afraid Benji's had an episode." A pause, then, "No, it was worse than that. He's going to need to be picked up."

While Aunt Min said something on the other end of the line and the nurse listened, a small wet slap sounded from across the room. It had been so faint it was almost inaudible, but when Benji looked down, Lemon Freckle was lying on the floor. The fish flopped once or twice on the bright white vinyl and then lay still. Its gills opened and closed a couple of times before stopping. Its bulging fish eyes, once glassy-black like little beads, were gone, completely scaled over.

"Where do you think your granddad might have gotten off to?" Nurse Hardesty asked from her desk in the other room. "I hate having to pull your aunt out of work."

Inside the tank, the remaining fish wriggled blindly. Their eyes were gone as well.

CHAPTER

TEN

Jodie trudged up the road just outside Oracle Springs and played frogger with on-coming traffic. He crossed the highway directly under the glare of a snarling fifteen-foot boar in studded leather. The remarkable plywood beast loomed like a nightmarish hallucination astride a sleek, red chopper advertising AJ's Road Hogs Bar and Grill. It was a point of interest in a viewless section of town, even if the bar itself wasn't much to write home about.

Housed in a steel Quonset hut with a rickety apron of wooden planks as a front porch, Road Hogs appeared more like a field hangar for aircraft than the roadhouse it was, but the establishment's main draw wasn't the architecture or even the monstrous sign. A row of smokers and grills, as black and sleek as a fleet of locomotives, rested in the grassy yard behind the bar.

The bar's owner, AJ Mader, was a genuine BBQ master. People came all the way from Bentonville and even Little Rock to get a taste of his brisket and burnt ends. On weekends, it was all but guaranteed that the parking lot would be filled to overflowing, but it wasn't a weekend, and the parking lot was nearly empty when Jodie arrived.

The only vehicles around were a white van with a decal of the bar's biker pig logo and a mustard-colored Toyota Celica belonging to AJ's sister, Alison, who at that moment was slicing lemons behind the bar counter. When Jodie entered Road Hogs, she wiped the juice from her hands across the rhinestone-covered pockets of her low-slung jeans and stepped away from her station to give the man a warm, if slightly stiff hug.

"Let me get a look at what they done to you up yonder." She pushed him away as quickly as she had embraced him. "Got a few more grays but still ain't gained a pound of flesh." Alison retreated behind the bar before Jodie could answer, eager to put a couple of feet of hickory between them now that the initial greeting was over and done with.

"You're looking real good yourself, Al," Jodie said, taking a seat at the end of the bar.

"It's nice of you to say, Jodie. But just so you know where we stand, flattery isn't gonna get you free food. We're not offering a friends and family discount these days." She gazed at him appraisingly, pursing her lips until they all but disappeared into a thin line. "Nothin' on the house, got it?"

"We still talking 'bout the food?" Jodie chuckled, but Alison's face didn't register so much as a smirk. "Fair enough, Al." Jodie nodded, then ordered a beer and a burger.

Alison took the ticket into the kitchen and didn't return until the food was ready, leaving Jodie alone to watch muted cable news on a small flatscreen and listen to some local show on a small portable radio Alison kept behind the bar.

"Ms. Reynolds is a recent transplant to our neck of the woods and a lawyer by trade, but we won't hold that against her...much."

"I left my practice when I moved from St. Louis," the guest corrected. *"I'm a former lawyer at best, Mike."*

"I suppose a former lawyer is better than a practicing one, right, listeners?"

Alison finally emerged from the kitchen. "I told AJ to hold the tomato and lettuce because of how poorly you and vegetables get on."

"Never cared much for rabbit food." Jodie lifted the top bun from his burger and inspected the patty before adding more ketchup.

"Eat up while it's still hot." Alison turned down the radio and returned to her lemons.

Jodie watched her work while he ate. She hummed as she sliced the fruit—a quiet, tuneless melody which rang pleasantly in Jodie's ears. He would glance at the TV when she looked over at him, pretending he wasn't enjoying the way she pushed her long auburn hair back from her face every time it fell past her ears.

"You seem glum, Jodie-boy. Min finally ask you to start splitting utilities?" Alison finished slicing and put the knife down. Her boots thumped heavily against the scuffed wooden floor when she walked over to a small glass-front fridge and placed the bowl of lemons inside.

"Sounds like a whole army stomping through the place. You still wearin' them same old shitkickers, Al?" Jodie peered over the edge of the counter at Alison's worn leather biker boots.

"I am. What of it?"

"Nothin'. Guess I should thank the Lord some things in this world never change, but you ever consider wearin' a pair'a sandals or what have you?"

"Nope."

"Min says you're seeing what's-his-name up at the hatchery."

"From time to time."

"Yeah?" Jodie set his burger down and settled his elbows on either side of his plate. "So, go on. Tell me what he's got that I don't got. I know you're achin' to."

"Not that it's any of your business, Jodie Burden"—Alison reached over the counter and handed him a napkin for his fingers—"but he's got a job, to start."

"Never took you for a gold digger, Al."

"Gold digger? You can go shit on a shingle, Jodie. Wantin' a man who isn't gonna sponge off me doesn't make me a gold digger. I've worked too damn hard for what I've got to let some raggedy deadbeat breeze in and help himself."

"I'm no deadbeat, Al. I'm lookin' for work."

"No one asked you to state your case. What you do is your business now." She heaved a crate of glasses onto the counter. "But if you was to ask me, I'd say you oughta go back to Cassville. Get your old job back and set your grandkid up in a school where no one knows what he is."

Jodie raised his eyebrows. "And what is he?"

Alison slapped the countertop with both hands. "Jesus! I meant he's *your* grandson, last name Burden. You know I didn't mean nothin' else. All I was suggesting is that you go back to where you and he got a chance at some sort of normal life."

"You tryin' to get rid of me, Al?"

"I'm trying to save you some trouble. You're washed up in this town, and everyone knows it."

"Are you included in that *everyone*? 'Cause if you are, that's plenty fresh. I seem to remember I was more than good enough for you once." He took a chance and winked at her.

"Never could take us seriously, could you?" She sighed and began wiping the damp glasses dry with a dishcloth. "Yeah, I do believe you were good enough for me...once."

"You sure know how to gut a man, Al. Want me to put my nuts on the table so you can cut'em right off and store'em with your lemons?"

"Listen here, Jodie." Alison shook the dishcloth at him. "You can tell yourself I'm some bitch all you want, but *you* were the one who left, and I understood it, even then. Everything you and Jaelynn went through and her disappearing afterward—I *got* it. You took off, and I never talked shit or listened to them that did. I turned a deaf ear to all of it and defended you when I could. I still do."

"Don't do me no favors, Al."

"That's easy enough to say, I suppose, after I done you about a hundred over the years."

Tires scraped the gravel outside, and the rumble of diesel engines, which had been growing louder, cut out, creating an abrupt void which brought Jodie and Alison's conversation to a halt. They looked to the entrance when car doors slammed and deep voices floated into the Quonset. Al pulled her phone out of her pocket and checked the time.

"Road and loggin' crews come in around now for lunch."

"I know. I was hoping to ask Ellis about some work."

Alison raised her eyebrows. "Work? You're gonna *ask about some work*? Smooth as all that."

Her face went slack, and her green eyes, heavily rimmed in black liner, turned cold. She leaned across the bar top toward him, sliding her arms along the scratched wooden surface until she was so close that her elbows were right alongside Jodie's on either side of his plate.

"I'm gonna do you one more favor, Jodie. I'm gonna give you the best goddamn advice you ever got, and if you're smarter than you look, you'll listen this time. Pack up and go. Get out of this town. It don't want you no more." She moved down the counter a ways, putting some distance between her and Jodie.

A herd of men in work overalls and neon vests tromped into the bar. It might have appeared like she was ignoring him, but Jodie knew her intentions were kinder than that. She was hoping to draw the crew's attention away from him, to keep their sights pulled in another direction.

The smell of the men—that of tar, sawdust, and manual labor performed under an unrelenting southern sun—preceded them. It was a dense cloud of blue-collar musk that filled the Quonset hut as the men filed toward the barstools. They moved in a pack, half a dozen or so of them—a motley blend of discharged military and former cons—who took their seats in a line at the bar.

Each and every one of them noticed Jodie. Some of them looked once and quickly glanced away, while others stared keenly, devouring him with eyes hungry for a fight.

Alison, having witnessed more than her fair share of brawls in her time behind the bar, slapped a coaster and a bowl of nuts down in front of each man before anyone had time to consider taking offense to present company. Jodie, for his part, waited until each man had gotten comfortable in his seat and was busy cracking peanut shells before he opened his mouth to address the man nearest him.

"I heard your crew might be short a man or two, Deems."

Ellis Deems, grayed and grizzled and well on his way to sixty years old, was not known around town for diplomacy. The man hadn't walked away from a fight since he left school in the ninth grade, but right then, he was doing his best to ignore Jodie. He rubbed his belly and wiggled his bushy salt-and-pepper eyebrows at Alison.

"JD got the smoker up and running yet, Alison?"

"Been here since six, tending the hickory, Ellis." She spoke loudly, likely hoping her voice would cover up Jodie's physical presence as well as anything he might say. Alison winked at the foreman. "I'm not surprised you can't smell it over your own rank odor. Must be that godawful aftershave Linda keeps buying you for Christmas. She's a smart woman. Does it so no other woman'd have you. Keeps you all to herself that way."

"Marco Petite said you was shorthanded this season."

Alison turned and looked at Jodie in disbelief. The smile slid from her face, like grease off a plate. She would have kicked him with those boots of hers if she could have reached him.

"Anyone hear a dog barking?" asked a man whose safety vest read "Tank" across the back in black electrical tape.

David "Tank" Egon was a mountain of burly flesh and freckles, bald as a baby on top but sprouting hair on his back that could have easily been mistaken for a rust-colored sweater. Jodie hadn't seen him for a couple of years, but in that time, the man had gotten bigger if anything. Tank threw his head back and emitted a few short, deep barks, and the rest of the crew laughed.

"Burnt ends all 'round, I guess, Al. Side of fries times six. And give ol' Leonard a salad. He's watching his girlish figure." Ellis slapped the back of the man next to him, who was the eldest of the crew and the slimmest by a mile. He snorted at his own joke, then took a napkin from a stack on the counter and blew his nose into it before swiveling his head toward Jodie.

"Marco said—" Jodie began.

"I know what Marco said. I heard you the first time." Ellis threw out a glare which made him appear more ursine than human. "I mean to say, I *heard* you, but I guess I couldn't believe you'd said it. You tellin' me you want to work with us?"

"I need a job. Ain't many around that pay worth a damn."

Tank nudged Leonard, who in turn elbowed the man next to him, and the whole crew—Bullfrog Petty, Quake Womack, Buckie Cochrum—turned in their seats to watch the show.

With a nod, Ellis Deems said to Jodie, "Marco told you right. I am short a man or two. Lambo Beshear moved up to Eagle Rock, and Aikin Tapscott went and busted six ribs and a thigh bone doin' God knows what while stoned out of his mind."

Ellis tossed his soiled napkin onto the counter. With a quick nod to Alison, he indicated she should take care of it for him.

"I've got three times more work than I got hands to do it. There's openings for a stump grinder and a flag man, and I need someone to drive a backhoe. Thing is, I got no openings or need for the kind of shitstorm that hirin' you would rain down on my fuckin' head. I bring you in, and I guarantee that news lands on Samuel Lauderback's desk before you've taken your first piss break.

"What do you think Lauderback's gonna say when he hears that I've brung Joseph Burden onto my crew? How you think he's gonna feel? How you think he's gon' goddamn re-act when he hears I hired the man who called his kin all them nasty names, the man whose daughter tried to ruin his son's life, dragging him through court and claiming all kinds of lies against him?"

"Wasn't lies."

"Way I hear it...the way Lauderback tells it—"

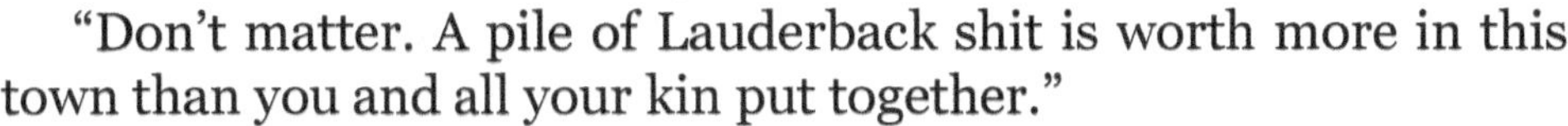

"Lauderback is full of shit, him and his son."

"Don't matter. A pile of Lauderback shit is worth more in this town than you and all your kin put together."

Jodie stayed silent. He stared, dumb and motionless, at the bottles behind the bar. Jodie didn't even turn his head when Ellis's stool scraped the floor and the man stood up. He watched Ellis's hulking shape approach out of the corner of his eye and smelled the man's breath when Ellis leaned over the bar next to him.

When Ellis spoke again, his voice was low, silky with warning and oozing danger. "You been gone awhile, Burden. I sure hope you didn't forget how things work around here. It'd be a real tragedy if you had." He pushed Jodie's plate with half-eaten burger toward the interior edge of the bar. "Pour me another Bud, Alison, if you don't mind, and you can clear our friend's plate. He's done eatin'."

Alison hesitated, but Jodie gave her the faintest of nods, and Ellis returned to his seat. Jodie slid a ten-dollar bill across the counter, then stood and turned to leave.

"Welcome back, Burden. We'll see you 'round," Ellis called.

"Oh, and also, Jodie," Leonard chimed in, with a tone that might have passed for friendly. "I come acrost a dog out in the woods earlier. Was out not too far from your place, clearing scrub. Shepherd lookin' thing. It's dead. I wondered if maybe it was yourn."

Jodie stopped about halfway from the exit. "Was it a bitch?"

"Mighta been," Leonard replied. "Hard to tell, considering the state I found 'er in."

Jodie bit his lip. That was how it was in Oracle Springs when your name was Burden: Pigs got shot and left to rot, chickens ended up headless, and dogs showed up dead in the woods.

"Thanks for the heads-up, Len."

"Don't mention it."

"I'll send your regards to Mr. Lauderback and his boy," someone called after him.

It might have been Buckie, but ultimately, it didn't matter who said it. They were all the same. A pack moving as one. A monolithic cluster of slack-jawed apes with half a brain to share amongst them.

Tank and another man snickered into their beers, and Jodie's hand curled into a fist, almost of its own accord. It would have been six on one, though Tank counted as two. Jodie would have gotten his ass beat for sure.

"You got something to say, Burden?" Tank called over his shoulder.

The whole crew watched. Alison had gone rigid as ice behind the counter. Everyone waited on a knife's edge, wondering what would follow.

Jodie cleared his throat and unclenched his hand. "Only that I best go get my dog, shouldn't I?" He pushed open the door and stepped outside while laughter erupted behind him. Jodie bent forward, hunching his shoulders to guard against its sting. Laughter hurt less than a broken nose and knocked out teeth, he supposed. "Fuck 'em."

Outside, the air was muggy and thick. Three black pickup trucks were parked side by side in front of the roadhouse, heat from their engines still flowing off their glossy hoods in waves. Jodie pulled a switchblade out of his pocket and knelt beside the front wheel of the first vehicle he came to. He ran the blade slowly and lightly over the tire's surface, letting the knife's tip catch in the small cracks and grooves of the dark rubber.

He had raised his elbow for better leverage when there was a high-pitched *woop*. When a sheriff's car pulled into the lot, Jodie stood up and snapped the knife shut, sliding it back into his pocket before stepping out from between the two trucks.

"Hang on there a tic," the lawman inside the cruiser called out. He pulled up alongside Jodie and stopped. Sheriff Dwight Hardesty lowered his sunglasses and peered at Jodie from under the brim of his dust-colored campaign hat. "Where you off to in such a burnt hurry? Everything all right?"

"Nothing wrong, Sheriff Hardesty. Why would there be?"

"I was wonderin' 'cause I saw you on the ground back there, Burden." The sheriff tilted his head so the light fell across his forehead. Hardesty's eyes were bright and blue above high cheekbones, and his nose was narrow but prominent. It was as though each feature was fighting for the starring role on his face. "You drop something?"

"Thought maybe I'd lost some spare change."

"I heard you were in town, but I didn't know if I should believe it," Hardesty said. "Anything particular bring you back?"

"Got my grandson now. Figured I might raise him up here at home, where things're familiar."

The sheriff nodded and sucked in his cheeks, making his craggy face appear even more angular. "I was sorry to hear about your girl takin' her own life. Suicide's a real boot in the ass, and there's lots of it goin' 'round these days. I had one out on double E th'other day. Another not more'n a month ago. Goddamn opioids and politics driving people out their minds. You headed home now?" He sounded both hopeful and threatening.

"I heard that my dog mighta died out in the woods. Gonna go see if I can collect her."

"Well, heck." Sheriff Hardesty slapped the door of his cruiser. "That's a real shame. Good dog?"

Jodie nodded. The sheriff removed his hat and tossed it onto the front seat.

"Good dog's worth its weight. You set right there. I got something for you." The sheriff climbed out of the SUV, went to the back, and raised the gate. He dug around a bit before pulling out a folded piece of plastic, which he held out to Jodie.

"What is it?" Jodie asked, his arms folded across this chest. He made no move to take the item from the sheriff.

"Body bag." Hardesty waved it at Jodie. "For your dog. It's a torso bag. Kid-sized. Luckily, I don't have much call for the little ones. I can spare it if you can use it."

"This what the county pays you for these days? Driving 'round, handing out party favors on the taxpayer's dime?"

The sheriff's arm dropped, and he frowned. "I'm headin' to your neighbor's place, actually. Judge Tanner's wife called dispatch. Mandy May. Couldn't understand a word she was saying. Just garbled bullshit, so I figured I'd best check it out. You haven't seen or heard anything strange out your way, have you?"

"Would it matter if I had? Doesn't seem like my word or my family's counts for much 'round here."

The sheriff snorted. "You really are a pissant, aren't you, Jodie? I was gonna offer you a lift, but I doubt you'd take it, seeing how little sense you got."

"You thought I'd take a ride from you?" Jodie laughed. "No Burden ever climbed willing into any vehicle with no lawman, even if the lawman is as crooked as you, Hardesty. I always wondered... Lauderback got you on a 1099? How's all that work?"

Unruffled, the sheriff squinted up at the sun. It had cleared the top of the Quonset hut, and Hardesty stared at it like he was trying to make out the time of day.

"We do what we have to, Burden. This world doesn't always give our druthers much of a nod, does it?" His lip curled into a disdainful sneer. "Doesn't pay to rock the boat, a fact your family mighta done well to remember over the years. Take the bag at least." He threw the body bag at Jodie, who let it bounce off his chest and fall to the ground. The sheriff climbed back into the SUV. "Enjoy your walk home." He tipped his hat before placing it back on his head and putting the vehicle into reverse.

"Will do. Tell your wife my sister sends her best." Jodie raised his voice to make sure the sheriff heard.

"Someday, you'll learn when to shut the hell up, Jodie, else that mouth a yourn gonna get you killed." The sheriff rolled his window up and hit the siren before speeding down the road in a storm of red and blue lights.

Jodie waited until he was out of sight before he bent down and picked up the body bag.

CHAPTER

ELEVEN

Leonard Trumbo hadn't said exactly where in the woods he had seen the dog, but Jodie figured he had a pretty good idea where to look. He didn't wait until he reached the turnoff toward home before climbing the crumbling embankment along the highway and plunging into the unruly thicket beyond. There, the treed hillside was steep, and Jodie had to turn sideways to keep himself from pitching headlong into the ravine. Even so, he slipped and skated hazardously down the slope, grabbing saplings to slow his momentum, until the moss-covered roof of Keller's sawmill came into view about a hundred yards ahead.

Jodie dropped the last five feet or so off the rock ledge running behind the mill and landed on all fours. He eyed the aging edifice from a crouch. Creeper and snoutbean snaked their way over the siding like green cords, and moss covered the splintery planks, but the structure had held up over the years Jodie had been away. An idle waterwheel dripped algae like a green beard, though it, too, was in one piece and gave the impression that, with the aid of a single shove and a steady current, it might yet turn and bring to life the titanic sawblades inside the mill.

Jodie spat his disappointment onto the ground. He had hoped to find the old place tumbled down or burned up, looking more like a ruin than it did. Seeing it so whole, so erect, made his head feel tight. As far as he was concerned, the building was a flinty scar on the landscape. It was sour milk and shattered china, stale bread and moth-eaten wool. It was everything rotten, pickled, broken, and empty.

He came around to the front, where the wide, black wagon entrance gaped, doorless and ready to swallow Jodie when he stepped up to the threshold. Jodie rested his hand against a post while his eyes adjusted to the dark. Light filtered down from the hole a young sycamore had torn in the roof, leaving specks of brightness like stray cinders on the mill floor.

He asked me to go to the mill with him, Daddy. Said he only wanted to kiss me where no one else would see.

If there had been any justice in the world, Keller's sawmill would have gone up in smoke by then or at least been torn down sometime before Kennedy was president. Instead, it sat abandoned and forgotten for nearly a century before being rediscovered, like most lonely old places, by lonely people: drug users, drifters, sad teenagers, and runaways.

No one seemed to know who owned the building, nor did they express any interest in organizing its demolition—not even to break it apart and sell to one of those reclaimed lumber outfits from the cities up north. Someone with the right entrepreneurial spirit might have looked at the better wood beams and posts and seen coffee tables and bar tops, but in Oracle Springs, few could have been bothered.

Jodie reached up and slapped the lintel overhead, imagining it whittled down into a sign hanging in someone's kitchen. "Live, Laugh, Love," it might read—a fine joke. There was no life or laughter in these boards. There was no love in this hulking ruin of a building. Only pain, despair, and ruination.

But there was no dog either. Dead or otherwise.

A quick glance was all Jodie needed to know for sure. The men would have left her out in the open for him to find, for shock value. Maybe Leonard had been telling the truth. Maybe he had happened upon the dog out in the woods.

Hidden Children

Jodie turned to leave, the corners of his eyes pinching protectively against the sun's light when he glanced upward. A murder of crows—sleek onyx scavengers—were carving circles on a faded blue cotton sky. The half dozen birds formed a bullseye, which Jodie only had to follow to a clearing near a fallen elm, where he found Miss Mouse.

The dog hadn't been dead for long. She couldn't have been—she had trailed Jodie to the front door after Min and Benji left and Lucas Tanner had waved goodbye earlier that morning. Jodie had shooed her away with his foot and shut her out of the house. He hadn't wanted her near him.

His mind was already on Bolivar—on The Elms—and all he could see when he looked at the dog was her red-stained muzzle. *Ate the boyfriend's brains right out of his skull like Alpo*—that's what the cop on the scene had said.

It couldn't have been more than an hour or two since he had last seen her, yet here she was, looking like a thing dead for days. Her flesh stretched away from her bones in ribbons. Her tendons, pink and shiny like bubble gum, were pulled outward over the ground in a bright tangle. She had been torn apart, practically turned inside out. And then there were the insects. They had found her already.

Not the advance troop of ants, always first to arrive, but worms, which was odd, Jodie noted, considering how newly dead the dog was. Worms and maggots needed time to hatch in a carcass, and there had been no time for that.

Jodie pulled the body bag the sheriff had given him from his back pocket and unfolded it, fighting the impulse to mentally thank the lawman he so detested. He laid it on the ground alongside what was left of the dog. If only the sheriff had seen fit to give him a pair of latex gloves as well. Jodie grabbed Miss Mouse by the hind leg and pulled her toward the bag. The ball of her hip joint popped free, and Jodie stumbled backward, the dog's rear limb still in hand. She was already rotting apart.

Jodie could almost believe he had made a mistake. It couldn't be Miss Mouse. This was someone else's dog or a stray. He dropped the dog's leg onto the bag and knelt beside the animal. Jodie held his breath and worked his hand around in the sticky fur until he located a collar in the ragged mess, then spun it around to read the tags. He wiped the engraved name with his thumb: *Mauser.*

A fly perched on the back of his hand. Jodie flicked it off, but two more landed on his cheek, and a third buzzed around his eye.

He swatted them away and watched while they flew to the trunk of a nearby tree, where they melted into the ranks of an army of their brethren.

Jodie became aware of the humming buzz of wings. Around him, every tree was wrapped in a writhing sheet of insects, like a glossy green and ebony bark. The swarm must have numbered in the millions. Jodie had never seen anything like it, at least not outside of a dream, and he wasn't sure how he had missed them before.

He hopped to his feet, flapping his clothes and shaking his limbs. Jodie imagined a host of creepy-crawlies working their way over his body. He moved quickly, grabbed a stout branch from the clearing floor, and used it to push the dog toward the plastic bag.

Miss Mouse flopped lifelessly from one side to the other. Her head lolled over, exposing a Blackwing drawing pencil protruding from one eye.

CHAPTER

TWELVE

There was only one bedroom in the Burden family's small home. It was more of a lean-to tacked onto the back by Min and Jodie's great-great-grandfather, Linus, for the purpose of hiding rotgut away from the prying eyes of the law. There was a bank of windows which had been cut in later, after the moonshine business went belly-up, and a large oak bed nearly filled the entire space. It was in that room, hanging off the back of the house like a parasitic appendage, that Jodie found Benji sitting alone on the edge of a mattress which sagged like a soggy tuna fish sandwich.

"You awake, little man?" Jodie asked.

Dumb. The boy was sitting up, wasn't he? The sun had set long ago, and the room was dark, but Jodie didn't need to turn on the light to see that. It was a good thing too because some things were easier to say in the dark.

"Got something to tell you—a hard thing, I suppose, but you need to hear it. Something's happened to your Miss Mouse. I'm afraid she's gone. She's run off."

If Jodie had been thinking more clearly, he might have wondered about the regularity of a child Benji's age sitting alone, so quiet and so still for that long, in a room as black as pitch.

"Aunt Min is about to start dinner. I hope you're not still feeling sick."

Across the bedroom, the mattress springs creaked, the rusted old coils telling Jodie that the boy had shifted on the bed.

"No use sulking over a lost dog. We can get you another if you want, a puppy even—one you can raise up yourself."

There was a long stretch of silence before the child spoke.

"She's out there." Benji's voice was the flat edge of a knife, so dull it made Jodie's heart throb, and for a second, he forgot they were talking about the dog.

"Yeah, somewhere...maybe. Don't sound so glum, little man. She'll find her way to someone nice, I'm sure."

Jodie turned his head as Benji came around from the far side of the bed. His slender form was nothing but a dark outline passing the window before disappearing into shadow at the edge of the room.

"Not Miss Mouse. *Her*."

Jodie felt a stab of surprise and looked back to where Benji had been sitting.

The boy was still there, exactly where he had been before. Jodie could make out his outline clearly. But if Benji hadn't moved, who or what had pulled Jodie's eyes across the room when it passed by the window?

A burst of cold exploded inside his chest, sending little tickling ribbons of ice shooting through his veins. He slapped the wall clumsily, groping for the light and missing it. His fingers fluttered over the wood paneling until they found the switch and flicked it upward. Light flooded the room, and the knot behind Jodie's ribs loosened.

Benji sat on the side of the bed, staring straight ahead, his feet dangling over the floor. There was no one else there. At least not *inside* the room.

Jodie squinted at the window beyond the boy, but all he could see with the lights on was the room's bright reflection in the glass. He was on edge—he'd cop to that—but hell, the whole town was. Every damn person in Oracle Springs was buzzing about what had gone down at the Tanner's place that afternoon.

Patricide. Right up the hill from the Burden's cabin. And the killer still on the loose.

"You shouldn't sit here, alone in the dark. It ain't right," Jodie stammered. A sense of ridiculousness began to creep over him. Imagine a grown man shitting himself over a trick of the light. "And you shouldn't worry too much over the dog. Ain't gonna change anything. I'm sure she's doing all right wherever she is...you know?"

Benji didn't answer, although his lips were moving. Silently, they formed words apparently not meant for Jodie, like the child was talking to someone who wasn't there or who was but Jodie couldn't see.

"Stop that muttering now, y'hear?" Jodie tried to sound firm and not frightened while he recalled the distinctly human shape which had passed by the darkened windows. "That's enough of that. Why don't you come on out now and watch one of your shows while your aunt finishes getting dinner ready?"

He led the boy out into the living room and settled him on the couch in front of the TV. Benji, sitting alone in the middle of the sofa, looked like he was floating away on a raft, the lone survivor of a shipwreck. Jodie grabbed a bottle of whiskey and a glass from the old china hutch before sitting down at the kitchen table.

Min was at the stove, heating up a couple of cans of pasta rings in sauce. "How'd he take the news about the dog?"

"Well enough."

"It's done, then. Poor old thing." Min stole a glance at her brother and the bottle on the table in front of him. "That my good whiskey?"

"Didn't know you had any that was good."

Min snorted and turned back to the stove. "Didn't say anything about the bad business up at the judge's place, did you?"

"Why would I bother him with that shit?" Jodie poured himself three fingers and didn't waste any time making them disappear.

"Lucas Tanner was kind to Benji. Not many are. There was a consideration between the two of 'em, and people'll be buzzing about what happened today, from Oracle all the way down to Bentonville. Benji's bound to hear something. Judge Tanner and his wife aren't any ol' folks."

"*Wasn't* any ol' folks," Jodie said.

"Last I heard, his wife was still alive."

"Mandy May Tanner. There's a real piece of work."

"You're tellin' me. Still, wouldn't wish what they're saying that boy did to her on my worst enemy." Min turned down the heat beneath her saucepan, the contents of which had begun to sputter and spurt. Red sauce splattered onto the stove and onto Min's hand, which she wiped on her shirt with little thought to the stains. "Honestly, I can't believe he'd do it." She shook her head. "It don't make sense. Lucas always seemed so gentle."

"You mean he always seemed so queer."

"You think anyone who's set foot in a museum or hair salon is queer, Jodie. You know what I mean. It's hard to believe he'd be capable."

"He's human. That makes him capable." Jodie poured himself another shot of whiskey. "If I've learned one thing, it's that we're all a bunch of crazy shitheads waiting to blow our tops."

"Oh, come on. Something real bad would'a had to go down to make him do his folks like that."

"I can tell you right now what happened. Boy got sick of his father's bullshit—tryin' to force him into a life he didn't care for. I'm telling you, that kid fought his way free in the only way the judge left him. He said to me this very mornin' that he was going to tell his pop he didn't want to study law anymore. Sounds like that went over real well, don't it?" Jodie leaned back in his chair.

"To hell with that, Jodie." Min craned her head to the side to make sure Benji was still engrossed in his show. "Nice boys—*gentle* boys—like Lucas don't go hacking their father's heads off with a machete over something like that."

"A saber. It was a Confederate saber."

"'Course, it was. Family heirloom, I suppose."

"Aren't they always?"

"They say Judge Tanner's head was taken clean off, and his wife, Mandy May, was near gutted and left for dead on the hall floor. No, a boy doesn't do something like that to his mother outta nowhere." Min began ladling pasta O's and sauce into bowls.

"*He was a quiet type.* Isn't that what they always say when shit like this happens to rich folk? *Kept to himself. Never any trouble. No idea he had it in him.*"

"It had to be someone else. Tanner ran a tight court. He could have pissed off any number of sickos with axes to grind."

"Then why did he run, Min? Why didn't the boy go to the sheriff and tell him what he saw?"

"How do you know he ran? I heard all the cars were in the garage. The boy could have been taken, or maybe he's buried in a sinkhole somewhere. Hardesty's making assumptions, and so are you. That man came out here with his mind already made up, just lookin' for a reason to pin it on the boy so he can close the case and get on with other things. Exactly like every other missing person case in this town."

She took a bowl of pasta over to Benji and used the remote to turn the television volume up some before returning to the kitchen and setting the remaining two bowls down on the table. "You're doing it again, Jodie," she said. Min took a seat across from her brother, who was staring at the boy on the sofa.

"Doing what?"

"You're lookin' at him like he's something you tracked in on your shoe. You want to tell me why?"

"I don't mean to look at him funny. It's only that he was there in the house when she died, when Jaelynn shot herself and her friend. He tried to clean it up."

"I know. You said already."

"Did I tell you he was up to his elbows in her blood, like he'd took a bath in it? It was in his hair, on his face, right down to the soles of his feet. He looked like he'd been tramping through a slaughterhouse. Lord, Min, what'd he do? Roll around in it? Smear it all over himself? Now, when I look at him, that's all I can see—her blood all over him. In my mind, he's all slathered up, redder than a barn, and I see her brains on the floor and that damned dog wolfin' 'em down...

"I'm glad the dog is gone, Min. God help me, I am. But Benji—" He couldn't bring himself to say it out loud, to confess to his sister that he had considered leaving the child with protective services. "I look at that boy and all I can think of is my baby's sweet face blown clear off and everything that might have brought her to that moment when she pulled the trigger. Then I start wondering if maybe it was me. Maybe I failed her."

Min let out a low whistle. "You need to be careful. If you're seeing those sorts of things, even thinking 'em, you better believe that he knows it. Sometimes, I think he knows every goddamn thing we think, and that can't be good for him."

"What the hell are you talkin' about, Min?"

Min threw her spoon down next to her bowl with a clatter. "Don't play dumb, Jodie. You've noticed it too. He knows things he shouldn't know, couldn't *possibly* know. He hears things that ain't been said. He's like she was. He's like Jaelynn. And he's like Memaw."

"You're full of shit, woman. You been working at that hippy-dippy witch shop too long. You're starting to believe the BS you hock to them tourists, and you sound like your boss, Paula, with her emporium full of crystals and oils and charms—with her so-called yarb doctoring and what have you. Crock. Of. Shit. And you wonder why I moved away from this goddamn town."

"I'm telling you, Jaelynn knew things. She knew when it was gonna rain before it rained. She knew when someone was going to stop by for a visit before they even turned off the highway. She was like Memaw and, according to Memaw, her mama before that. And like our mama before she took off and left."

"What you know about our mother could fit on a postage stamp. Don't talk to me about that woman. I don't need to hear no made-up bedtime stories about Mercy Burden and her magical ways."

"A *come-before*—that's what Memaw called her," Min said, ignoring her brother. "She knew what was coming before it came."

"A *come-before*? More like a *come-and-go*, I'd say, considerin' how she ditched us and all. Our lovin' mother stuck around about as long as your jaundice."

"You're the worst, Jodie Burden. You know that? The worst. And you're the one who's full of shit because you know what I'm sayin' about Jaelynn is true. She had the family gift."

"Gift, my ass. Jaelynn knew it was going to rain 'cause there were clouds in the sky. That's common sense—something not everyone has in spades, I guess. And since when did we have people stoppin' by to visit, unexpected or otherwise? This dang family has been about as popular as skunk musk in a radiator since long before you and I's born. Folks have always given our kin a wide berth."

"She knew." Min pointed her finger at Jodie. "She knew about Carrie. Before any doctor did, Jaelynn knew."

Jodie slammed his fist onto the table, making the bowls and Min's spoon jump and clatter. "Stop your goddamn pickin' and leave Carrie be. So what? So Jaelynn knew her mama was dyin'? Maybe it was that obvious. Maybe I didn't notice or didn't *want* to see. Tell me, Min, which sounds more like to be so: Jaelynn was some psychic mind-reader, or I was a lousy husband who didn't even notice his wife was dyin' right in front of him?"

"Listen, Jodie," Min said, reaching her hands across the table toward his.

"Naw, you listen to me, Minerva. Supposin' Jaelynn had sight, supposin' she was a come-before, like you say...What good did it do her? How come she couldn't see what that fella was like, huh? How come she couldn't see what he was going to do to her? Explain that to me."

"Which fella?"

Misery flashed over Jodie's gaunt, gray face, making him look a decade or more older than his forty-two years. "Either of 'em. All of 'em. The one that raped her and knocked her up and the one that scared her so bad she had to shoot him. They were all the same, weren't they? Just out to get theirs and fuck everyone else—each selfish bastard there to pound a couple more nails in her coffin." Jodie folded his arms over his chest, his narrow shoulders hunching forward, his chest growing concave. "You think she knew all that was comin' her way and did nothing to stop it?"

"I guess it doesn't always work the way you want it to. Second sight or ESP, whatever you call it, maybe it's not that simple," Min suggested.

"ESP." Jodie rolled his eyes, then leaned closer to the table and his sister on the other side. "What do you know about ESP? You don't even have fuckin' gaydar. Trailin' after Sheila Hardesty like she's some kinda lesbo. I seen you makin' eyes. People are gon' talk."

Min shot daggers at him with her eyes. "People are always gon' talk. It's your choice to listen to 'em or not. As usual, you got the wrong end of the stick, but it sure would be nice one of these days if, seein' how you're my brother and all, you might think to ask me about it *before* you fall hook, line, and sinker for local gossip. I swear, sometimes it's like we've never met. You really believe the shit the town says, you of all people?"

"What am I supposed to think, Min? I've never seen you with a man." Jodie slumped back into his seat while Min rose out of hers. "Simmer down. I'm not sayin' that makes you what they say you are, but a person could see where they might get the idea."

"You've never seen me with *nobody*, Jodie, man or woman. And everyone 'round here's gonna get sore knees from all the leaps to judgement they're makin'." Now it was Min who folded her arms over her chest. "Seems like the only person don't got a heavy interest in my love life is me. Go figure."

"Either way, it ain't gonna end well. You're a Burden too, and happily ever after never works out for any of us."

"You're such a hypocrite, Jodie, lecturing me on appearances and things that don't end well. You trying to tell me you didn't go sniffin' 'round after Alison Mader today at her brother's bar? Lookin' for work, my ass. Like any of them crews'd take you on and risk pissing off Lauderback himself. All I was trying to say before is that you can't lie to a kid like Benji, and if something's on your mind, he's gonna know it. Best thing is to be honest with the little guy. He's hurtin' plenty, and it's okay to show him you are too. Let it out sometimes."

Jodie looked over at Benji on the couch. Seeing him there, watching TV with his head cocked at a familiar angle, made Jodie's heart ache. It might as well have been fifteen years earlier and Jaelynn sitting there on the sofa, so alike were the mother and son.

"I can't do it, Min." Jodie shook his head. "I can't let it out. If I do, there'll be nothing left of me."

CHAPTER

THIRTEEN

During the night, Jodie was pulled from his sleep by an intense thirst. His head ached from the whiskey he had drunk at dinner, and his tongue seemed as swollen as one of the fat white grubs which gnawed on the roots of the vegetables Min tried to grow—the ones that always seemed to shrivel into sad tufts of straw. The glass of water he had left on the table beside his bed was empty—he couldn't recall when he had finished it off—but, in the silence of the cabin, water dripped.

It fell from the bathroom tap or maybe the kitchen faucet, in drips which had to be as big as butter beans. They hit the rusted drain cover like a tin pan drum. The sound was torture, increasing Jodie's thirst ten-fold and driving him from his bed, even though his head felt like it was trapped in a vise.

He padded his way down the hall and past the couch where Benji slept. The boy's breathing was soft, rumbling like a kitten's. In the kitchen, Jodie turned on the faucet, which hissed and spat water so noisily, pipes groaning in harmony, that Jodie feared he would wake the whole house. He let the fixture run, however, while he filled a glass and drank it down before filling another.

Each time he finished a glass, Jodie remained as thirsty as he had been. There was a briny taste in his mouth, like he had been drinking salt water from the ocean. He held up his glass to inspect it. The water was dark.

Suddenly, the taste made sense.

Jodie dropped the glass into the sink. It wasn't water he had been drinking but blood—a blood so red and rich it appeared almost black in the darkened cabin. The sink was splattered with the same thick ichor as well. Jodie backed away, wiping his hands on his shirt where they felt damp with gore.

The front door blew open, and a quiet rustling crept inside the house, the delicate whisper of a breeze through dense foliage. Jodie stepped toward the door, intending to shut it before Benji woke.

From the opening, the forest summoned him with a sigh, and instead of closing the door, Jodie stepped outside to meet its call. He climbed down the steps to the drive and stood alone beneath a moon and stars so close he might reach up and touch them. The universe, usually resolved to proving to Jodie how tiny and insignificant he was, grew smaller.

It was as if the cosmos had realigned and drawn inward, twisting and collapsing while they fixed on Jodie as their new, true center. Even the trees seemed to silently pick up their roots and move a step closer. This world around Jodie was narrowing, forming a tunnel which funneled him into the woods.

A path wound through the forest like a silver ribbon. It stretched out before Jodie, and beyond it, on all sides, strange white flowers grew, mirroring the scattered stars in the heavens. They glowed in the moonlight, unfurling and opening in waves when Jodie passed, like the tiny mouths of baby birds waiting to be fed.

Snakelike vines overhung the path, reaching down from the encroaching trees in twisted tendrils, straining toward Jodie. They, too, possessed those curious blooms—the white flower mouths— which seemed to snap and nip at the air.

Curious, Jodie reached out to the bloom closest to him and found it hard and rigid to the touch—more like bone or cartilage than plant. He plucked the blossom from the vine and held it close to his face to inspect it.

It *was* made of bone—tiny white bones, like fish ribs or bird legs, complete with little claws at the tip. In the center of the bone flower was a pistil, like a flat red chicken's tongue. Jodie reached out to prod it with his finger, but it snapped closed. He dropped the flower onto the path and watched while it wilted and decayed. It turned to dust before his eyes, and from that rose a figure as white and gleaming as the bloom had been.

The ivory dust became a woman.

Smooth as porcelain, she moved like moonlight, spreading over the path toward Jodie. Her eyes were as pale as her skin, though not entirely blank. There was a faint ring of iris lurking there, a ridge of the lightest sky blue, and it was fixed upon him. Her gaze was fast and unflinching, but when she was a little more than a breath from Jodie, she turned away.

Her body contorted like a sliver of light on a clear ocean floor, and although she was smooth as marble everywhere else, where her spine should have been, her skin was ragged and torn. She was a vessel split open, with a jagged rent running from the nape of her slender neck to the curve of her lower back. The chasm resembled the split in a rotting tree or log, and it held only darkness within.

Shadows crept out, like black oil bubbling up from a fissure in the earth. They moved through the air, reaching for Jodie, enveloping, swallowing him until he was lost in a night as dark as pitch.

There was no longer light in any direction. The stars and the moon were gone.

Jodie understood he had fallen into that crevice in the woman's back and was now lost in an abyss within her. She was infinite, all around him with her darkness, but even darkness had degrees. Upon this matte black canvas were oily shadows. Like night on night or black on black, they caught the light from some unseen source and gleamed around their edges until they became wiggling threads and bands of dancing onyx within the ebony world.

Hundreds of these shadows, maybe more, surrounded Jodie and flowed through the unlit ether inside the woman like vague wraiths. Jodie could not fathom the exact nature of these veiled forms which crept and crawled toward him. They encircled him, prancing and swirling, alive, with their ragged panting, their agonized breathing.

They snorted and stamped the closer they came. Things with cloven feet, things with snouts and muzzles. Jodie spun around, looking for escape from the ranks of the shadowy congregation, but the hungry band growled from all corners of the darkness.

Jodie's panic rose until cool arms embraced him. The pale woman was there—a vision of her within the other, like a nesting doll. She was a shield between him and the legions of invisible beasts. Slowly and fluidly, she changed in his arms.

In the midnight land of monsters, she was one thing and then another. She was Jaelynn. She was Jodie's mother. She was Alison Mader and more. She was his first schoolteacher, a waitress he had met in Branson. His wife, Carrie. Yes, she was Carrie in her sundress, in a hospital gown, then naked and beckoning to him.

Can you hold me?

Jodie *was* holding her, wasn't he? She pulsed in his grasp, and her skin felt like water.

"Yes. I can hold you." His voice was a moan, and he tightened his embrace, but she wriggled away like a snake.

Not like that. She took his head in her hands and cradled it, tilting it this way and that. *Can you hold me here?* Her long fingers probed the shape of his skull. *Are you strong enough to become?*

When she pressed her palm against his chest, his heart seemed like it might burst.

Many try, but none ever last.

"I can hold you." Jodie gasped. Despite the coolness of her touch, heat flooded his body. It radiated through his torso and into his limbs and groin.

I am in you, and I am of you, Joseph Burden. You are chosen, and you will have blood and dominion if you choose it.

With one of her hands still over his heart and the other around his skull, Jodie's vision sharpened. The creatures surrounding him came into focus—a bizarre and hellish company of men, women, and beasts. They were distorted and broken, bent backward and twisted, spliced and joined like bad experiments. Their flesh had rotted away, and their bones shone in the darkness, which grew less impenetrable, lit by the clarity the creature had bestowed upon him.

Jodie shrank back at the sight of these monstrous creatures who sniffed and tasted the air, sensing him although they could not see him. They were all blind, their eyes gone—torn out or shriveled in the sockets—and their eyelids scarred over and sealed shut. They pawed the earth, writhing or bucking. Their twisted forms seemed determined, trying to convey something to Jodie, a message or a warning.

They cannot hurt you, the bone-dust woman whispered. *You needn't fear them.*

"What are they?" Jodie's voice was hoarse.

They are hidden things and lost things. Things that could not hold me.

"Are they dead?"

They are immortal now. I have made them so. When they grew too weak to contain me, they fell to darkness, and in darkness, they will live forever. But you...you will never know this sorrow. You are strong, Joseph Burden. Her palm pressed harder against his chest.

"You got me wrong. I ain't strong at all." Jodie gasped. His ribs cracked, and a searing pain joined the heat coursing through his body, radiating from where the creature's hand rested. "I'm weak. I'm stupid. I ain't got nothing to offer you. Nothing."

I see you, Joseph Burden, as I see all of your kind. You call to me. You shine through the darkness. You are everything. You are skratti.

"I don't know what that means."

Born of witches. You are a doorway, able to hold the hidden ones in their truest form and bring them forth. The others—man and animal—fall to dust before the old god's children can ascend.

Jodie tried to protest. He tried to scream but couldn't.

The woman pushed her hand into his chest, tearing through his skin, working under his muscles until her cold, thin fingers wrapped around his heart and squeezed.

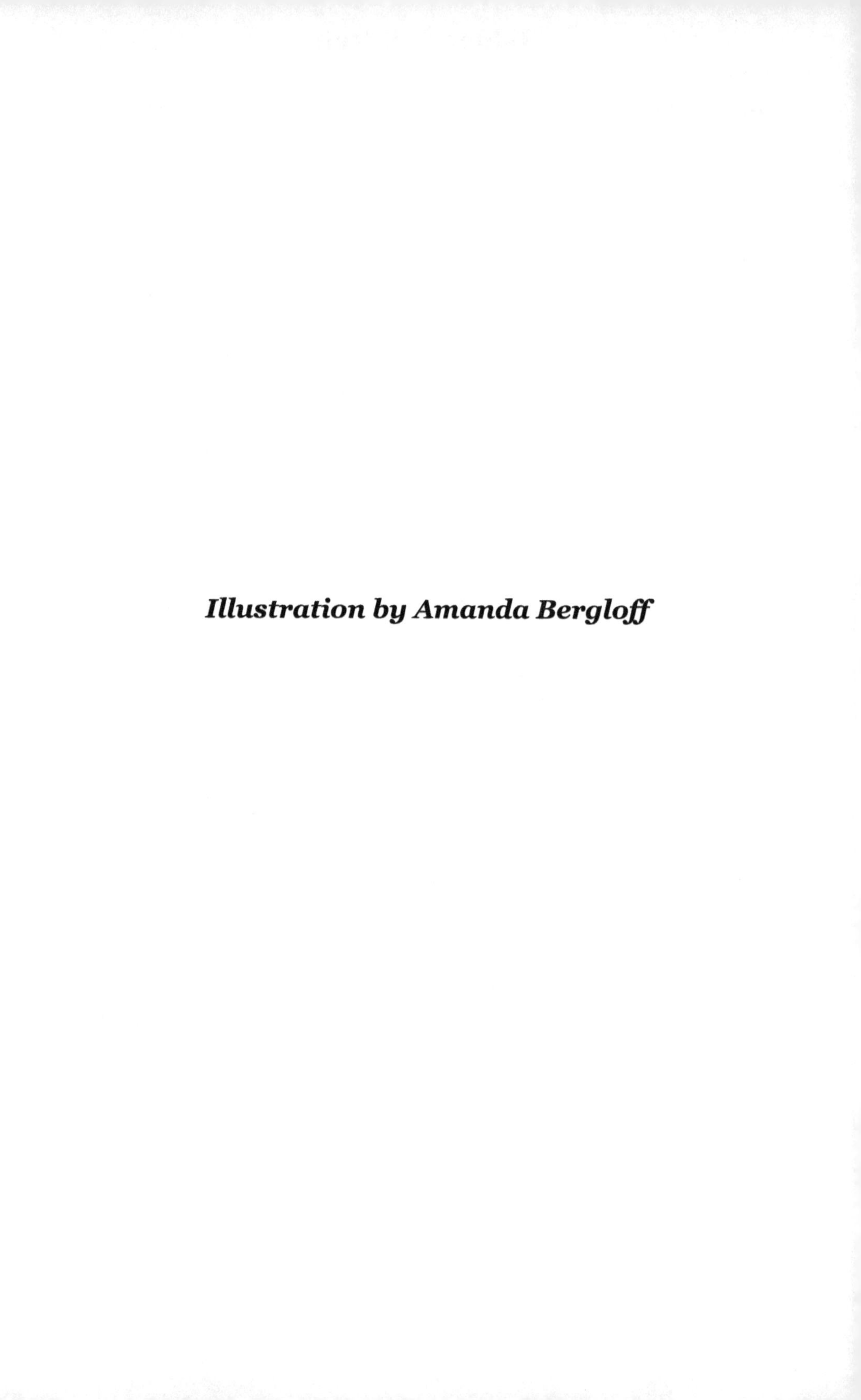

Illustration by Amanda Bergloff

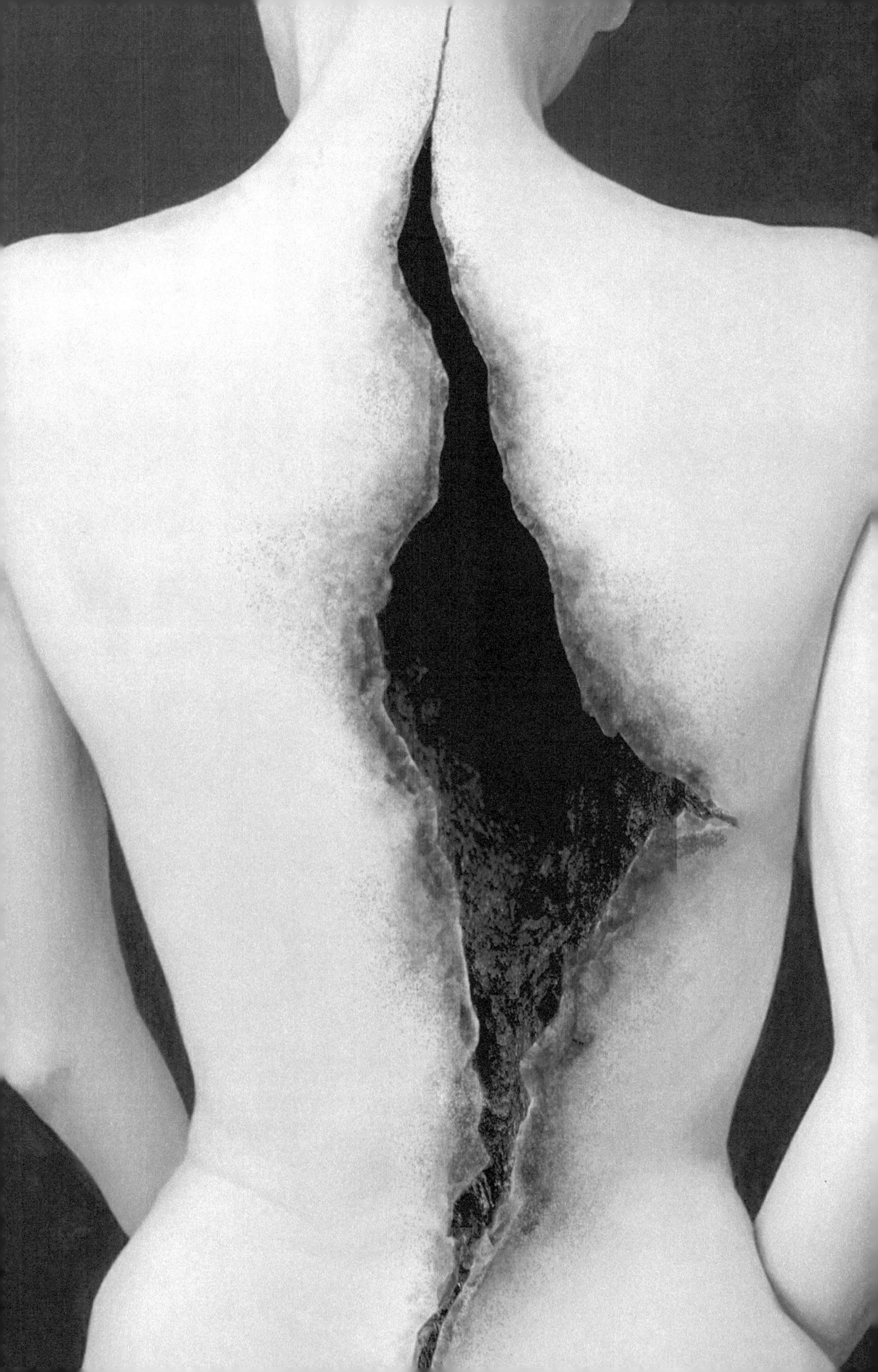

CHAPTER

FOURTEEN

A shadow fell over Jodie's face and blocked the morning light, sending the final fragment of a dream skittering out of his head like a scared rabbit.

"Goddamn, Jodie. Get up." Min's voice was a locomotive rattling through his dreamscape. She was on a tear about the window, something about the glass.

Yes, grousing about a mark or smear.

Jodie was drowsy, and the reason for his sister's consternation was less clear. She sounded upset, but he found himself struggling—and failing—to care. He flung his arm over his face to block out the light and his sister's nagging.

Jodie reached into the back of his mind and searched the nebulous haze for any remaining shred of the dream he had been having, but the images had faded to nothing. Until Min spoke, he had been far away. Waking up had been like coming back from a trip but doing so too fast, plummeting in an out-of-control elevator, or screaming down a hillside in a car without brakes toward the inevitable short stop. Jodie had whiplash.

Spiritualists and holy rollers had talked about out-of-body experiences, and though he had never set much store by that kind of thing, for the first time, Jodie could imagine what it might feel like. His chest hurt, and a disorienting fog clung to him.

"You want to tell me what you think happened here?" Min asked.

Jodie opened his eyes a crack. She stood over him like a vulture, pointing to the window on the other side of the room.

Jodie fought twisted sheets to sit upright in bed, and his sleep-addled brain tried to wrap itself around what he saw. "Bird hit the window?" There were several streaky smudges of red on the pane of glass.

"That's a handprint, Jodie, a bloody one. No mistakin' it."

"Lord, Minerva." Jodie yawned and stretched. A twinge rippled down his sternum, and he remembered the woman from his dream— the creature, how she had reached inside him all the way to his core. He patted and prodded his chest. His ribs were solid, but he had indigestion. "Why're you pissin' all over *me*? It ain't my handprint."

"Did I say it was?" Min strode to the window, knocking the bed hard with her leg, jarring Jodie mid-yawn. "Prints are on the outside."

"What's your point?"

"Someone was out there last night, someone with blood on their hands."

Jodie blinked drowsily in response. "What d'you want me to do about it?"

Min's jaw dropped, and one eyebrow shot up. "Oh, gee, I don't know. Maybe get up off your ass and check it out for starters."

"That mess ain't goin' anywhere." Jodie leaned back against the headboard. "I'll check it out once I've had my coffee. Could be animal prints."

"Animal prints?" Min followed her brother's gaze to the window, where five perfect red fingers met a clear palm mark. "Call Sheriff Hardesty." She shook her head and spun on her heels, crossing the room to the door. "With all that happened up the road to the judge and his wife, the sheriff's gonna want to know about this, and I ain't gonna sleep right until someone checks it out. I don't aim to end up with my head on a shelf, just so you know," she said from the hall.

"You think it's the Tanner boy?" Jodie swung his legs out of bed and called after his sister. "Last night at dinner, you were sayin' he couldn't have done nothin' wrong. Now you're worried about him coming down here and finishin' you off? Which is it, Min?"

When she didn't answer, Jodie heaved himself out of bed and went to the window for a closer inspection.

The rising morning temperature had already dried the prints on the glass and turned them more brown than red, but it was clear enough that the marks had been made in blood and nothing else. Jodie placed his hand over the windowpane, lining it up with the outline on the other side. His palm was wider, and his fingers were stubbier. Someone with long, slender hands had made these.

"Artist's hands," Jodie said under his breath, considering a small purple blood blister on the tip of his finger. Someone had been outside the window in the night, watching him while he slept—while he dreamed. Or maybe the prints had already been there when he went to bed and he hadn't noticed them.

Jodie recalled the shape he had seen passing the window in the dark, the one he had mistaken for Benji.

Min appeared again in the hall outside the door. "Maybe I'm wrong and it is Lucas who attacked the Tanners. Is it possible there was something really messed up goin' on in that house that we didn't know about? Sure. On the other hand, maybe Lucas is dead too and the person who killed him and his father and attacked Mrs. Tanner is still wandering around. All's I know is, we have to look after Benji. His safety is number one in my book."

"You think I don't feel the same?"

"I never said you didn't. I just don't know that you give his special circumstances as much consideration as they warrant. All these goin's on aren't good for him. He's sensitive to this sort of thing."

"Oh, Lord. You still on about him readin' minds and shit?"

"No. I'm talkin' about what happened to his mama. He's seen enough of this world's ugly already."

"Well, hell. If he's being weird, keep him home from school. Don't send him back there if you think he's gon' do something squirrely and make a fool of himself again. Let him watch TV and settle down."

"I have to work. You gonna watch him all day?"

Jodie scratched his ribs through his undershirt. "I would, but it looks like I need to go see the sheriff about these handprints, don't I?"

"You are the worst, Jodie, the absolute worst, you know that? I don't have time for your bullshit this morning. I'm late to open the shop as it is, and I still have to drop off your grandson at school." She slammed the bedroom door hard enough to rattle the windowpanes.

The glass, with its enigmatic markings, quivered, and Jodie was, once again, alone, his only company the fast-fading memory of the woman he had dreamed of the night before.

CHAPTER

FIFTEEN

Olivia Reynolds unloaded the last box of books from her silver sedan and carted it down a twisted set of stairs to the landing behind Paula's Emporium. There was less than four feet between the back of the building and the tall limestone retaining wall holding the mountain at bay. Olivia knew this because she had measured it with an app on her phone while she waited for a shop employee to show up and unlock the door.

She had also measured the height of the retaining wall and estimated the angle at which it tilted: ten feet and a precarious seventy-five degrees. A former law professor of hers had once said she had a meticulous mind, and it was undeniable that she had a head for details, along with an unending desire to know and categorize. Research, observe, and absorb—that was her MO. A move to a new town and state and the end of her law career hadn't changed that.

One of the first things she had observed upon moving to Oracle Springs was that the hills of the town weren't a continual slope but rather a series of narrow steps. Locals called them *benches*. Olivia wasn't sure if the mountains had formed naturally in such clear-cut terraces or if they'd had help from early settlers. A geologist would be able to say, but Olivia didn't know any in town—didn't know *anyone*. She had to assume God had done all the cutting and creating and the settlers had handled the embellishing when they threw up their rickety shacks and ramshackle abodes.

Beyond the crisp, stair-like incline of the mountain, there wasn't much order to Oracle Springs at all. It set Olivia's perfectly straight teeth on edge—the way the town's streets ran up and down at angles, zigzagging this way and that, hardly ever meeting at a proper ninety degrees. The houses, too, had been built with a reckless disregard for geometry or the laws of gravity. Their architects—novices and amateurs, it appeared—had given zero thought to the dangers of mudslides, and the structures hung on for dear life, appearing tethered to the rock face by vines alone or glued there with green moss.

Yes, Oracle Springs was chaos on a miniature scale, to be certain, but at least it didn't pretend otherwise.

The larger world was just as mad, just as irrational, but it hid behind an orderly façade and a myriad of sensible pretenses, which Olivia could no longer stomach. That was what she tried—and so often failed—to make her friends back in the city understand when they asked what the hell she had been thinking moving to Oracle Springs, where she was undoubtedly the only Black woman in a ten- or twenty-mile radius. Everywhere a person went, chaos and hatred bubbled under the surface, but in Oracle Springs—that harum scarum little town—the crazy sat right out in the open, along with the bigotry.

Olivia balanced the box of books on her hip and pulled open the door to the rear stockroom of Paula's Emporium. It was full of out-of-season items and extra merchandise piled in stacks so high they were as likely to collapse as any hillside or retaining wall in town.

The shop beyond wasn't much tidier. It looked out over the cobblestone streets of downtown Oracle Springs, long and narrow—about as wide as the front door plus a display window. It wasn't the sort of place Olivia would have considered setting foot in back in St. Louis. All kitsch and very little quaint, it was littered with a busy mélange of tacky souvenirs, offensive tchotchkes, and random housewares. The place cried out for a little brand management.

Olivia set her box of books down on the countertop next to a rack of dreamcatcher key chains and looked up in time to watch a truck with a large Confederate flag hanging off the back pull up in front of the café across the street. "Good ol' boys assemble."

"What?"

Olivia hadn't meant for the shopgirl to hear her all the way up at the front of the store.

Shopgirl? No. Olivia made a mental correction. The shopgirl was Olivia's age—early forties. Hardly a girl. Saleswoman, clerk, store associate—all these would have been more appropriate titles. Either way, she had spoken louder than she meant to.

"Sorry. I find I talk to myself more and more these days." Another few months of living like a hermit in the cabin she had inherited from her uncle and Olivia would be conversing with trees. "I meant the men across the street."

The woman had stopped working when Olivia first spoke but now went back to removing a display of lingerie from the front window without bothering to look at the men in question. "They're headin' out to look for Judge Tanner's kid," she said.

Olivia tried to remember her name. It was an uncommon one. *Minerva.*

Olivia had met her once or twice before when she came in to speak with the store owner, Paula, about stocking the book she had written. Paula had called her something shorter, though. *Min.*

The nickname suited her. Min—minnow, minimal, miniscule. The woman gave the impression of someone who tried to make herself small in general and did her best to go unnoticed.

"The kid went missing yesterday. They're goin' to try to track him down."

"I heard about that." Olivia leaned back against the countertop while several more trucks pulled up across the way and a handful of men got out. "What's the deal? Are they looking to rescue him from something or string him up? I mean, I'm not into Westerns, but I've watched enough to know a posse when I see one."

Min shrugged. "I suppose they'll figure it out when they come acrost him. It'll depend on their mood...and how much they had to drink."

She opened a box and removed several cocoons of tissue paper and bubble wrap. Based on the shape, Olivia guessed the bundles held mugs and shot glasses. Min unwrapped them all and stacked them in the front window. There was something about her, with her quiet awkwardness, that Olivia liked. And at least she was someone to talk to.

"That's quite a transition." Olivia watched Min pull the first of two four-foot-tall aliens out of the next box in her stack. She gathered that these little green men, with wide-black eyes and glowing rubber skin, were meant to take up residence in the space previously inhabited by the two wicker mannequins in lacy white bustiers. "Underwear to UFOs and aliens."

Min chuckled. Her laugh was hoarse and throaty, rusty even. "The underwear was for the newlyweds. They come for the bed and breakfasts 'round here from spring through summer. We sell them all sorts of things—lotions, handcuffs…The fuzzy kind *and* the metal ones. It all comes down in the fall."

"And fall is for aliens?" Olivia asked, trying to make sense of it. "Because of Halloween or something?"

"Because of the alien nuts. There's a UFO convention comes to town end of September. It's our biggest tourist event, and then ghost tours pick up closer to Halloween. This stuff's not big with the locals, but the tourists like it."

"So I gather," Olivia said. "I did a podcast a few weeks back on local lore. You know, the Ozark Howler, the Nixa Hellhound, the legend of the Gowrow. It got a lot of play but probably not from the local crowd. That stuff's about as popular as I am around here."

"Lucky for Paula, the tourists buy enough to pay the mortgage this time of year. That's why she changes up the merchandise."

"If it doesn't glow, it's got to go."

Min hopped out of the display window. She was shorter than Olivia had realized and slender to the point of skinny. Min all but disappeared behind the wicker mannequin when she wrapped her arms around it to dance it back to the rear of the store.

"*If it doesn't glow, it's gotta go.* Tell that one to Paula. She'll have a sign made up." She set the mannequin in a corner opposite Olivia, right next to a shelf displaying edible lotion, books on the Kama Sutra, and magnetic bumper stickers that said: "Just Married." After that, she returned to the front of the store for the second mannequin, which she also carted past Olivia, but this time, she headed into the storeroom.

"Watch out you don't trip over the books back there," Olivia warned. "I left a second box with another couple dozen copies inside the door."

"I see 'em," Min called from the back room.

"They're all pre-signed. If you don't think Paula would mind, I'll put a couple out on the shelves. And I've got a box of blank ones here by the table for the signing on Saturday."

Min joined Olivia at the counter. "You can leave a few by the register. I'll try to push them as I ring people up."

"That would be great. Honestly, though, I don't think you'll sell too many."

The stack of glossy books was ridiculously high, a towering monument to futility. It wouldn't matter how long she camped out behind the card table Paula had set out for her, Olivia would be lucky to move a tenth of the copies she'd had printed. It didn't matter, though. Sales were not the point of the whole endeavor.

Min followed Olivia's gaze to the table and mistook her dark look for one of disapproval. "I'll dress it up before Saturday so the ripped top don't show. We've got a couple tablecloths in the back."

"The table is fine. I'm just aware that there is a limited market for my book here in town. I agreed to go on a local radio show, thought it might have been good publicity, but it was just a waste of time. The host mostly wanted to talk about how I stood out here in Oracle Springs." Olivia's dark skin warmed with a flush, and the muscles at the back of her neck tightened. "And my clothing. Funny how men like him have no interest in women's clothing until someone wants to wear men's suits and a fedora. Then all of a sudden, they're experts in ladies fashion."

"Didn't like your hat, huh?" Min asked, taking in Olivia's loose-fitting slacks and double-breasted blazer.

"No, he did not." Olivia nodded grimly. "It's all right. I wasn't expecting Radio Mike and I were going to be best friends."

"What's the book about?" Min picked up a copy, turning it over in her hands, and Olivia felt a little stab of indignation that the woman hadn't read it yet. "*Under Their Skin.*" She read the book title out loud.

"It's about a late relative of mine, Dr. Hezekiah Reynolds. He owned the cabin I inherited from my uncle last year, the one I'm living in now."

"True story?"

"True as they get."

"I don't read much, but it looks real good."

"Thanks." Olivia smiled, even though she was pretty sure the woman hadn't meant it.

Min set the book back on top of the stack and returned the grin, but her eyes were already wandering to the display window and her unfinished work.

Olivia leaned over and rested her elbows on the counter, making herself comfortable. She couldn't quite bring herself to leave, even if she had done everything she came to do. All that awaited her back at her cabin was her late uncle's collection of Clive Cussler novels.

After depositing a couple of dollars on the countertop, she took a chocolate bar from a box next to the register. Caramel nut. Not her favorite, but in the interest of not having to return to an empty house, she unwrapped it and nibbled while she spoke.

"Hezekiah Reynolds was my great-grandfather—add a great or two—on my mother's side. He ended up here in Oracle Springs back in 1889."

Min glanced once more at the window and her uncompleted project. "What'd he come here for?" she asked finally.

"It's a weird story, one that goes all the way back to just after the Civil War. There were a lot of mangled humans around then looking for miracles, and it became known that the spring water in the Ozark mountains had healing properties. It most likely had to do with the minerals picked up from the surrounding soil—kind of an early vitamin infusion before people really understood vitamins—but the word spread, and people started showing up in droves to drink it and bathe in it, hoping to cure all sorts of ailments."

Min frowned. "I guess I don't know much about that."

"There isn't much to go on in Oracle Springs, as far as written history goes. Eureka Springs and Berryville have done a better job preserving their historical records. I really had to dig to find stuff on Oracle." Olivia picked a nut out of her molar. "As people started coming to the springs, they built a railroad to accommodate the influx and to bring in lumber to build hotels and healing resorts— early health spas and medical tourism essentially. The whole region was set to take off in a big way."

"Oracle Springs never had any big resorts or fancy hotels."

"I know. It was headed in that direction, like the other towns, but then it all went to pot. Something happened that shut the town down right as it was about to blow up like its neighbors. People

who came here started getting sicker, not healthier. It didn't matter why they came in the first place—TB, rheumatism, cancer. One by one, they succumbed to a mysterious wasting disease. No one knew what it was, but it was fast and fatal, and it didn't take long for people to start pointing fingers. Some blamed the water. Others said the disease was linked to livestock, and they culled herds and flocks until there were barely any animals left."

"Poor things."

"It didn't help either. Things got worse, and in 1889, they really started going downhill. The doctors gave up and moved out, and the undertakers moved in. The neighboring towns got scared, and someone tore up the railway. I guess they thought they could contain the spread of whatever this was that way. A handful of local businessmen tried to get the government to send someone down to investigate, but the Spanish-American War was on at that point, and the powers that be weren't going to expend much energy on an out-of-the-way spot like Oracle." Olivia paused to take one last bite of the chocolate bar and wrapped the rest back up in its shiny cellophane.

"Trash is back here if you need it," Min offered.

"Thanks." Olivia deposited the wrapper in the can and continued. "This is where my grandfather got involved and what my book is about." She checked to make sure her fingers were chocolate-free before opening a copy of the book and flipping to a page with a black and white tintype of a distinguished-looking man with a dark complexion and hair that was white at the temples. She held it up for Min to see. "Hezekiah was a scientist who spent most of his professional life in the Caribbean and South America documenting and researching the New World Screwworm. Do you know what those are?"

Min shook her head.

"Awful things. The screwworm fly lays its eggs in an animal's open wounds or even sometimes the bellybuttons of newborns. The larva that hatches is different from any other type of maggot in that it feeds on living flesh rather than dead. Once it's inside its host, it burrows in, twisting deeper and deeper, hence the name *screwworm*. It eats the animal alive from the inside out...and not only animals. The Latin name for the New World Screwworm is *Hominivorax*. It means *man-eater*. It'll live inside a person, devouring them until their flesh is covered with sores and falling off, and that pretty much fit the description of what was happening to people here in Oracle. Victims had large sores, missing flesh... And observers reported seeing what looked like worms crawling under the afflicted person's skin. There had also been mention of large fly swarms in the area. Hezekiah heard about it and came up to see if the screwworm fly was causing all the trouble."

"Was it? Did he guess right?"

"No. Hezekiah managed to collect a few specimens, but they weren't *Hominivorax*. They weren't like anything he'd ever seen before. He left some sketches he made in the cabin. If I hadn't seen other drawings of his, I would have figured he should have left art to the professionals, but the man could draw. His sketches of these flies show they had an abnormal number of legs. Some had one set of wings; others had two. None of them had any eyes, just bulging masses of tissue covered with some sort of membrane. He thought it may have been a new species, one previously undocumented but similar to the screwworm in behavior. He sent off samples to the government, but they still refused to act. Hezekiah was hooked on the idea of figuring this out by then, really obsessed. He bought a cabin and moved into town. At the time, he was the only Black man living in Oracle Springs and probably the most educated person around, so that went down about as well as you can imagine."

Min nodded. "How do you know all this anyhow?"

"He kept journals and documented everything. My uncle left the journals to me with the house. Hezekiah wrote about how the town shut him out, treated him like a pariah, even though he was trying to help them. People refused to speak with him, and the ones who did quite often told him ridiculous tales of possessions and curses. Superstition ran rampant. The mayor brought in a group of men from Bentonville called *witchmasters*. These men were like paranormal investigators, as near as I can tell. I found some good references to them in Vance Randall's writings from the 1920's. Ridiculous, really. Things got pretty heated. There were lots of accusations, and then Hezekiah disappeared."

"Disappeared how?"

"Vanished. No trace of any kind. He left behind a wife and child who were living in South Florida at the time. He hadn't wanted his family anywhere near the town when people were dying, but he wrote to his wife often. When the letters stopped, she got concerned. She sent her brother to look for Hezekiah, but he came back with no news, so then she went herself. She was a fierce woman and tried her best to get the authorities to look into the disappearance, but she had no luck."

"I hadn't heard any of that," Min said. "About your uncle, I mean."

"If Hezekiah had been white, you might have. History tends to want to erase us when it can. That's why my family fought so hard to hang onto this cabin. It's not about inheritance. It's about taking a stand and saying *we're still here* to the descendants of the people who killed my relatives."

"You think the folks 'round here killed him?"

"You doubt they did?"

Min shrugged. "Wouldn't put it past them. They killed my great-great-grandpa. That would have been a bit after your doctor uncle's time. His name was Linus. Linus Burden. They strung him up from a tree about a mile from the house."

"There you go," Olivia said with a resolute nod.

"In all fairness, though, ol' Linus wasn't any doctor, and he was caught trying to pour strychnine in the town's water supply."

"Why would he do that?"

"He was either drunk or gone 'round the bend. According to the stories my memaw told, he was an odd one, even by our standard. He claimed he was trying to kill a water demon that wanted to wear him like a Sunday suit. He said it had chosen our family and owned us and the only way to be free was to kill it. Everyone ignored him until he tried to take out half the town. They hung him 'til he was dead and rotted, then tore him down and threw him in the deepest pond. The family hadn't had much luck digging a well that lasted longer than a season, so the deep pond—the big pool at the base of the hill by the house—was their only source for water when the smaller pools dried up in summer. Linus's body left it poisoned for months."

"That's sick."

"It's how things were done back then."

"No, it's murder. If you excuse past injustices rather than condemn them, history will repeat itself. You have to kill that kind of thinking. Drown it back to hell. Your uncle was probably schizophrenic. He needed help. My uncle deserved tenure at a good university. A government grant, maybe. Let's not try to paint that into a prettier picture than it is. This Saturday, I'm going to sit out on the sidewalk with my book, talking about the past." She slapped the cover. "Maybe I don't sell a single copy, but I'll get under people's skin a little, make them think a little harder about some things. Make them take the blinders off."

"You think it's gonna change their minds about anything?" Min curled her lip, and her eyes flashed.

For the first time, Olivia recognized in her a bitterness, a quiet rage, not unlike her own.

Min continued before Olivia could respond. "Any ideas the people in this town got are all pretty much burrowed in, like those screwfly worms you were talking about. I know firsthand. Nothing ever changes. Some folks get away with anything, while other get blamed for everything. That's how it is for my family. If you listen to the talk in town, the Burden women are all whores, and the men are lazy good-for-nothin's. Farther back you go, the more creative folks get. They accused some of us of being witches. Who knows, maybe those witchmasters you mentioned came sniffin' around my kin's door back when folks were getting sick. More recently, like not even thirty years ago, they were calling my memaw a witch, said she made milk go sour and could take the shape of a hare when she felt like it."

"A hare, as in a rabbit?"

"Yep."

"No shit? That must have come in handy around Easter time, huh?"

"Right." Min chuckled before growing serious again. "They killed every last pig and chicken she tried to raise, and once or twice a month, a group of men would get to drinkin' and decide to use the front door for target practice. Family must've had at least a dozen different front doors blasted to splinters over the years. Did you know that Burden wasn't even our last name originally? It was Bourdon, but that somehow got changed to Burden in the town register."

"I'm guessing that was no accident."

"No one in the family has ever assumed it was."

"I should interview you for my podcast. Sounds like your family has an interesting history."

"No, I couldn't be on any show. It doesn't pay to stick your head out like that in this town, not when you're a Burden. I keep a low profile, and folks leave me alone. I start talking about diviners or yarb doctoring and people'll start saying I made a pact with the devil."

Olivia almost laughed but stopped herself in time. The woman was serious, and she might not have been wrong. When Olivia had lived in St. Louis, she wouldn't have believed people still bought into these old superstitions, fearing the devil like he might appear in the flesh. Even she, who had seen some strange things in court, assumed society had come farther than this, but that was before she had passed a couple of signs bolted to a fence around a cornfield, which ran alongside the highway from St. Louis toward the mountains.

"Beware Witches and Homosexuals," the first sign read. The second said, "They are the children of Satan." It would have been comical if it wasn't so sad.

"You think we're funny." The woman was perceptive. Olivia was sure she hadn't smirked, not even a little bit, but the woman had picked up on something, and her brown eyes had gone stony.

Olivia worried that their connection, the first tenuous link she had forged with a real local, was in danger of snapping. She sighed. "Not you, Min, but there are a lot of backward people in Oracle Springs. I haven't exactly received the friendliest of welcomes. Now, I have no problem with superstition in general—each to his own—but I take issue with the racism and the bigotry, and I can't help but see that it's all connected. These things are born from a place of ignorance, and ignorance kills. It killed my great-grandfather and maybe yours too. It needs to be called out for what it is. That might not earn me many friends, probably fewer friends than my book will earn dollars." She sighed. "Writing doesn't pay what legal work does."

"You still take on any cases?" The stormy look in Min's eyes vanished, replaced by a needy gleam. Based on the woman's reaction, Olivia had uttered a magic word of sorts. "I mean, you're still a lawyer, right? You still got the—what d'you call it—the bar?" Min asked.

"I'm still a member of the Bar Association and licensed in Missouri, but I don't practice. Not in over a year."

"You ever deal with custody issues? Like if someone who isn't a kid's parent or even grandparent but is still related could get custody from another family member?"

"Are you thinking of suing someone for custody?"

"No...I mean, I don't know." Min stopped herself and pressed her lips together so tightly they pulled inward and disappeared.

"You know what, forget it. Forget I said anything."

And there it was. The thread had snapped. Min smiled, but it was a smile for customers, formal and obliging. It was the same tight-lipped grin Olivia got from strangers she passed on the street.

The phone rang. "I gotta answer that," Min said.

"Don't let me keep you," Olivia replied flatly. She moved away from the counter, over to the shabby card table and the stack of books.

Under their Skin. She would have to remember to bring a pillow to place on the metal folding chair Min had set out for the book signing, or her ass would be sore before noon.

Olivia planned to sit out there all day—all weekend—staring down every redneck who passed by until she was sure she had gotten under *everyone's* skin.

CHAPTER

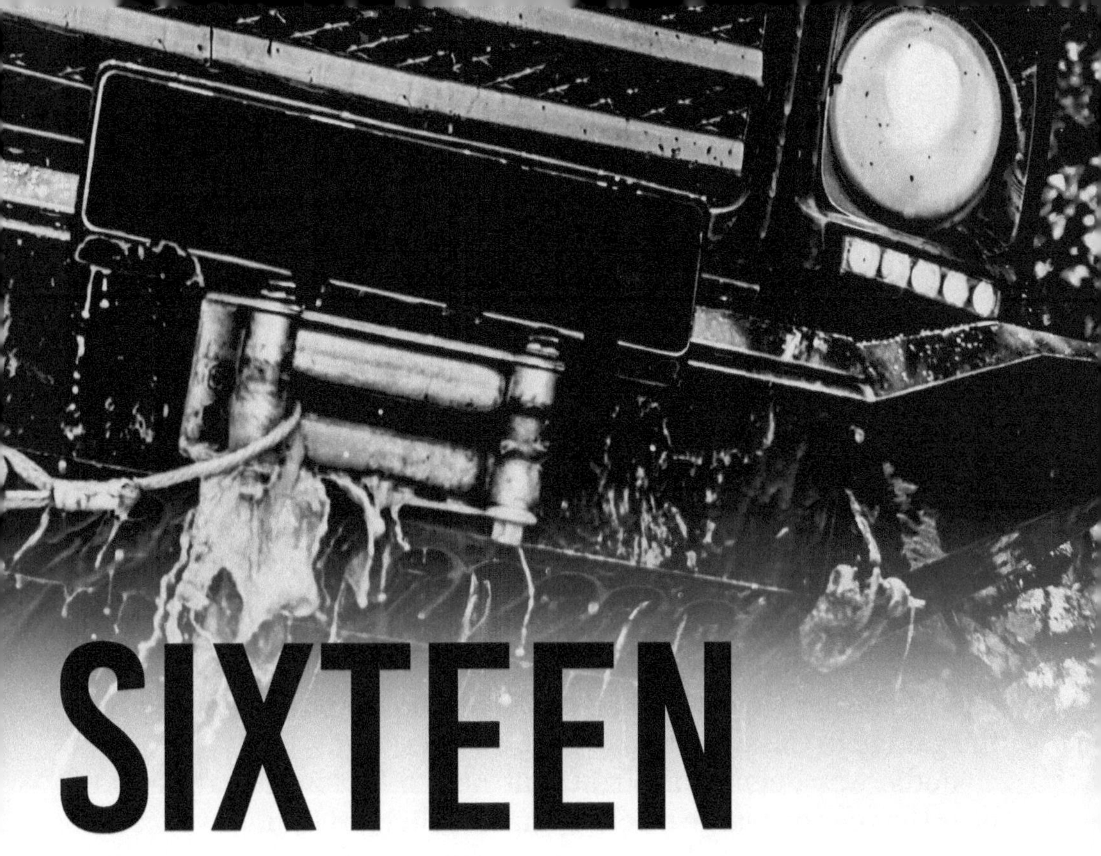

SIXTEEN

The bloody prints on the window of Jodie's bedroom had definitely been human. More disturbing than that, though, was what Jodie had found on the ground beneath the window. Lying in the dew-dampened earth were strands of human hair, dark like the Tanner boy's, and skin.

No, not skin.

Chunks of flesh. Long strips of rotting tissue, like a coyote had gotten a hold of something but lost his appetite and left half of it behind.

Jodie's stomach had churned, but he managed to bury the gory mess in a hole near where he had interred Miss Mouse. It was only later, when he was halfway into town, that he wondered if maybe it hadn't been such a good idea. He had buried the proof that something hinky had gone down. The sheriff would hardly believe him without it—hell, there was a chance the sheriff wouldn't believe him *with* proof.

The whole endeavor might turn out to be pointless, and he would have walked all that way for nothing.

Jodie ducked around a road sign. He was still five miles from town. Min had ordered him to get after the sheriff about those handprints, then left him with no good way of doing that. Without wheels to get into town or a working phone, it was like she expected him to send up a smoke signal. Only it was worse than that. She expected him to walk all that way—more than twelve miles there and back—to speak with a man whose corruption had helped put Jodie's daughter on the path to an early grave.

Jodie kicked a rock and sent it winging down the hillside. He bet Min hadn't thought about that.

A little bit of consideration was all he wanted. And, if she would let him borrow the damn truck from time to time, he could drive into Bentonville and donate plasma. There was good money to be made selling plasma, if he went often enough. With some cash, he could get his phone working. And he could put down a deposit on another beater since he'd had to sell his old car to one of the guys at the garage in Cassville to pay back a loan.

Jodie was deep in thought, but not so lost in it that he didn't hear the roar of a large truck on the road behind him. It was coming up fast. He moved a shade closer to the shoulder to make room for it to go around, but a moment or two later, the truck still hadn't passed. The sound of the engine had grown quieter, and what had once been a roar was now little more than a growl, low and throaty.

The vehicle was creeping along behind Jodie, like a big cat stalking a gazelle. Jodie's body tensed. His every nerve was singing while he waited on the pounce, for the knife-like claws in the back.

It came soon enough.

Something heavy—a full beer can, maybe—struck him in the back of the head. There was a metallic thud, a searing pain, and an explosion of tiny twinkling stars behind Jodie's eyes.

Sparklers on the Fourth of July…Fireworks overhead reflected in his daughter's big, baby doe eyes…

Jodie's knees buckled, and he tried to remember why he had been on the road in the first place. Then he blacked out.

Hidden Children

In the half-light of dusk, young Jaelynn approached, purple popsicle juice staining her chin and dripping down her elbow. Barefoot and dirty, she and Lucas Tanner flew past Jodie and down the road in front of the cabin. They shrieked, waving their frozen treats in one hand and the sparklers Jodie had given them in the other. Flecks of light scattered into the dark in their wake, and the sparklers made spitting noises, like angry cats.

Jodie leaned back in a plastic lawn chair, moving his bare feet away from the heat of a low charcoal grill. Carrie, his wife—alive and all honey-sweet vitality—with the cancer only beginning to eat her from inside, danced toward him. Her sundress clung to her legs, and she smiled at Jodie over a platter of bloody meat for the barbeque.

Large fireworks—copperheads, whistlers, and blinkers—burst in red, white, and blue showers, which blossomed against the black velvet night. Holt Tanner—Zeus Almighty in his mansion on the peak above the cabin—hurled a thundering barrage of fireworks against the sky. The delighted guests crowding Tanner's Olympian decks clapped and cheered but were drowned out by each subsequent volley of incendiaries.

Below, Jaelynn screamed and covered her ears with both hands when the display reached its crescendo and the sky lit up like day. She abandoned her sparkler and popsicle, the latter melting into a sticky, black pool on the ground.

"Don't worry, baby girl. Daddy ain't gonna let nothin' happen to you," Jodie promised, but the vow was broken into so many pieces by the sound of explosions.

Jodie's head hit the truck bed with a bump. It jarred him awake and rattled his brain enough to let him know it wasn't entirely swollen. Heavy tools inside the storage chests on either side of him clanked and thumped while the truck—the one which had been tailing him—bounced over the rain-carved ruts of a crumbling road. Hogtied and unable to keep from pitching and rolling around, Jodie bounced into and off of an unknown companion.

There was another man with him in the back of the truck.

Jodie came nose-to-nose with him long enough to recognize the fear written over the man's face before they each hurtled away to opposite sides of the bed. When they rolled back toward each other again, they avoided eye contact—not scared enough to ignore the awkward intimacy of being so close to a complete stranger.

Jodie had never seen the man before, and he wondered if he had been away so long that he no longer knew all the other pariahs in town. It was a small if not elite club. Then again, this man didn't appear to be local. He was bound and gagged like Jodie, but someone had shoved a rag into his mouth as well. If he was local, they wouldn't have bothered. They would have trusted that their victim knew there was no point in screaming. Not a single soul in town would take two minutes to call the law once they saw who was driving the truck and then reasoned out who had sent them.

The truck stopped, doors slammed, and the back gate opened.

"Mornin', Ellis," Jodie said. "How's things, Tank?"

Ellis Deems reached over Jodie and grabbed his bound hands.

Jodie whistled. "Whoee...If I had to guess by the smell, Ellis, I'd say you had shit for breakfast. You ever consider adding mouthwash to your dental routine?"

"The only one who's gonna eat shit is you, Burden." Ellis cheerfully let go of Jodie's arms. He took a break from dragging him to the edge of the gate in order to run his fingers through Jodie's hair. When he had a sufficient grip on it, Ellis raised Jodie's head and brought it down hard against the metal bed.

Rough hands rolled him off the truck, and Jodie landed face down in hot gravel.

Boots crunched against the small stones, and Jodie opened his eyes. He closed them again in pain when one of those boots collided with his stomach, knocking the wind out of him.

Jodie couldn't breathe. He was drowning, dropping like a stone in a rain barrel, sinking deeper. One of life's losers. He might have belonged there at the bottom of that barrel, but he was not alone.

The same boot which had connected with his stomach now struck his back, and Jodie's vision blurred. He gasped and stared up at the sky, like he was looking up through the surface of water. All that golden sunshine and blue haze a rippling blur.

Someone else—some*thing* else—was with him in the depths.

Not alone. Never alone.

Two pale arms snaked through the water, and a slender hand caught hold of Jodie's, suspending him and keeping him from hitting that bottom.

You are chosen.

Then two rough hands, anything but slender and pale, grabbed Jodie's arm and pulled him off the ground. Jodie gasped, able to breathe again, able to hear Tank Egon ask Ellis, "You want Burden or the other'n? Don't make no difference to me."

"You take th'other. Leave Burden with me. Boss wants to see him."

CHAPTER

SEVENTEEN

Jodie's shoulder popped in its socket when Tank wrenched him up to stand in front of Ellis Deems. The big man let the smaller one dangle like a fish on a line for a second or two before dropping him onto his feet. Jodie swayed back and forth, but Ellis had a hold of his bound hands by then and managed to keep him upright.

Ellis prayed he wouldn't be rewarded for his efforts by getting a load of vomit on his shoes. He waited for Tank to grab the other man out of the pickup's bed.

Once Tank had the second man in hand, Ellis marched Jodie across the gravel toward the large house beyond the circular drive. Made of raw timber and rough-hewn slate in mossy greens and grays, the sprawling home had the feel of a rustic mountain lodge or ski resort, complete with hand-carved oak doors leading into a rock-clad entryway.

Ellis had always felt the urge to look around for a check-in desk when stepping into the place. The architecture, along with the tufted leather sofas and tribal-patterned cushions and rugs, made him think of the hotel in that old movie *The Shining*. The house was a scaled-down version of The Overlook, with touches here and there which were pure Ozark.

Animal head trophies, their eyes fixed and staring, watched from their mounts high on the walls above the spacious living room. They were silent witnesses to the parade of captor and captive, and Ellis reminded himself it was better to be the predator than the prey. He quickened his pace and pushed Jodie ahead of him.

It had to have been Ellis's imagination, but the heads seemed to turn when he passed, following him with their beady eyes.

A long hall lined with family portraits and framed vacation photos led to the very back of the sprawling house. Ellis shoved Jodie through the door at the end of the corridor and into an office, where Samuel Lauderback sat behind a glossy oak desk bigger than Ellis's bed. He was busy at his computer when they entered.

Chiseled and tan, Lauderback had the look of an aging cowboy, a polished Marlborough Man in a crisp plaid shirt tucked into fitted jeans. There was something Hollywood about him, Ellis had always thought, like he was straight out of central casting, and even though they were close in age, both nearing sixty, Lauderback seemed a decade younger than Ellis. He lacked the dings and dents and perpetually worn-out appearance which aged the other man and was trim and tidy, where Ellis was flabby and disheveled. The man's close shave showed off strong features and what Ellis's wife would have referred to admiringly as "a healthy layer of collagen."

Samuel Lauderback was a high-headed man, a gentleman farmer and one of the last of the large-scale family growers in the area who hadn't sold his holdings to the Chinese, which Ellis respected. And although Lauderback had never served time in the armed forces—not like Ellis himself all those years ago—he had a military bearing, ramrod straight and hawkish, which made Ellis Deems want to stand up a bit straighter in his presence.

Ellis loosened his grip on Jodie, who headed for a leather wingback opposite Lauderback's desk as though he was there for a Sunday social call.

Poor misguided asshole.

He caught Jodie by the arm and jerked him back to the center of the rug, pushing him down onto his knees before Lauderback could look up and see where he was headed. It was a mercy, really. It wouldn't do the man any good to appear too forward or cocky. Lauderback would make him pay for it in spades.

"I presume I ain't here for a friendly chit-chat, then," Jodie said.

Ellis shook his head. Jospeh Burden—always with the smart mouth and no mother wit.

"You presume whatever you like, Mr. Burden. It's a free country." Lauderback's voice was a low drawl scraped over gravel, raw and rough, like that of a conservative talk show host. He looked up from his computer and removed a pair of silver reading glasses, rubbing the marks they left on either side of his nose. Lauderback set the glasses down next to a picture of his daughter astride a prize-winning horse.

Ellis wondered where the girl was. Where did Lauderback send her and his wife when he had Ellis bring folks like Jodie Burden around? All those years of doing the dirty for Sam and Ellis hadn't seen hide nor hair of them, except at social events and around town.

Jodie wasn't as interested in the photo of Hope Lauderback as Ellis was. He was taking in a different picture, one which hung on the wall behind the desk.

Grainy and sepia-toned, it showed a large open-air building housing a line of metal vats. The vats were surrounded by a dour crew of sturdy women in aprons and overall-clad men with wrinkled, peach-pit faces and eyes lost in squinty folds of flesh. Some of Ellis's kin were in that lineup.

The Deems clan had worked for the Lauderbacks as long as anyone—and most certainly Ellis—could remember. Farmers and farmhands, cannery owners and canners...Theirs was a shared history, Ellis liked to believe. It made him feel important and helped him justify some of the more distasteful things Lauderback asked him to do.

"You know what that is, Mr. Burden?" Lauderback asked.

"A cannery," Jodie answered.

Ellis wanted to slap the man, for his truculence and to shut him up—to stop his impertinent greening. That was the sort of disrespect which would inspire Lauderback to ask Ellis to do something he would feel bad about later.

Lauderback seemed calm, however. His blue eyes were bright and clear. "A tomato cannery, to be exact. My family's own. That's the original building, torn down back in '75. We raised tomatoes

and canned them commercially on this farm right up to 1967. Ours was one of the last of the Ozark canneries operating before the industry died in the region. We survived longer than most."

He reached up and straightened the picture, although it hadn't appeared crooked to Ellis.

"Look at them. That's history right there. More than that, even—that's the backbone of America. Hardworking families who carved out a living in an unforgiving climate, taking nothing but what the good Lord gave them and turning it into something real, something lasting." He held out his hand, palm up, and made a fist, like he was grabbing something tangible and not just air. "You think that resonates, Ellis?"

"Sounds good to me, Mr. Sam."

Lauderback swiveled to the computer on his desk once more and donned his glasses, peering through them at the monitor while he typed. "Something real. Something lasting." He stabbed his index fingers at the keyboard, his hunt-and-peck brand all cockerel aggression and no uncertainty. "Need to have something about rebirth maybe...reconnecting to a more honest era, a more industrious time. Or how about: *America, a land of producers, not parasites*? What do you think, Mr. Burden?"

"I think you sound like you're running for mayor or something."

"Not mayor, Mr. Burden, and not me. My son, Sam, Jr., has another year of law school. Once he's done, he can work for a year or two in the city, take on the right cases, and gain a little exposure. A following, if you will." Lauderback waved his hand without looking up. "I don't expect you to understand or, frankly, to care. I can't imagine civic duty is something you know much about." He finished typing. "Bottom line is, within the next five years, Sammy'll run for Congress. After that, well, sky's the limit. The party's changing. It needs fresh young stars like Sammy. So does the country."

Lauderback pushed his heavy chair behind him and rose like a king from his throne. He strolled past Jodie to the window. The man smelled of cedar and freshly cleaned leather—a scent which whispered of gentility and class to Ellis.

"If you look out that window, you know what you'll see, Mr. Burden? Tomatoes. Ten acres of heirloom Arkansas Travelers and Cherokee Purples." The burnished glow on Lauderback's tan cheek wasn't half as warm and rich as the pride in the man's voice. "You ever raised tomatoes, Burden? Pain in the ass. Finicky. The insects love 'em, and farming organic takes the patience of a saint, but the point is that we do things in keeping with the old ways around here. It's about celebrating our heritage. I don't raise tomatoes for the money—I got acres of soy up north for that, acres I could have sold to the Chinese, like the rest of my neighbors, and made a shit ton a' money—but the point is...Oh, goddamn, Ellis. I've forgot my point."

"It's all for Sam, Jr., Mr. Lauderback," Ellis said, proud to contribute but aware that Lauderback, sharp as a tack, forgot very little. He had brought Ellis in on the conversation to remind Jodie he was there—the heavy was still in the room, as it were, and the smaller man was outnumbered.

"Right. Thank you, Ellis. It's all for Sam and my girl, Hope, too. I raise tomatoes as a backdrop, Mr. Burden, to create the right platform. I'm setting the stage for Sammy's rise in the political world. When I had the cannery rebuilt, I didn't do it for this."

Lauderback gestured to a pyramidal stack of cans in a display cabinet against the wall. Each can bore a label which read: "Clay Hollow Cannery, Oracle Springs. Arkansas's Finest."

"I'm hemorrhaging cash. Did you know it costs me a dollar twenty for every can I turn around and sell for a buck eighty-nine? Chicken scratch. But it's not about that. Come here." He jerked his head toward the glass, granting Jodie permission to rise and join him beside the window.

There was something about it which made Ellis shiver—the two men surveying the one's kingdom. He could almost see the power and a sheer force of will radiating off Lauderback, like heat off a hot tar pavement. Something was building, a tension or an energy, but what it was, Ellis wasn't sure yet.

"Looka-here, all the way down towards the woods. You can see the shine on that new cannery roof. That there's American gold. This place is a slice of apple pie. It's all part of the plan: family farm, family values. Hardworking folks come up from nothing and look at us now. Bring me one of them there cans, Ellis, if you wouldn't mind."

Ellis opened the case and pulled out the topmost can, careful not to disturb the remaining tins or topple the pyramid. He lobbed it to his boss, who caught it, then tossed it lightly in one hand as if testing its weight.

"So many pieces to put in place...A goddamn jigsaw puzzle is what it is, but it's my legacy. It's what matters most."

He had barely finished speaking before he wound his arm back and swung hard.

No pause. No warning. No hesitation.

It took Ellis by surprise, even though he had long since forgotten to be caught off guard by anything Lauderback did. The can struck Jodie in the jaw and across the mouth, splitting his lip wide open. The force of the blow jerked the man's head sideways, and Ellis cringed.

Jodie dropped to all fours on the ground, where he hunched over and curled in on himself, like an animal with the heaves. Lauderback loomed over him.

"Like I said, Burden, we do things in keeping with the old ways around here."

Jodie spat blood, and Lauderback placed his hand on the back of the man's neck, forcing his face into the wool rug. Ellis wondered if, up that close, Jodie would be able to notice the rust-brown blood stains embedded in the intricate Navajo pattern. On occasion, Ellis himself had been tasked with cleaning up those stains, but no amount of scrubbing ever seemed to remove them completely from the bristly wool yarn.

Lauderback was practically sitting on Jodie by then. His weight on the man's torso seemed to make it hard for Burden to breathe. Jodie was wheezing and gasping while Lauderback leaned forward and hissed in his ear.

"Back in my grandpa's day, if a man came 'round threatening your family and your reputation, that man ended up bloody in a ditch or sunk in the creek with a bullet in his brain." Like a preacher spewing brimstone warnings and promises of damnation, Lauderback was breathing holy fire. "Yessir, I've got fourteen brand-new, stainless steel steam tanks down in the cannery, and I will put you in one, son. This is my promise to you, my vow before God, and you can take that to the bank."

Lauderback stood and surprised Ellis once again by not putting his boot in the man's face. The corners of Jodie's mouth had pulled back, revealing bloody gums and pink teeth. He grinned like a submissive dog waiting on the next blow to fall.

Lauderback could have taken the pained smile as mockery, but he must have known it was a grimace.

"My family didn't get where they got by being soft or letting troublemakers push them around. Now, I want you gone, and I want that boy, Benji—or whatever you call him—gone too. Showing your face in this town, bringing that little bastard around, is an insult to me and my son. It stirs up old rumors—ugly things that ought to remain dead and buried—and threatens everything I have planned for Sammy. He's the best thing ever to come out of this backwater, and he doesn't need whispers and gossip of past indiscretion and boyhood foolishness coming back to tarnish his shine. I won't have it. I'm not going to let one night and the accusations of some white trash tramp ruin a promising future. I'll lay you out cold before I let you take that from him."

If they had been outside and if Lauderback had been a less cultured man, Ellis figured he would have spat on Jodie. As for the man on the floor, there was a look in his eye Ellis recognized. It was that of a man who knew when he had been licked, when he had been beaten, when the hill was too steep and he had nothing left in the tank. So why, then, did something change?

After a moment or two of nothing—of bottom-dog submission—Jodie lifted his battered head. It appeared he was going to try to stand.

Ellis's body tensed in preparation for something. A counterattack or escape maybe. He watched Jodie warily, but the man didn't move further off the rug. Instead, his eyes rolled around in his head, darting this way and that while he searched the room. Ellis couldn't guess what for.

Then he realized Jodie was listening to something.

Ellis strained to detect what the other man was hearing. What came through was a faint ringing, a whine like the sound of a distant tornado siren. It was almost a song, as fine and thin as the string of drool connecting Jodie's bloody mouth to the rug.

Jodie's lips began to move, mouthing words Ellis couldn't hear or understand, and it made him uneasy.

His grandmother had told him stories about the Burdens, not Jodie specifically, but his relatives. According to her, they were a dirty clan of conjure folk who spoke the devil's language. Some of them, she had said, threw no shadow, having sold their souls for dark powers. According to her, they commanded familiars—strange creatures bound to do their bidding—and where there was trouble in Oracle Springs, one could be certain a Burden was behind it.

It was said that they burned dead infants to make charms from the ashes and stole milk from their neighbors' cows by wringing the liquid from a clean dishrag into a bucket while the poor beasts' udders shrank and shriveled. But that had been generations ago, Ellis reassured himself, there in Lauderback's office. Nowadays, the Burden were a bunch of good-for-nothings who couldn't get their acts together.

"You had better listen to me, Burden." Lauderback hadn't noticed Jodie's mumbling. "You get on up outta here and take that little retard with you. I'll give you the week to disappear, but if you're wise, you'll pack up a hell of a lot quicker. I promise, there will never be anything here for you but the pain I will rain down on you and your family. I will scald and skin you like a tomato and bury your sorry remains in my fields. My family will eat the fruits that grow up out of your rotting flesh. I will devour you. Do you hear me? I will crush you like an insect." To hammer home his point, he swatted at a fly which had landed on the wall beside him, mashing it against the plaster.

Lauderback wiped the remains of the insect off his hand with a handkerchief he had pulled from his pocket and nodded once more to Ellis, who was obliged to drag Jodie to his feet yet again.

Ellis huffed like a steam engine beneath the dead weight, without anyone to help him. He hoisted Jodie up and over to the window when his boss beckoned. Jodie's head hung low, but he raised his eyes, and the three of them watched Tank Egon and Buckie Cockrum frog-walk another man—Jodie's companion from the truck bed—out of the barn and toward the fields.

The men stopped before the rows of tomato-covered trellises. While Tank held the man in check, Buckie raised a gun and aimed it at the man's head. A muffled shot sounded through the double-paned windows of the office, barely louder than a book snapping shut. Jodie jumped all the same while Ellis marveled at the quality of the glass.

Tank and Buckie then dragged the limp man out into the field, where they disappeared among broad-leafed plants almost as tall as their heads.

"Think on this, Joseph Burden. I let that man die with his skin on. You won't be so lucky."

Lauderback grabbed Jodie by his hair and raised his drooping head off his chest.

Ellis was so startled he almost let go of Jodie's arms.

Behind ragged lips and chipped teeth, Jodie's mouth was a wide, smashed grin. It was a devil's mask he wore, and behind that crazy, wrecked nightmare of a smile, Burden smirked like a crazed fool.

"Feast for crows," he whispered in a voice Ellis didn't recognize. "In the end, you're all meat." He turned to Ellis, his eyes pale and glazed—milky, as though a thin membrane had grown over his corneas. "I've seen your charred body. I've seen the thing that you become, Ellis. You won't stop it once the bargain's made."

Ellis looked to Lauderback like a fearful child looks to a parent. Lauderback had always made it clear he found mental instability and disability distasteful for the plain old reason that he feared it might be catching. He took a step back.

Jodie's deranged jabbering had made the great man as nervous as it did Ellis, and his discomfort showed in a narrowing and sideways flicker of his eyes. "Get this babbling idiot out of here," he ordered. "Remember, Burden, you've got a week to make yourself scarce."

Ellis hauled Jodie out to the front drive and dumped him into the back of the truck, alone this time. Jodie moaned but continued to smile up at Ellis from the bed.

I've seen the thing that you become.

What the hell did that mean? Ellis gnawed on his fingernails while he drove toward town. His wife had warned him to stick to road work. She said they would find the extra money to make ends meet some other way, and for the first time, Ellis wondered if she hadn't been right. Every time he looked in the rearview mirror, he expected to see Jodie sitting up, grinning at him with that horrible smear of a mouth through the rear window.

As it was, the image was imprinted on his brain, and all the way back to town, he heard that voice that wasn't Jodie's.

You won't stop it once the bargain's made.

CHAPTER

EIGHTEEN

AJ Mader's pristine white T-shirt bore a sloppy streak of blood across the front. The paper-wrapped packages of raw beef he carried from the roadhouse van through the bar to the kitchen had sprung a leak. In addition to the smear on AJ's shirt, there was a trail of drips from the front door through the roadhouse, which would have to be mopped before the restaurant opened.

"You sit there long enough, Al, and I'm gonna have to put you on the menu," he called out to his sister, who was perched on the bar top with a phone pressed to her ear.

Alison stuck her tongue out at her brother and swung her feet like a child, trying to make out her son's voice over the static on the line. She hated how far away he sounded and the fact they rarely had a good connection between Oracle Springs and the base in Oklahoma. Alison sipped her Coke, which had gone flat while she had been on the phone, and let him do most of the talking. His stories about basic training left her feeling giddy and proud.

AJ returned from the yard, a streak of black charcoal now criss-crossing the dab of red on his shirt. With one hand, he held out a plastic bag of trash to his sister, and with the other, he gestured for the phone.

"Here, you say hi to your uncle while I get back to work. We'll talk next week, and Thanksgiving's 'round the corner. I bet they got you all thinned out up there, but I've got big plans to fatten you up while you're home. I'm going to send you back to base lookin' like a little butterball."

AJ wagged his head back and forth and snapped his fingers.

"I know, I know," Alison said. "Okay. Here's your uncle. He's been waiting. Bye, baby. Love you. You're the best thing I ever done." She traded AJ the phone for the trash and hopped off the counter.

Outside, her black, buckled moto boots sank in the loose gravel while she dragged the trash bag to the dumpster in front of the restaurant. Her mood was lighter than her stride, and she felt like whistling until a movement in the corner of her eye stopped her in her tracks.

A deer stood a few feet from the edge of the woods beyond the parking lot, frozen like a sculpture made of snow. Its fur was the exact same color as its ivory antlers.

Alison stood stock-still, as motionless as the deer, hypnotized by the creature's glacial beauty, until a chill wriggled up her spine—a feeling as frosty as the animal's arctic coat.

"A sign," she whispered, but the deer's ears pricked up anyway.

Alison held her breath, afraid of scaring it further but also just plain scared. She didn't set much store in the superstitions of the older folk in town, but a white deer was a startling thing. Alison had read once or heard somewhere that a creature like that was an omen. A good one or a bad one, she couldn't recall.

Alerted to her presence by some small twitch or sound, the animal turned its head toward Alison, who inhaled sharply when she caught sight of its eyes. Pupilless and staring, they bored into her, unflinching oily discs of white in the deer's skull.

The creature pawed the ground and shook its head, swinging its intricate, bony rack of antlers.

Tires squealed, breaking the spell the animal had cast over Alison. She turned her head and caught a glimpse of a black truck peeling out of the parking lot. When she looked back, the deer was gone. No sign of it at all. Not even a flicker of white between the trees or beyond the smokers.

A groan sounded from behind the dumpsters. Alison dropped the trash bag to the ground and approached cautiously.

"What in God's name?"

Jodie sat slumped against the metal side, bruised and bleeding. Alison lowered herself to her knees in the gravel beside him.

"What the hell happened to you?"

"I ran into a little trouble on the highway," Jodie slurred through swollen lips.

"You get hit by a truck or somethin'?"

"Or somethin'."

"You need a doctor. Come on. I'm goin' to bring my car 'round. Do you think you could crawl in if I get it close enough? Or should I go get AJ?

"It's okay. I'm fine." Jodie tried to stand but fell back against the dumpster. A bloody string of spit oozed out between his busted lips.

"You're *not* fine. That eyebrow's gonna need stitches and...Good Lord. Lean forward."

There was a smear of blood on the side of the dumpster where Jodie's head had been resting. He dropped his chin to his chest while Alison felt through his hair and along his scalp with tender, probing fingers. She found a pronounced welt and a flap of torn skin.

"This doesn't look good, Jodie. You need to see someone 'bout this."

Jodie shifted his head away from her touch. "Don't trouble yourself, Al. Just some ice'll do. I'd ask for a beer too, but I ain't got my wallet on me."

"Ha. I guess your funny bone ain't broken then. I don't see why I bother worryin' about you, Burden. Clearly, your head is so hard it's made of granite. You're one stubborn ol' dumb shit. I should let you bleed to death in the parking lot then, huh? Bet you a hundred bucks you got a concussion. Who did this to you? Do I need to ask what you got into, or is it the same pile of shit as ever?"

"No comment." Jodie took on a pious tone, closed his eyes, and leaned his head back.

Alison glared as though she'd like to smack him.

"I thought as much. Goddamn it! Let it go before you end up murdered."

"Now you sound like Lauderback himself."

"Is a grade-A shitstorm what you're looking for? You tryin' get even now or something? It's never gonna work out for you. You'll keep going 'round and 'round with that man until you're dead."

"Or until *he's* dead."

"I am not hearing this." Alison pushed herself off her knees, but Jodie reached out and grabbed her by the wrists before she could stand.

His pale face was filled with a sudden flush, and the golden flecks in his eyes stood out. The brown seemed to have drained away.

"You keep asking me why I'm back, Al. *Why'd you come back? Why'd you come back?*" he said, mocking her in a singsong tone. "I couldn't have answered before today, not even if I'd wanted to, but I know now. I came back for him."

"For Benji?"

"For Lauderback. I'm going to make that man sorry. I'm going to make everyone who had anything to do with what happened to Jaelynn sorry—from Lauderback to that shitstain of a son of his, right on down to the men he sent to threaten her to keep quiet about it."

"I knew you were dumb, Jodie, but I never figured you were crazy. You can't seriously be considering taking on Lauderback. You wouldn't get a quarter mile down that road before Hardesty slapped your ass in jail on some trumped-up charge and then *only* if you were lucky. You'd be just as like to end up sunk in a crick. People like you don't touch people like him, and your life ain't gonna be worth ten cents of God-help-you if you so much as try."

"I don't know, Al. Something tells me this is my moment."

Flies from the dumpsters found them where they crouched on the ground. They zeroed in on the scent of Jodie's blood and circled. The buzz of their wings was an incessant drone Jodie didn't seem to notice.

With her hand still clasped in Jodie's vise-like grip, Alison shook her long hair, flicking it like a horse's mane, to keep the insects from landing on her face.

"I can't explain it. It's a feeling. Maybe it's her—Jaelynn—trying to tell me something. I don't quite know, but I'm sure I've never felt anything like it before. I've been pulled back here. Things are turnin' around, and this time, for once, maybe a Burden is gonna get his."

"And here's me thinking you were actually lookin' to give your grandson a better life." Alison ripped her hands away from him. "You don't give a rat's ass about that little boy's welfare. This is all to get back at the Lauderbacks—father and son. That's the only reason you came back."

"Well, there's also the barbecue. Where else I'm gonna find short ribs like AJ's? Known in three counties as the best."

"Oh, shut up, Jodie. You're not funny. You know, there was a time, right after Carrie died, when I wanted to love you. I thought maybe God'd forgive us for what we done while she was sick, but you couldn't get your head out of your ass then, and apparently, you can't now either. I chalked it up to grieving before, but now I don't know if you got a death wish or if you're bad at life."

"I don't expect you to understand, Al," Jodie said, all trace of mirth evaporating.

He looked out across the field with such concentration, to the exact spot Alison had seen the deer, that she turned her own head to see if the creature had returned.

"You don't know what it's like, havin' everything taken from you when you know you deserve better. Something's happening. Change is comin', and things are going to be different, one way or another." Jodie staggered to his feet, clutching his arm to his ribs. "You mark my words." He lurched forward.

Alison moved aside so he could pass. She watched him limp across the lot, then up the highway.

Alison had the uneasy feeling she was watching someone who was already dead.

CHAPTER

NINETEEN

Benji's backpack was a stone set over his legs, holding him down. He shifted his body, trying to get comfortable on the sticky truck upholstery, but Aunt Min had already fastened his seatbelt. Benji couldn't move more than an inch or two. Adding to his immobility was the heat of the day.

Inside the vehicle, the air was warm and thick, like honey. It enveloped Benji and wrapped him in a viscid embrace. It was not an unpleasant sensation. The child missed the feel of his mother's arms around him and would have been keenly unmoored had the day been cooler and the atmosphere less close.

Aunt Min and Nurse Hardesty were talking outside the truck, their voices muffled and cottony through the cracked window. The pounding of blood in Benji's ears threatened to drown them out, but he didn't need to listen to know what they were saying.

"I'm sorry I had to drag you away from work, but I couldn't get a hold of your brother. That's two days running now."

"It's all right. I would have been here sooner, but I had to wait for Paula to get back to watch the store. She understands. She's known Jodie a good long time, and Lord knows I've worked for her enough years to earn a little grace. How does it work, though? Do you keep records of who you called when a kid got sick and who showed up to get them?"

"The attendance office keeps track of pickups." Nurse Hardesty looked at Benji through the window. "I take note of the medical stuff: temperatures and symptoms and the like. That little boy ran quite a fever. His teacher said he came in from recess a little red in the face. She didn't think much of it because a few of the kids had been teasing him earlier and she thought maybe he was flushed from crying."

"He doesn't," Aunt Min said. "He doesn't cry. Ever. Not since..."

"Right." The nurse shot another glance Benji's way.

It was quick, but Benji sensed the emotion behind it. *Curiosity.* Nurse Hardesty would jump at the chance to open his head and dig around in there a little, like a kid in a sandbox with a spade.

"Anyway, Miss Pettijohn checked his temp in the classroom, and it was 101, but by the time she brought him down the hall to me, it was closer to 103. With it climbing that fast, there has to be something going on. I'd recommend taking him to urgent care."

"We're still tryin' to figure out insurance. Jaelynn hadn't signed him up for Medicaid, near as we can tell. We got Tylenol at home, though. I'll try that first. Maybe a cold bath would help."

"Maybe." The nurse nodded, somewhat skeptical. "But if it looks like he's getting worse and the Tylenol isn't cutting it, don't wait too long to take him somewhere. At the very least, give me a call. You've got my number."

Aunt Min and Nurse Hardesty walked around the front of the truck, and Benji followed them with his eyes. His head felt oversized and heavy, like it was packed with wet sand. It swiveled atop his skinny neck, but he found it easy to track the nurse. She was wearing bright pink scrubs which made Benji think of blinking, neon signs.

The two women paused in front of the truck's sun-scarred hood. Benji allowed their voices to drift away from him, no longer trying to catch the words floating through the glass like iridescent bubbles. Nurse Hardesty brushed a fly off Min's shoulder, sweeping her hand down Min's arm. The downy soft hairs on Benji's own arm bristled in response, as though the nurse had touched him instead.

There was something akin to a fib squatting—toad-like—behind the gesture. It was all warts and ugliness, and he wanted to warn his aunt not to trust it. The nurse seemed kind, but more than that, she was curious. Benji felt her eyes on him whenever he passed her in the hall. She watched him with the same curiosity with which he watched beetles.

Benji reached out his small hand and touched the window. The glass felt wobbly. If he tried, he reckoned he could push right through to the other side...or the *Otherside*. The *Otherside* was a world all on its own, one bearing resemblance to the real one but different. It was a place which should have been a dream, even if it didn't feel like dreaming when Benji had been there.

Once, back in Bolivar, in the home he shared with his mama and Tyler, Benji had gotten mixed-up somehow and found himself there for the first time.

He had been lying on his back in the bathtub, staring up at a speckling of greenish-black mildew coloring the bumpy ceiling. His mama was sitting on the toilet next to the tub, reading a tabloid and watching him so he wouldn't drown in eight inches of bath water while he submerged himself up to the edges of his eyebrows.

Benji's hair, in need of a trim, floated away from his face and then back, like swaying pondweed. The surface tension of the water tickled. Benji liked the way he could hear the TV in the living room coming through all muffled, making the actors sound like they were speaking an alien language.

He wriggled his body like a fish.

Water washed over his face, and then Benji was falling backward into depths much deeper and darker than the bath. As he sank, tiny bubbles rose off his body. He tried to follow them toward the surface, swimming with all his might, but something was pulling him down.

The surface receded. High above that, the moldy ceiling of the duplex bathroom had been replaced by the stone ceiling of a cave. Benji looked down at a pile of white bones below him. In the center of the bones, a place where the water was deeper still—a deep dark hole like an eye.

It was a doorway to a world he could barely describe: an inky realm of desolation, a place made of screams and moans, a palace of darkness, a prison. Sounds of terror and pain were woven into it, as if it were an oily black fabric made of misery itself. The knowledge of this rippled through the water, surrounding Benji, who understood and felt the weight of all that despair.

He also sensed *her*.

She was there with him. This was where she lived, where she was trapped.

I see you, Benjamin Burden.

Benji startled, panicking. Water filled his mouth, and he choked.

The path is made. The thread is formed. In this moment, we are joined.

Images came to Benji, flashing hot and red behind his eyes. She-wolves and sirens, demons and half-women, but also some kind of a mother and a child, a host and its parasite.

We are one and the same.

Benji was inside her, and she was inside him. Around them, the cave was warm and red—bloody as a womb. This was her world, the creature's. She was its queen, and as surely as Benji saw her, she saw him.

We are joined. I will come to you—the future you—when I am the future me. I see you now, but I wait for you as well.

Benji attempted to understand, but his surroundings were growing wobbly once more. He struggled to comprehend the creature's words, but before he could, two arms reached down from above the surface. They grabbed him and pulled him up.

He coughed and sputtered while Jaelynn dragged him from the bathtub. She shook him and thumped his back hard.

"Are you trying to drown yourself?" Benji's mama wiped the water from his face with a towel.

He was back in the bathroom. The creature was gone. All that was left was the faint scent of pennies.

Benji stood next to the bathtub, dripping all over his mama's tabloid magazine. The pages warped and puckered when water slid off Benji's small body.

"What on earth were you doin'? You can't scare me like that."

Jaelynn wrapped him in the towel and held him close. He closed his eyes and leaned his head against her.

"You still with me, little man?"

Always and forever.

CHAPTER

TWENTY

"Jesus, you're hot." Min shifted the backpack off Benji's legs and opened the truck door wide to let some air in while she unbuckled him. They had arrived back at the cabin. "I'll run you a cold bath when we get inside."

The boy didn't answer. He was asleep. His long, dark eyelashes, normally so prominent against his pale skin, stood out less with his cheeks flushed and ruddy. His lids quivered, indicating he was dreaming, and his lips were pushed out. Benji resembled a baby rather than the kindergartener he was.

This might have been what he looked like when he was a toddler, Min supposed. But she had no way of knowing. Min hadn't been there, and Jaelynn had sent no pictures after she took off without warning in the middle of the night, with her newborn son.

Initially, Min had suspected Jodie was hiding photos of the boy from her. She would never put it past him to be that unkind. He had even implied for a time that he was in contact with Jaelynn, made it seem like she checked in with him now and then. It had taken Min six months or more to realize it was all bullshit.

Jodie hadn't heard a peep from Jaelynn—hadn't seen hide nor hair of her—since she drove off in his car with Benji strapped in the backseat, alongside a loaded shotgun. He had lied, either to make Min jealous or so folks wouldn't know Jaelynn had run away from *him* as surely as she had fled the town, the folks in it, and the insults which followed her.

A familiar flash of bright pink pulled Min's gaze from Benji's sleeping face. She turned her head in time to watch Nurse Hardesty disappear behind the cabin.

"Sheila?"

Min looked around, perplexed. There was no sign of the nurse's car, which made Min wonder if she had imagined the woman, maybe mistaken a flash of a bird's plumage—a Scarlet Tanager's, perhaps—for the nurse's brightly hued scrubs. She didn't wonder long because, moments later, a voice floated to her from within the shaded glen beyond the rear of the cabin.

Someone was calling to her.

Min. I'm over here, Min. Come to me.

The forest was quiet. All the animals within it had fallen eerily silent, so there was no mistaking the voice.

It was Sheila Hardesty's.

Min refastened Benji's seatbelt so he wouldn't topple out of the truck, left the door ajar so he wouldn't overheat, and followed the call into the woods. A few strides past the far corner of the house, she stopped.

Nurse Hardesty stood on the narrow dirt path snaking beside the old outhouse. Her back was to Min, and she appeared to be staring into the dense thicket.

"What are you doing here, Sheila?"

The nurse didn't move a muscle or respond, and Min hesitated, unsure if she should approach the woman. A breeze rustled the leaves overhead and lifted Min's hair from her shoulders. It played softly over her face and her bare arms, but the nurse's long ponytail barely stirred. Where Min's shirt ruffled and flapped when the gust intensified, Sheila's scrubs remained inert and unmoving, like she was frozen or fixed in stone, statue-like.

Min's hands began to sweat, and she felt the sun beating down on her, even though she was standing in the shade. "Sheila?" The name was a question. "Why are you here?"

"You want him, don't you? You want him for your own." The nurse's voice was slow and muffled, as though it was coming from a great distance, traveling through water, even.

"What are you talking about?"

"You want the child."

"Benji?" Min looked back at the truck. The door was still open, and she could see the boy through the windshield. The gray tint on the glass cast an unhealthy-looking pallor over his skin, but Benji was still resting peacefully.

"He could be yours."

Min shook her head. "He's Jodie's grandson, his direct kin."

"I could help you." The nurse was whispering, but her voice sounded clearer than before and closer as well—so close she might have been inside Min's head.

"You mean, you'd testify in court?"

The nurse nodded.

"You'd say I'm the one comes to get him when he's sick and all that? You'd say I'm the responsible one and help me if it got ugly? Jodie would fight it—tooth and nail, he would."

"I'm sorry that I had to call you at work, but I couldn't get a hold of your brother. That's two days running now." The nurse repeated the words she had spoken earlier that day, like an old answering machine or an automated phone system playing a recorded message.

Instead of giving Min hope, the way the nurse spoke set Min's teeth on edge. It was a canned response. Prepackaged and inorganic.

Something was off. And the nurse still hadn't turned to face her.

"*Together*...together...together, we would win."

A tingling, creeping sensation began to work its way up Min's spine all the way to her scalp, where it made the hair on the back of her neck rise. She felt cold.

Something about the woods was wrong.

An irregular thrumming sound wove its way around the trees like a fog. The animals were still hushed, and although Min hadn't noticed it until then, there was a rancid smell on the wind, a sour funk she couldn't put her finger on. It was familiar and foreign at the same time, much like the forest suddenly seemed. She took a step back toward the house and the truck where Benji slept.

The woods around her heaved.

The earth lifted like a dock carried on the swell of a lake. The trees and the rocks and deadfalls around the cabin rose as well. It was as though the forest had taken a breath. It had inhaled and left the remaining air thinner.

Min's head spun. The colors around her intensified: Leaves were greener, acidic even, tree bark shone like silver, and the clay soil was red like blood. Moss glowed incandescently. Sunlight fell over everything in oily, pearlescent shafts. All of nature seemed… *unnatural.* These woods were Min's home, and yet the place was unwelcoming and strange to her.

"Turn around. Turn around so I can see your face," she demanded.

The figure didn't move. "Tell me what you want, Minerva Burden, and I will see that it is yours."

Min drew a shuddering breath, and the knot growing in her stomach tightened. A warning her grandmother had given her when she was younger jumped into her mind. *Don't speak your wants to the wind…*

"For the devil himself may hear." The nurse completed the old woman's adage, sending Min's thoughts racing.

Why would Sheila Hardesty have followed them home? Why not say what she needed to before, at the school? Where was her car? Min knew the answers to all these questions as surely as she understood that the thing on the path in front of her was *not* Sheila Hardesty.

It wasn't even human.

If Min looked closely, it appeared worn through in places, like a threadbare blanket.

"Who are you?" Min's voice was barely louder than the wind rushing through the tall grass. She took a step toward the house, keeping her eyes trained on the thing near the woods. "*What* are you?"

A wave of terror stole over Min's body. Before her was a changeling, a mimic, something which could take the form of another. It was a walking deception, a living lie—fraud made flesh.

Her grandmother had told her tales of shapeshifters and shadow people. According to the old woman, the hills were full of creatures which could take the form of others. They hid in the woods and caves, with no definite shapes of their own. Like water, they were able to twist themselves up to resemble just about anything. It was…

"Backwoods trickery." The creature that looked like Sheila

Hardesty was staring right at her.

Min hadn't even seen it move—not exactly. It was more like it had inverted, twisted in on itself until its front was its back and it was facing her. With her heart in her throat, Min got her first good look.

It was the same height and weight as Sheila Hardesty. It wore her clothes and had the same hair, right down to the last strand, but it did not have the nurse's countenance. What peered back at Min hardly counted as a face. It was a smear, a white blur with a cruel, slash for a mouth and stark, pupilless eyes.

Min staggered backward, desperate to get away from it. She tripped over something and caught herself against the house. It was the body of Miss Mouse, which lay uncovered and exposed. Something had dug her up. The plastic body bag was torn open, and a pencil protruded from what was left of the pet's eye. Min's stomach churned, and she tasted bile.

In the split-second she had allowed herself to be distracted, the thing pretending to be Sheila had moved closer. It was only a stride or two away, close enough to touch her if it were to reach out.

If it were to reach out.

For the first time, Min noticed how abnormal and elongated its arms and legs were and didn't understand how she could have overlooked it before.

As if to confirm Min's estimate of the length of its limbs, the thing raised its arms and extended them. It flickered, like a television broadcast losing signal or a bad digital image. For less than a blink, it appeared to fragment into thousands of humming, buzzing particles.

Not particles.

Flies.

"Good God." The fearful knot in Min's gut rose into her throat. It was a solid lump that made her gasp. She wheeled around, attempting to run, and collided with Jodie.

Min almost screamed when she saw him, not recognizing her brother at first. His face was so smashed up that he looked like a different person. Or maybe not *even* a person.

"Jodie, there's a—" She turned back, finding herself staring at an empty path. "I saw...something." Her words trailed off while she scanned the woods.

Whatever she had seen was gone.

"What're you doin' creepin' around back here?" Jodie asked, ignorant of her distress.

"Nothing." Min caught her breath. "Nothing at all. What happened to you?" She tried to steady her voice while she swapped her fear for surprise at the sight of her brother's wounded face.

"You diggin' the dog up?" Jodie had noticed Miss Mouse.

"That wasn't me. It was...coyotes maybe. Probably. I heard something...Came back here to check it out." Min couldn't tell him about Sheila. She couldn't tell him what she had seen. He would only use it like he used everything else—as ammunition against her, bullets and bombs of nastiness to spit out whenever he felt the need to wound and make her bleed. "What happened to your face? Did you get 'round to talkin' to the sheriff?"

"You trust that asshole way too much. When are you going to learn that the law ain't ever gonna do nothin' apart from make it worse for folks like us?" Jodie nudged the dead dog at his feet with the worn toe of his boot. "Me and you are a couple dogs to kick." He shook his head. "We don't need Hardesty. I've got this handled."

"You've got it handled? Your hamburger-face says otherwise." She jabbed her finger at Jodie's shoulder, which she noticed he was nursing somewhat.

"Don't touch me." He slapped her hand away.

Before Min could reply, a howl broke through the air.

"No! No!" The panicked wail was almost inhuman, more like a wounded animal's cry.

"Benji." Min's hand flew to her cheek. "I left him in the truck."

She and Jodie took off at a run but skidded to a halt in unison at the edge of the drive.

Benji was standing in the middle of the gravel path. A cloak of glistening black flies swarmed his body. They crawled over him from head to toe, crept along his mouth and hovered around each of his nostrils, clung to his eyelashes and buzzed in and out of his ears.

"Holy shit." Min rushed forward and dropped to a squat. She waved her hand over Benji's face to shoo away the insects and shake them off his clothes and hair.

The boy didn't see her. Nor did he notice the flies covering him or the ones Min had mostly brushed away.

"No!" he screamed again, his glazed eyes fixed on the forest.

"You showed him the dog?" Jodie asked Min.

"Like I would. Benji, look at me. What's wrong?"

The flies were gone, but Benji was sweating and pale. Even his brown eyes looked lighter in color.

"Don't," the boy said. He raised his hand and pointed his small index finger at Jodie. "Don't play with her. Her games are bad. She doesn't trade fair."

Min touched his forehead and then his cheeks. "You've got a fever, little man. You're not making sense."

"It's *her*. She's doin' it. Pawpaw Jodie knows. But she's a liar. She was only s'posed to have Tyler. Just him. I told her she couldn't have Mama." Benji shook his head at Jodie. "You want to trade her, but she's a liar-pants-on-fire."

"Shut up, boy."

"Jodie!"

"He's talking a load of shit." Jodie wrinkled his nose.

"You'll see her too, Auntie Min. The *real* her. Not one of the faces she makes out of flies or the faces she steals." Benji stroked a strand of Min's hair which had fallen over her shoulder. "You'll see her without her mask, and then you'll know. She's ours and we're hers too. Always."

"Who, little man? Who is ours? What's that mean?"

"Her. We're her family, but she doesn't need all of us."

"Need us for what?"

"*One to have and one to hold.* That's what she said. One to make the door and one to be with her forever. The other one can *go to hell*." His eyes were glassy and blank, his face blanched apart from two bright red spots on his cheeks.

"He's burnin' up," Min said to Jodie. She wrapped her arm around Benji.

His knees buckled, and he folded like a rag doll into her arms. Benji pressed his feverish cherub's face against her chest, threatening to burn a hole all the way down to her heart.

"Do you think he'll be okay?" Min looked to Jodie, who stared at the boy with a look of grim intrigue on his face. "Did you hear me, Jodie? Should we take him to the clinic?"

"Why're you asking me?"

"Because you're his grandpa! He's your responsibility."

Jodie snapped back to attention with a porcine grunt. "He'll be fine."

"What was he talkin' about? *Who* was he talkin' about? He said you knew." Min eyed her brother with doubt. "What's he mean, Jodie Burden?"

"How the hell would I know? Boy's hallucinating or somethin'. It's all fever bullshit. He's delirious. You heard him."

Lies. Lies were all Min heard when Jodie spoke. They slipped from his mouth like spittle, but if she listened closely, she could hear the hum as well, the same one which had been there minutes earlier in the forest. It seeped out of him, along with his many deceptions.

Jodie leaned down and placed his own hand on the child's forehead. "Like you said, he's burnin' up."

Before he could pull his hand away and stand up, Min reached out and made to lay her palm against Jodie's forehead. He jerked away from her, but not before she felt the heat radiating off his brow.

"I said *don't* touch me."

CHAPTER

TWENTY-ONE

Sheila Hardesty closed out the last of several research articles she had been reading on her laptop. Autism, Tourette's, or epilepsy could all present in any number of ways, but none of them seemed a perfect fit for five-year-old Benjamin Burden.

The nurse leaned back against the upholstered headboard of her bed and rubbed her temples. As a rule, she didn't bring her work home with her—her husband, the sheriff, brought enough for the both of them—but the boy's condition was getting worse, with two fits in as many days, and it was more interesting than the cases of sniffles and head lice she usually dealt with.

And yet maybe she was reading too much into it. Hear hooves? Think horses, not zebras. She had learned that in nursing school. The simplest explanations were often the best.

It had been only a few months since Benji had witnessed his mother kill her boyfriend in self-defense and then take her own life with a shotgun. Maybe that was all this was.

Sheila stopped herself.

That was all this was—as if it was some little thing.

More aptly, that was *everything* this was. Trauma. A case of pediatric PTSD. Thinking it was anything other than that, something hereditary, was narrow-minded suspicion growing out of the fact that Nurse Hardesty knew where the boy had come from.

Product of rape. The phrase made the boy sound like the watermelon Sheila had sitting on the countertop downstairs in the kitchen. It sported a sticker proclaiming itself a "Product of Texas." Still, it was better than "Rape Baby," the name bandied about by local busybodies.

Sheila wouldn't let herself use either phase out loud, though she had thought both of them plenty. She couldn't help it. Sometimes, when she was around the boy, she even felt a pull and a tug in her mind which wanted to bring those words right up to the surface. When that happened, she worried she might accidentally blurt out something inappropriate. Sheila had never, as far as she knew, come across another child conceived that way.

It had started with the Oracle Springs High School homecoming game—the game where the previous year's varsity football team returned to play against the new varsity team. Sammy Lauderback, Jr., a recent graduate and son of a prominent local farmer, had driven down from his college in Kansas City to take up his old position as quarterback. He asked a sophomore named Jaelynn Burden to accompany him to the dance after the game.

Nothing about that was unusual. Sheila had attended Oracle Springs High School herself, and it was common for former players to ask current students to the dance. It was the only way they could participate since that event was exclusively for the student body and their dates.

Sheila didn't suppose anyone remembered who won the homecoming game that year, but what happened afterward was locked into the town's collective memory for life. Jaelynn Burden accused Sammy Lauderback, Jr. of driving her out to Keller's sawmill after the dance and raping her there.

It set tongues wagging in overdrive, as did the investigation which followed—followed and then went nowhere. Sheila had still been in nursing school at the time, and she missed the initial frenzy of gossip. It wasn't until she came home and then met and married Sheriff Dwight Hardesty that she learned about the scandal in detail.

Confidentially, Dwight had told her the accusations were likely true and that most people in town believed the girl, though none would dare say so. Sammy Lauderback, Jr. had been a hellion as a youth and had left a wake of stolen fishing boats, missing rifles, and property damage behind when he graduated. There wasn't a soul in Oracle Springs who would claim to be overly fond of the eldest child of Lauderback, Sr., but the case was *he said, she said*, and there hadn't been enough concrete evidence to suggest the encounter wasn't consensual.

The birth of Benjamin Burden nine months later hadn't changed that one bit.

Downstairs, the front door slammed, and heavy footsteps sounded on the stairs. Sheila snapped her laptop closed.

"Dwight? Is that you?"

Sheriff Hardesty blew through the door of the bedroom without answering. He smelled of damp underarms and irritation, like he had been sitting too long in his own crotch sweat on the leather seat of a hot patroller.

"Things are going to hell in this town." He dropped his badge and holster on the bed near Sheila's feet and began unbuttoning his shirt. "I shoulda known it wasn't the end of it when the McKenzie girl went missing weeks back. It's going to be a nightmare."

"Worse than usual?"

"Judge Tanner getting whacked like he did already put us over the top, but there's more coming. I'm sure of it. There's a mood in this town like I've never felt. It's in the air. People are on edge, and it's got all the old timers grumbling. I swear, every crank in town has been ringing me up. Gracie Moser has flies on the walls of her garage. Apparently, this warrants a visit from yourn truly. Woman's ninety years old and can't see all the way to her own fucking toes, but she can see flies all over the side of her garage. *Lord help us, it's the apocalypse.* The woman ought to be put out of her misery. She wasn't even the first senile coot to waste my time today. Rick Harbison said the crows were acting funny. Crows, for God's sake! Like I don't have enough to do."

"Any breaks in the Tanner thing? The investigation? Anyone seen or heard from the son yet?"

"Nothing." Hardesty peeled off his sweat-stained undershirt and dropped it on the floor next to the rest of his clothes. Now he was stripped down to his socks and skivvies. "You're being careful, right? You're carrying the gun I gave you? Way the loonies in this town are talking, you're likely to have to fend off the boogeyman or Satan himself these days. You think you know people—" He pinched the bridge of nose and closed his eyes, something he did when he was getting a headache. "What you got planned for dinner? I'm starving."

"Nothing yet. I only got in a minute ago."

"Well, you know me. It doesn't need to be anything fancy. Just the usual mess." Dwight kissed her neck roughly and ducked into the bathroom.

The shower taps squawked, reminding Sheila of seagulls over the Gulf of Mexico. The water ran, splashing against the porcelain sides of the tub, and she thought of waves against the shore. She picked up her phone and opened her photos.

The latest shots in there were of the vacation she and the sheriff had taken to Gulf Shores, Alabama, before the school year started. It hadn't been more than a few weeks since they got back, and Sheila had managed to hang on to the glorious memory of the salty wind in her hair and the sand between her toes all the way up until the previous Tuesday.

On Tuesday, she had gotten stuck in a never-ending afterschool staff meeting, and the recollection began slipping away from her in a rush of stress and monotony.

Ocean sunsets. Margaritas. The day cruise they had gone on. Sheila swiped through the pictures, hoping to regain some of the warm feeling the trip had inspired in her. The more photos she flipped past, the more she considered opening her laptop back up and booking another stay over Thanksgiving break. It would be too cold to swim, but there was always the hotel hot tub and spa, and anywhere was better than Oracle Springs.

Sheila stopped when she reached a photo her husband had taken of her. She was lounging on the hotel bed, nude, with her hands barely covering her breasts.

In the shower, Hardesty groaned. It was the sound he made when they had sex, which hadn't happened since their return from Gulf Shores. Back home, they were different people, and some things didn't seem to work.

She placed her thumb and index finger on the phone and watched herself grow larger in the field. The hotel room disappeared, and her naked body filled the screen. Sheila tweaked the filter on the photo, making the freckles on her chest and shoulders disappear, and darkened the tint until she seemed extra tan—exotic even. She was a different version of herself in the photo, someone she didn't know but might have liked better.

Of course, it was only a filter, an illusion of transformation.

Very little in Oracle Springs actually changed—not the sheriff, not the people, not Sheila. It seemed that the citizens of the tiny hamlet were determined to keep the place as boring as possible, resisting anything new or different with an almost religious zeal.

There was a pervasive air of guilt and fear which hung over the town and had for as long as Sheila had lived there. Where it came from, she didn't know, but it chafed and rubbed like new leather shoes and filled her with...*ennui*. That's what it was. Ennui—one of the fancy words she had learned when she was in college up in St. Louis, before she came to Oracle Springs, the town where the official story was that it was always horses, never zebras—by decree and local ordinance.

God, she wished something interesting would happen one of these days.

She saved the changes to her photo with a needling sense of boredom pricking at her mood. Her thoughts turned back to Benji Burden and to the boy's great-aunt, Minerva. Sheila had heard almost as many stories about Min as she had about Benji. The two of them set the town's gossip mill churning, and Sheila could see why.

Pent-up frustration and dissatisfaction wafted off the woman like a gas. There was something ticking inside her which was likely to go off at any moment—at least, that's what Sheila assumed. No one could be that repressed and not be ready to explode, right?

That was interesting, at least. Both Min and Benji were a welcome change from the monotony of small-town nursing, wiping snotty noses at the local elementary, and acting prim as the wife of a public official.

An impulsive idea struck the nurse, and she pulled the nude photo back up on her phone. Sheila took a deep breath, selected a number from her contacts, and hit send. Just like that, the picture of her caressing her breasts in a hotel room went hurtling into cyber space.

"Let's see what you make of that, Minerva Burden," she said with a satisfied nod. "And you too, darlin,'" Sheila added, speaking to her husband in the shower. Then she dropped her phone next to the sheriff's gun and badge, sure he would be unable to resist the opportunity to unlock it and check up on her, to sort through her texts and emails.

A fight wasn't the same as a vacation, but it was something to stir the air and get sluggish blood pumping. Plus there was always the chance Min might reply with something equally interesting.

That thought satisfied Sheila in a way she had not been in some time.

She slipped out of her scrubs and into a long T-shirt and baggy shorts. "It's too damn hot to cook, Dwight. You feel like chicken salad?" she hollered at the bathroom door.

CHAPTER

TWENTY-TWO

Later that night, Jodie sat upright in bed. Darkness and pain hovered over his smashed face like storm clouds. The two forces battled and pushed in on him, leaving Jodie disoriented and irate.

Night had crept across the gravel drive to knock on the little cabin's door hours earlier, but Jodie's bruised cheekbones and eye sockets, along with his busted teeth, radiated hurt and kept him from sleep. He found it more tolerable to sit up against the headboard than to lie down, so he leaned back against the splintery oak and stared into the crushing dark.

The pills Min had tossed at him before bed didn't half cut the agony, and what little relief they had brought wore off shortly after he had taken them. Jodie figured he might have made out better with a bottle of whiskey than a bottle of aspirin. At least the drink might have done more to suppress the incessant ringing in his head.

There was a whistling noise which hadn't stopped since Lauderback's office, and Jodie was less inclined to believe it was tinnitus than a call to action—a high-pitched ballad of blood and vengeance. It was a wrathful siren's song which had dogged his heels all day and drowned out everything but the pain. Currently, it was keeping him from sleep as effectively as his stinging flesh and aching teeth.

There had been someone else in that office, a fourth party joining him, Lauderback, and Ellis. Jodie had felt a presence, sensed it skirting the corners of the room, skulking around the costly furniture and over the handwoven rugs. It was a silent witness to his degradation and humiliation until it had spoken to him, whispering delicious promises in his ear.

Those promises were all that kept Jodie from weeping like a baby when Ellis hauled him to his feet and dragged him to that window. But now what? Was something supposed to happen? The air was buzzing with possibility and potential, like it did before a storm, but Jodie couldn't quite deduce what it all meant.

He climbed stiffly off the bed, shuffling out of the dark and down the hall to the living room. There the TV flickered and played mutely to a sleeping audience. Min snored softly on the couch. She cradled Benji's head in her lap, her face slack and weary-looking. The boy moaned a little in his slumber, but his eyes remained shut. Jodie reached down to place his hand on his grandson's cheek but felt the heat radiating off it before he got within inches.

In the china cabinet, he found the remaining stores of Min's whiskey. The good stuff was gone, but what was left would do. Jodie consumed it straight from the bottle, and while his head still ached, the savage thoughts there became quieter. He drank more and his vision grew fuzzy.

The room was a blur of gray and blue light, but an idea was taking shape in his mind. There was something he needed to do, something he had failed to accomplish years ago.

A sacrifice is in order.

Armed with purpose and the bottle of whiskey, Jodie stumbled to the front porch, where a dented metal grill sat in the far corner, collecting spiderwebs. He shoved it out of the way with his foot and found a rusted can of lighter fluid beneath. It was the same tin he had bought before he left Oracle Springs for Cassville, and it was at least half full. Jodie hoped it would be enough.

He hopped off the porch and made his way down the hill, to where the road's black pavement melted into rocky clay and the

woods began.

A few yards into the moonlit forest, Jodie found himself in a wild grove of dogwood, along with the mosquitos. He hadn't bothered to put on a shirt before he left the cabin, and the insects buzzed around his bare torso, landing on tender, exposed flesh and foundering in a heavy layer of perspiration. Jodie was sweating, though the air was fresh and carried a nip which indicated the arrival of cooler seasons.

The sun was not even a glow on the horizon yet, but the inkiness of the night sky over the eastern ridge of the hollow had begun to fade ever so slightly. A solitary coyote was singing his final paean to the night, feeling the approach of dawn deep in its primeval core.

The animal called out like a town crier to the unseen beasts and hidden creatures of the hollow—the hunters and their prey— warning them that it was nearly morning and all was well. Or not well, perhaps. There was a trespasser amongst the trees, after all, an invader picking his way down the hillside with a teetering but determined stride.

Jodie ignored the animal howling on the ridge above him and stopped to gather a few small scraps of wood and some dried brush. He continued to fill his arms with desiccated forest litter while he pushed deeper into the woods. Jodie had collected a substantial armload of branches and twigs—as much as he could carry without dropping the whiskey and lighter fluid—when Keller's sawmill came into view.

The building loomed large, a crippled leviathan hunkered down in shadows. It stopped Jodie in his tracks. He took a moment to reflect. A stolid, physical reminder of past wrongs, this place was a personal affront to Jodie and those he loved most.

This was where Jaelynn's end had begun, where the threads of her life had first started to fray and unravel, and a voice in Jodie's head told him he was a fool to have let the place stand, to have borne the insult for as long as he had.

Rape. Assault. Such violations must not be allowed a monument.

With his collection of sticks and branches in arm, he gazed into the dreary interior of the mill. Shadows fought against the dawn at the building's doorway. They patrolled the threshold on shaded velvet paws but couldn't stop the mix of moonlight and early morning blush creeping over the floor. Nor could they stop Jodie from marching inside and dropping his armload of sticks at the base of the western wall. This was the area farthest from the stream and the moldering waterwheel, likely the driest and most apt to burn.

The pile of sticks didn't amount to much in that vacuous space—it was barely higher than Jodie's ankles—but he was too determined and too drunk to give up. He used his feet to push dry leaves and old sawdust into a mound beside his little heap of kindling.

Jodie was still dancing the leaves into place when a tapping noise drew his attention to the rear of the mill.

He turned around and stared into the darkness, unable to make anything out in the impenetrable gloom. Jodie tilted his head and listened a moment before issuing a warning.

"Whoever's back there, this is your eviction notice. You best move your ass to greener pastures 'cause it's about to get hot in here."

His suggestion was met by silence. The mill was quiet, inhabited by nothing other than ghostly shadows and old secrets.

Jodie returned to kicking his leaves but, before long, was interrupted once again.

This time, there came from the back of the mill a muted scraping sound, like someone dragging something across the floor. Jodie whipped around and stared into the cavernous old building. There was a chittering in the rafters—the warning cry of a possum or raccoon. He scanned the beams above for glowing eyes but failed to see the thing moving toward him in the darkness.

When he cast his eyes down from the roof and saw it—*truly* saw it—Jodie realized he had been looking right at it before.

A tall, thin shadow watched him from a distance. It stood so still, so statue-like, that Jodie had thought it was part of the mill itself—a sawed-off post or a beam which had fallen and landed perpendicular maybe.

He stared at it for a good long time, hoping his eyes would adjust to the dark enough for him to make out what it was. It didn't so much as twitch, and Jodie was hard-pressed to accept that it had been the source of the noise he had heard until it shifted suddenly and he nearly leapt out of his skin.

Whatever it was, it had taken a step. A single pace forward, dragging one of its legs stiffly and making the papery scraping sound Jodie had heard earlier.

Jodie froze, but the lanky shadow continued to drag itself toward him. As it drew closer, Jodie saw it for what it was—organic and alive, upright like a human, like a man, but moving as some sort of broken robotic thing.

"Stay where you are. Don't come any closer." Without taking his eyes off the advancing form, Jodie reached into his pocket for his knife but came up empty-handed. He had left his blade at home on his bedside table.

A weak band of light stole in through the open wagon door and fell across the floor. Jodie's heart fluttered and rose in his chest, as dry and weightless as the leaves at his feet, when the creeping thing stepped out of obscurity and into the light.

"The hell?" Jodie said breathlessly.

A rotting corpse with livid purple skin stretched over shiny red-black muscle...The thing standing before Jodie appeared to be made from darkness itself.

Jodie stepped back while it moved across the mill floor, scraping along with the awkward herky-jerky motion of a marionette. It didn't matter that he didn't have his knife. He would have been too afraid to use it.

Jodie's hands shook, and he dropped the whiskey bottle. It landed with a shattering crash. He stumbled over the tin of lighter fluid, opening and closing his mouth like a fish, and backed away. Jodie gasped but didn't seem to be taking in any air. His head spun.

What he was looking at was Lucas Tanner—what was left of him anyway.

The young man was a living nightmare. His hair and scalp had peeled away, and cowl-like folds of skin gathered at the base of his skull. A crest of white bone glowed like a halo over the remnants of a face hanging in ragged shreds. Lucas's arms and legs had been stripped down to muscle and sinew, and his abdomen bulged behind a thin membrane of tissue, as though all his organs had sunk inside his body and were preparing to burst through the remaining flesh. They pressed out and down, ready to fall to the floor with a splat at Lucas's feet while he walked toward Jodie, all his tendons pulling and twisting in the open air.

When he was close enough that Jodie could see his veins, black and varicose, squirming like nightcrawlers over his body, he lifted his gleaming, rancid chin, and Jodie got his first good look at the man's face.

Skin gaped and drooped around his orbit, and one of his eyes was missing. The remaining orb was milky white, as if covered by a heavy cataract or scar. Jodie's mouth dropped and Lucas's did the same, mimicking or mocking Jodie's astonished gape. With his mouth open, Lucas's tongue lolled out, mottled and purple. Most of his teeth were missing, as was part of his throat. Long, shiny vocal cords showed like exposed satin strings.

Monster.

The word stole into Jodie's brain and became a scream while the thing lurched toward him. Lucas's rotting limbs picked up speed, and he zeroed in on Jodie, who felt trapped in molasses and moved backward like a snail.

The distance between man and fiend grew shorter.

The dead thing was emitting a gurgling noise Jodie had mistaken for water earlier. It was not unlike the sound the lighter fluid made as it ran out of the rusted tin in glugging waves at Jodie's feet. Another step or two and the thing that was once Lucas Tanner would be between Jodie and the door, blocking his only way out.

Time finally unfroze, and Jodie scrambled backward, able to move but only as well as he might in a bad dream. He couldn't seem to pump his legs fast enough and barely managed to skate past the approaching menace and out the mill door. Jodie scurried across the clearing and plunged blindly into the woods, where creeping fingers of silvery mist wrapped around trees and whisps of gray haze swirled beneath his pounding feet.

Stricken with panic, he tore through a labyrinth of saplings and stout forest giants, not caring in which direction he went. A branch snapped close behind, and he looked over his shoulder.

The rotting body of Lucas Tanner was still in pursuit. It flew through the woods after him, matching his pace as easily as any living hunter might and following too close and too quick for something which appeared so wrecked and ruined.

Jodie raced on, glimpsing a low-hanging catalpa bough a fraction of a second before he collided with it. It struck him across the gut with such force that he was lifted off his feet and deposited onto his back in a heap on the ground. There he rolled around like a turtle, trying to catch his breath and unable to stand.

Lucas, ragged and rotting, appeared above him.

All Jodie could do was retch and cower. He rolled into a ball and pressed his forearms together tightly to cover his face, like a child holding a blanket over their head in the dark. But even if Jodie couldn't see the thing standing over him, he could smell it.

The rank odor of decaying flesh wafted off the revenant in sickening waves, growing stronger as the judge's son leaned down. Jodie's gorge rose.

Something small and light dropped onto his forearms, tumbling off to the ground beside him.

And then...nothing.

The foul smell dissipated, and the birds began to tweet and call in the woods again. A grackle chirped and whistled reassuringly in a branch above him.

Jodie pulled his arms away from his face.

He was alone.

Lucas was gone, and so Jodie lay on the damp earth. The moisture from the ground wicked into his shirt until he couldn't tell the difference between the dew and his own cold sweat. He rested there until his breathing returned to normal and the sky shifted from gray to gilt-edged blue. Then he sat up and looked around for whatever it was Lucas had dropped.

Beside him was a corsage—a single, pink-tipped rose and a spray of baby's breath bound with a white ribbon.

Jodie held the flowers up to the light and marveled at their freshness and familiarity. They should have been wilted or turned to fragrant dust, but they were as intact and pristine as they had been the night Samuel Lauderback, Jr. pinned them to Jaelynn's homecoming dress.

The flowers had survived somehow, fresh and unmarred by time, while the girl who had worn them had not.

It seemed a miracle to Jodie, or better yet, it was a promise.

CHAPTER

TWENTY-THREE

Jodie shimmied into the kitchen with an appetite and dug a box of waffles out of the freezer. Despite the thrashing he had received the day before, he felt good—a post-adrenaline buzz maybe, left over from the night before. His body was covered in bruises, and the gash on the back of his head still stung, but he barely noticed it.

He patted his shirt pocket and felt the small lump—the corsage Lucas had dropped. Although somewhat wilted from his body heat, it hadn't disappeared. He hadn't dreamt it or the dead man, and in the comforting light of day, Jodie had reached the conclusion that young Tanner's appearance, however disturbing, had been a sign. It was an indication that cosmic forces were finally on his side.

"Since you ain't goin' in to work today, mind if I borrow the truck?" he asked Min, sliding a frozen waffle into the toaster. The kitchen immediately smelled like burnt bread from the crumbs in the catcher, which never got emptied.

"Why? Where you gotta be?"

Where you gotta be? It was none of her business. Like Min wasn't hiding something of her own.

Jodie had noticed the way Min had jumped when he came in and how quickly she set her phone face down on the table. Seemed everyone had their little secrets. The thought almost set him to giggling.

Again, he felt his breast pocket. Jaelynn's corsage was still there. Like a scab he couldn't resist picking or a cracked tooth he couldn't stop tonguing, Jodie couldn't seem to leave the tiny bunch of flowers alone.

"Figured I'd run over to Fayetteville to the plasma bank," he said brightly, aware that Min was still staring at him, waiting for an answer. "Give the red to make some green. Could help with a bill or two."

"You figure you got enough left in you to donate? Looks like a fair amount mighta leaked out yesterday."

"You're funny. I still got plenty. The techs'll be happy to see me. They know I got the good stuff. Universal type and all that shit." He felt giddy inside. "They see me comin' and they roll out the red carpet." Jodie straightened up, standing as rigid as a royal servant might, and waved his arm majestically over an imaginary rug.

The crease between Min's eyes deepened to a knife's cut when she frowned. "What's got into you?"

"Dunno. Just slept well, I guess."

"Slept well? You'd have to be in a coma to feel that good. What gives?"

"What gives with you? You been sour as grapes since I got home yesterday." Jodie slipped behind her chair, prodding her between the shoulder blades without warning when he passed, knowing she would flinch the same way she had when he first came into the room. "Something making you jumpy today? You sound like you want to play twenty questions, so let's start with you. What's going on with Minerva this morning?"

"Nothing." She scowled and tried to shrug off whatever Jodie's touch had set off in her. "I guess I need to swap mattresses with you or something. Then I can be Mary-Full-O-Sunshine."

"That reminds me...I was gonna suggest Benji take my bunk for the day. Go on and tuck 'im into the big bed, where he can stretch out. Then you can watch TV in here without worrying about disturbing him." He took the waffle out of the toaster, tossing it from one hand to the other to avoid burning himself while he looked for a clean plate.

"That's about the most considerate you ever been, Jodie Burden. Now I know you're up to something."

"Don't look a gift horse in the mouth, Min. You're likely to get bit." Jodie grinned, his swollen smile hitching toward one side, before he opened his mouth wide and took a large, loud bite of the crisp waffle. He didn't even feel his broken teeth anymore.

"Fine," Min said, shaking her head. "You carry him in there, though, since you're feelin' so good."

CHAPTER

TWENTY-FOUR

The springs inside the old mattress creaked. From the kitchen, Min called down the hall to Jodie, trying not to sound as nervous as she felt.

"Make sure the window's locked. You know, just in case."

Even though she was sure by then she had imagined the events of the previous day, every time she passed by the bedroom on her way to the toilet, Min worried she would see that thing wearing the nurse's face peering in at her from the woods.

"It can stick sometimes, so be sure it's caught good and proper."

She dug around in a small plastic basket, the kind they served fries in at old diners, until she found the keys to her truck. Min tossed them to Jodie, who plucked them out of the air with one hand when he came through from the bedroom.

"He's all set. Still sleeping, sweet as pie." He held up his hand when he saw Min about to speak. "And yes, I checked the window."

"Okay then. Try not to leave the gas tank empty when you bring 'er back this time."

"You got it." Jodie gave her a thumbs-up and danced his way to the front door.

"Be sure to give me a call if you're gonna be too long. If Benji takes a turn for the worse, I might have to consider running him into urgent care."

Jodie stopped his prancing. "You might have to consider *nothing*. It's not your call, Min. He's my grandson, and I'll decide when he sees a doctor." His jubilance flagged. It was the most aggrieved he had sounded all day.

Min set her jaw and turned away, staring hard at the trivets hanging above the stove. "Well, shit, Jodie. Why don't you lift your leg and piss on the boy to mark your territory? Tell the world he's all yours that way."

"You don't know nothin' about it, Minerva."

"Don't I? Seems to me, we've been here before."

Jodie's wife, Carrie, had been dead only a few short months when Jaelynn had made the mistake of calling Min "Mama." The girl had been young and her mother recently deceased, so saying it still came naturally. It had been such a small thing, such a minor slip of the tongue, that Min didn't give it much thought at first.

Making a point to correct the girl would have felt like a cruelty, but then, the more she thought about it, the more Min had realized she didn't *want* to correct Jaelynn. A nice warm feeling had settled inside her. She allowed herself to consider what it might be like to have a child of her own, a daughter not too unlike her niece. For once, Min didn't chase those thoughts away, but let herself consider the what-if.

She had still been thinking about it when Jodie met the child's casual slip with a back-handed slap across the face.

"That woman ain't your mama," he had yelled while stabbing his finger at Min. "Your mama ain't with us no more, but—I shit you not—her body's gonna spin in the grave if you go 'round disrespecting her memory like that. You don't replace the people you love. You don't throw 'em over because they're dying. Don't ever let me catch you callin' another woman *Mama*. You hear me, girl?"

Min had barely had time to cast Jaelynn a sympathetic glance before Jodie shot his hand out and grabbed Min's, capturing it in his rough palm as quick as a lizard snatching up a fly. He squeezed the ball of her fist in his own until she thought the bones in her fingers would break.

Hidden Children

It wasn't like Jodie to be hurtful, not physically anyway, but there was something poisonous burning in his eyes. His voice was soft and dangerous, like a rattlesnake's shake.

"She ain't yours. Ain't never gonna be."

"I never said she was."

"She has a mama—in the cemetery maybe, but still her mama."

Min had tried to free her hand, but he held on tight. "You're making mountains outta nothin', Jodie. She didn't mean any harm by it."

"It ain't that simple. You know what people in town say about us. How do you think they're gonna twist it if the child starts calling you, my own sister, *Ma*? Think about how that'll sound. Folks think we're weird enough as it is."

He had still been gripping her hand, and Min began to simmer. With each throb of her limb, her blood ran hotter until she was near to boiling. Their collective anger became a current of electricity riding a circuitous loop. One twin's rage had fed off the other's, growing stronger, hotter, and deeper, until the wire hook holding up a decorative trivet on the wall above the stove snapped and the ceramic plate fell. It landed on the rear burner with a crash and dented the heating coil.

Jodie had let go of Min's hand with a jerk.

The trivet had survived, but the coil still bore the indentation, and something between brother and sister had fractured irreparably that day. From that point on, they danced around each other with suspicion, as if one would try to take something from the other before all was said and done.

As for Jaelynn, she never made the same mistake again, and Min had done as Jodie ordered and backed off. Only now that Jaelynn was dead, it left Min to wonder if it had been the right thing to do. Maybe if she had refused to give in, Jaelynn would still be alive. All Min knew was that she wasn't going to make the same mistake twice.

She waited until she heard the engine rev and the truck start up the hill to the highway before picking up her phone and opening the picture she had hidden from Jodie—the one Sheila Hardesty had sent her the night before. Min wasn't sure what to make of it, but it did complicate things.

"Damn it, Sheila." She slapped the table hard enough to make the salt and pepper shakers bounce.

If Min sued Jodie for custody of Benji, she would need witnesses who appeared unbiased. A school nurse would have been ideal, but there was nothing impartial about that photo. Clearly, the nurse had been listening to gossip about Min, to the rumors which had floated around town.

Min snorted in contempt. Just because someone didn't have a fella didn't mean she wanted a gal, and while the picture the nurse had sent made Min feel a great many things, turned on wasn't one of them.

A vehicle came down the road from the highway. Min listened while it approached, but the engine lacked the percussive tambourine-like rattle her own truck produced, so she knew it wasn't Jodie returning. The noise grew louder and then softer again when the car or truck turned up the hill toward the Tanners'.

Min deleted the picture from Sheila—she had seen enough—and went to check on Benji.

He was sleeping soundly where Jodie had left him in the back bedroom, breathing deeply with his lower lip sucking in and puffing forward on the exhale. His dark lashes stood out on his pale cheeks, and he had balled his hands into little fists.

Min felt his forehead. He was warm but not as feverish as he had been the day before, so she decided she would let him sleep rather than wake him for another round of Tylenol. As she backed away from the bed, she noticed something tucked under the mattress.

It was a sheet of paper wedged in between the mattress and the wooden slats below.

Min bent down and tugged on it until it came free. It brought with it a cascade of crayons as well as more paper. The pieces scattered over the floor at Min's feet. Each had been scribbled on, and almost all of them had that damn black triangle Benji kept drawing, except the piece in Min's hand. On that one, Benji had drawn a stick figure.

Min stared at the crude scribble, and her heart began to beat faster. Her hands trembled, making the paper quiver, and the figure danced on the page. It stared up at Min with empty eyes and grinned at her with a razor-cut mouth.

This was the face of the thing she had seen in the woods, the thing masquerading as Sheila Hardesty.

Min collected the rest of the papers from the floor, placing them on top of the stick person—the stick *thing*—so she wouldn't have to look at it while she carried everything through to the kitchen. She pulled an earlier drawing Benji had done off the fridge, then sat down at the table, her hands continuing to shake. Min laid the black triangles out first.

Side by side, they looked like a jagged row of black teeth. Something about them was familiar, though.

Min wracked her brain, trying to call into focus a thought or an image which wanted to dart away from her, like a tadpole in a pond.

A black triangle. A black pyramid. An opening.

The opening to a cave, Min thought. *The cave at the bottom of the hill.*

She hadn't gone there in years, but she recalled it well enough. All those days she had spent playing with Jodie by the big pond, the drowning pool...The cave beyond it a dark triangle reflected in the water...

Someone had issued a dare. Who would go inside? Then Memaw's voice and a scolding, the promise of a hiding.

Don't let me catch you in the caves. Some aren't caves at all, but doorways to places you don't want to go. Blood like ours is precious in these places, like gold or like...keys.

Min shuddered and swept the pages away, pushing them to the far corner of the table. She laid the sketches of the stick figures side by side. They were almost identical to one another—both crude and simple, bereft of detail and features. The only difference was that, in one, Benji had drawn himself alongside the black stick figure.

Benji had added details to the sketch of himself: a nose, ears, clothes, even shoes. He had given himself brown eyes with a black dot for a pupil. His skin was tan crayon, and his shirt was red.

Benji hadn't drawn featureless stick figures because he couldn't draw anything else.

He had drawn this other figure that way for a reason.

Because that is what she looked like, right down to the long, thin tail Min could now see poking out from behind the creature's leg.

She set the drawing down again, feeling lightheaded. Min had been holding her breath for some time and emptied her lungs of dead air. The sound of her exhalation was a gale force wind blowing through a barn roof vent, and every other noise in the cabin—each drip, whoosh, creak, and thump—was amplified.

Everything was louder to Min's ears, except the insects and the birds outside. They had fallen silent. Beyond the cabin's four walls was a dead zone.

Min jumped when something large scuttled beneath the floor.

Instinctively, she stamped her foot against the wooden planks. Some animal or another was under the house, making a nest out of what little insulation there was left, rooting around, digging...

Digging!

"Goddamn, Jodie," Min said. "Who buries a dog right next to the house?" She leapt out of her chair. "Might as well leave her carcass out on the porch and let the animals have at it. Save havin' to rebury her every damn day."

Min charged out the door and around to the back of the cabin, where something gray and gold had heard her coming and bolted. An animal whipped past her, brushing her calf, and Min hopped to the side. It disappeared into the scrub at the edge of the woods before she could get a good look at it. She had to hotfoot it a second time when another streak of mottled gold whizzed past her on the right.

"Jesus!" she said, regaining her balance.

A coyote bitch, skinny and mangy, paused a few feet away and looked back at her. Its sallow eyes were drained of color but full of resentment.

"Get! Get goin'!" Min kicked a clump of dirt toward the animal, who dodged it and darted after her mate.

For good measure, Min lobbed another dirt clod at the pair, then realized she was disturbing the earth Jodie had shoveled over Miss Mouse. Min was standing on top of the dog's grave.

One dusty paw was exposed, telltale claw marks around it proof the coyotes had been digging.

Min knelt and pushed the displaced dirt around the dog's foreleg, patting the mound smooth before standing back up. She stomped her feet toward the brush a few times, in case the coyotes were still there, before she went back inside and locked the front door behind her.

Securing the door was an unusual precaution in the Burden house but one Min had been taking ever since the incident up at the Tanners', despite Jodie teasing her about it. As soon as she bolted the door, she reached down for the shotgun her memaw had kept beside it, forgetting that it wasn't there—hadn't been for years.

Min would have laughed at her own foolishness if something didn't feel so wrong in her gut. That knot was pulling tight again, and a tingling, pricking sensation played over her skin until her arms were covered with tiny goosebumps.

Jaelynn was a come-before, like your mama, Mercy, was. She always knew when a visitor was coming.

The suddenness with which Min realized she was not alone was like a punch to the side of her head.

CHAPTER

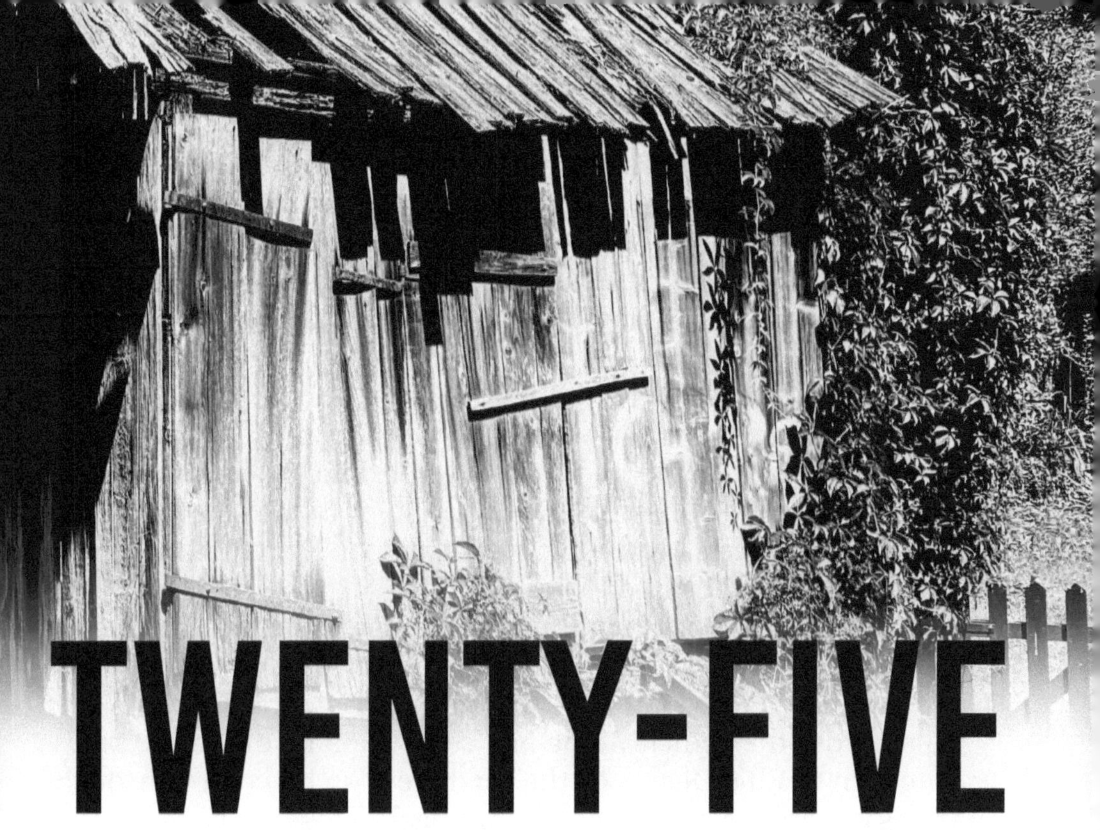

TWENTY-FIVE

With a tank of gasoline sloshing in the back of the truck, Jodie swerved off the main highway and onto the dirt access road leading to Keller's sawmill. The sun was not yet at a noontime high, but it flickered through the trees overhead and washed the road with spangles of soft, dappled light. The air was warm, but the trees along the road had begun to change color seemingly overnight. Here and there, a leaf stood out, a garish scarlet among its green brethren, like it had been dipped in paint or in blood.

Jodie had the window down, and a breeze whipped his hair over his forehead. But it did little to cool his skin or dry the sweat gathering between his shoulder blades and dampening his shirt. He felt feverish, and he blamed Min.

She had put the idea that he might be sick in his mind, with all her worrying about Benji. Kids caught colds. They ran temperatures. It was as normal as scraped knees and bloody elbows. Jodie hung a skinny arm out the window and slapped the metal door panel, humming to himself while he whipped around the last curve in the road before the mill.

He slammed on the brakes.

The truck skidded to a halt not a hundred yards from Ellis Deems's big black Ford, which was parked in front of the mill.

Jodie threw the gear stick into reverse, backed up past the last bend, and killed the engine. He watched the road for a minute or two to see if anyone had followed, but when no one appeared, he climbed out onto the road.

In the back of the truck was a plastic gas can. It was big and new and very full. Jodie had purchased it and its contents with a couple of twenty-dollar bills Min had kept hidden in the glove box for emergencies. Jodie heaved it out of the truck bed and skulked into the woods.

He made it back to the mill under cover of tree and stopped at the far edge of the scrabbly, bald clearing before the wagon door. There he hid in a thin stand of saplings and waited.

Apart from the vehicle Jodie had seen when he drove up, there was no sign of Ellis Deems or the road crew, so he inched through the trees in a crouch and prepared for a dash across the barren path. Jodie was about ready to take off when Tank Egon came lumbering out of the woods a hundred feet or so to his left.

The man resembled a cinnamon-hued brown bear, with his red hair and incredible heft. He was towing a dried-up old log, a dead-fall long since gone silver with age and sun. Ellis Deems trotted after him carrying a pack of smaller branches, which stuck out on either side of him, making the man look like a porcupine trailing a larger beast. They dragged the log and branches into the mill and disappeared into the shadows.

Jodie remained in place but shifted his position so the mill's roof blocked the sun's glare. He was able to make out the shapes moving around inside.

There were five men in the mill, including Ellis and Tank. The rest of the crew—Bullfrog, Quake, and Buckie—stood around a giant pile of wood they had collected and deposited in the center like a raggedy altar. By the time Ellis and Tank added their contributions, Jodie figured the bunch of them must have cleared the forest floor of nearly every branch, twig, and dead-fall.

They had been working on their little project all morning—that much was apparent, though less clear was the reason why. Jodie couldn't seem to work it out.

Staying low, he went in for a closer look, taking cover alongside the building.

The mill's wooden siding had warped over the years, and it bowed out like ribs, leaving gaps between the boards which a man's head might fit through. Jodie peered into one of these openings and was able to get a clear look at what Ellis and the boys were doing with their heap of sticks and logs.

The road crew had piled the deadwood into a mound and stood around it like statues. Not one of them moved, but they all emitted a humming noise. Only the sound wasn't coming from their mouths or throats. It rose right from their chests—from deep inside their bodies. Before Jodie could wonder about it too much, the same noise came from somewhere to the side of him.

Leonard Trumbo wobbled out from behind the mill. He had taken off his work vest and wore nothing but his white undershirt, which he had sweated through until it was translucent. Leonard carried a gas can, not unlike the one in Jodie's hand, and appeared to be of a similar mind to Jodie, splashing the can's contents up and down the side of the mill.

He didn't notice Jodie and carried on dousing the mill with gas while he drew closer. The smell of petroleum intensified. It burned Jodie's sinuses and his throat. He waited until Leonard was within arm's reach before he spoke, keeping his voice low so the men inside the mill wouldn't hear.

"S'goin' on, Leonard?"

Leonard lifted his head and stared at Jodie, his gaunt face an unreadable mask.

"Lauderback ask you to do this?" Jodie continued in a whisper. "He ask you to torch the place?"

Leonard looked past him, dead-eyed and unresponsive.

"What gives, Len?"

"Jodie?" Leonard blinked, just now seeing Jodie for the first time. "Where'd you come from?"

Something wriggled below the man's eye, making the thin, bluish skin of his lower eyelid twitch. It snaked itself all the way up to Leonard's lower eyelashes. The same was happening under the skin of his scrawny neck and boney chest.

"You okay, Len?"

A tear leaked out of Leonard's eye. It slid off his cheek and dropped onto his white shirt, where it left behind a pink-tinged, oval stain.

"We got to pay, Jodie. What we done was wrong. I knew it then, and I know it now. I never had a daughter, but if I did and someone treated her the way we did your girl, tried to terrorize her and fright her into silence, I'd...I'd..." He didn't finish. His eyes glazed over, and his face went slack. The only movement was the tiny things rippling below the surface of Leonard's sweaty skin.

"What's happening to you?" Jodie asked.

"I don't know," Leonard said, his voice chock full of misery. "There's a voice in my head, and it won't stop screamin' at me." He slapped his ear with the hand not holding the gas can. "*Blood for blood.* Over and over. *Blood for blood*, she says to me." He made a fist and pounded his ear so hard his knuckles cracked. "*Blood for blood.*" Leonard raised the gas can, shut his eyes, and began pouring the contents over his body, dousing his clothes and hair.

Jodie jumped back. "You gone crazy, man? What are you doing?"

Leonard stopped howling and looked at Jodie, but his stare was blank—*beyond* blank. His eyes had gone white. Jodie watched while he pulled a lighter out of his pocket.

"Call her off, Jodie. Tell her we're sorry."

"Easy, Leonard," Jodie said breathlessly.

"Don't let her do this to us." A fly crawled out of Leonard's mouth, which now drooped at one corner like he'd had a stroke. The man didn't notice the insect. He raised the lighter and held it close to his gas-soaked T-shirt.

Jodie didn't have time to say or do anything before the older man flicked the igniter and pressed the flame to his chest below the pink tear stain.

"Len, don't!"

Jodie's shout came too late and was drowned out by the sucking sound the flames made when they caught the man's clothing. He erupted in a fury of red and yellow fire.

Leonard Trumbo was instantly transformed into a human torch. He turned from Jodie and ran. His screams melted into the roar of the blaze enveloping him, and he swept along the side of the mill like a comet. The trail of gasoline he had poured earlier lit and became a fiery tail.

Dried grass and weeds at the base of the building sparked like fuses and sent probing fingers of flame shooting up the siding. The old planks caught, and in seconds, the entire structure was alight.

Jodie ran toward the front of the mill, away from the fireball that was Leonard Trumbo. He stopped in time to avoid colliding with Tank Egon. The big man was also on fire. He barreled out of the burning sawmill like a small sun and fell to the ground near Jodie's feet. The smell of barbeque, matching one of A.J. Mader's famous grills, filled the air.

Inside the mill, three glowing forms twisted and writhed atop the wood pile. Buckie, Quake, and Bullfrog burned and screamed, dancing in pain on what was not an altar, but a pyre.

While Jodie stared, Ellis Deems came tearing out of the mill, not as far engulfed in flame as Tank, but burning and half-crazed with panic and agony. He saw Jodie.

"Help me." His voice was a thin, ribbon-like wail above the squeal of the fire and the sharp creaking the mill made when its beams began to weaken and sag. He charged toward Jodie, who realized he was still holding his own gas can.

"Get back," Jodie yelled, but Ellis kept coming. Jodie spun around and made for the pond.

Ellis followed, howling senselessly.

Jodie reached the farthest edge of the clearing where the hill cut away, dropping a sheer fifteen feet to the ground below. He skidded to a stop and turned.

Ellis was still bearing down on him, the man's face a mask of melted, blistering flesh.

Jodie realized for the first time that it wasn't Ellis's screams he had heard but his own. Ellis's cries had stopped when his tongue began to roast. Caught between the burning man and the cliff, Jodie threw the only thing he had at Ellis—the gas can. It hit Ellis and exploded. An eruption of flame blasted Jodie over the cliff's edge.

He flipped once in the air and landed on his back a frog's hop from the base of a waterfall flowing from the millpond above. The impact knocked the wind out of him, and he lay there, waiting for Ellis to come toppling after him, crashing like a fiery rocket to earth. The only things Jodie saw, though, were flame and smoke rising over the treetops.

The mill's old water wheel groaned. There was a squeal and a splash as its metal mooring broke and it dropped into the pond, sending a tidal wave surging over the stone ledge. In an instant, what had once been a leaky-faucet trickle became a roaring falls. Water burst past the rocks' edge in a white-capped torrent, and a stinking, stagnant spray fell over Jodie and the creek beside him.

The slow-moving brook was now a wide, raging river. It swept down the hill, tearing at the brambles along its banks and picking up branches and dark silt from the shore.

Jodie sat up and crawled toward the angry creek. His body ached from the fall, and his cheek and one arm stung where flaming drops of gasoline from the gas can's explosion had hit him and seared his skin. He dipped his hand in the current, cupping his palm and bringing a shallow measure of water to his face.

While he lay with his throbbing forearm in the stream, a figure appeared on the ledge above him.

Jodie looked up, expecting to see Ellis or Leonard, charred black and half-melted, but what he saw instead made his heart leap for a different reason. Jaelynn, in her pink homecoming dress, stood on the rocks over Jodie's head.

He slipped on his knees across the mud, drawing closer to the cliff, never taking his eyes off the girl. If he did, she might disappear, and he would find she had been nothing but a mirage born of smoke and sunlight glinting off the water.

She leaned forward, her body extending dangerously far over the cliff's edge. There was no cushion of leaves or moss below to soften her landing if she fell, only jagged rocks which stuck out like bad teeth above the surface of the creek water. Jaelynn raised her arms and leaned her head back. She looked like a bird about to take flight.

"No," Jodie shouted.

His daughter stepped off the ledge.

CHAPTER

TWENTY-SIX

Min was not alone in the cabin. *He* was there. The man had let himself in while she was out chasing the coyotes. She sensed him long before she smelled or heard him coming up behind her.

He grabbed her around the middle, pinning her arms to her sides. She threw her head back, hoping to strike his nose or cheek with the back of her skull, but he anticipated the movement and buried his face against her shoulder.

"Easy...Easy if you know what's good for you."

His voice was muffled, his breath hot, damp, and eighty-proof through the fabric of her shirt. His gun in its holster pressed into her back.

"I want to talk to you," Sheriff Hardesty slurred, so drunk mid-morning that Min figured he must have started before the sun had even come up. "We got to sort this out...like...gentlemen...'cause we all know you're no lady, Minerva-erva-erva."

"We can do that, Sheriff." Min nodded earnestly. "Honest,

though, there ain't that much to talk about."

"You get off lookin' at pictures of a man's wife?"

"No. Never. Sheila musta sent that on accident. I didn't look anyhow. I deleted it. There. My phone is on the table. You can check it."

"I know about you, Minerva. I know what you are," he said, licking his lips. "You're a pussy lover. A carpet muncher." He jerked her closer while he spoke. His gun—she *prayed* it was his gun—pressed harder into her back. "It ain't right. What kind of man would I be—what kind of husband—if I let you pervert my wife? She's a good Christian woman, for the most part, and she's mine. You don't get to dirty that up with your sin...your whatever you call it."

The sheriff spun Min around, and his sour breath blew straight into her face. The damp spot on her shirt where his saliva had collected was already growing cold. His pale blue eyes, half-open and watering, darted this way and that, but his jaw was set so firm and square Min thought his teeth would crack.

"You know"—he sniffed, his nose red and swollen—"you aren't bad to look at, Minerva. I forget that you aren't all that old, even though you are almost a grandma...You and your brother raising that kid together...You could still make some fella a decent wife, if you fixed yourself up a little. You got nice eyes."

He slid his hand up her back until his fingers were buried in her hair.

"Seems like such a goddamn waste to me." He clenched his hand into a fist, pulling her hair, and mashed his face into hers without warning.

His lips were wet against hers. She stumbled helplessly along with him while he dragged her to the couch and flung her down like nothing. Like she weighed nothing. Like *she* was nothing. Then he was on top of her. He straddled her and pinned her down. His face might have been all crazed anger and venom at that point, but Min only saw the gun. It was no longer in the holster, but in his hand and inches from her chest.

"Please," she said, keeping her voice low. "There's a little boy sleeping on the other side of this wall. He's already watched his mama die. He don't need more blood in his life. Please think about him."

"I love my wife," the sheriff howled—a love-sick wolf.

"I know you do. And she loves you. This was a misunderstanding.

No one meant nothin' by it."

"She's not a pervert." He jabbed the muzzle of the gun into Min's sternum. "She's what I get—my reward—for having to put up with inbred peckerwoods like you and your fuckin' brother. The meth heads and the damn fentanyl fiends...messin' my town up so I can't hardly recognize the place some days. I gotta deal with all that. It's all on me. No one else is gonna clean it up. I deserve something nice." He raised the gun and wiped his nose on the sleeve of his uniform.

"You do. I know you do, Sheriff." Min took a deep breath. "So don't do nothin' that you're gonna regret. Let's talk about it. I'll get you a drink. We can talk it out."

Hardesty looked down at her and blinked hard. He frowned as if he was surprised to see her beneath him and wasn't quite sure how she had gotten there. After a couple more blinks, he swung his leg over so he was no longer straddling her, though he remained perched on the edge of the couch.

Min still didn't dare move.

"I've never done anything like this before." Sheriff Hardesty sighed. "That woman makes me so crazy sometimes, you know? It's not your fault." He sounded almost sympathetic. "You can't help the way you are. It's TV and Hollywood telling everyone they're homos."

His red-rimmed eyes roved over her face and came to rest on her hair, disheveled from where he had grabbed her.

"I've never had a problem with you, Minerva. I've known you a long time, and I don't think you're like your brother. You're better than him. You keep your head down mostly. That's smart." He pushed her tangled hair away from her face with a heavy, sweaty hand and tapped her forehead with the muzzle of his gun.

Min nodded and smiled up at him, but small, continuous waves of shivers had set her body to vibrating. Shock was setting in.

"I hope you don't take it personal, the things I've had to do. Now and back then, with your niece too. I know it didn't always shake out fair for your kin, but a wise man knows which side his bread is buttered on, and my mama didn't raise no fools."

"I understand," Min said through chattering teeth.

"I figured you would." He smoothed her hair down over her shoulders. "You seem like a woman who understands...things. I can help you, if you want."

"Help me?"

"Sure. Maybe you don't have to be this way. Maybe you could change. You got soft hair," he said, though he had stopped stroking her strands and had placed his hand on her thigh. "Maybe you just need someone to help you see how good it can be, you know, when you're doing it with a man."

Min's eyes grew wide. She opened her mouth to scream, but before she could make a sound, Sheriff Hardesty clamped his hand down over her mouth.

"Damn it. I didn't say I was gonna do you without your say-so. I'm not like that. For Christ's sake, I'm the friggin' sheriff. I just meant that if you wanted to see what it was like, I could help you out. Who knows, maybe you aren't as gay as you think. You ever consider that?"

He let go of Min's mouth and rubbed his temples like his brain was beginning to throb, like he was sobering up a little.

"I don't know. It made sense in my head."

Min made a small choking sound, and the sheriff glared at her.

"Calm down already. I said I'm not here to hurt you. I only...I need you to stay away from my wife, hear?" He set his gun down on the table in front of the sofa.

Min shook her head violently. She grabbed his arm, burrowing her fingers into the muscle. The blood had drained away from her face, and it felt numb.

"What's wrong with you now?" Sheriff Hardesty asked.

She raised her hand and pointed.

Lucas Tanner—the gory remainder of him—stood in the living room, halfway between the sofa and the front door.

The sheriff fell back across Min, emitting a sputtering sound and gagging. Min caught a whiff of bile and guessed he had thrown up in his mouth. Hardesty reached for his gun in its holster, forgetting it wasn't there.

Lucas advanced, preceded by the stench of him. The foul odor overpowered the scent of Hardesty's vomit and hit Min in the face. Decaying meat and clotting blood—Lucas Tanner smelled like death and looked like it too. His rotting mouth hung open, his jaw connected by a few fraying tendons, and an oily reddish-black substance oozed over his moldering lips.

"What the fuck is that?" Sheriff Hardesty bellowed.

The tower of leftovers which had been Lucas stepped closer. The muscles remaining on his face switched, glistening and raw. They pulled up, lifting whatever flesh was left near Lucas's mouth and exposing the few molars he still had in his upper gums. It was as close a thing to a grin as a creature like that could make.

Never in life had Lucas appeared so cruel. This was no longer the young man Min had known.

Hardesty leapt to his feet, wrenching Min off the sofa. He gripped her by the arm and held her in front of his body. The sheriff was clinging to her for support and positioning her like a shield between him and the dead man.

Lucas took a slow, shuffling step forward. His movements were drawn out, unhurried. He might have appeared to be a mindless, animated corpse—and a blind one at that, with only one blank, white eye left—but he seemed to know Min and the sheriff were trapped. There was only one way out, and it was directly behind him.

The sheriff remembered his gun on the table and bent down behind Min to pick it up.

"You stop right where you are! Don't you take another step!" Hardesty sounded like he had marbles in his mouth, spraying saliva all over the side of Min's face and neck while he hollered. He pressed in behind her, raised his gun over her shoulder, and took aim.

Shots exploded while the sheriff emptied the gun into Lucas.

The blasts rattled the delicate bones in Min's ear, deafening her and throwing off her balance. She reeled, and the room spun like a carousel.

The bullets hit Lucas's rotting body, and the dead boy exploded with an unearthly roar Min heard even over the ringing in her ears. Lucas burst into a vapor of black flies and a bloody mist, which filled the room like an expanding star or supernova, shattering the front window and splitting the doorframe as it poured out of the cabin.

The sheriff pushed Min out of the way and rushed for the door. She staggered and followed him out of the house, after the buzzing cloud of flies swarming across the road and into the woods on the other side. Their tiny beating wings, numbering in the millions, kicked up a cloud of red dust and bent trees backward with a gale force. The other insects screamed, and birds cackled and cawed from the brush.

The sheriff stopped at the bottom of the porch steps and aimed his empty gun at the trembling forest.

Min had made it halfway down the stoop when a monstrous black crow, limp and lifeless, landed on the step next to her. Another fell on the one below, stopping her in her tracks. She looked at the sheriff, who threw his arms up to cover his head in time to avoid being hit in the face by an obsidian-feathered bird.

More and more of its black-cloaked brethren rained down on him, dead. Their lifeless bodies pelted him and drove him back to the house.

A gray sedan pulled into the drive, and Olivia Reynolds stepped out of the vehicle into the full force of the avian deluge, which quickly covered the car's hood and roof with dead birds.

Safely under cover, the sheriff turned on Min. "This is you doing this. I know all about your fuckin' family. I heard the stories. Conjure folks and white trash devils. Criminals! What the hell did you do to me?" He pounded on his head, as if trying to wake himself from a bad dream. "What did you give me? LSD? S'that what it was?"

Still deafened by the gunshots, Min didn't have to be a lip-reader to understand what the sheriff was saying. She was a Burden, and she knew the drill.

"This isn't me. That was Lucas Tanner," Min said. "You saw him too. That was Lucas. What the hell happened to him?"

"*What the hell happened to him*? Nothing! Nothing we know of because that wasn't Tanner. That was a fuckin' hallucination. You did something to me. What the hell did you do?"

He grabbed Min by the arm, but Olivia was striding across the bloody gravel drive, with its minefield of dead birds, and swatting away flies. She made a beeline for the porch.

"Hey! Get your hands off her. What are you doing?" Olivia pulled out her phone and pointed it at the sheriff, already recording as she climbed the stairs.

"Mind your own damn business," Hardesty yelled. "I'm the law."

"Start acting like it then. God Almighty, as a lawyer, I met a few unprofessional cops, but you take the cake. Bring it down a notch, or this ends up on the internet. You got it? You really want the world seeing you like this?"

Sheriff Hardesty looked at the phone in the woman's hand. "Why don't you tell the world what she's done? She's a...a damn witch or something. She drugged me." He turned back to Min. "I always knew there was something wrong about you, Minerva Burden. You're just like the rest of your suggins family."

Hidden Children

He was running out of steam now, out of hot air, and he sounded like a balloon deflating with a whine.

"You poisoned me or drugged me. This is all you. Mrs. Moser's flies, Rick Harbison's crows—all of it. It's you and that brother of yours too. Unnatural is what you are." He rubbed his swollen, red eyes with his fists. "Can't even trust my own senses around here nomore."

"Unless you plan on charging Ms. Burden with something, something other than being a witch or...what was it—*conjure folk*? I suggest you head on out of here before you go viral, Sheriff."

Hardesty took one last look at the camera and pitched himself down the porch steps, limping up the road to his vehicle, which was parked around the bend, almost out of sight.

"Un-fucking-believable," he muttered, kicking a limp bird out of his path. "Crazy people in this town." A branch cracked in the woods along the road, and the sheriff shied away like a spooked pony. "Goddamn Burdens!"

CHAPTER

TWENTY-SEVEN

Jaelynn stood at the lip of the stone spillway by the sawmill pond. She spread her arms wide, like an angel's wings, set one foot out over the edge, and then jumped. Jodie reached out as if to catch her, but she didn't fall. She hovered.

Something floated behind her, holding her aloft and keeping her out of the spray of the surging water. Jodie couldn't make out what it was from where he stood, not even when it pushed Jaelynn forward, well past the cliff's edge and over the creek below, before lowering her slowly to the forest floor.

Jodie scrambled to his feet. "Jaelynn?"

"Daddy?"

"Jaelynn, my baby girl, you're alive."

"Daddy, are you there?" Her big eyes were wet and empty. They stared off, covered by a white cataract-like film.

Jodie's stomach dropped. "I'm right here, baby girl. Can't you see me?"

"Daddy, I'm...I'm real sorry." Jaelynn's words had a familiar ring.

Daddy, I'm...I'm real sorry. Jodie had heard this before. She had said this to him on the phone right before she killed herself.

"What's happening to you, sweetheart?"

"I killed him, Daddy." She called him "Daddy" but still hadn't looked at him. Her marble-like eyes were trained on the distance, at a point somewhere over his shoulder.

A sob found its way up from Jodie's chest into his throat.

This wasn't his daughter. This was something playing the part of Jaelynn, reading her lines like a script. Whatever it was, it spoke words from the past—words already dead—hollow echoes.

Yes, an echo.

That's what this was, Jodie thought. It was an echo of Jaelynn.

"You and I have done this before," he said. An emptiness crept into his voice.

Jaelynn's echo ignored him, as he half expected it would, and the rerun played on with wooden, robotic performances.

"Tyler. I shot him. You don't believe me. Are you there, Daddy?" She didn't even wait for him to answer. "I can't go where they won't let me see my son. I can't go. I can't go anywhere. Trapped. Where they won't let me see."

That wasn't right. They were off-script. Just when Jodie was sure that all this double could do was repeat what had already been said, something had changed.

"I can't go. I can't go." Jaelynn was repeating herself like a damaged record with the needle stuck in the groove. "Can't go. Can't go."

"Stop. Stop it!" Jodie held his hands up to his ears. "Please stop," he begged.

The needle unstuck. "He's all I got. I can't go where they won't let me hold him. Let me hold him. Let me be his mother."

"No. That's not how it went...That's not what she said. It's...wrong. You're wrong. You're not her. You're something else."

The false Jaelynn finally turned her head toward Jodie, her white eyes staring, boring holes in him, but she went on without mercy.

"I could see it. It was in his eyes. No one believed me. *You* didn't believe me." Her voice was no longer sweet and breathless, but sibilant and vicious. "I couldn't listen to them say all those nasty things again. Callin' me a liar and worse. Bitch. Cunt. Dirty whore. You didn't stop them, Daddy. Why didn't you stop them?"

"Why are you doin' this to me? What are you?"

Hidden Children

The mimic moved toward him, but it was her words, not her form, which beat him back to the cliff face. Jodie fell away, shrugging and shrinking, sinking into himself, while this cruel copy of his daughter continued to spit poison in his face.

"Do you think I wanted him to do what he did all those years ago? Do you think I wanted him to lay me down on the dirty mill floor and do all those things to me, to hurt me? Do you think I asked for it? Do you think I *liked* it?" She advanced, pushing Jodie back another step. "I almost killed myself that night. Did you know, Daddy? Did you know I wanted to die, even back then?"

"You never said." Jodie pressed his back against the cold, wet stone beside the waterfall. He could retreat no further. "You should have told me."

"If I had, you wouldn't have believed me. You never believed me. I had to kill myself so you would know I wasn't lying."

"Don't say that." Jodie took a ragged breath. "I believed you." His heart was hurting him more than his arm, his burned cheek, or any of the other scrapes and bruises he had acquired in his fall.

"A part of you always wondered...Did I ask for it? Was I the slut they said I was? Don't pretend it's not so. When it was over, after he'd finished with me, I went down to the bottom of the hill. Covered in dirt and seed—*his* seed—I went to where the stream deposits all the trash and garbage and sorrow it gathers as it runs through the hollow. I went to the bottom of the hill, where our misery and the things we'd like to forget collect in a deep pool in front of the cave that sings. You've been there, Daddy. You know the place. I went to where things end and where they begin."

Jodie had almost forgotten the shadow lurking behind Jaelynn, but now he noticed it again. It was emitting a strange hum, and on closer inspection, Jodie realized it was not a single thing, but many things, millions of parts making a whole. It was a mass of flies, a shifting cloud fusing with Jaelynn's image, which was some sort of projection, a play of light on shining iridescent wings—a hologram of sorts.

"I tried to jump, but something held me back," the vision of Jaelynn said.

"You knew you couldn't do that to your old man," Jodie said, even though he understood more fully than ever that he was not speaking to anything human. "You knew you couldn't leave me like that, not after we'd lost your mama too."

"I was going to do it." She spoke lightly, carelessly. The words landed like wasp stings. "Something else stopped me. Physically stopped me, I mean. It wrapped around me and held me back. I could feel it inside, searching, tasting."

"I don't understand."

"Of course, you don't. But *she* did. She knew. It was my blood that awakened her." A dark trickle wound its way down Jaelynn's leg from beneath her party dress. Like a river on a map, the crimson streak kept on running until it crept over her foot and dripped into the stream, where it formed a blushing burst of pink. "A witch's blood is a valuable thing. It is the key. It has the power to awaken, and awaken she did. She rose through the water and felt the spark."

"What spark?" Jodie asked. The image of Leonard Trumbo catching fire danced before his eyes.

"Benji. The seed had barely been planted but already was beginning to grow. He called out to her, and she answered. They had met before. She had been waiting for him."

"Called out to who?"

Jodie took a step toward Jaelynn, but she moved away. Shadows fell across her face, darkening her complexion until she was an underexposed portrait of herself. She was fading. Jodie was losing her, and it threatened to tear him in two. He didn't care if the face he saw was real or not. It was her face, and he had missed it.

"Forget it. It don't matter. Just come home, Jaelynn. Come back with me, please. Whatever you are, it's fine with me. I want you back, baby girl."

"I can't." She shook her head. Her hair blurred at the edges, like a cloud drifting apart where it was thinnest. She floated closer to him. "I'm not real, Daddy."

Already, she was disappearing, turning to flies and absorbing into the column. Jodie found himself pleading with a pillar of insects to bring his daughter back.

"I don't care. I want you...I want you home."

"You cling to an illusion. You chase the dead." Her voice was cold now, nothing like Jaelynn's. "You are empty, and you want. Want, want, want. Why not seek something attainable, Joseph Burden, son of Mercy, child of Linus?"

The cloud of insects shifted, taking on a new shape, and Jaelynn became Alison Mader.

"I can't bring your daughter back—not as she was. That is beyond me. She is gone, and all you can do is mourn." Jodie stifled a sob, and the thing which looked like Alison frowned. "Sorrow is a weak emotion. It is a stone around your neck that will sink you if you let it."

"How can I stop feeling what I feel? Don't you think I want to?" Jodie pulled at his hair, at his clothes. "It eats me up. It makes me so I can't even see no more. I'm walkin' around blind. I'm like a goddamn wind-up toy walking into fuckin' walls over and over again. It never ends. First Carrie, then Jaelynn. Why?"

He pounded at his chest and slapped at his face, hoping this thing in front of him would see the stone already residing inside him, made of petrified hurt and hate and regret. Jodie needed understanding, needed forgiveness. He struck himself until he was so weak that he dropped to his knees.

"I'm sinkin', but I ain't got no strength to fight it. It aches. It's a dog chewin' me up inside, gnawing on my guts. I can't take it no more. I don't deserve this."

"Don't sink without a fight. If you must go down, taste blood before you drown."

He hadn't seen her bend or kneel, but she was eye level with him and drawing closer. She placed her hand—Alison's hand—on his chest and pushed him until he was lying on his back on the ground. His whole body felt petrified. He was powerless to move, and she crawled over him like an animal, sniffing him, sensing him, tasting him, as though making some determination as to his general makeup and being.

"There is great sorrow inside you, yes, but there is rage too, and there is power in that rage if you embrace it."

"How? How do I do that?"

The thing that looked like Alison Mader reared her head back. She appeared to grow larger, every bone in her body lengthening.

"*Rap. Rap. Rap.* God came knockin'. Let me in, Joseph Burden." She stroked his face with clammy fingers, and her words rose to a high-pitched hiss, like a snake's sigh. "We are alike, you and I. We are the hidden children, kept from the light, denied by our makers, trapped by circumstance. We both have suffered, but I am strong, and you are weak. Cast off your weakness and become a man, become a father."

"I *am* a father."

"You *were* a father. Your daughter is dead, and her killers walk the earth, rich and fat. They live while she does not. What kind of father would allow that?"

Jodie had no answer.

Up close, the thing in front of him didn't look as much like Alison Mader as it had before. Her features were blurred, her mouth thin and hard-set. Jodie's body was growing numb, either from fear or from shock, maybe both. His limbs were heavy, and he felt as though he was sinking into the ground, unable to move while the earth held him in place.

The thing that was Alison but was not Alison hovered over him, rocking back and forth. If his body hadn't been so numb and he hadn't been so stupid with fright, he might have been able to tell if he was making love to this creature or not. But he only knew that something was emptying him out.

It was carving out who he was, who he had been, and filling him with something new, something that was not Jodie Burden, something powerful and raw. It continued until it seemed he might burst.

Rap. Rap. Rap.

"Open the door, Joseph. Let me in and I will give you justice."

Jodie's arms were deadweights. They felt tethered to the ground, but he managed to lift them anyway and wrap them around the creature. Her skin twitched and jerked beneath his touch. A thousand insect wings tickled his palms. He slid his hands over her until he reached her back and could feel the gaping chasm beginning at the nape of her neck and running the length of her torso, confirming what he had already known—she was the creature from his dream.

With his arms around her, he fingered the ragged flesh rimming the yawning gash and ran his hand the length of the opening. The creature's raw, tattered skin rippled at his touch, and the space began to widen.

White skin pulled back. The flies shifted. It was as though the creature was turning inside out. Her body opened and unfurled. Darkness spread outward.

Jodie reckoned he should be terrified.

A smarter man would have been.

"Why are you helping me?"

"Because you will help me in return."

"How?"

"I will give you justice, and you will give me life."

"You look alive enough to me."

The creature smiled. "I desire real life beyond the drowning pools and the cave, beyond my prison. I desire to be flesh, not flies. The butcher's month approaches, the Month of Slaughter, when the earth will be wetted with blood and dark things grow strong from its nourishment. The time is coming, and I must have life. I offer you a trade. I cannot bring your daughter back, but I will help you destroy this man, the one you hate, this father who has everything you do not."

"Lauderback."

"That is what you want."

"Yes. I want to kill Samuel Lauderback, the goddman son of a bitch whose son raped my daughter and who used his money and power to cover it up."

The creature nodded. "I will help you find justice. Find me in the darkness where I lie, and I will give you blood."

CHAPTER

TWENTY-EIGHT

The metal roof of the Clay Hollow Cannery was aglow when Jodie climbed the rocky trail from the highway onto the back half of Lauderback's land. Lit up, the roof was a beacon visible for miles.

It took Jodie a moment to realize that this building wasn't on fire too, that the sun sinking lower on the horizon was reflecting off the new steel. The gleam offset the darkness of the woods, deepening the shadows beneath the trees. It was there, in the insect-filled gloom, that Jodie waited, crouching low with his heart hammering, his eyes on the entrance to the cannery.

Minutes crept by.

A bridle path wound close to Jodie's hiding place, and a teenage girl on a chestnut mare rode by after a time. Neither animal nor rider noticed him. He remained quiet and motionless, inhaling the stench from the wastewater lagoon.

Finally, Samuel Lauderback, Sr. strode down the walk and climbed the steps to the cannery. Only then did Jodie raise himself on aching legs and stalk toward the building the man had disappeared into.

Homespun and rustic from the outside, the cannery was all business within, filled with modern machinery and the latest technology. Everything was stainless and sterile, from the wide tables with rollers for sorting the tomatoes to the big industrial vats for steaming and storing and the intestine-like tubes and chutes, which squirted stewed tomatoes and paste into cans. Jodie's footsteps sounded heavy on the spotless floors and reverberated off the equipment when he entered.

"Where the hell have you been, Ellis? I've been calling you half the day." Samuel Lauderback turned around. His face curdled like old milk when he saw Jodie. "You're a bad penny, Mr. Burden. If you've come to ask me to give you more time to get out of Dodge, I'm afraid I'm going to have to disappoint. You got six days."

In reply, Jodie pulled his knife out of his back pocket.

"I see." Lauderback let out a sigh and shook his head with an air of irritated resignation. "It's like that, is it? You really are dumber than you look, Burden." In no particular hurry, the man took off his checked overshirt and hung it on a nearby hook.

Wealth hadn't made Samuel Lauderback soft. The fitted undershirt he wore revealed a physique a much younger man would have been proud of. The farmer was more than capable of delivering on any physical threats he made.

A toolchest sat on one of the stainless steel sorting tables. Lauderback flipped it open and pulled out a large wrench.

"You've made a big mistake, Burden. Come nosing around here like a stray dog and you're going to get put down like a dog."

"I'm not anyone's dog," Jodie said, "especially not yours."

Lauderback shook his head slowly, but, as if someone had hit fast-forward, the man's easy pace went triple speed. Without a breath of warning, he lunged.

Jodie just managed to jump back in time.

The breeze from Lauderback's wrench kissed his face when the tool whizzed past, barely missing his cheekbone. Lauderback grinned, even though he had failed to connect with his target, and Jodie felt an extra surge of adrenaline. Broken bones weren't his adversary's goal. Lauderback was playing for keeps and aiming for his head.

In turn, Jodie lashed out with his knife, swiping at the man's chest, but Lauderback was ready on the backswing.

The wrench sailed through the air once more, and again, Jodie had to leap away to avoid getting his skull cracked open. He danced back a step or two, then sprung at his opponent, coming in low with his blade.

Focusing on Jodie's head had left Lauderback's legs wide open. Jodie slashed at his thigh, drawing some blood but mostly ire. Lauderback looked down at the thin smudge of red on his heavy jeans and back at Jodie. His hard eyes glittered.

"You're goin' to wish you hadn't done that, son."

"Your son's a rapist, and I'll deal with him next."

"You're already dead, Burden." The man raised his weapon and charged at Jodie like an enraged bull.

Jodie stood his ground and thrust the knife out as Lauderback brought the wrench down. The heavy metal tool hit Jodie's hand and sent the knife spinning. It landed with a clatter before skittering away and stopping somewhere under one of the scalding tanks.

Jodie tucked his throbbing hand to his chest, sure it was broken, and darted after the knife.

"You lose something?" Lauderback chuckled.

He followed Jodie toward the tanks, swinging the wrench back and forth lazily. Jodie spotted the knife glinting beneath the silver vat and scrambled for it. Lauderback raised his wrench high, then brought it whistling down, but Jodie ducked under the steam-washing table.

The wrench hit the sheet metal top with a deafening gong and left behind a dent, marring the mirror-like surface. Jodie darted behind one of the larger vats, wedging himself in between the tank and the wall, no closer to his knife than he had been before.

"No way out now." Lauderback whistled and strolled closer to Jodie's hiding place.

It was true. Jodie was trapped.

The man's suede boots squeaked on the freshly washed floor.

Jodie leaned against the wall and planted one foot before the other against the metal tank. He braced himself and pushed until the vat wobbled. Jodie grunted and shoved, and the tank tipped over.

Tomato mash and pulpy juice dumped out in a wave between him and Lauderback. The other man's face turned as red as the seed-filled slop spreading over the floor. Lauderback dropped the wrench and charged through the mess, grabbing Jodie by the throat and lifting him right off his feet.

"It's better like this, Burden. I'll use my own goddamn hands." He held Jodie aloft by the neck.

Jodie kicked his feet, skimming the floor and slipping over the red sludge. He gasped and wheezed, and his vision went red.

"You're done, you pathetic pissant."

Jodie's eyes bulged and darted this way and that, looking to every corner in the room for salvation, for the assistance he had been promised.

This was wrong. It wasn't supposed to go this way. This wasn't justice like the creature had spoken of.

"Daddy? Are you all right?"

From across the cannery came a voice so sweet Jodie thought, for a moment, it was Jaelynn. But before he could choke out her name, Lauderback answered.

"Everything's fine, Hope. You go on up to the house, sweetheart, and help your mama get supper on."

Lauderback's daughter, the girl Jodie had seen earlier on the horse, was tall like her father, with sun-kissed cheeks and wind-blown hair. Sixteen or seventeen years old at most, she hovered inside the doorway of the cannery, surprise and concern glowing like twin stars in her cornflower-blue eyes.

"I said go on home now, Hope."

The girl turned a quarter of the way toward the door, looking for all the world like she intended to do as her father had instructed. But then...

"Are you sure I shouldn't call someone?"

Lauderback waved her off with one hand. "You run along now, like a good girl." He spoke with a tremor.

The man was afraid for his daughter—not for what might happen to her, but for what she might see him do.

Instead of leaving, the confused girl took a step closer to her father, followed by a second. When she reached the ring of pulpy tomato slop, she stopped, the toe of one shiny leather riding boot nudging the crest of the red juice. She pulled her phone out of her back pocket and held it up.

"I could call the house."

"No. I've got this handled. I'll be right on up after you. I promise. I have to finish talking to Mr. Burden here." He set Jodie down and eased his grip but didn't take his hand away from Jodie's throat. "Go on."

Hope was still frozen, with her phone halfway to her cheek. Lauderback smiled to reassure her, but the grin faded quickly. The man's face went slack and gray, a change so pronounced that Jodie looked to see what had caused the shock.

Behind the girl, something was rising.

A woman, made up of countless humming insects, emerged from the crimson slop covering the floor. The teenager slowly turned to see what her father was gaping at, but already, the red figure towered over her. She barely had time to utter half a scream before a buzzing, scarlet hand shot forward and reached deep into her open mouth.

Hope gagged and choked, then fell silent, her mouth filling with sauce-coated flies. She flailed her arms, not sure what to grab onto or how to fight the onslaught of a million tiny foes moving as one. The girl dropped to her knees while the insect-woman reached deeper within.

The figure's whole arm was inside the girl now, so far down Jodie imagined she could tickle the girl's kidneys if she had a mind to. Hope's legs slipped and jerked in the viscous sauce, refusing to remain beneath her. With a spasm, she fell onto her side, grabbing at her throat, with the red woman on top of her, still pouring into the girl until the figure finally disappeared entirely into that pretty rosebud mouth.

"No!" Lauderback, forgetting Jodie, ran to his daughter.

Hope lay still, face down on the floor. Lauderback rolled her over, bellowing at the sight of her staring blue eyes and her red-ringed mouth, which was locked in the contortion of a silent scream. He pulled her to his chest, clutching at her lifeless body and rocking her like a baby, his white shirt growing ever more red.

Jodie caught his breath and limped forward, bending down to retrieve his knife now that his attacker was distracted. Quietly, he limped toward the door. All the fight had run out of him the moment Hope Lauderback, so young and innocent, hit the floor.

Beyond the threshold was Hope's horse. It was tethered to one of the porch posts, whinnying and bucking, its nostrils flaring as the smell of death wafted through the open cannery door. It saw Jodie and reared up with a snort.

Jodie hung back, afraid of the large beast and its stamping

hooves. Behind him, Lauderback wailed.

"You did this. Goddamn you, Joseph Burden."

Jodie spun around and ducked. The other man, who was on his feet again, swung wildly at him with two meaty fists.

This time, Lauderback didn't bother to aim his blows. With his face contorted with rage and pain, he plowed into Jodie, knocking him backward and grabbing him around the neck with one arm. Jodie's larynx compressed, and he whipped his hand up defensively. He had almost forgotten the knife he held until it sank into Lauderback's throat.

The man let go and staggered back, clutching at the handle protruding below his ear. The weapon hit the floor, followed almost instantly by the farmer, who landed on his knees not far from his daughter's body.

Jodie watched while Lauderback grew paler and his slouch deepened. Blood ran down his shoulder, and finally, he toppled over.

Jodie closed his eyes, picturing Jaelynn standing on the cliff. Below her, the creek flowed red with blood.

A sloppy, wet sound snapped him back to attention. A few yards away, Hope Lauderback was struggling to her feet.

Awkward as a new colt, she slid this way and that, all knees and elbows. The flies which had choked her crawled beneath her stained skin, holding her up and animating what should have been her lifeless body. She was a puppet, suspended by the insects inside her rather than strings.

Jodie stared, aghast, when she spun around to face him.

The girl took a first faltering step in his direction, testing the strength of her legs. Satisfied, she attempted another. Wobbly as a willow, her movement across the floor was a monstrous herky-jerky dance, strange and rubbery. It disgusted Jodie. He wanted to look away. Jodie didn't want to see the creature, the way she raised her wavering arms and examined her new hands, opening and closing them like crab claws while she grabbed at the air.

"What did you do to her?" Jodie asked.

Hope's head jerked. She dropped her arms and stared at him with white eyes.

"It's what you wanted." Her speech was slurred, as though her tongue were a foreign object in her mouth.

"I wanted to kill Lauderback. You said you'd help me."

Hidden Children

Teeth like ruby-red pomegranate seeds flashed when the creature that was once Hope Lauderback grinned. "I said I would help you destroy him. What father is not destroyed by the death of his child?"

"Goddammit. She was just a kid. I wanted Lauderback and his son to pay for what they did to Jaelynn, not this girl. She had nothin' to do with it."

"You wanted justice. A daughter for a daughter. That sounds right to me." The creature had reached Lauderback's body now and looked down on him. "You can still see it in his eyes—the misery. Look at him and tell me that's not what you felt, Jodie."

She was close to him and smelled like metal, but she was soft and fluid when she pressed against him, easily conforming to his shape.

"This *isn't* what I wanted." Jodie struggled against her embrace.

"But it is. Your heart cried out for blood. Blood is what I offered, and blood is what you took. This was our agreement."

He pushed her away, his palms coated with blood and the spilled tomatoes. "If this is what I wanted, then why do I feel so goddamn wrong about it?"

"Maybe what you asked for was not all that you wanted. Maybe there is more." She spoke softly, almost kindly, no longer stumbling over her words. Her movements were becoming more refined as well. She was mastering her new form.

"What about you? You got what you wanted. Life, wasn't it?" Jodie gestured toward her perverse new body, turning his head at the same time so he didn't have to look at it.

The creatures face crumpled. "This isn't life!" she exclaimed. "This is flies and rotting flesh. This vessel won't hold me. It will fall apart, like they all do. Like your daughter's lover and her friend from the woods, each one faster than the last as I grow."

"As you *grow*?"

"As I grow stronger. You make me stronger, Joseph Burden." She stepped close again and stroked his cheek with a wet, sticky finger, leaving a streak of red from his cheekbone down to his chin. It might have been Jodie's imagination, but already, her fingers felt colder than before. "Your thoughts and dreams strengthen me. With your help, I will once again possess a true form, not this sad reflection of what I am."

She leaned forward and spoke softly, as though imparting a dear secret.

"The real me, the part that can be whole and permanent, sleeps in the water. It waits for an appropriate vessel."

"In the drowning pool where Jaelynn went?"

"Beyond that. In the cave. Where *they* tried to contain me and keep me and use me."

Confused, Jodie shook his head. "Who's they?"

"They are the ones who call themselves masters—witchmasters—whose bones now decorate my prison."

"What are you?" Jodie whispered, fear coursing through his body and making him numb.

"I am the red mother. I am the oracle. One of the hidden children born of the raw god in the Month of Slaughter. I am known by many names, but I am you and yours now, and you are me and mine. We are bound, you see." She tilted her head shyly, it seemed. "I have named myself for you even. I am Seph."

"Seph? As in *Joseph*, like me?"

She nodded. "Your family is my family. When I came to you in your dream, you crawled into me, as your kin have done before, and like them, you saw the darkness in which I exist and recognized it as the same darkness that exists in your heart and in your soul. We are matched, you and I."

She brought her stained mouth closer to his. He saw that she meant to kiss him. Jodie jerked away, horrified.

"It wasn't supposed to go down like this. I'm not supposed to *feel* like this still."

"The pain will never stop, Joseph, son of Mercy. It is all you will ever feel, as long as you are trapped in human flesh. Only I can change that. Only I can set you free. Come to me. Find me in the pool inside the cave. Find me at your mother's grave."

"My mother ran off when I was a kid."

"Lies. Her bones rest with me. Close your eyes and I will show you."

Jodie hesitated.

"Do it. Close your eyes and I will give you sight."

Jodie pressed his eyes shut and stared into the reddish glow at the back of his eyelids until something appeared.

"Tell me what you see."

"I see a cave with a red wall...red walls and a bright blue pool."

"What else?"

"There's a girl here and some men."

"Look closer."

"The girl looks a little like Jaelynn."

In fact, the girl looked *a lot* like Jaelynn—or maybe like Min but without the hard edges. She wasn't either, though. The girl was younger than both, fifteen at most. She was pink and shiny-fresh, like a rose, but she had the same dark hair and pale skin all the Burdens had.

"Dear Lord, is that—"

Jodie opened his eyes, but Seph commanded him to close them once more. She pressed her wet hand over his face until he saw the cave and the girl again.

"Watch."

The girl was crying. The reasons why came to Jodie jumbled up like puzzle pieces in a box. Someone had lied to her. Someone had betrayed her. Jodie could feel the emotion like salt in a cut.

There was a man. There was a baby—

No, there were two. Him and Min.

They were waiting for her, waiting for their mother. The girl before him was Mercy Burden, the woman he had been led to believe had abandoned him all those years ago, who instead had been led into a cave against her will by a group of men who eyed her like hungry wolves.

One of the men, the eldest among them by the looks of it, took her by the elbow. "It's time, Mercy."

"Please, I want my babies. They're only little. They'll be so hungry by now."

"It's too late for that."

There was a ripple in the clear pool behind Mercy, a shimmering disturbance which snaked out with purpose toward the gathering of humans—the men and their captive. It reached the edge of the pool, but instead of dying like a wave on a beach, it gathered energy, taking shape and rising.

The shape became a woman who grew more solid while she ascended until she was white as bone, with a sleek and reptilian body. She heaved herself up and over the lip of the pool.

Rather than the reticulated knobs of a backbone, there was a gaping split, like a tear in the fabric of a shirt ripped up the back. The woman's clawed hands tore at the dry dirt of the cave floor when she propelled herself forward, crawling rapidly like a dog on all fours, moving toward the men who did not see her and Mercy who now saw everything.

The girl screamed. She pulled away from the men and tried to run, but they caught her by the arms and held her tighter than before. They spun her around and forced her down onto her knees. Still, they failed to notice the woman-creature moving like an animal across the sandy cave. Their focus was on the girl whose brown eyes were wide with terror.

One of the men pulled a knife from his pocket and flicked it open. It was a dagger-like blade, sharp on both edges, with a vicious, pointed tip. Showing no hesitation, he crouched next to Mercy and stabbed it into the back of her hand, pinning her to the cave floor.

Mercy hadn't seen it coming. When the blade pierced her hand, she howled but never looked down, not caring about the source of her pain, only the advancing creature.

Blood seeped out from beneath her palm, oozing between her fingers and forming a pool around her hand, which the woman from the water began lapping up like a dog as soon as she drew near enough. Mercy shied away, but the man pushed her lower. The creature darted beneath Mercy before her chest reached the floor.

Jodie assumed Mercy might disappear into the dark place running the length of the creature's back the same way he had. He thought she would fall into the terrible crevice and be swallowed up. But when the girl's body met the creature's, it was the figure who disappeared, absorbing upward into the girl instead.

Still on her knees, with her chest and face low to the floor, Mercy bucked and pitched, her back rising and falling convulsively, her long mane of soft brown hair sweeping the floor and turning gray with dust. The eldest of the men, whose face was half-hidden behind a grizzled goat's beard and whose teeth were like long yellow corn kernels when he smiled, reached down and grabbed her by the back of her neck. He hauled her up to standing, as if she were a puppy he had lifted out of a box by the scruff.

Mercy raised her chin to meet his leering gaze and bared her own teeth. She had a child's set, small and round, like little white pearls in her mouth, but her eyes were no longer her own. They were not warm and flecked with amber stars, but white and empty.

When she spoke, it was not with the voice Jodie had heard her use to plead with the men earlier. Her words rang out like discordant bells and reminded him of the noise an old car's engine made when shot metal ground against metal. The bone-white woman was inside the girl, using her tongue, her vocal cords, to make sounds no man or beast of this world had ever uttered.

One of the men gave a whoop and a holler. "Goddammit, she's done it! The witch brung up the oracle, just like the old timers said." He punched another younger man joyfully in the shoulder. "You sure picked a ripe one."

The younger man was almost as pale as the creature nesting inside the girl. He rubbed the stump of his left arm with his one remaining hand, looking on grimly while the other men celebrated the girl's possession.

Jodie moved across the cave, drawing closer to the mother he had never known. "What's happening to her?" he asked Seph, peering into Mercy's young face and her empty eyes.

"She is becoming."

"Becoming what?"

"More," the creature said bluntly. "You can be more too. You have her strength. You are the one who will give me life beyond the water. Find me in my hiding place and I will give you peace. I swear it. All you have to do is let me in."

"And if I say no, then what happens?" Jodie asked.

The image of the cave flickered.

"There are others. Your family is blessed. Even the smallest of you possesses great strength."

"The smallest? You mean Benji?"

"I felt him sparking to life inside your daughter's womb as she stood by the water the night he was conceived. I sensed him—the boy who had already crossed time to be with me on the *Otherside*. I called to him, and in turn, he called back to me, his cells quickening at the sound of my voice." Her face turned flinty and hard. "I offer you peace, Joseph Burden, in exchange for what I most desire, but if you are too foolish to take it, I will find another way. You must make your choice."

Once more, the cave became clear in Jodie's mind. The men who had brought Mercy to the water began to shout, but their cheers of celebration turned to cries of horror. From inside the girl whose lips and tongue formed strange and unknowable words, whose face moved like cold wax, came an ancient song of destruction and ruin.

Jodie understood the melody, the words emanating from his mother's soul—in his heart and his mind, he understood all too well.

Take them. Have me, but take them all too. Take them all to hell.

The men's screams grew louder, and the clear water of the pool turned red with their blood.

"Do you see now?" Seph asked.

The images of the cave faded away, and the interior of the cannery came back into sharp focus.

"Do you see the power that could be yours? Your mother saw. She made her choice. You must do the same."

With those final words, the flies animating Hope's body burst free. They poured out of her, escaping through every path they could find or make. They took to the air, stained with Lauderback blood, and left the girl's corpse a tattered wreck on the floor.

Jodie knew he should be leaving too—running from the scene if he were smart—but he searched the cannery until he found a tarp to throw over Lauderback and his daughter. Before he covered them up, he rolled Lauderback onto his stomach so that whoever found them wouldn't have to gaze upon the horrible look on the man's face, the one which had fixed itself there when he watched his daughter die.

There was no way to hide the horror the girl had become, though.

When at last Jodie heard a car coming, he tore himself away from the pair, slipping from the cannery while dust from the approaching vehicle rose like a sail over the rows of tomato plants.

CHAPTER

TWENTY-NINE

The battered front door of the Burden cabin swung sadly on its broken hinges. The latch was cracked and the frame splintered. Curtains in the front room billowed on the evening breeze through the shattered window. Min watched from the sofa, waiting for Jodie's return.

Olivia Reynolds set a cup of coffee down on the table in front of her.

"Is it me, or is it getting dark?" Min asked, ignoring the beverage. She took a sip from a tall glass of whiskey she had let go of only to refill again and again since the sheriff had driven away that morning.

Olivia took a seat next to her and gazed out the destroyed window. "It's getting later. That's what usually happens when it gets later."

"I don't know why Jodie isn't back yet. He should have come home ages ago. His grandson's sick, for God's sake."

"I checked on Benji a few minutes ago, remember? He was sleeping."

"Do you think that's normal? Him sleeping so long?"

"I wish you'd let me make you something to eat. You haven't touched anything all day, and that"—Olivia pointed to the glass of whiskey in Min's hand—"isn't going to do you many favors on an empty stomach."

"You won't find much of anything in the kitchen, apart from cereal. Maybe some frozen waffles." She rubbed her neck where the sheriff had gripped it earlier and tried to remember what else she had in the fridge.

Olivia frowned so deeply her eyebrows nearly touched. "I wish you'd let me document what the sheriff did to you. You've got bruises, and we need to get photos while they're still fresh." She looked directly at Min before adding, "If he hurt you anywhere else, though, we'll need to go to the hospital for an exam."

"He didn't hurt me anywhere else. Didn't get the chance."

"I'm glad I came by when I did."

Min looked up at Olivia in mild surprise, like she was seeing her for the first time that afternoon. "Why *did* you come by?"

"I had something to give you," Olivia said. "It's nothing much. Just some information I dug up regarding non-parental custody cases, after what you said in the store yesterday, after you asked me about it."

"I did what?"

"Asked about custody. You asked if I knew anything about it, so I brought you case notes, statistics. Yesterday, you said—"

She stopped. Min's eyes had drifted, refocusing on the drapes and the busted door.

"You know what? It can wait. What I'd really like to discuss now, if you're feeling up to it, is what the hell I saw this morning."

"Just Hardesty bein' an asshole."

"I mean the cloud of black flies and the apocalyptic rain of dead birds that dented my half-new Subaru."

"Oh...that." Min slumped back against the sofa. "I'm not sure I know what that was, not for certain."

"I'd love to hear your thoughts on what it might have been, then."

"You'd never believe it."

"Try me." Olivia crossed her arms over her chest and leaned against the couch too.

"Lucas Tanner, Judge Tanner's son, showed up while the sheriff was here."

Olivia opened her mouth in surprise and to speak, but Min held up her hand.

"If I don't spit this out quick, I'm not going to get it out at all. Lucas was...not right. Not right at all. I don't think he was alive, I mean. I know. I know." Min waved her hand. "I know how that sounds, but what walked into this house was dead—livin' dead, if you follow."

"Like a zombie?" Olivia asked.

"I don't know. Maybe. Sort of? You saw how freaked the sheriff was. That wasn't unwarranted, I can tell you."

"Okay. That's a lot to swallow. What was the sheriff even doing here? Let's back up and start with that."

"He came to tell me to stay away from his wife. He got this wrong idea in his head about the two of us. Then Lucas showed up, and I'm not even sure what happened next. I think the sheriff shot at him, and that's when he kind of...blew up...into flies."

"So, the flies were...Lucas? A twenty-year-old human boy blew up into *flies*?"

"I wouldn't believe it either if I hadn't seen it with my own eyes, but..." Min shrugged.

Olivia stared at her for a minute before looking around and sniffing the air.

"You smell somethin'?" Min asked.

"Yes. I smell rancid meat and something coppery but not gas. There could still be carbon dioxide, though. That's odorless."

"You think something made us hallucinate? A gas leak?"

"It makes more sense than exploding zombie-boys turning into swarms of flies, doesn't it?"

"Were you hallucinating too, then? We all imagined the birds out there?"

"Maybe gas killed the birds. It could have been coming from outside the house. Are there any chemical processing plants around here? I don't know the area well."

"There's nothing like that here. Closest thing is a dog food packaging plant ten miles away." Min leaned back on the couch next to Olivia and took a drink of her whiskey, then chased it down with a second, larger gulp.

Olivia watched her swallow the amber liquid and stare off into space. "I agree, there's something strange going on. I couldn't begin to guess what, but I do know that I'm not leaving you alone until your brother gets back. Do you know where he is?"

"No. Where he said he was goin' and where he's actually gone are probably two different things." Min smiled wryly. "Feel free to stick around, though, until he gets back. You might come up with some ideas for your podcast. A day in the life of a true billy. Be warned, though. If you hang around with me for too long, people'll start to talk."

"What will they say?"

Min turned to her. "You been in this town six months now, right? Why don't you tell *me* what they'll say?"

"Fair enough." Olivia nodded. "Any truth to rumors?"

"My memaw used to say, 'You just ain't one way or t'other. God didn't pick your path, Minerva. He set you down at the fork.' Well, contrary to popular belief, I'm not interested in forkin' anyone, man or woman." Min snorted bitterly at her own joke.

Olivia remained silent.

"Don't see how it hurts anyone, but I guess it makes me a wrong one to some. How about you?" Min nodded to Olivia's outfit while she took another sip of whiskey.

"The suits?" Olivia straightened the gray waistcoat she was wearing and smoothed the pressed linen trousers over her thighs. "No, I'm straight. I love men. I love everything about them, including their clothes."

"I wish I was brave enough to dress up like that every day."

"There's a backhanded compliment, if ever there was one." Olivia chuckled. "I'm going to check on Benji once more, and then I'll make us up something to eat, even if it is just frozen waffles."

"You know he was born in that room?" Min stared at nothing while she spoke. "Jaelynn is the only one of us in the last five generations who wasn't. Carrie, my brother's late wife, insisted on going to the hospital. She was a cut above us Burdens. Don't know what she saw in my brother. He tried to convince her to have Jaelynn here to save some money, but Carrie wouldn't hear it.

"Probably for the best because Jaelynn was a big baby and Memaw wasn't with us anymore. She was the real deal, Memaw—a midwife and a real talented yarb doctor. I almost strangled coming out when my mother gave birth, but Memaw saved my life. After she passed, we were all clueless. Lucky for everyone, Benji shot right out, tiny but healthy.

"Come a little sooner than expected, but that worked out well too, his being early. I don't think Jaelynn coulda taken much more. Kept saying she worried the baby would have *his* face. It was a relief when Benji come out looking one hundred percent Burden, in all ways."

"Worried the baby would have *whose* face?"

"Sam Lauderback's."

"The farmer and tomato guy on city council?" Olivia's eyes grew wide. "I've run into him before. He's pushing sixty."

"Not him; his son. He took Jaelynn to a dance and then out to Keller's sawmill. Things went bad. Jaelynn was a strong girl, but a person can only take so much. She loved Benji from the start. I probably should have seen it comin', though, the way the town's feelings towards her sat heavier after he was born. She could take the hate for herself, but not for her boy. The night she took off was a rough one. She stole Jodie's car and our memaw's shotgun. That gun had sat right there for three generations." Min pointed to a narrow strip of wall between the front door and the window. "Still seems strange to see it gone."

"I'm so sorry about your niece."

"It's my own damn fault. Jaelynn was Jodie's girl, and I should have known better than to get attached. It's no good gettin' attached to anything that belongs to Jodie Burden. It all ends up broken in the end. If I was smart, I'd start my own family. Then it wouldn't hurt so much to watch Jodie get his and throw it all away." Min shrugged. "Guess that wasn't in the cards for me."

"Why not? You're still young. You could have a kid."

"Someone like me?"

"Absolutely."

"Not in this town. Not in this state. It wouldn't be so hard to accept if I didn't have to watch Jodie get it all and then fuck it up so bad."

"Who the hell are you?" Jodie stood in the doorway, his body framed by the wrecked opening. His eyes flicked from Olivia to Min and then back again. "And what are you doing in my house?"

CHAPTER

THIRTY

Jodie tried to shut the front door behind him several times before realizing the frame had split and the latch was broken. "What the hell happened here?" He glared at Min. "I'm gone for a few hours, and the place falls apart." He stomped his way into the house toward the kitchen.

"Why are your clothes all red?" Min sniffed the air. "And why do you smell like a hot dog?"

"Or like spaghetti Bolognese," Olivia added, inhaling as well.

"I don't know you," Jodie said to Olivia before turning to Min. "What're you bringing strangers around for? What's she doing here?"

"*She* is here looking out for your sister," Olivia answered, "while you were missing in action the whole day."

"Where were you?" Min asked.

"What's it to you?" Jodie grabbed a towel from the kitchen counter and wiped his face before he pulled his stained T-shirt over his head. Bare chested, he glowered at Olivia, daring the stranger in his house to stare.

Olivia turned away with a roll of her eyes. "I'll go check on Benji again," she said to Min.

"What in God's name happened to you?" Min asked after her guest had disappeared down the hall. "Weird shit has been going on all day, and you're nowhere to be seen."

Jodie turned his back to her and began scrubbing his face and arms at the kitchen sink.

"Benji's still sick, if you're interested. The sheriff showed up and—"

"Hardesty was here?" Jodie froze, covered in white lather up to his elbows. "When? When was he here?"

"Let me finish, damn it," Min said. "Not too long after you left this morning, the sheriff let himself in—had a real bug up his ass—but while he was here, Lucas showed up."

"Lucas Tanner is dead."

Min looked at him sharply. "How do you know?"

Jodie frowned and clamped his mouth shut. He was burrowing into his silence like a toad in the mud.

"You've seen him too, then," Min said. "You know what happened—what he's like now—don't you? He was here. Made like he was going to attack me and the sheriff, but then he burst apart. Turned into flies."

Jodie snorted. "Bullshit. You've finally cracked...wide open, by the sound of it." He shot her a truculent look and began rinsing his arms and shirt under the tap.

"You know it ain't bullshit, Jodie. Something happened to Lucas, and something is happening to Benji. I only hope it ain't the same thing."

"What d'you mean?" This got Jodie's attention. He turned off the tap and dropped his soaked shirt into the basin. "The kid's just under the weather, right?"

"Benji's not well. He's still sleeping. Got a real bad fever off and on. And he's talking to himself—him, the boy who says nothing. I've never heard the boy say more'n eight words at a time, and now, every time I check on him, he's rambling. He was going on about his mother or *a* mother, but I've never heard him call Jaelynn that before. She's always been Mama. I don't think he's talking about Jaelynn. There's something out there. I can feel it like I felt Hardesty earlier. I don't care if you think I'm crazy. Something is coming."

"It's already here," Jodie mumbled. He looked at the knife he had pulled from his pocket. There was dried blood on the blade and trapped in the rivets. He plunged it into the water and started scrubbing it.

Before Min could ask him what he meant, headlights flashed against the far living room wall. Tires crunched on the gravel drive. Min and Jodie swiveled their heads to the front window in unison.

"Who's that?" Jodie asked. "Who else you invite 'round?"

"No one," Min said.

Olivia appeared in the hall.

"Hit the lights," Jodie ordered.

Confused, Olivia flipped the switch on the wall next to her, dropping them all into darkness. Jodie crept to the busted living room window and peered into the dusky front yard.

"Benji still feels hot," Olivia said. "I think he's hallucinating. You really should consider taking him—"

"*Shhh*. Someone's out there." Jodie waved his arm at her.

"What's got you so damn spooked?" Min demanded.

"I said quiet!"

A car door slammed shut, and footsteps sounded on the drive.

Jodie threw his back against the wall between the door and the window. "Dammit. Min, go see who it is and what they want."

Min nodded, but even before she reached the doorway, someone called out. Someone who had lived in Oracle Springs long enough to know you didn't approach a person's front door in the dark without announcing yourself first unless you wanted a face full of buckshot.

"Jodie? It's Al. You in there? Min? Anybody home?"

"It's Ali Mader," Min said. "You can hit the lights, Olivia."

Min waited until the room was bright again before she rolled her eyes at Jodie's paranoia—she wanted to make sure he didn't miss it. Jodie poked his head out the busted window, confirming that what Min said was true, before stepping onto the porch to meet Alison.

"Thank God you're here, Jodie," Alison said as soon as she saw him. "Please tell me you've been here all day. Or better yet, you've been sittin' in some bar where plenty of folks saw you."

"I've been around, Al. Why?"

"That ain't gonna be good enough, Jodie."

Min joined her brother on the porch. "What's going on?"

"Sheriff Hardesty was at the bar today." Al picked her way over the dead birds littering the walk, a look of confused disgust on her face. "He blew in this morning and sat there most of the day, getting shitfaced like I've never seen him do. Leastways, not while he was in uniform."

Min looked back at the doorway where Olivia had appeared, and the two women traded glances.

"Deputy Carlson came to get him half hour ago—almost had to gather him up off the floor. Carlson said the sawmill burned down. Gas cans laying around mean arson most likely, but there's bodies inside too."

Jodie stiffened. Alison didn't seem to notice, but Min sensed his body go rigid next to hers.

"They found Ellis Deems's truck out front. They're saying it's probably the whole crew in there—all dead. I overheard while I was bringing coffee to funnel into the sheriff. I think Carlson would have injected it directly into the man's veins if he'd known how. He was a wreck, trying his darndest to sober Hardesty up, because, in addition to all that, they got a call that something went on at Lauderback's place."

"Carlson say what?"

"No. Must have been something big, though, if he was ready to drag Hardesty out there, as tanked as he was."

"So, why're you here, Al? If you came all this way to accuse me of somethin', you better spit it out."

"What the hell, Jodie?" Alison paused at the bottom of the porch steps and wagged her head in disbelief. "I came here to warn you. Folk's—not me, but folks—are saying you must have had something to do with all this."

"Why me?"

"It don't take a detective to figure out that much. The sawmill burned. Something's amiss with Lauderback. It's adding up in people's minds. They're even thinking you might have had something to do with Judge Tanner now, saying maybe you blamed him for certain folks not going to trial."

Alison's voice rose with every count she listed, and Jodie winced. He hopped down the steps to join her, keeping his own voice low while he spoke.

"You don't need to shout, Al. Everyone on this here green earth don't need to hear you."

"Wouldn't matter if they did. Everyone in town already knows something's up. People in the bar started yapping as soon as

Carlson dragged Hardesty out. Your name was floating 'round before they'd pulled out of the parking lot. Please, please, tell me this isn't what you were talking about yesterday. I know Linda Deems. Leonard Trumbo's son married my cousin. All those men had families, Jodie. They didn't need to get all burnt up. Six bodies, they found. Please tell me that wasn't you."

"You gotta even ask me that, Al? I know Ellis Deems has a wife and kids, and Tank's got a little boy down in Bentonville he visits when he can. And Leonard...I never had nothin' against Leonard Trumbo. Nothin' much anyway. If the man's IQ was Fahrenheit, he'd freeze vodka. They didn't treat my family right, but they were following orders. I know that. I wasn't looking for any of them to die."

Alison lunged up the steps and hugged him. Her relief was a warm, tangible rush which flowed out of her. She pushed him back and smiled. "I didn't want to believe any of it, but you were acting so weird yesterday. You've been on edge, so I didn't know what to think." Over Jodie's shoulder, she noticed the cabin's busted-out window and door for the first time. "Hey, what happened to—"

Her voice was suddenly drowned out by a clattering from above.

A large sheet of corrugated metal which had been nailed to the roof, a patch to keep the rain out, detached just below the ridge line. It slid noisily over the rotting, shake shingles, picking up speed while it plummeted. It dropped over the edge of the roof and fell vertically.

For a split second, Jodie's view of Alison was blocked by a flash of galvanized silver.

When Alison reappeared, she looked different. There was a deep, meaty V where the smooth line of her shoulder should have been, and her arm hung limply at her side. The sheet metal had hit her shoulder and ripped clean through skin, tendons, and muscle. It had split her clavicle in two and sliced through Alison all the way down to the swell of her breast.

Alison's face turned white, and she staggered to the side before toppling forward.

Jodie caught her. "Min! Help me."

"What the hell was that?" Olivia ran down the steps but stopped when she got a good look at the woman and her injuries. "Jesus Christ."

Quickly, she unbuttoned her vest and pulled it off. Olivia

kneeled next to Jodie and Alison and pressed the garment against the woman's wounded neck and shoulder. Alison moaned.

Min peered up at the roof to see if anything else was about to come down before joining them. "The explosion earlier today must have knocked some of the sheets loose," she said breathlessly.

A cluster of black birds congregated where the scrap had been. Min watched nervously while they grew in number, materializing as if from nowhere.

"We have to get her away from here," Min said. "She needs the hospital. I'll get the keys. Jodie, where'd you put them?"

"Grab mine," Olivia said. "They're in my bag. We'll take my car since she's blocked your truck in."

It was true. Alison's yellow hatchback was parked close behind Min's truck.

"Hurry! Help me get her onto the back seat," Olivia ordered Jodie, who was too stunned to move.

He stood there with his mouth agape, unable to focus on anything but the seeping wound in Alison Mader's neck and the blood forming a pool beneath her.

"I didn't ask for this," he said under his breath.

"What?" Olivia said.

"I'm coming with you."

Olivia shook her head while keeping the pressure on Alison's shoulder. "Bad idea. If what she said was true, the police are going to be looking for you. For questioning, at the very least. You showing up at the hospital, with her in this state, is only going to make it worse. I suggest you wait here and think about where you were this morning and afternoon and try to figure out how you can prove that if asked."

"Someone needs to stay with Benji," Min said, sailing out of the house with Olivia's keys in hand.

"Your brother can do that."

Min looked confused, but Jodie shook his head.

"It's not goin' to look good, Min, if I show up with her all injured like she is. Not if the town's out for my blood already."

"I don't want to let go of the wound," Olivia said. "You drive, Min. Just help me get her into the car. We're wasting time."

Olivia kept her now blood-soaked vest pressed against Alison's body while Jodie lifted the woman around the ribs and dragged her to the sedan.

On the roof ridge above them, the crows continued to gather silently, watching the people below and forming a line of black, which stood out indelibly against the sky, even in the growing dark.

CHAPTER

THIRTY-ONE

It was Benji's second visit to the *Otherside*, although he didn't remember falling through this time. He couldn't recall anything more than feeling hot and a dizzy while waiting for Min to get him out of the truck and bring him inside. Benji might have gotten himself out of the vehicle at some point and maybe stood in the drive, screaming, but that part was fuzzier.

Despite that, his second trip over hadn't been as much of a shock as the first. He wasn't in the pool, but in the cave, where the pool was. It was a strange place, with its red walls and funny smell, though it wasn't as lonely as it had been the first time down in the dark water, with only *her* for company.

Things were happening all around him. Every event which had ever taken place inside the cave was playing out in front of Benji, and it was like watching a hundred TV's at once. Even the walls were alive and moving. Strange lines and shapes appeared and disappeared on their slick surface. Drawings, like those a caveman might have made, flickered in and out, like images in a flip book.

Men in animal skins stepped into his vision and then out, followed by people wearing the kind of old-fashioned clothing Benji had seen in picture books about pioneers and settlers. These people brought women to the cave and gave them to the creature. She rose from the pool when they came and traded secrets for the lives of the women. They called her Oracle, and sometimes, she would try on the women they brought, like a woman tries on a dress, but it was a dress which fell apart too soon.

Groups of men in more modern clothing arrived and did the same. They brought women who they called witches, and these women didn't fall apart like the others. The men were learning.

Their offerings survived with the creature inside them. Sometimes, they even lived long enough that the men grew fearful and pushed them into the water to drown. Of all the visitors to the cave, Benji liked these men the least. Each of them was black-eyed and solemn, and they brought girl after girl, bleeding them before throwing their bodies into the pool.

Once, they brought a man with skin much darker than Benji's. He had black hair and eyes of the lightest green, like a cat's. Benji liked this man and the way he roared at the ones who cut him, but the man didn't bring the creature up from the water, so the men slit his throat and left him to rot on the cave floor.

Sometimes, Benji recognized himself in the cave. Sometimes, he saw his grandmother, Mercy. He knew it was her from the way she looked—so much like his mama and Min. The creature went inside her, and when this happened, she spoke to Benji without moving her lips.

Your future and your past are colliding. The time is right. You must make your choice.

It was strange, seeing himself across the cave and realizing he was in two places at once. He watched while the creature reached out with the grandmother's dead hand and drew a circle in the sand, pointing to one side and then the other.

You are there. You are then. We are here. We are now. She connected the two points with a line. We are joined. Now and then. Always and forever.

The circle was time. Benji knew he could be anywhere on that circle, anywhere and somewhere else besides. He could be here and there, one side or the other, in two places at once or, as he was now, in one place at two different times. And so could she.

Right then, she was on the floor in front of him, cloaked in a decaying body. She also stood behind him, smelling like...tomatoes.

He felt the heat from her body and the buzzing emanating from her, as it did from the swarms of flies she commanded. This version of her wore his mother's appearance, much like the other had worn Mercy's and the other the traveler's.

I will come to you—the future you—when I am the future me, she said.

Benji wasn't sure which of them had spoken.

"Why do you do that?" he asked.

Do what?

"Make yourself look like her, like Mama."

So that you desire to come to me.

"Aren't I here now?"

No. You are asleep somewhere else. I am not here either, not really. She cast her pale eyes down.

"Where are you, then?"

The creature nodded sadly to the pool, and Benji went to it, leaning over the stone edge until he could look into its depths. The water was sparkling clear, and he could see everything within: eyeless fish, shining pebbles, and even a small, heart-shaped pendant. But it was the dark eye, that black portal, in the center of the pool which held his attention, hypnotized him, and pulled at his soul.

I am banished, the creature said mournfully, *pushed out by the new gods to make way for their new creations, forced to surrender my place in the world to accommodate your kind. Now I am trapped, hidden away in the dark always.*

"It's awful." Benjie shuddered. He couldn't help himself.

Set me free, then. Show me which door you would have me go through. I give you the choice.

"I don't know what that means," Benji said.

Across the cave, the other Benji extended his hands to Mercy, and she reached back for him.

It was you, coming through and finding me here, who showed me when I could be.

"You mean *what* you could be?"

The creature shook her head. *No. You helped me find the moment out of all these moments. You helped me find the* when. *I saw you, and you became the fixed point on a constantly spinning wheel. You showed me when it would be possible. Now choose the doorway and let our journey together begin.*

"The doorway is Papaw Jodie or Aunt Min, isn't it?"

Yes. She nodded eagerly. *I leave the choice to you. Decide and we will be together.*

"But what will happen to them, the one I pick? Where will they be after you go through them?"

They will be hidden. Tucked away, like I have been these many years.

"I don't want that. I don't want them tucked away, not either of 'em." Benji shook his head, wary of the flies amassing on the walls and ceiling.

Whether you choose or not, I will have my witch. The creature grew taller while she spoke, spreading out until spaces became visible between the pieces she had cobbled together to look human. *One of them will make the bargain for you. They are undecided now, but that will change. Before long, I will lead one of them to me, and I will be free.*

The flies which had been gathering took to the air. They formed a swirling tornado-like cloud, filling the cave before they poured out of the opening in the ceiling. The creature herself broke apart, shattering into so many more insects and following the cloud into the sky—a fast-moving storm streaking away over the darkening horizon.

CHAPTER

THIRTY-TWO

Min leaned as far over as she could, pressing her ribs onto her knees. She recalled having heard that bending over like that helped a person breathe when they felt like they were going to hyperventilate. An elderly couple across the ER waiting room stared at her, but they were little more than a blur. The paperwork the nurse had asked her to fill out for Alison was an illegible mess.

"Any minute, A.J. Mader is going to burst through the door and start tearing folks new assholes until he finds out what happened to his sister," she said to Olivia, who had returned from a search for a vending machine.

"Have a coke." Olivia offered Min a can, which she took from her with shaking hands. "It isn't your fault."

"I hope her brother agrees with you. He's gonna want Jodie's head on a plate."

"If I were Jodie, I'd be more worried about the police right about now."

"You think the police are gonna show up?" Min looked at the doors once more.

"Not yet, maybe. Sounds like they have bigger fish to fry, and the doctors seem to buy that this was an accident. It *was* an accident, right?" Olivia didn't sound too sure. "The odds of it coming down like that, right where she stood…"

"So many strange things have happened today. This turning out to be an accident seems unlikely to me. I know the roof looks like crap—we've been patching it with pounded scrap for decades—but as ugly as it is, it's sound. I get up there myself at least twice a year and check it out. Otherwise, it leaks, and I end up getting a shower while I sleep." Min raised her soda to her lips, but a fly landed on the back of her hand before she could take a sip. Her eyes widened.

"It's only a fly." Olivia waved her hand over Min's to scare the insect away. "What? What is it?"

Min's eyes were fixed down the hall, beyond the ER waiting room. She stood up.

"Where are you going?" Olivia grabbed their things from the row of seats and followed her.

"You hear that?" Min asked, setting a deliberate path down the hall, like a bloodhound tracking a clear, fresh scent.

"All I hear is the voice in my head saying, 'Go home, Olivia. Leave these crazy white people to their crazy white people shit.' Why I'm not listening to it, I don't know."

They turned down another corridor.

The second hall was narrow and much less busy than the main passage, with its constant parade of doctors, nurses, and techs. A row of unused gurneys and empty carts lined one wall, and the few doors along the other were mostly wide open, the rooms beyond empty and dark. Down at the end of the hall, one door was cracked, revealing a band of weak light shining within.

Min made a beeline toward this door and paused outside. Olivia caught up and grabbed her arm when Min reached out to open it.

"We should go back to the waiting room, in case someone has news about your friend."

"It's coming from in here. I can hear it."

"Hear what?"

Min shook off Olivia's hand and gave the door a shove. A single florescent tube light flickered above a hospital bed. The rest of the room was dark, apart from the blinking, flashing lights of the life support systems and heart monitors attached to the person in the bed. The patient was unconscious, like a fly trapped in a spiderweb of IV lines, monitor cords, and tubes.

"What are we doing here, Min?"

But Min didn't answer. She was focused on the patient and slowly approached the bed. Olivia took a chart from the plastic holder mounted on the wall inside the room.

"*Amanda May Tanner*," she read. "Oh, hell. Is this the judge's wife? The Tanner kid's mom?"

"Do you hear it?" Min stood by the side of the bed, so close she could have reached out through the lines and tubes and touched Mandy May's hand. "It's coming from her."

She leaned down, bringing her ear closer to the injured woman's bandaged chest, which rose and fell in a rhythm determined by the breathing machine next to her.

"I don't think this woman is in any condition for visitors, Min. We really should go."

"She never cared for us Burdens much." Min looked up at Olivia while keeping her head close to Mandy May's chest. "She didn't want us as neighbors. Hated that her boy played with Jaelynn when they were kids. Got even worse after what happened to Jaelynn. She worried people were gonna think Lucas was Benji's father."

"Well, her son tried to cut her in half, like a juice orange, so I'd say karma paid her back." Olivia joined Min at the bed and leaned over as well. "Doesn't look like she's going to be bothering anyone anytime soon. You ever see anyone so pale? She's got something in her hair."

Olivia reached through the medical rigging and pinched something out of Mandy May's platinum candy-floss hair. She held it up so she and Min could inspect it.

"It's a little worm or larva or something." As Olivia said it, Mandy May's eyes flew open, and she shot her hand up, grabbing Olivia's wrist tightly. "What the fuck!"

Startled by the sudden movement and Olivia's cry, Min took a quick step back into a metal rolling cart. The cart tipped, and Min toppled. She hit the floor in a clatter of stainless steel instruments.

Olivia struggled with the patient, who had seemed so lifeless seconds before but now possessed an almost inhuman strength. "Get her off me," Olivia screamed to Min.

"Olivia." Mandy May's eyes had flashed open. They were glassy white orbs in her wan face. "Olivia Reynolds."

Olivia's face turned gray, and she stopped fighting. "How'd you know my name?"

"Olivia Sadie Reynolds. Daughter of Carol, born of Albert, born of William, son of Hezekiah, whose bones rot in a cave. I know why you are here. You are the last of your line, and you seek the truth."

"Min, what is this?" Olivia twisted her arm, trying to loosen Mandy May's grip, but was too stunned to do much more.

Min remained on the floor beside the damaged cart, too afraid to move or speak.

"They thought he was a witch. Hezekiah, a healer with skin so dark—they thought he must have magic to match, those ignorant fools."

When Mandy May's words hit Min's eardrums, it felt like a live bee was bouncing around in her head.

"Those who called themselves witchmasters brought him to the pool and invited me in with his blood, but they flung him into the water when he failed to speak the words they wanted to hear, when I failed to come through. All these years, you've searched for him. Know now his body rests with me."

Mandy May sat up in one swift movement, her back ramrod straight, those white eyes staring directly ahead. She looked like a ventriloquist's dummy when she started to speak again.

"Strong was his rage. He may not have been a witch, but he was willing." Her head swiveled slowly toward Olivia.

"You're a crazy bitch. Let me go."

"*Rap. Rap. Rap.*" Mandy May looked directly at her now. "God is knocking, Olivia Reynolds. I tire of my prison. Ymir, the god who created the world from nothing but his own cries, tells me my time has come. Help me and I will give you vengeance. We will drink the blood of those who held Hezekiah under and watched him drown."

"Those men are dead."

"But their blood still runs through the veins of others. The son of the son of the man who killed Hezekiah Reynolds still lives."

As she spoke, worms—tiny white wriggling maggots and shiny black larvae—crawled out of her mouth. They fell in clumps onto the sterile white hospital sheets and dropped onto the floor beside Min, who scrambled to her feet. They worked their way over the bed toward Olivia, who still struggled to wrest her arm away from Mandy May.

Hidden Children

The heart monitor began to squeal. It made a loud, continuous beep, and the green line rising and falling across the screen dipped, then ran flat and straight. Mandy May Tanner was on her knees on the bed. She pulled Olivia close.

Rot emanated from her mouth. Red-black saliva dribbled over her lips while she screamed out, "Help me reach the door and together we will kill them all, beginning with the witchmaster. His father was the son of the man who killed your kin. He carries his blood."

"Let me go." With a final jerk, Olivia wrenched her arm away from the woman whose own limb tore from her body at the socket. Olivia gasped, and Min stared in shock.

"This body will not hold," Mandy May shrieked. "I need the witch. Bring her to me. She is the door. Bring the witch to the cave." She stared Olivia down with slick, dead eyes. "Together we will make her see. We will make her let me in."

She turned on Min in a flash, clawing at her chest and face. Min shoved her hard. The woman's rib cage collapsed like a flimsy wicker basket. Mandy May fell back onto the bed, her chest a concave trough, like a bowl filled with writhing insects.

"Let's go." Olivia grabbed Min, who could only stand and stare at her hands and the crawling things which covered them.

Mandy May, broken as she was, stirred. Her claw-like fingers grabbed the sheets, and she pulled herself toward the edge of the bed.

"Go now!" Olivia ordered, dragging Min to the door.

Mandy May writhed and glowered at the fleeing pair. At the door, Min turned back, even though Olivia continued to pull at her.

"Know this, Minerva Burden...In the end, your brother will not falter. One of you will give me life, and he has already begun to bargain. The door is opening. I only need one. The other is surplus."

With one last twist, she rolled over the edge of the mattress. Her body hit the floor and appeared to shatter, breaking apart like a ceramic pitcher and spilling its contents. Worms and flies, beetles and black-winged moths, scurried over the tile.

The flying insects took to the air as Min leaped into the hall and slammed the door shut.

CHAPTER

THIRTY-THREE

Olivia and Min bolted down the corridor and plowed directly into a security guard.

"What's the rush, ladies?" he asked when they pushed past him. "You been in with the judge's wife? That room is off-limits."

They ran on, paying little attention to the man. Min thought he might come after them when they didn't stop, but she heard him head down the hall toward Mandy May's room instead. She knew what he would see when he reached it: the bloody mess of bones and flesh on the floor, the insects.

The sight must have stunned him because Min and Olivia were already through the waiting room and at the door to the parking garage before they heard him shout.

"Get back here. Stop!" followed by, "Someone call the police!"

Olivia's sedan was parked a few bays down from the revolving doors. They almost had their car doors open when the guard appeared some distance behind them.

"Freeze!" he yelled.

A bullet ricocheted off a concrete post beside Min.

"Crap," Olivia said.

"Keep your head down," Min instructed. "These rent-a-cops train on tin cans. He couldn't hit a moving target if it had a tail and he was trying to make squirrel stew."

"What the hell does that mean?" Olivia asked, throwing herself into the driver's seat.

"I don't know," Min confessed, joining her inside the vehicle.

"Do me a favor and shut up for a minute while I get us out of here." Olivia threw the car in reverse and backed out of the parking spot, then shifted gears and floored it toward the exit.

The guard fired again. The bullet hit the corner of the rear windshield, shattering it and sending a shower of glass onto the backseat, which was still soaked with Alison Mader's blood.

Half a block from the garage, the highway came into sight, and Olivia turned onto it, speeding back in the direction of Oracle Springs. "Look in the glove box," she instructed Min while the hospital lights faded behind them.

"What am I looking for?" Min asked.

"You'll know it when you find it."

Min opened the glove box and felt around until her hand hit something hard and cold. "A gun? What d'you want a gun for?"

"I want you to throw it out the window. Get rid of it. If the cops pull us over and I have a gun in the car, it won't be good."

"Why do you have it then?"

"Because Oracle Springs is twenty miles from the national headquarters of the KKK."

"What if I throw it out and then we need it?" Min cradled the gun against her chest, unwilling to let it go. "There was something in that hospital room, inside the judge's wife. What if it follows us?"

"Fuck. Fuck!" Olivia slammed the steering wheel. "This is it. I'm going to be shot. Arrested, if I'm lucky. Disbarred. I'll never be able to go back into law now. I should have known. This is how it happens. I should never have come down to this backwoods shithole."

"You might want to get off the highway."

"Don't tell me what I want. I want to *not* go to jail. I want to live. How about that?" Despite her anger, Olivia did pull off the main highway. The car sailed onto a smaller, deserted side road. "They probably have a fleet of patrol cars heading our way. *Be on the lookout for a lanky piece of trailer trash and a Black woman who couldn't mind her own damn business."*

She slowed the car down to take a sharp curve and tried a few measured breaths. Min started to speak, but Olivia held up her hand to stop her.

"For the second time today, would you mind telling me what the fuck happened to us back there? What did she mean by 'your brother has already begun to bargain?' What are you people into?"

"Believe me, I plan on askin' Jodie just that. I think he knows what this thing wants and why it's here—or at least has some sort of idea. I'll wring his scrawny neck to get answers, if I have to," Min promised.

Though, it was Olivia who grabbed Jodie by the shoulders when he met them at the door once they arrived back at the cabin. She shook him so hard his head wobbled on his thin neck.

"What the hell is going on? What aren't you telling us?"

"I don't have to tell you anything. I still don't even know who you are." Jodie had put on a shirt which wasn't stained red with blood and tomato sauce, and he straightened it primly after Olivia let go. He turned to Min and asked, "How's Al? What'd the doctors say?"

"Everything you touch breaks, Jodie Burden." Min stood by the door, her head bowed and her shoulders slumped. "You destroy anything good. I don't know how, but this is you. It's all your doing."

"What's that supposed to mean? Is Al gonna be okay, or isn't she? They can patch her up, right?"

"*Patch her up.*" Olivia shook her head. "Like she's a tire or a pair of old pants. A woman is dead."

The color drained from Jodie's face, and he looked to Min. "Al?"

"Not Al," she reassured him. "Mandy May Tanner. She spoke to us, but it wasn't really her. There were all these flies and insects inside her, and even after the heart monitors went off and she was dead, she was still moving." Min caught the look which passed over Jodie's face. "You know what I'm talkin' about, don't you?"

Jodie retreated to the couch. The bottle of whiskey Min had been nursing earlier was almost completely drained.

"I might." He flopped down onto a cushion and dropped his head into his hands. "Okay, I do know. I don't know what it is exactly, but I know what you mean. Lauderback, his daughter—I'd bet what happened to them up at the cannery ain't a far cry from what happened to Mandy May. Lucas too."

"Hope Lauderback is dead? She's just a kid," Min said, shaking her head. "Do you know what's happenin' to Benji?"

"No."

"If you do and you're not saying…he could be in real trouble. He could end up like them."

"He won't. She doesn't want him for that."

"She?" Min's tone was grim. "*She doesn't want him for that?*"

"Near as I can tell, she's taken some sort of liking to the boy. He's special to her somehow. We all are."

"You seem to know a lot. That must have been quite a conversation you and this thing had," Olivia suggested.

"Oh, God, Jodie. What have you been doing?"

"I didn't know it was gonna end up like this, honest. I wanted Lauderback to pay for what he did. Threatening Jaelynn and making her run, to help out his son. She said she could help, if I was willing to trade with her. Can you blame me? The only way Jaelynn was gonna get justice was if something came along to level the field, and it did. For once, I—"

"Oh, fuck you, Jodie!" Min said. "You're messing with shit you don't understand, shit none of us understand. It's crazy, and—I don't care what you say—it's hurting Benji."

"We can't take him to the hospital now," Olivia noted. "It's not safe there, but we've got to do something for him. For us too. Mandy May—or rather that thing inside her—mentioned the *witchmaster*. Do either of you know who that is?"

Min's eyes widened. "No, but you do. You mentioned it at the store. Remember? You said the town called in a group of witchmasters from Bentonville to look for the root of the sickness way back when."

"Sounds like they might have found it. What we saw happen to Mandy May sounds exactly like what happened to the people in 1889, only accelerated a thousand times."

"When you were researching your book, did you figure out who any of these men were? She said 'the son of the son' and all that. The kin of the man who killed Hezekiah Reynolds is still alive."

"I didn't find any names, and it wasn't really the focus of my work. I actually might have an idea, though." Olivia appeared more surprised than anyone. "I interviewed a cryptozoologist from Fayetteville on my podcast once."

"Lord, is she even speaking English?" Jodie asked Min.

Olivia ignored him. "This woman studies strange creatures—she

called them cryptids. They're local legends basically, like the Ozark Howler and something she called the Nightshade Bear, which I hope to God I never run into. Her research led her to a local man, a crazy old hermit type. He called himself a witchmaster and claimed to be a sort of expert on all things magical and unusual.

"He actually approached her one day when she was in town doing research, seemed excited when she told him her name. He invited her back to his cabin to look at an old book, a registry that he called 'the ledger.' Apparently, it listed local families with occult ties going back generations, and he claimed her family was in there. The whole exchange spooked her, and she didn't go with him, but she said the man goes by the name 'Yellow Pete.'"

Jodie scratched his chin. "They call Old Pyron Leahy Yellow Pete."

"I think Memaw used to call him Sulphur Pete, actually," Min said. "She hated that man with a passion. If I remember correctly, his wife died a few years back, and Paula sent him a condolence basket from the store. She knew Pyron some."

"If anyone fits the description of crazy old hermit, it'd be him." Jodie nodded.

"I think it is him. I asked around and tracked him down after the podcast," Olivia said. "I wanted to see this ledger the woman mentioned. There's so little written about Oracle Springs from back then that I hoped he might have some information about the outbreak. I wondered if maybe Yellow Pete's ancestors who arrived about then might have run into Hezekiah. I'm not one to put my trust in a talking corpse," she added caustically, "but if what Mandy May said was true, it sounds like they did."

"We need to go see him." Min had one foot out the door already.

Olivia looked somber. "He's a first-rate asshole. I went to his house, and he stood on his porch with a rifle. Wouldn't even let me out of my car. Called me a few names which I won't repeat."

"He's involved in this somehow. I can feel it," Min said. "And this thing seems to have it in for him. Maybe he knows how to stop her. We have to go see him."

"You really think that's wise?" Jodie asked. "Seems to me like we've got enough of a mess *without* bringing a known crazy man into all this. You've heard the stories, Min."

"Your friend Alison is barely alive because of this thing," Olivia pointed out. "Your grandson is sick, and that's probably down to whatever this thing is too. She's the cause of all this trouble. While I'm not particularly eager to darken that racist asshole's doorstep again, if he has any idea how to stop this monster, then I'm all for making the effort."

"Someone has to stay with Benji," Min pointed out.

"Him. He can." Olivia nodded to Jodie. "I want to see this man, this *witchmaster*, to find out what he knows about Hezekiah, and I don't trust your brother, Min. I'm sorry, but I don't. You and I will go together. He stays with the kid."

Jodie shrugged. "Don't matter to me. You go and talk to Leahy, Min. Find out for both of us what the hell is goin' on. If this has something to do with why Jaelynn died, I need to know it."

CHAPTER

THIRTY-FOUR

yron Leahy's house, little more than a shack, sat deep in the woods, as far from the center of town as the Burden cabin, only in the opposite direction. It was a tumble-down mess of logs and mortar which seemed to have developed a disagreement with each other over the course of the years and were now trying their best to separate.

The round timbers sagged, and the clay that had once sealed the gaps between had long since crumbled away, rendering the place about as airtight as a colander. The abode reeked of neglect despite the elaborate collection of bleached antlers and rusted horseshoes adorning each exterior wall.

"This is about where I got to the first time I came by," Olivia said when they approached the front walk. "Right before Mr. Leahy burst out the door with a shotgun and started spewing racial epithets."

"No sign of him yet. We're off to a good start, I guess."

They reached the porch without incident. Olivia nudged Min

and pointed upward. A dead screech owl hung above them, its wings spread wide and nailed to the heavy wooden lintel above the front door. Olivia grimaced.

"It's good luck," Min explained, unperturbed.

"Not for the owl," Olivia replied.

Min raised her fist and knocked on the paint-worn door. A breeze swept over the porch, carrying the scent of a not-too-distant storm and whispering urgency to the women.

"Hello?" Min called out to whoever might be inside. Her voice echoed against darkened windows and silent walls.

Ropes strung with dried Devil's Root swayed and rustled like brittle paper where someone had swagged them over the windows and beside the door.

"More good luck charms?" Olivia asked, and Min nodded.

"Memaw used to do the same."

A scraping noise from the side of the cabin drew the women to investigate. They leaned over the side railing. A dead bodark tree stood beside the house. Its rigid, twiggy fingers scraped against grime-encrusted glass, like nails on a blackboard.

"Min." Olivia pointed to the wood beyond the cabin, where something dark and lumbering, monstrous and covered in what appeared to be matted fur, was emerging from the closely bunched trees. "What the hell is that?"

"Someone wearin' a ghillie—homemade, by the look of it." Min waited until the man was closer to shout out to him. "Pyron Leahy? That you?"

"Ho," he called back in affirmation, plodding up the path in no real hurry.

The man carried a bundle of something furry and dead, which he hung from a brutal-looking hook next to the door after he reached the porch, leaving it to dangle while he pulled off the shaggy hood of his hunting attire.

"What'd you want?" His face appeared as wrinkled and pore-ridden as a morel mushroom, but overall, he had the look of an overgrown sorrel bush, with a great shaggy beard and wolfish-gray hair that hung long and wild to his shoulders. It made wearing the fibrous ghillie hood seem almost unnecessary.

Min started to speak. "I'm—"

"I know you. All you Burden folk look alike. Any fool could see it." He slipped the ghillie suit off. Beneath it, he wore a sweat-soiled undershirt and a pair of sagging blue jeans. Pyron Leahy opened the front door and went inside.

Min and Olivia hovered on the porch, unsure if they were meant to follow.

"You come here for a reason or just plan to stand around like dumbshits, waitin' for the rain?" the man called gruffly from somewhere inside the cabin.

Min and Olivia exchanged quick glances before stepping, one after the other, into Pyron Leahy's living room. They had to duck under the low doorframe and found themselves squeezed in amongst a great collection of furniture. Tables, chairs, cabinets, and curio cases cluttered the small space and trapped the stink of rotten food and damp earth between them.

Across the room, Pyron flicked on a single lamp, which did little to fight off the gloom hovering over everything. But it did assist Min and Olivia in finding their way to a clear corner, where they were less likely to trip over a cardboard box or a pile of old newspapers.

"Hate to bust in on you like this, Mr. Leahy," Min said, "but we had a question or two we was hoping you could answer."

"I knew your memaw." Pyron Leahy raised a salt-and-pepper eyebrow and gave Min the once-over. "She had a problem mindin' her own business too." He struck a match against the stone fireplace, and it fizzed to life. Sulfur—the smell of it rose above all the other odors in the room and emerged as conqueror, if only for a second. "Never did care for me none, but there was plenty folks in Oracle who didn't care for her neither."

"Folks said she was a witch."

"They was wrong." Pyron shook his head and threw the lit match into the fireplace, where it caught a clutch of crumpled paper on fire. "I never know'd that woman to throw a curse. She was a yarb healer, had some of the seer in her, but that's all. She didn't cotton to the craft, and she made no pacts. She might have been a witch, but she sure wasn't a practicing one. Now that daughter o' hers, your mama—she was a different story."

He shuffled to his chair—a battered wingback which stood in the center of the room facing the hearth and the fire beginning to glow. It was the only uncluttered spot in the entire chamber and the sole place where the floor was visible for any stretch. There, strange dark stains covered the wooden planks, which hadn't seen a coat of varnish in decades.

Pyron Leahy placed his shotgun on the floor beside him and stretched his arms over his head, emitting a satisfied groan. He only had one hand.

The stone ledge was wide enough for a person to sit on if they didn't mind roasting their backside, but Min took her place where Pyron indicated she should. Olivia drifted to the corner of the room, somewhat forgotten by their host.

"What are these?" she asked of several chalk outlines covering a stretch of wall not hidden by furniture. Someone had drawn a chain of nearly life-sized figures holding hands, like a string of paper dolls, over the rough, timbered walls.

Pyron didn't take his dark eyes off Min but seemed to know what Olivia was asking. "Witches—draw 'em in ash, drive a peg awl into the wood where their hearts would be. Stops up their magic for a time. Takes the cuss off."

Olivia was about to say, "You're joking," but stopped herself when she remembered all she had seen that evening. If there was ever a day to suspend her disbelief, this was it. She ran her finger over the black outline and looked at the tip. It was coated in a dusting of charcoal.

"So, it's true. You're what they call a witchmaster around here? You stop witches from cursing people or performing black magic?"

"I do my best." Pyron grinned at Min, showing her his long yellow teeth. "Effigies like these help some, but they're useless on a real powerful witch, and there been a few 'a those 'round here. The bloodlines in Oracle are strong. Something 'bout the land and the water makes conjure-folk real potent—gives 'em an extra jolt—though I couldn't tell you why."

"How much of a jolt? How strong can these witches get?"

"Eh." He grunted and wrinkled his bulbous nose. "Don't matter much these days. I ain't seen many true witches 'round here the past few generations. Just a handful. Most don't even know what they are. I can see it in 'em 'cause I know the signs to look for, of course. A particular shape to the skull. A knobbed finger joint. A fleck of fire in their eyes."

"If there was a witch like that, what sort of power might she have? What sort of things could she do?" Min asked, shifting on the hearth.

"Well, a powerful witch does more than throw the odd witch ball and cast sorry love spells. She can transfigure herself, take the form of animals, and make folks sick to death without use of poison or root. She can destroy a fortune or make a fella rich if she has a mind too."

"Could a witch control a body, living or dead?"

Pyron Leahy leaned forward in his chair. "You mean, like zombification? Only a mighty powerful conjurer could do that. I ain't never seen it myself. Only heard tales."

"How do they do it?"

"Spells. Charms. Animal sacrifice."

"But how do they actually *do* it? Do they ever use insects as a part of it?"

A change came over Pyron's face. He shrank deep into his chair, resting his head against the high back and staring at the ceiling in silence for what seemed like ages. Min looked to Olivia for guidance, but she went back to inspecting a bell jar full of dead orange and gray regal moths.

Pyron coughed and shook himself out of his trance. "What you're talkin' about is somethin' entirely different." He leveled his gaze at Min. "What have you seen, girl? Flies? Worms and the like? Crawlies that work their way under a man's flesh to make him sit up 'n move." He wiggled the fingers on his one hand at Min. "Then tear him apart from the inside out?"

"Yes." Min was breathless. "Like that."

"No."

"*No?*"

"That was no witch who done that. Witches are folks with gifts. Terrible gifts sometimes, but they have limits. What you're talkin' about is not a witch, but a creature, a thing of darkness, a hidden being—evil and malicious as hell."

A shiver ran up Olivia's spine.

"They're rare. You come across them now and then, hiding in trees and rocks and in water too. I've only ever seen one with my own eyes, and the water is where she rested—where she slept. The water is where she waited." He had grown increasingly distracted, disturbed even. Pyron flicked his tongue over his lips as though his mouth had gone dry, and he worked the frayed arm of his chair with nervous fingers.

Olivia used the moment to slip into the kitchen unnoticed. The ammonia-laden funk of nesting mice met her inside the room, and a pile of filthy dishes greeted her from the sink and countertop. Roaches scuttled away from her feet when she walked to the window at the far end.

She looked out onto the rear of the property and noticed wooden stakes planted in the ground. They formed a line parallel to the woods, and atop each one hung an animal skull and a twisted rope of what Olivia assumed must have been dried intestine. The sight combined with the smell forced her to turn away and burn a blue streak back to the living room, where Pyron Leahy was still talking.

"She came from the shadowlands, from hell, or the *land of mist*, as my grandpappy called it. She's a cave-dwelling monster who's been here since before anyone can remember. The natives knew about her. They saw her for what she was and let her be. They called the hills around where she lived the *empty place* and disowned it long before the white settlers came and took the land for their farms and homesteads. The new folks who arrived stayed away as soon as they realized what she was—what she could do."

"What could she do?"

"Enter into human flesh." Pyron gazed into the flames burning behind Min. "She could pass through blood and possess a person—take their body for her own."

"That's what I saw," Min said, leaning forward. "I think I saw this thing do that."

Olivia paused by the kitchen door. Next to her stood an old cabinet filled with junk. She wiped the dust off one of the glass-paneled upper doors and leaned her forehead against it, trying to identify the oddities on the shelves. Tiny dolls made of twigs and strips of fabric. A little clay dish filled with what appeared to be fingernail clippings. Hand-cast bullets and carvings of animals and children. All old. All dusty. All weird. But none of it told Olivia anything she wanted to know.

She sought a connection to her great-grandfather. There had to be a clue to Hezekiah's disappearance somewhere in all this trash. That was the reason she had come to this disgusting old cabin.

"What you saw was infection, not possession," Pyron told Min. "This creature sends her emissaries—insects usually—into a body. They can jump from one host to another or go into animals too—small ones in general, sometimes more than one at a time. The creature controls them from a distance, but she's tied to the water, trapped by some ancient magic or curse. She can only leave it in a sort of spiritual fashion, visiting folks in their dreams, where she comes to them in the form of a woman with a tail and an openin' in her back."

"Like a sore?"

"Like a rip in the sky, a hole in the universe. She swallows people up inside the darkness she holds there. That's the power of her possession. It's how she frees herself from the water. She's got to find the right sort of person, and then it's like nothing you've ever seen before." His black eyes, dim and watery with age, lit up. "She needs to find a witch. A true witch. And once she's found them, they fall into her, into that hole in her back, and they become one, intertwined and interwoven like thread. Then hold onto your ass because she starts to whisper."

"What does she whisper?"

"The secrets of creation. All the mysteries of space and time. The things she says could make kings out of paupers and gods of mere mortals—not that this is what she's always done, what she's always been used for. The settlers who discovered her, religious sorts, didn't know she could tell them the future, but they learned pretty quick that they could use her to root out witches in their midst. She draws them to her, and the proof is in the possession. Only a witch can hold her. Anyone else is ripped apart like tissue paper."

"You believe that?" Olivia looked up from the cabinet. She had been inspecting a small wire cage which held what appeared to be a shriveled animal's heart with three rusted iron nails through it. Olivia set it down and wiped her hands on her pants.

"I don't *just* believe it. I've seen it." Pyron didn't look back at Olivia, but he tilted his head in her direction. "The only way she gets out of the water is to possess someone. The only way she stays out of the water is to possess a witch. She has no body of her own, or if she does, it can't survive here in this world. She must have a witch, someone with power beyond an ordinary human's, who can act as a proper receiver. And then she can tell the future. That's where the name of this town comes from—Oracle Springs. Not many know that these days, but it's all writ down in my people's ledger."

He waved his hand toward the back of the room.

The ledger. Olivia searched for anything that looked like it could be the record Pyron spoke of. There were no books on the shelves in front of her—not in the upper cabinet behind glass, anyway—but she hadn't yet looked in the lower shelves. She squatted and pulled open one of the wooden doors.

"Once folks figured out what she could do, they started asking her to tell them things. Small things at first, like would there be enough rain that year or were they right to damn up a certain creek or river. They'd ask her about politics too, money and other business matters. And once they knew what they needed to know, they'd hold her under until the demon abandoned the witch's body. Kept everyone safe that way."

"You mean, they'd drown the witch?" Min asked.

"Weren't no witch by then. The witch was gone. Just the demon remained, fused with the witch's flesh, and the longer she stayed, the stronger she would get. Might seem cruel to you, but they couldn't let her out of the cave. Dangerous thing, this demon. No good lettin' her run loose."

"Why? What would it do?"

"Nothin' helpful, you bet your sweet ass."

"You don't know? You don't know what it does or what it wants?"

"I never bothered askin' her direckly. At first, the way my kin and I saw it, she was a beast. A thing. You might as well ask a dog or a horse what it desires. As long as she told us what we wanted to know, that was good enough for us. Only, after a time, she started getting stronger. She drew power from the land and witches on it. It got so's you couldn't count much on what she said. She began to lie, and we started to see that she had business of her own in mind. But you can ask yourself what does any evil thing want? Destruction, pain, and suffering, most like.

"The early settlers must have figured that out too 'cause they gave up going to see her—forgot about her, really. That's part of her power. She casts a cloud over these here hollers that blinds folks, makes 'em overlook all the strangeness. That shit don't work on me and mine, though. A witchmaster has defenses against that kind of thing. See these?" He leaned closer to Min and opened his black eyes wide, pointing to them. "Black. So the spells can't creep in. It's all games to her, but I ain't playing.

"The one time this creature had her way, I watched her rip my family into pieces in that cave. Took everythin' in me to wrestle her back to the water and drown her to hell. We let her get too strong, and we didn't calculate the power of the witch we brung to her. I chose the girl myself—pretty lil thing." He closed his eyes and inhaled, a tiny smile playing at the corners of his slack mouth, as if he smelled something sweet. "Mighta considered runnin' away with her more than once. She had me so twisted up in her charms, I held my family off—wouldn't let them take her until after her babies come. They were eager to start the ritual, but I felt I owed her that much. That mighta been my mistake. Gave her too much to live for, too much to kill for."

Those black eyes staring at Min grew watery, and the old witchmaster settled back into his chair.

"She was so young and small—just a slip of a girl. We never thought we'd have any trouble handlin' her, even after the demon was inside, but somethin' went wrong. The ritual always went like clockwork. Let the demon and the witch join as one, then, just before the witch's eyes turn completely white—that's the sign to look for—drown 'em both. But never, never spill the witch's blood after that, especially if there's a second witch around. That can release the creature, and she's like to make the jump from one to the other."

"You keep calling it a *she*?"

"Yes, *she*. A demon bitch—a succubus to drain the life right out of a man. She claims to be the offspring of one called Ymir, an ancient creator god from the northern myths, older than Woden, who's sometimes called Odin. Far as I'm concerned, though, she's the mother of lies."

Olivia opened the last of the lower cabinet doors, the only compartment she hadn't yet searched, and smothered a sneeze. It was full of dust and cobwebs but also contained several large books which seemed promising.

Pyron droned on, bending so far toward Min, who also leaned forward, that their noses were almost touching.

Olivia pulled the first book from the cabinet. She flipped through the initial few pages and discovered nothing more than a collection of pornographic photos dating back to the 1970s. Olivia swore under her breath and shoved the book back in the cabinet. The next text she picked up was some sort of dictionary of the occult—interesting and forbidding-looking but not handwritten, as she assumed the ledger must be.

Olivia rummaged through the stack, finding each book to be a disappointment until she reached a heavy leather-bound volume with no title or author listed on the cover or spine. She opened it and discovered a series of names and dates. Lines connected the entries in a sort of web, and Olivia thumbed through several pages

before she realized she was looking at something like multiple family trees.

She flipped ahead, scanning for certain dates. The years advanced, and Olivia's head begin to sing. She drew closer to the year of the outbreak, the year Hezekiah had disappeared.

1889. Arrived in Oracle Springs at the behest of Alderman Tark Williams. The year was divided by seasons on the page. Olivia ran a shaking finger down the columns until she came to the last lines of summer.

And there it was.

Hezekiah. His name was written in bold, scrolling black ink, but what did it mean? Beside it was a sloppy scrawl of broken sentences.

Qualities noted. Ancestry unknown. Taken to the water.

That was it. There was nothing more. Just a smudged black X in the last column.

What qualities? Olivia wondered. *What water?*

She turned the page, hoping the entry continued onto the next, wishing for more, anything other than that simple black X. Olivia turned to the back page, and several small plastic cards fell out onto the floor. She picked them up. They were driver's licenses, each card bearing a picture of a different woman.

Six licenses. Six women. Olivia looked up. Six witches on the wall.

Six outlines with wooden pegs in their hearts.

"How did you stop her from getting out when the ritual went wrong?" Min asked Pyron.

"By the skin of my teeth!" Pyron exclaimed. "By the Lord's mercy."

"But you *did* stop her. You know how."

Min's voice betrayed her excitement, while across the room, Olivia couldn't remember what she had been looking for or why. Her legs were shaking, and the room began to spin. Everything around her blurred together, but a few things, certain items, jumped out.

The lamp next to Olivia, for instance, with its dried leathery shade. The light glowed through it, pink and tan. Fleshy. She didn't even need to look closer to recognize the veins and wrinkles running through it and a black mark near the seam—a tattoo maybe. The shade was made of human skin.

"The best way to stop her is to prevent her from starting in the first place."

"She's already started."

"No. She's just playin' with you. She's sent out her emissaries, but the real demon slumbers in the water—trapped there until a witch's blood is spilt. What have you seen? Birds? Flies? Bodies kept alive by her for a time until they fall apart? They're trifles. Little tools she uses like puppets. They're her servants and carry her messages to and fro, but these hosts can't hold her for long. They can't contain her. The bigger the host, the quicker they fail. The more bodies she tries to take on, the more it drains her. She needs a witch with power to feed off and a willing one at that— someone who won't fight her, someone she can merge with, whose flesh and soul will accept her. And she needs blood to spill before she can enter. The blood is the pathway. Until then, there's only so much she can do, only so much power she can wield."

Hearing almost nothing Pyron said, Olivia staggered back against the log wall.

Skulls. On the fireplace. Coyote or dog skulls mostly, but one human. One *undeniably* human. She had missed it before. All the while, its empty eye sockets had been watching, peering out from above Min's head. The thing had practically been screaming at her. How could she have overlooked it all? Bones wrapped in hair and hide. Dried fingers on a shelf.

Oh, God. An eyeball in a jar. Talismans. Tokens. *Trophies.* This man wasn't mastering witches; he was killing women.

The foul black stains on the floor appeared to spread. They grew larger and wider, reaching out toward Olivia's feet like an oil spill in the ocean. She felt she would pass out at any moment.

"Min, we need to go." Olivia sounded strangled. "Now."

Min didn't hear. "What was the girl's name?" she asked Pyron. "Who was the little witch you took to the demon all those years ago?"

The witchmaster flashed those corn-kernel teeth once more. "Mercy. Mercy Burden.

Upon hearing her mother's name, it was Min's turn to reel. She tried to stand but teetered back toward the fireplace, her head narrowly missing the heavy stone mantle. Olivia was there by her side—just as shaky, just as shocked—taking her by the arm and pulling her in the direction of the door.

"Hold on now. You really think I could let you two leave? You," Pyron said to Olivia, "pokin' around back there, diggin' into things you don't understand, thinkin' I wouldn't notice. And you..." He turned to Min while he rose to his feet. "She's waitin' for you. You're her doorway. She's sensed you and your brother, and she thinks her time has come. It's almost autumn. The nights are gettin' longer and the days colder, and man fears the coming frosts. That's when she's strongest, and so I have to be strong too.

"I was weak all those years ago. I couldn't bring myself to kill Mercy's children. I couldn't destroy my own flesh and blood, but I see now that was wrong. The time has come to end things before she finds a way, before she lures you to her with all her promises and lies. As long as there is a witch nearby, none of us is safe from her."

"I'm not a witch. I don't do spells. I didn't make any pacts," Min argued. "I wouldn't even know how."

"It's in your blood. She smells it, and she's marked you, pact or no pact. I am sorry, daughter." But he didn't look sorry, and his yellow smile hadn't faded or shrunk a bit. "There ain't no other way. The creature is risin', but she doesn't know she still has Pyron Leahy to reckon with. I kill you and that brother of yourn and there ain't no more witch for this parasite to latch onto. With any luck, she'll sink back into her watery hole for another forty years."

He picked up the shotgun resting beside his armchair and pointed it at Olivia.

"I'll do your friend quick, and when it's your turn, I'll make it clean. A witch's blood is too dangerous a thing to spill."

CHAPTER

THIRTY-FIVE

In the cave, the air shifted. Something was different.

Benji had moved. His sleeping body, the one he longed to return to, was being taken somewhere. Although he hadn't repositioned an inch inside the cave, he felt dislodged or displaced and knew he no longer lay in Jodie's bed in the Burden cabin. He wondered if not knowing where his body was would make it harder to get back.

The thought made his blood run cold, and he tucked his knees into his chest until he formed a small ball curled against the lip of the bright blue pool. Shadows of past and future, figures from times before and times to come, floated around him.

Mercy was still there. He had watched her die over and over again, killed each time by the man with one hand. She was a come-before, and just before she passed yet again, she whispered to him.

Someone is coming.

A dark form loomed at the mouth of cave. Its shadow pulsed against the ruddy walls. It swelled like a growing bruise against the red. Benji waited, holding his breath. Behind him, the water in the pool bubbled and churned.

Something was rising.

Benji heard a moan.

On the side of the cave, someone from the past or maybe from the future lay bleeding. The cave was full of the dead and dying. Benji couldn't keep track of them anymore. It might have been a victim of *hers*, or it might have been a victim of the men with the long beards and the yellow teeth who often appeared, sometimes with Mercy, sometimes without. Benji had witnessed them drown a dozen people or more since he had found himself in the cave. Sometimes, it was the same person over and over.

Witch, witch. Bleed the witch. Raise the oracle. Make us rich, they chanted. The more he heard it, the dumber it sounded to Benji.

Someone is coming. Something had been released. It was happening. Benji leapt to his feet.

"Stop," he shouted. "I didn't choose! I didn't pick one. I swear, I didn't."

CHAPTER

THIRTY-SIX

A loud bang reverberated around Pyron Leahy's small cabin. Min, Olivia, and even Pyron cringed at the sound. Min reached out for Olivia, who grabbed her chest, feeling for a wound but discovering herself unharmed.

Pyron hadn't fired the gun. The noise they heard had been a crack of thunder from the storm, which had finally arrived.

That and something clattering down the chimney.

Claw and talon scraped brick. Velvety wings beat against stone, and the cabin suddenly filled with birds. Ravens and crows poured in from the fireplace opening. Sparks tumbled, and the fire flickered as the birds' wings fanned the blaze.

Pyron's tiny cabin seemed to erupt in flame and feathers. He dropped his gun to the floor and grabbed at one of the birds when it swooped past him, clawing at his shoulders and face. Olivia threw one arm over her head and grabbed Min. Before man or beast could stop them, the two women sprinted out the door. Birds streamed through the opening with them.

In the kitchen, a window shattered, and something larger barreled in, upsetting the rancid pile of dishes which crashed to the floor. Pyron threw open the inner door, aimed his gun, and fired. The blast from his weapon peppered the cabinets with shot and sent a small coyote tumbling backward. Its dead, dish-rag body hit the cabinet below the sink and dropped onto the pile of cracked dishes and glass.

Pyron ducked back into the living room, where he stamped out the cinders smoldering on the floor in front of the fireplace and then stuck his head out the front door in time to watch Min and Olivia speed up the drive in Olivia's car. The women departed in a cloud of black birds and torrential rain. The forest, alive with the howls and cries of animals and insects and the raging wind through the trees, shrieked and railed at their fleeing taillights.

His many years of experience with witchery and bedevilment told him what the beasts and creatures of the woods were saying. *She is here. She is here.* The natural world could feel it—the rise of something otherworldly and unwelcome. The dark thing Pyron dreaded most was stirring. He felt it in his blood the same way the animals could. She had awakened, just as he had feared she might.

Pyron bolted the door behind him and returned to his chair and his fire. He didn't bother to right the lamp the birds had upended. The glow from the fireplace was all the light he needed. It cast a ruddiness onto the walls and illuminated the many sketches and carvings he had made over the years.

Each outline on the wall represented a witch no longer walking the earth, but while he once had felt a ripple of satisfaction in his gnarled old soul at the sight of them, Pyron now cursed these images. He could almost hear them. They were crying out. Calling to *her*. Asking her to punish old Pyron for what he had done to them. Age had dimmed his memory some, but his hand still felt the warmth of their skin, still knew the soft pliability of their tendons and flesh when he squeezed their necks and snuffed out their wickedness.

A cawing from behind made him spin in his chair, and he peered around its winged back at a crow, fat and glossy, who perched on the open door to the kitchen, scrutinizing him with beady black eyes.

"It takes more'n a few birds to scare Pyron Leahy." He stood and reached for the barrel of the shotgun leaning against the side of his chair. "I'll dash your brains in and leave you for the rats."

Hidden Children

He swung for the bird with the butt of his rifle, but it fluttered away in a flash of onyx and glossy blue-black feathers, easily avoiding the assault. It landed with a soft rustle beyond the wavering light at the edge of the fireplace hearth, where it was lost in the creeping darkness.

"You can go back to hell, to the demon who sent you, and tell her Yellow Pete knows what she's after." Pyron took one step toward the corner where it had flown and heard someone laugh.

More than birds rested in the shadows beyond the hearth.

"You can tell me yourself," a voice said.

Like unbalanced scales, rising on one side and dipping on the other, Pyron sank into his chair when the creature in the shadows stood up.

"It's you," he gasped.

"Yes. Truly me. I am free."

Free. The word sent chills bouncing down Pyron's knobby old spine, and he sat up straighter in his chair, trying to hide his fear from her, even though he knew she must have smelled it on him already. Fear had a pungent aroma, one Pyron knew well. He had smelled it back in Vietnam, mingling with the smoke from the fires in the villages he burned.

Had smelled it on the witches he had hunted like animals.

Had smelled it in the cave forty-two years ago, when he first came face-to-face with his visitor on the night she tore his family to pieces and he had barely managed to escape.

She had already killed them all—father, brothers, uncles, elders. The demon had left them mangled and crushed on the cave floor. She would have done the same to him, but he had grabbed her, tackled her without thinking, and in that moment, he had realized how much stronger her body had grown.

It was like grabbing onto steel or stone, not the tender young woman he had first taken on a prickling bed of needles and leaves in the woods and later enjoyed again and again in the back seat of his car. The creature he held that night was no longer Mercy Burden. Pyron had wrapped his arms around her and felt her teeth sink into his neck, but he didn't let go. He staggered to the water and pulled her in with him.

Pyron had taken one final gulp of air before they dove headlong into the pool, wrapped in each other's arms. His last hope had been that she, unprepared for the plunge, would run out of breath before he did. They sank slowly through the water, but it was a race to survive. He must outlast Mercy's body or die there in the pool of bones before the demon was expelled.

Pyron had barely made it. The light had left Mercy's eyes a second or less before the transition was complete—before the demon had completely taken over her flesh. He had released his lover's body and watched it drift down into the black center of the pool while he struggled to the surface. But Pyron was no longer the strong young man he had been that night when he had fought her off, and he now felt the icy fingers of fear twist deeper into his soul. He leaned closer to the fire to burn away the cold terror coursing through his veins.

"It's been an age, hasn't it?" Pyron's visitor crouched in front of him, blocking the fire's warmth and casting a twisted shadow. "You aren't looking so well these days."

The creature looked around, taking in the lampshades, the bones, and the hellish drawings on the walls.

"You've been busy all these years, Pyron. Where did you find space to put them all? You didn't sink their bodies in my pool or the rivers that feed it. I would have smelled them." She sniffed then—an animal catching a whiff of carrion on the air.

Her eyes narrowed, and a sly smile spread over her pale, distorted countenance. Pyron winced. Her face was a living mask—rubbery and wrong but animated, nonetheless.

"Beneath the house," she hissed. "Oh, yes, I hear them now." She clucked her long, red tongue at him. "You buried them in the earth where you thought I wouldn't find them. Tell me, how many did you find were truly witches?"

"I couldn't take any chances. If there was even a possibility that one would make their way to the cave, I couldn't risk it. I had to destroy them." He spat as he spoke.

"Excuses, Pyron. Lies."

Pyron's mouth dropped open, but the creature held up a long finger to silence him.

"I've seen into your mind. I know the things you've done. Evil. *Yellow Pete*. Why did they call you that?"

"It was a nickname. In the army, everyone had one."

"I see your past as clearly as I see you now. They called you Yellow Pete because of the man you shot—the one you skinned and wore like a pelt."

"Lotta people did a lotta bad over there. Those yellow bastards did the same to us, worse even—torture. It was war."

"But *you* liked it." She looked at him, her face still human enough that he could read her emotions and knew she was pondering something. "I wonder why you let your children live? Any child of Mercy Burden's was a risk. Don't tell me there's a sentimental bone somewhere in this body of yours." She leaned in close, running her hands over his legs and up his body, then gripped his arms tightly. "Maybe I should see if I can dig it out, add it to my collection."

He gasped when she pressed her strong fingers into his elbow joints, forcing them into the grooves between bones until he thought they would dislocate. "I know you. You make deals. Give and take. You like a bargain."

"You don't have anything I want."

The fire crackled, though there was very little log left—only blackened char—and the room felt hotter than it should have to Pyron, who had been chilled moments before.

"I could help you," he said, licking his lips, straining to speak through the pain in his arms. "You been in that cave a long time. You don't know what it's like out there now."

"As far as I can see, man doesn't change much. He lacks the imagination required for rebirth."

Pyron squirmed in his chair. "You're right. Folks don't change. They'll hate you, just like they've always done. They'll fear you, and they'll hunt you down like a rabid dog. They'll find a way to destroy you or at least send you back to hell, where you come from."

"Like you did when you drowned the mother of your children? You must have seen the exact moment the fire left her, the second her soul departed. Did you see me then too? Did you see me drift away as that perfect body that you made useless floated down into the dark? I saw you Pyron. I saw into your soul. It's charred and clotted with crawling, creeping things. Maggots and death beetles."

"Shut your mouth, demon," he spat. "What I did to Mercy *was* mercy. The men who come for you will do worse. They'll come with weapons you can't imagine. You won't last long. They'll send you back where you belong, back to hell where you came from, as soon as they see what you are."

"The witch has accepted me. This body will last, and so will I. This world will once more be my home."

"You don't know nothin' about this world. You don't know nothin' about being human," Pyron snarled. "You'll give yourself away, and they will end you. Humans are bloodthirsty things. You and me both know it. When they get through with you, you'll be nothing but one more pile 'a bones hidden in the dark."

The creature laughed. "Hidden things don't stay hidden, Pyron. They cry out to be found. Listen, Pyron. Listen." She cradled his chin in her hands, her clammy palms, and stared into his darting eyes.

He smelled pennies, moldering copper, and he heard *them*. They moved beneath the house, pushing dirt away. Pushing clods and clumps of earth. Shifting and clawing. And then there came a tapping. A scratching at the floorboards beneath his feet.

"*Rap. Rap. Rap.* Your hidden children call to you. Open the door, Pyron. Open it and join them." The demon rose, her haunches appearing bowed for a second, more animal-like than human. The creature balled her long, slender fingers into a fist and reached high, then plunged her hand down through the moldering floorboards at Pyron's feet, releasing a cloud of dust, along with the smell of decay.

Immediately, the witchmaster saw them. All of them. The witches. The dead women. They peered up at him from the hole the demon had torn before him, as if from the mouth of hell. Their fearful, white-bone faces glowed in the dark recess below the house. They had been waiting.

Now they poured through the opening, their clothes tattered, stiff and stained with the fluids which had seeped out of their bodies while they withered and rotted beneath him all those years. Pyron raised himself from his chair, but they were on him, pushing him back. Their hands were fleshless claws, talons, tearing at him, ripping his flesh from his body.

"God is knocking, Pyron." The fire lit the creature from behind. Only her grin, devilish and wide, was visible. It gave off an unearthly gleam from the shadows covering her face. "It's time to answer."

CHAPTER

THIRTY-SEVEN

The flock of cawing, scratching black birds swarming after Min and Olivia was unshakable. The creatures dove and swooped at the windshield, their talons scraping at the roof of the sedan. The women cringed and ducked while they sped away from Pyron Leahy's cabin of horrors, but it wasn't only birds they had to contend with.

"Look! Over there in the woods." Min pointed, and Olivia peeled her eyes away from the road, looking to the tree line.

Strobing flashes of gray, tan, and white showed between the trees at the road's edge. Coyotes and foxes, along with deer and smaller beasts too numerous to count, stampeded through the woods like a herd of animals fleeing a fire. Predator and prey had thrown in together in a single-minded cause and raced alongside the car, maintaining their distance while also keeping pace.

When the car reached a curve and Olivia took her foot off the accelerator, one of the deer, a large buck with an eight-point rack, altered his course sharply and veered toward the car.

He plowed into the driver's side. Glass shattered, and the creature's antlers, hard and sharp, stabbed through the window. Olivia ducked closer to Min, jerking the steering wheel, and the car fishtailed on the slippery road.

"Go faster," Min hollered.

Olivia floored it, and the deer flailed. His antlers caught in the window opening, and over the sound of the rain and car's engine, his hooves pounded and tore at the pavement.

"Shake him loose," Min said.

The animal thrashed and flailed. Olivia jerked the wheel back and forth. Tires squealed and slipped, but the big creature twisted free and fell to the ground. Min turned around in her seat, watching him stagger to his feet again.

"Jesus, that was close." Olivia swept broken glass from her shoulder and lap. "An inch more and that deer would have made me his pin cushion."

"It doesn't make sense. Pyron said the creature didn't have this much power. He said she could control insects or smaller animals a few at a time."

The side road merged into a larger thoroughfare, and high retaining walls sprung up to separate the roadway from the wooded hillside. Atop these dark, stone buttresses, the packs and herds continued to amass. Some animals still raced the car along its course, but many more took positions on the rocky ledges above the motorway, watching the vehicle from a distance, silent and unmoving as gargoyles.

Olivia eyed them through her open window. "I guess we must have leveled up."

"It's wrong." Min shook her head. "She shouldn't be able to control this many animals, not big ones."

"*That's* what bothers you? Quantity?" Olivia squinted, trying to count or at least estimate the number of beasts above them, getting nothing but a face full of rain for her trouble. "Does it matter how many there are? Bambi attacked us. Heckle and fucking Jekyl are after us—there's a childhood nightmare come to life. And you're wondering how a man with lampshades made of human skin could be wrong about a tiny-ass detail? Somehow, it doesn't surprise me that someone who described murdering women as 'putting down witches' might not be the most reliable source of information. Probably because—oh, I don't know—he's batshit crazy!"

"Olivia?"

"What?"

"Olivia!"

She looked back at the road and slammed on the brakes in time to avoid plowing into a line of deer stretching all the way across the highway. The women rocked forward as the car came to an abrupt stop in front of the animals, which stood shoulder to shoulder, flank to flank—a proper, regimented army forming a barricade across the pavement.

"Are you seeing this?" Olivia asked.

Min nodded.

Either the temperature had dropped or the animals were putting out some extraordinary heat. Their breath was visible around them while they exhaled incredible, silvery clouds of air. Steam wafted off their backs when raindrops fell on their hides, and a heavy mist seeped out of deep wounds in their bodies and from their eye sockets, which were empty and cavernous.

"I don't think these things are alive," Min said.

"Dead or alive, they can move their asses." Olivia rammed her hand against the steering wheel to sound the horn.

The noise didn't faze the animals. They held their ground.

A large doe pawed the earth and took a step forward, challenging the women. Olivia put the car in reverse and backed up, then shifted into drive and took a deep breath.

"What are you doing?" Min asked.

Olivia hit the gas and sped toward the doe.

"You ever played chicken before?" Olivia drove the car straight at the animals, and Min braced for impact.

The deer didn't move, and at the last minute, Olivia spun the wheel hard. The tires screeched yet again, and the car swerved and pitched. Olivia steered it ninety degrees to the right and headed down a smaller side road.

"Guess we lost that round, and now we're taking the long way back."

The line of deer appeared in a chain formation on the road behind. Olivia watched them in the rearview mirror. The animals took a few small steps down the hill but showed no sign that they were about to give chase.

"That's what I thought." Olivia snorted, turning back around.

Min pivoted in her seat as well, but they both saw the towering mass of fur in front of them too late to do anything but plow straight into it.

The car's airbags exploded with a bang, and the weight of whatever they had hit came down on the hood, forcing the nose of the car to the ground and bringing the entire vehicle to a sudden stop.

Min's ears rang. Something dripped down her face, running into her eyes and over her lips. She was bleeding, and her chest hurt.

The car door opened. Cool air flooded in. It was a relief at first, but then someone yelled. Olivia was shouting. *At* her. Tugging at her. Pulling her from behind the airbag and out of the car. All Min wanted to do was remain still, to curl up around her aches and her pains. But Olivia was asking her something—where did she put the fun? The fun?

No, not the fun. *The gun.*

Min's voice sounded slow and slurred to her own ears when she said, "Under the front seat."

Olivia let go of her, and Min staggered. There was a popping not unlike the sound the airbags had made when they deployed. Olivia was firing the weapon. Min wiped blood out of her eyes and tilted her chin to the sky to let the rain wash the rest away. When she looked back at her friend, a surge of adrenaline brought everything into focus.

The car had hit a bear.

The animal's fur and flesh were torn and scabrous, but the wounds were already oozing and foul. The injuries hadn't come from the collision. The bear peeled itself off the hood of Olivia's vehicle, and she fired the gun at it two more times in rapid succession while it approached. One bullet struck it in the gut and the other in the chest, but it kept coming.

"Nightshade bear," Olivia hissed, her eyes wide with fright.

Like the deer at the top of the hill, the beast exhaled smoke, and steam emanated from its old wounds, as well as the bullet holes and a large gash where it had hit the fender of Olivia's car.

"I think it's already dead," Min mumbled, catching a whiff of rotting flesh.

The beast drew closer.

"Not enough." Olivia pulled the trigger again, but the gun was empty. She fired over and over, but all the weapon produced was a feeble clicking noise. Olivia wound her arm back to throw the gun at the bear, when the animal stopped.

Inexplicably, it turned in the direction of the deer and lumbered up the road toward them, away from Min and Olivia.

"What's happening?" Min asked, as confused as she was relieved. "Where's it going?"

"I don't know." Olivia dropped the gun to her side.

"Did you see the way its ears moved? Something's calling it."

"Good riddance, Smokey, is all I have to say. Come on." Olivia didn't take her eyes off the bear's retreating back while she waved for Min to follow her. "I don't have a damn clue where we are, but I assume we've got a long walk back, and I'd like to get as much distance as possible between me and that thing as quickly as possible, got it?"

CHAPTER

THIRTY-EIGHT

Min and Olivia trudged down the hill toward the Burden cabin, so soaked they couldn't get any wetter. They no longer bothered to wince when the rain ran down their faces into their eyes and when it formed chilly rivulets whisking down their necks and rolling between their shoulder blades. Clouds covered the moon. They could barely see one another, but they heard each other well enough—the *slish slosh* of wet sneakers and loafers squelching with every step.

The pavement on the side of the road had split and crumbled. Min stepped in one of the ruts and her ankle rolled, but she kept going, picking up the pace even when the black outline of her cabin came into view below. All the lights were out. The house was a small box, a squat package, wrapped in darkness. It appeared that no one was there or that something had happened to the people who *were* home.

Benji. Jodie. Min's guts lurched. Had the animals been there too? She set off at a run.

Olivia jogged behind her. They arrived at the cabin one after the other, then rushed up the steps and inside. The lights were off, but the TV was on. It flickered, giving enough of a glow to illuminate Jodie stretched out, prone on the sofa. His skin appeared waxy and gray, and Min's heart pounded like it might beat its way into her mouth...until her brother turned his head.

"What took you so long?" he asked.

"We would have been back sooner, but we got invited to a picnic with Yogi Bear, and it seemed rude to refuse," Olivia said. "My car's totaled. We had to walk. Your sister can tell you what happened because I'm not sure I even know."

"The house is dark from the road," Min said. "I thought something might have happened to you...to Benji." She flipped on the light, and both she and Olivia sucked air over their teeth.

Jodie's gaunt face appeared drawn and pale. He wore an expression of weariness which deepened all the furrows and frown lines on his brow and around his mouth. Jodie looked ill and aged and had sweated right through his shirt, which clung to his thin body, nearly see-through it was so damp.

"What's happened to you? Where's Benji?" Min started toward the bedroom, but Jodie stopped her.

"The boy is fine. I checked on him a minute ago. It's Alison. It was on the news right after you left. She died at the hospital."

"Oh, no," Min groaned. "They announced it on TV?"

"They didn't name names, but they said a woman brought in earlier had died and that the judge's wife passed as well. A guard is being treated for something...Shock maybe. They're linking it to two women who fled the scene earlier today." Jodie nodded and resettled into the sofa cushions—a dismal bump on a log. "I reckon that's you two."

"You *reckon*, huh?" Olivia leaned back in amazement, her eyes blazing. "You *reckon* anything else, like what you're going to do about that, considering this is *your* mess?"

"Calm down a sec. Let's think about things." Min placed her hand on Olivia's arm, but the woman shook it off.

"No. This asshole is calm enough for the both of us," she said, gesturing to Jodie. "*It's all linked to two women*, he says. Well, it's linked to you too, pal, and I'm not going down for this. None of this is my business *or* my problem."

"You're shivering," Min pointed out.

"I shot a goddamn bear—a walking-around-dead bear. I'm fucking peeing in my pants, Minerva Burden. This is bad. Do both of you not see it?" Baffled, Olivia stared at the brother and sister. "I don't believe it. Is this what it's like being a...a Burden? Shit like this happens regularly, huh? Monsters and demons and *runnin' afoul of the law*? Is that what you hayseeds call it?"

She backed away from the pair while she spoke, hitting the dining table and knocking over a stack of torn paper—drawings made by Benji.

"Let's go upstairs and get you some dry clothes," Min suggested. "Memaw always said you can't—"

"Screw your memaw."

"I'm only saying you'll feel better when you're warm." Min held up her hands in surrender. "You don't have to do nothing you don't want to."

"Oh, we're *well* past that. You think I wanted any of this?" Olivia shook her head but followed Min up the open stairs to the loft above the living room.

It was several degrees warmer up there and stuffy where Min slept. Olivia stopped shivering almost immediately and looked around. Her chills were replaced by a strong sense of claustrophobia. The pitched ceiling began no more than a foot or two off the floor, and it rose six feet at most below the center peak, requiring a person to duck if they were standing anywhere but the exact middle of the room. Rain beat against the roof, so close overhead, and sounded like a xylophone. There was a mattress on the floor and a low dresser in front of the room's sole window, which Min went to and began to rummage through.

"I know it's not your style, but it should fit well enough."

Min held up a pair of jeans and a sweatshirt, offering them to Olivia, who took them from her with a sigh but didn't attempt to put them on. Instead, she stared thoughtfully at Min.

"This isn't my style or my world. I should never have come here. Here I was, thinking I'd make a difference. I was going to help you with your custody bullshit, but that boy wouldn't be better off with you." Olivia shook her head. "That boy would be better off a hundred miles from here, with a family that isn't so fucked up."

She pulled the sweatshirt over her head. Her fingertips grazed the ceiling despite the fact she had leaned over as far as she could. When Olivia straightened up, she noticed the stricken look on

Min's face.

"I'm sorry. I don't mean to be hurtful. I'm just...pissed off and scared, and I'm worried for the kid."

"It's all right." Min sat down cross-legged on the edge of her mattress. "You're probably right. Benji *would* be better off with someone else, with people who have their shit together. Even before all this craziness started, it was dangerous around here. You weren't wrong when you said this is what it's like being a Burden. We've got secrets, skeletons in closets, and bodies buried in shallow graves. We've got hushed-up births and fathers whose names aren't to be spoken aloud. We go missing. We get shot, poisoned, beat up, addicted, and sometimes, we even kill ourselves.

"Every generation is the same. We're odd and we're hated, and anytime something messed up happens, we get blamed. After all that happened tonight, I don't guess that's unwarranted. I told you I wasn't going to have kids because it wasn't possible the way I am, but that's a lie. I'm too scared. Havin' kids is like pulling your heart out of your chest and letting it walk around, all soft and squishy. It's not safe. For most people, tragedy is a possibility, but if you're born into a family like mine, it's a certainty."

"That's life." Olivia shrugged, too tired for sympathy. "I know plenty of women who have children who are fully aware of how unkind this world is. They have to be. They know they're going to send their babies out into a society that doesn't value them most days and seems intent on killing them some days, but they do it."

"I'm just tired of it all, I guess," Min said. "Tired of feeling scared day in and day out."

"You're not the only one." Olivia began to unzip her trousers, and Min turned her head away so Olivia could slip them off and then step into the jeans from Min's dresser. "They're a little tight, but if I don't breathe," she said, zipping them up, "they'll do."

"Min! Get down here!" Jodie called from the bottom of the stairs. "Benji's gone!"

"What?" Min rushed to the top of the landing. "How?"

"He's gone. He was in bed, sleeping. I didn't move him, and now he's gone."

The two women hurried down the stairs and into the bedroom. Sure enough, it was empty. Min dropped to her knees and searched under the sagging bed while Olivia looked in the closet, shoving Jodie's clothes aside to see if the boy had hidden behind them.

"Not here."

"He isn't in the bathroom," Jodie added, joining them. "He must have left the cabin."

Min spun around to face him, her mind full of accusation and resentment. "How's that possible? How'd he get out without you seein' him? How drunk are you right now?"

Jodie appeared flustered. His eyes darted around in their sockets, and he could barely stand. He leaned against the doorframe for support, extra slouchy and even more like a string bean than usual.

"I was watching the TV, and the thing about the hospital come on. It took me by surprise. It's...It's Alison. I know I shouldn't have been drinking, but...it's Alison." He looked like he would be sick.

He seemed so unwell, in fact, that Min stopped herself from cussing him out and instead asked, "You don't think that thing took him, do you?"

"How? I was right there the whole time." Jodie gestured to the couch.

"Could she have taken him out the window?"

"I don't know. I didn't hear anything."

"When did you last check on him? A rough estimate even?" Olivia asked, maintaining a greater degree of calm than her counterparts.

Jodie shook his head.

"Okay, well, it's clear he's not in the house, so we need to search the woods and road. He's little and not feeling great. We have no idea if this creature got to him or not. Benji might be alone, and if he is, how far could he have gotten? He might still be within earshot."

The three of them spilled out of the cabin into a light sprinkling of rain. The storm had eased off, and the moon had found a crack in the clouds. It shined down on the wet surface of the road, which gleamed like Christmas ribbon winding up the hill.

Min pointed a flashlight in that direction, searching for any sign that Benji had made his way toward the highway. Olivia turned on her cell phone light and worked her way around the cabin, waving the beam from side to side in hopes of locating the boy behind a shrub or tree. Her phone flickered through every window in the cabin, marking her progress around the small structure, but there was no sign of Benji—not until Jodie cried out.

"I've got footprints!"

Min hurried back from the road, and Olivia came around the corner of the cabin. Jodie stood beyond the drive, not far from the dead end. He hadn't brought a flashlight, but the women could make out his shadowy form pointing in the direction of the woods.

"The tracks head this way."

"Where?" Olivia asked, waving her phone over the muddy ground.

But Jodie was already striding off in the direction of the trees, leaving Min and Olivia scrambling to keep pace.

The ground was wet and slippery and the going rough, though Jodie didn't seem to have a problem with it. Min and Olivia lost him several times in the dark, and Olivia had to stop to scrape the muck off her shoes when they became too caked in it to continue.

"It's like following Hansel and Gretel into the woods," she said. "I keep waiting for a gingerbread house to appear. Only, if that crazy old man, Pyron, is to be believed, you and Jodie are the witches, so who is it we're going to run into out here at the end of a breadcrumb trail?"

"*Shhh.* I think Jodie's hollering."

They jogged toward the sound of his voice and found him, not far along, standing on the banks of the stream. Fat and swollen with rain, it had become a surging, growling, mud-and-stick-filled torrent.

"Benji couldn't have crossed this. There's no way." Min called to Jodie, who headed upstream along the bank's edge. "The water's so high there aren't any rocks showing. There's no steppingstones to get across."

Jodie doubled back. "That doesn't mean he didn't try to cross. If he did, he might have been swept away."

"Don't say that." Min was aghast.

The water was flowing fast, churning in violent eddies, leaving a layer of spume on the surface and a white froth gathering around the banks.

"Tears won't help find him. I'll head upstream," Jodie said to the women. "You two head downstream, to the drowning pool."

The drowning pool. Those words had never sounded so ominous to Min.

"If the water took him, that's where he'll be."

"Come on." Olivia urged Min gently. "The sooner we find him, the better."

They headed downstream as Jodie had instructed, following the water along the stepped slope to the bottom of the hollow. Each time they approached a ledge, the sound of the falling water grew so loud and disorienting that Min thought it might drive her mad. And whenever she and Olivia leaped from a stone step, she knew they would land ankle-deep in boggy sludge, with the risk of hitting something harder and snapping a leg bone.

The bottom of the hollow had never seemed so far away, and it began to feel less and less likely that they would find Benji when they reached it—or find him alive, at any rate.

They were over halfway to the basin floor and the creek's end when Min's cell phone rang. She pulled it out of her back pocket and stared at the screen like it was some alien object.

"Are you going to answer it?" Olivia asked.

"I forgot I had it with me."

The phone rang again. The high-pitched trill startled something in the trees, and Olivia ducked when whatever it was flapped past her head.

"Who is it?"

"Sheila Hardesty, the sheriff's wife."

The phone rang again, and this time, something larger moved in the thicket a short distance away from them.

"Answer it or put it on silent. Make it stop ringing before everyone and everything in this jungle knows we're here."

Min answered the call and put it on speaker. "Not a good time, Sheila."

There was a pause before the nurse replied. "I'm sorry, Min. I was looking for your brother. I tried him earlier, but the number says unavailable, as usual."

"What'd you need Jodie for?" Min frowned, and Olivia fidgeted impatiently.

The creeping darkness seemed to encircle them as soon as they were not walking. It pressed in and surrounded them. To stop moving was to risk being trapped by the tightening shadows.

"I thought he'd want to know that Benji is doing much better. His fever broke about forty minutes ago, and he's been perking up steadily ever since. He's even had a bite or two to eat."

"What?"

"I said Benji is feeling better."

"Benji is with you?"

Min and Olivia's eyes met.

"Yeah, Jodie brought him over and asked if I could watch him. Said it was an emergency. He looked so rough around the edges I figured it must be. Frankly, it got me worrying a little. After Dwight saw the picture I sent you, he got sorta crazy. I didn't mean for him to go charging off to your place half-cocked like that."

"Didn't you?" Min raised an eyebrow then. "No, forget it. It doesn't matter now. What did Jodie say when he dropped Benji off?"

"Only that he needed someone to take care of Benji. I asked him if you were all right, and he said you were but not much more. You know, it's not like Dwight to drink in the morning when he's working. If I'd have known he was going to hit the bottle like that... Well, he stormed out so fast there wasn't much I could do. I hope he didn't worry you or make a nuisance of himself. He gets so jealous."

Her voice contained a hint of pride, but Min couldn't bother to be annoyed.

"Did Jodie say anything else when he dropped Benji off?"

"He did, but I think he misspoke. I asked him where he was headed, and he said he was going to find Jaelynn. I figured maybe he meant you or Alison Mader—I heard he's been by the bar a couple times. I didn't pry further."

"Alison is dead. It was on the news."

"What? I haven't been watching. I've been looking after Benji. Oh, God, what happened? I need to call Dwight. I bet that's why he hasn't been home yet. Do you want me to bring Benji on by now?"

"Yeah. Bring Benji home."

"I am really sorry, Min, about Alison and about the picture. I shouldn't have se—"

Min hung up before Sheila could finish. "She has Benji. Jodie brought him to her."

"I heard. Shit. Why the wild-goose chase then? What's your brother playing at?"

"I don't know. Sheila said he told her to watch Benji because he was going to find Jaelynn."

"As in, your dead niece, Jaelynn?"

"I think Jodie mighta gotten an idea in his head and gone and done something stupid—*real* stupid."

Min was about to add "as usual" when a heavy oak branch whisked through the air and collided with Olivia's head. The tree limb hit with a sickening smack, and even in the dark, Min could see the shine of blood on the woman's temple when she toppled sideways to the ground.

"Olivia!"

CHAPTER

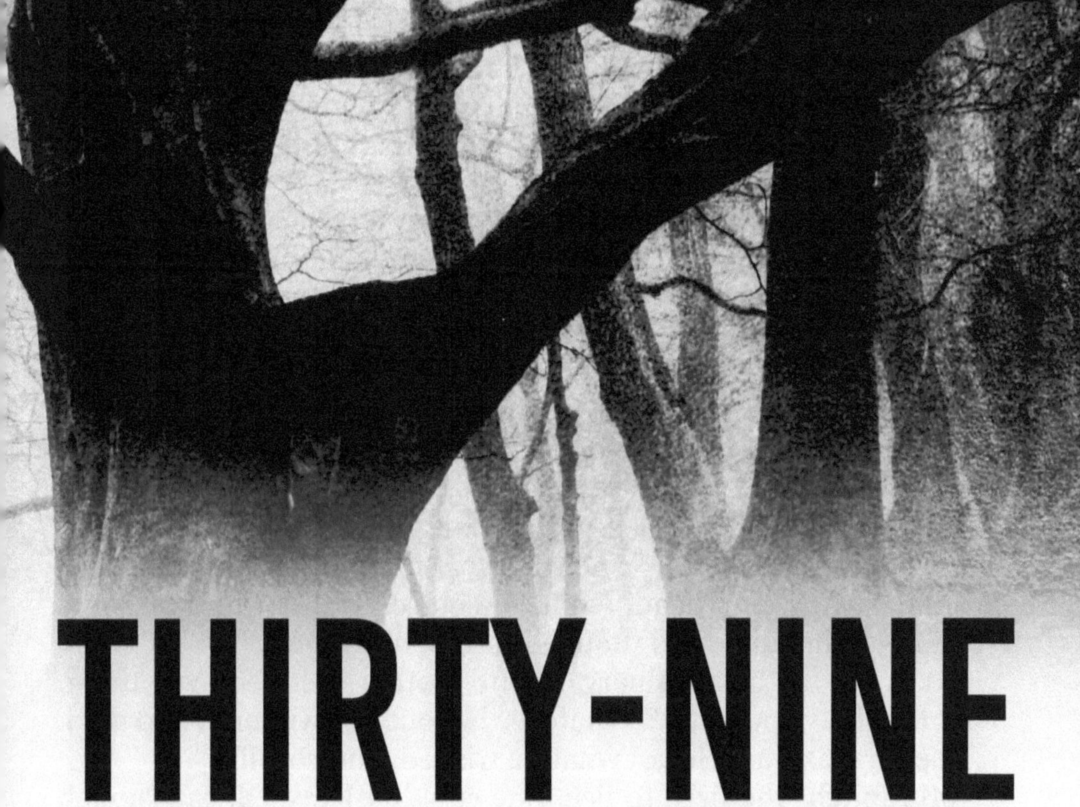

THIRTY-NINE

Olivia was gravely silent. She didn't whimper or moan, didn't seem to breathe. Min had no time to check if she was dead or merely unconscious, though. In front of her, a step or two beyond where Olivia had stood, was Jodie. He still held the branch and appeared even stranger in the moonlight than he had in the cabin.

"Jodie?"

He was pale, a thing made of white stone. "Jodie's been to the water, Min." His voice was a chorus of toads gathered beneath the house in the wet springtime, croaking and made of many parts. It was like more than one person speaking at the same time—Jodie and someone else inside him.

"What's happened to you?" Min asked with a gasp.

Jodie or not-Jodie chuckled. The sound was dry and mirthless. Despite the rarity of Jodie's usual laugh, Min would have recognized it easily, and this was not it.

"Jodie got what he wanted, Minerva. I told you he was ready to make a choice." The being looked up at Min with white eyes that weren't Jodie's. "He chose oblivion...He chose death."

"No, not Jodie. He didn't want to die." Min stepped back, twigs cracking underfoot.

The thing which looked like her brother advanced toward her.

"Not at first. First, he asked for vengeance. He thought it would heal what was broken inside him, but even after they were gone, all those men—burned and butchered—the sore still festered. It was the woman, though, Alison, who brought him to the water in the end. Her death drove him to me, and he begged for release." The creature reached out, palms up, as though presenting an offering. "It is done."

Min's heart had stopped beating, and her blood had turned to sludge. "You killed him?" She tried to wrap her head around this, around Jodie being dead, while she stared right at him or some version of him, distorted though it might have been.

"It is for the best, Minerva. Your brother polluted everything. Isn't that how you put it? Whatever he touched withered and died. It's better this way. He got what he wished, and so will I."

Min fought the urge to flee. She couldn't leave Olivia. Though the woman still lay on the ground, Min had noticed her chest rise. She had seen her breathing. Olivia was alive.

The creature raised her arms to the sky and sighed. "I want life, Min. It's all I've ever wanted, and I am so close...closer than ever."

Min edged nearer to her friend while the creature continued to speak to the night.

"I am Seph, the oracle for which your town was named. I am the demon the witchmaster warned you of. But more than that, I am the shadow, the unseen thing you've known was here all your life."

She turned now toward Min, her eyes like searchlights in the dark. They fell on Min, and at once, Min was rooted in place.

"You felt me coming, didn't you? All along, you've known it was only a matter of time. You waited for me, stayed while others left. Except you waited too long. Your brother came to me first, and we made our deal." She shook her head in mock sadness. "Poor Minerva. As usual, less for her and more for Jodie. Jodie-boy. St. Joseph."

As the words were repeated back to her in mockery, Min realized that Seph could read her thoughts. She would know Min had planned to run as soon as Olivia woke up.

Hidden Children

"Your brother's body is strong. He is a witch, like you, descended from witches I have known before. He will hold me." She wrapped her thin arms around herself and caressed her own long body. "Your brother and I are bonded now. Water and dust turn to clay. Together, we are something more, something stronger than we were. We are becoming whole."

Min could see this becoming while she listened to the creature and wondered why she hadn't recognized it before. She had been blind. Back at the cabin, Jodie had already begun to change. His gaunt, ashen face, his drooping, lanky posture—these had all been signs, and Min had missed them. In hindsight, he hadn't even sounded like himself.

Now Jodie's form was changing further. Joints were becoming more pronounced and increasingly knobby. Bones lengthened and stretched. Jodie's voice, the conglomeration of human and animal sounds Min had heard earlier, evened out until it was smooth and soft. Like the slipping of silk over skin, it flowed evenly. It was feminine, seductive even—nothing like Jodie's.

Could he really be gone, Min wondered, the prodigal son who disappeared and reappeared as he pleased?

The thing resembled her brother less and less every passing second. Jodie's hair, once graying at the temples, darkened and took on a rich luster. The lines on his face diminished, and his eyes were bright and pale. Min no longer recognized them when they gleamed at her, hard and unblinking.

No, this was not her brother. This thing had taken him. Min's fear was replaced by anger.

"If Jodie's gone, why the hell are you still here? Why don't you fuck off and leave the rest of us alone?"

She braced herself for the creature's answer, already knowing what it would be.

Benji. She wants Benji too.

Min steeled herself against the creature's words but not the physical attack which followed. Without warning, Seph darted toward her. Min barely saw her move; she came so fast.

Before Min could blink, the creature stood before her, so close Min could smell the heady, pungent aroma wafting off its pallid flesh. It was a scent which spoke to the strongest and most lasting of elements—not flesh or earth, but metal and mineral—enduring and hard.

At that distance, Min noticed that Seph's eyes were not entirely white. They possessed a small black pinhole of a pupil Min hadn't seen before, as well as a faint, raised outline of an iris, clear like water, with a few gold flecks floating in it. These features might have been leftovers—the last remaining vestiges of Jodie's eyes.

"I'm here for you, Minerva," the creature said. It was not the reply Min had expected. "There are still gifts to be had. Ymir, the father, the oldest of creators, is a generous god, and he blesses even the least of his children. What do you desire most? Let me hear you say it."

On the ground, a few feet away, Olivia moaned.

Min looked down. Her friend was lying in a bed of strange white flowers. Vines had wrapped themselves around her ankles and wrists, winding their way over her body. The forest had opened for Seph, and tiny blooms of bone sprang up everywhere her feet had touched while she walked toward Min. Trees shone silver and bent away so the moon and the stars could look down on her white skin, unobstructed. The forest was under the demon's thrall.

"I don't want this," Min declared, unmoved by the terrifying beauty enveloping the woods around her. "I don't want anything from you."

"Well, that is a lie." The creature smiled. She reached out and took Min's face in her hands. The demon didn't just smell like metal; her grip was like iron too. "You and I are not so different. We both want life. Not merely to possess it or watch it, but to create it. That is the ultimate power." She pressed in close once more and whispered in Min's ear. "Together, we can fulfill your dream *and* mine."

The creature ran her amphibious-looking hands over Min's sternum while she spoke.

Revulsion flooded Min's body and mixed with a rising terror until she choked on it. She thrashed and fought to get away, but the creature was strong—more so than Jodie ever had been. If Min had doubted that the thing her brother had become was not human, all uncertainty was erased right then.

Fighting Seph was pointless. She held onto Min like a squirming kitten, impervious to all her clawing and biting.

"You want this. I have seen it in your mind," Seph said.

She wrapped her long fingers around Min's skull, as though they were burrowing deep into her head, straight into her brain. Min's knees buckled, and she dropped to the ground. Seph crouched over her, still hissing in her ear.

"Legacy is what you desire. Someone to call you *Mother*...or"—she smiled malevolently—"*Mama*."

It was Jaelynn's voice, and at the sound, Min's body gave out completely. She toppled to the ground, with Seph coming down on top of her.

The weight of the creature—that iron-forged thing—pushed Min into the soft, saturated earth. Spindly, alabaster fingers, icy cold, crept over Min's body toward her belly and hips.

No, Jodie, no, Min thought.

The creature pulled at her clothes, tugging them down and away until Min was exposed and the cold earth pressed against her back and her thighs. Something inside her ripped away, releasing a flood of searing heat and pain.

She was dying or wished she was dead, but the pain continued. Confusing, disorienting agony. And whispering. The creature whispered all the while.

"I know what you want. I will give it all to you." Seph's words made Min's temples ache and set her teeth on edge.

Rocks and broken roots dug into her back. Sharp things prodded and stabbed at her, and the creature continued—continued to speak and continued to drive Min deeper into the ground.

"Did you know he wanted to die, Minerva? You shared a womb. You are connected. Did you feel it? Did you feel me when I entered him? Did you know it somewhere deep inside the hollow of your being?"

"No." Min let out a sob. "I don't want to feel it. I don't want this."

"It is done."

The creature sprang up so fast that Min gasped. The excruciating weight lifted, and the tearing inside her stopped. Before Min knew what was happening, the creature had gone, disappeared into the woods, leaving Min to curl into a tight ball on the ground. When she was able, she gathered her ripped and soiled clothing around her and rolled onto her stomach so she could push herself up to her knees.

She should have been running. Her attacker might return at any moment, but her legs felt stodgy and wooden, and she hadn't seen which direction Seph had gone. There was a risk of running toward the threat rather than away.

Min pulled at her rumpled T-shirt, which was bunched up under her bra. She caught sight of her stomach as she did. Beneath the skin of her abdomen, something moved inside her. It rolled and shifted, pushing the smooth flesh outward and forming something like a wave or a ripple.

Blind with tears and trembling, Min clutched her stomach and tried to stagger to her feet but failed. Hysteria welled up inside her. It wasn't real. It couldn't have been. It was more of the creature's tricks. If she could read Min's mind, then she could make her imagine things too. Min clawed and pressed at her stomach, trying to make whatever writhed there disappear.

"Min? What happened?" It was Olivia. She was on her feet, conscious, though blood streamed down the side of her face, forming an expansive stain on the sweatshirt Min had given her.

"I need to get to Benji before...she does. Help me get him, please." A sudden, vicious cramp in her belly stopped her, made her double over in the wet dirt on the creek bank. Min's vision blurred, and her head swam. She heard buzzing.

"What's that noise?" Olivia heard it too—the hum of a million insect wings.

They descended like a black cloud from high above the treetops. The swarm of flies was coming, a towering, humming wave of black and green which appeared ready to swallow Olivia whole.

"Run!" Min shouted.

Olivia's eyes and mouth opened wide. Comprehension struck her full force, and she realized the danger she was in. The giant wave of flies collapsed over her, and she disappeared from Min's sight for a moment before finally bursting out of the billowing wall of insects.

Olivia whipped the hood of her sweatshirt over her head to protect herself while she bolted up the hill, pursued by the flies. She waved her arms and whimpered, not daring to open her mouth to scream. In her mad panic, she forgot Min and vanished between the trees.

Dizzy with relief and pain, Min rocked backward and slipped into the creek, where an eager current swallowed her and began ferrying her helpless body downstream.

CHAPTER

FORTY

The current dragged Min down the hillside—away from the house and Olivia, farther from Benji. The swollen stream carried her like flotsam until she reached the pool at the very bottom of the hollow. There, the tide released her, spat her out onto the shore as if it had fulfilled some silent mandate from the creature who controlled it.

Min hauled herself onto the pebbled shore. She spat flecks of decaying leaves and creek bottom muck onto the warm stones and coughed muddy water out of her lungs before collapsing face down. While she tried to catch her breath, something nearby snorted.

There was a rustling, and Min lifted her head.

The animals which had chased her and Olivia on the road had returned. They stood along the banks of the pond, looking rather worse for wear. Since Min had last seen them, the dead herd had fallen further into ruin. Their hides and pelts were more rotted. Wounds oozed and gaped, exposing layers of white fat and livid organs. The bear was there as well, the holes from Olivia's bullets still visible.

Min pulled herself to her feet, and the creatures moved closer, tightening their ranks and blocking the path back up the hill. Retreat was her only option. Min fell back, away from the ghastly menagerie, to the bluff where a cave's triangular doorway beckoned. Promising warmth if not safety, it drew her in with a strange hum and an unnatural glow. A rocky passage unwound before her, its narrow twists and turns familiar, like something she had seen in a dream.

Min's wet hair clung to her neck, and her clothing felt tight. Her body still ached, and she reached out to the smooth stone walls around her, sliding her hand over their slick, barren surfaces for support and balance.

Something deep in the cave laughed. It knew she was there, sensed her while she glided down the passage, deeper into the folds of the cavern and into a round, open chamber.

A pool glowed as blue as an eye, its darkened center glittering with tiny lights, like stars. It was the opening to a different world or dimension, filled with the brilliance of comets and crawling with dark beings.

The power and spark of creation and absolute destruction lay submerged in the clear water, and from it all rose a tower of bone. The ivory structure appeared to float above the surface. It was both temple and altar—a monument to death constructed with the shattered remnants of Seph's victims.

In front of all this rested the creature herself—the demon.

The sight of her struck Min dumb. She lay on the ground, stripped of clothing, reclining against the pool's stone lip like the subject of a painting. This was not the snarling, vicious distortion of Jodie which had attacked Min in the woods. This was a female version of the man who looked incredibly like Min herself but longer of limb and pale as ivory. Her skin appeared elastic, malleable and rubbery, as though it could become anything. She was as fluid as the water she dwelled in and just as terrifyingly beautiful.

Seph's shoulders were heaving while she took in great, shuddering gulps of air. Her smooth gut expanded and contracted, and she rocked back and forth, emitting sounds very much like human sobs. The demon was crying, and it was most assuredly the strangest thing Min had ever witnessed.

Having been pushed beyond the boundaries of fear, she felt only curiosity and moved closer, wondering what color the tears of such a being might be.

From only a few feet away, she noticed just how greatly her brother's body had been transformed by the creature. The part which had made him male had pulled in close, almost disappearing.

"Is my brother gone then?" Min asked when she could almost touch the creature with her foot.

Seph lifted her blanched eyes to Min. "The becoming is almost complete."

"Why are you crying, then?"

"I weep because it is beautiful. *We* are beautiful." She blinked away her tears and gazed at Min. "Do not be angry with me. I have merely acted on Jodie's wishes. This is what he most desired."

"Bullshit," Min spat. "Jodie never would have said he wanted a thing like this."

Seph looked at Min with pity. "You still fail to comprehend my abilities. I see the world's hidden wishes, the ones too shameful to confess aloud. I see everything. I know what Jodie wanted."

Min's hands went to her middle, and she shook her head. "No. What you did to me, Jodie didn't want that."

"The need to own and to conquer, the desire to possess and dominate—all men have this, even the meek ones, even the unambitious ones. Jodie was a man, like any other."

"I won't believe it." Min still ached all over. She hurt in places she had never felt before—deep-inside places which the monster within her brother had reached and violated—and now she grew angry. "Jodie never would have done that, and Benji said you were a liar."

"Did he?" Seph smiled and sat up in a crouch, like an animal ready to spring. "He's a boy. How much can he know?"

"He's a Burden. He's got our gift of knowing. I know things too. Like I know why you're crying."

"Do you?" The creature cocked her head, amused.

"It's because you lied to Jodie. He isn't too happy with your little bargain now, is he? I'll bet those are *his* tears—his regular old human tears. He wasn't so thrilled with the fine print, or maybe he just changed his mind when he saw what you were about."

Min's pain made her bitter. It drew up inside her a good old hill-folk brand of onery, and she looked around for something to use as a weapon. All she found were rotting bones and Jodie's clothes, which had been dumped in a pile.

"It doesn't matter now." Seph rose, so tall.

Min hadn't expected that. She had been seeing eye to eye with her brother for forty-odd years, even when they didn't see exactly eye to eye. Now she looked up to meet his gaze.

"He made his choice, and the joining is nearly complete. He is tormented, and I feel it, yes, but it will not last long. He will learn to live with the truth of the bargain he made."

"What truth is that?"

"He is mine forever. I shall hold him inside me for an eternity." She turned her back to Min, revealing the chasm, the split running the length of her spine. "See for yourself."

Darkness swelled around them, filling the cave, and a sucking emptiness overtook Min. It drew her toward the creature, the same way she had been tugged along the cave passage. Like a magnet, it pulled at her, and then Min was inside the creature.

A spectral sailboat on a ghostly tide, she floated over a cold, glassy sea of shadows. Dark forms danced around her, twisting in the eternal night of the creature's sable world. They grew and shrank, pulsing while they floated around her. Min's own body expanded, reaching out and breaking apart into the ether.

An eternity seemed to pass, and then she was spit out of the darkness. Min returned to the light of the cave, where she gasped and shivered in Seph's arms.

"I saw them, the shadow creatures." Min was horrified to think that her brother could be one of those lifeless, lightless wraiths. "Who are they? *What* are they?"

"Everyone who has ever bargained. Everyone who has ever knelt on my altar and prayed." Seph waved to the blue pool. "Everyone who has ever begged me to make them more than they are. They are inside me, along with the beasts I have ruled and used. There are worlds inside me, Minerva," she whispered. "Worlds you've never imagined. Jodie is there now."

"He's trapped in there with the shadows, with those monsters?"

"Not *trapped* with them. He rules them. He asked for death, but I gave him a greater prize. I gave him dominion."

"If he asked to die, it was only because he wanted to be with his wife and his girl," Min said, backing away from the creature. "But he's not with them, and he never will be if he's in there."

She picked up the heaviest bone she could find from those littered about the cave. It was a sturdy-looking femur, and she brandished it over her head like a club.

"You think you can hurt me, Minerva Burden?" Seph chuckled. "I'll kill you where you stand. I warned you, didn't I? I only need one of you. The other is surplus."

Seph strode forward and knocked the bone from Min's hand as if it were nothing. It soared across the cavern and shattered against the stone wall. The creature grabbed Min by the neck and lifted her off her feet.

"You are nothing compared to me. You cannot win. You should have taken my offer back at the hospital. You could have saved yourself from so much pain, but you chose foolishly and have brought this upon yourself."

She let go of Min, whose legs buckled beneath her. Min landed on her back and grunted when her breath rushed out. Seph dropped to her knees and crawled over, pinning Min by her arms to the ground.

She was not so beautiful anymore, wearing a mask of rage, but there was no fighting her. Seph had been strong in the woods, and now she was even more so. Not like iron or stone, no. Now her strength was incomparable, like nothing Min had ever known or even imagined.

Min closed her eyes. There was nothing to do but wait for death, should the creature choose to deal it. She relaxed her muscles and allowed her body to go limp, but Seph released her. The creature sat up.

"You are wise to choose submission, Minerva. I can still use you." She placed her heavy hands over Min's stomach. "My spark is in you now. You have something precious within."

Seph pressed harder against Min's belly, and Min's insides responded to the demon's touch. Something pulled. It tugged and expanded. The tingling nervous sensation Min had felt a few times before in her life hit her.

Something was coming.

From within her own body, something was on its way.

"It's growing inside you already. You are the vessel. The Month of Slaughter, a time of life and death, approaches, and with your help, a new demon will walk the earth."

"No," Min moaned. "I won't give that to you. I will drown you back to hell. The witchmaster said—"

Seph's hands were on her throat again. "You take advice from a dead man. I killed the witchmaster. It was a debt long overdue.

You, too, owe a debt, Minerva. You should have strangled in your mother's womb. I saw your birth. I saw the cord around your neck, and I saw two paths flow from that moment. You lived and you died. I have seen a world without you in it, and I can make that world a reality if I choose."

Her grip on Min's neck tightened, and Min kicked her legs. Her feet slid up and down, making long tracks on the cave floor.

"Your struggle is pointless. I see in all directions. Whatever you do, I win." She laid her cold, pale lips over Min's and inhaled.

The little breath Min had left rushed out of her and into the creature. The cave grew even redder than before. The very edges of Min's vision seemed to be on fire. Her eyes rolled in their sockets, landing on the pile of Jodie's clothing lying near her.

There was a sliver of metal showing beneath the heap.

Jodie's knife.

Min reached out a leaden arm and pawed clumsily for the weapon. Her fingers brushed cold metal, and she grabbed it.

She flicked the blade open and swung it toward the demon, in the direction of those white eyes. Seph stopped it inches from her face. She grabbed Min's wrist and, with one violent shake, sent the knife flying from Min's hand.

"Have it your way. Show me your strength, witch, if that is what you want." She twisted Min's arm over her head and held it down against the ground. "Show me what you can do."

"Why are you doing this?" Min's shoulder ached, her elbow felt as it if it would pop, and her words were a ragged cry echoing off the cavern walls. "Why?"

"You of all people should understand. I want what you want, Minerva." The demon released her and stood up. "All those things you lay awake at night coveting, in your little nest above the world, I crave them too. I want a family, a legacy—more like me to be mine and call me theirs."

She reached down and pulled Min to her feet, clutching Min to her chest like she was a child's ragdoll. The creature began to sway, howling a devilish lullaby which chilled Min more than if she had screamed or ranted.

"Help me," Min whispered into Seph's ear. "Help me, Jodie."

Seph continued to dance Min around the cave. "Jodie is far away. He can't help you. He chose this."

"No. Not this," Min protested weakly. "You said he wanted to die, but this isn't death. It's something else, something worse. Jodie, this isn't what you wanted." She spoke to her brother, hoping that, wherever he was, he could still hear her. "There's no peace inside this monster. Fight it. Fight her."

Like white lightning, the demon struck Min on the jaw and sent her head rocking backward. Sparks exploded behind Min's eyes, and she stumbled, dazed and senseless, to the edge of the pool, where she collapsed against the stone. She spat blood and ran her tongue over her torn lip. Min had bitten right through it, but still, she managed to call out.

"She lied to you, Jodie. This isn't what you want. She's like all the rest, out to get hers and fuck the Burdens."

"You think it's that easy, Minerva? You think that you can call to your brother and out he will come? He and I are joined. I am in his blood now."

"Yeah, but the way I heard it, you don't just need a witch to live. You need a witch that's willing, and my brother don't seem so willing right now. I can feel it."

Seph contorted her face into an angry sneer, but the wild snarl quickly died on her lips. She gaped in wonder and then surprise, feeling it just as Min did.

Jodie was still in there. He was coming. Every nerve in Min's body told her he was on his way.

Seph sputtered and gasped. She charged at Min, who dipped her fingers into the pool beside her and touched something cold and hard. It was a bone, a sturdy one stripped of flesh, which had risen with the others.

Min pulled it from the water and swung, striking the creature in the temple when she charged.

Seph staggered but didn't fall. She grimaced and clutched her head. Something inside pained her. Jodie was knocking around in there, a bad houseguest, bringing things down from the inside. The demon kicked at Min, but her movements had grown slow, sluggish even, and the hands clawing at her torso were growing less talon-like and more human. She doubled over and groaned.

"I think someone is serving you an eviction notice." Min stood and retrieved the knife from where it had fallen. "I know my brother, and he didn't ask to be trapped forever in your darkness. It's time to hold up your end of the bargain. Let my brother go. Let him die, you bitch."

Min flicked the knife open and strode toward Seph. She ran the blade into Jodie's side. Using every bit of her remaining strength, she yanked it until she had dragged the knife all the way across his abdomen to the other side.

Slit open like a fish, Jodie dropped to his knees. Blood fell in sheets onto the sandy floor of the cavern, and Min knelt beside her brother, taking his face in her hands. The blood continued to drain out of him, and he grew paler, but the color returned to his eyes.

"Jodie! Talk to me, Jodie."

"You were right," he muttered through clenched teeth. "You were right about it all."

"Shit, you're gonna have to do better than that. Say somethin' that lets me know it's not the demon talking."

"Quit pickin', woman." Jodie's teeth chattered.

Min laughed, though she had also begun to cry. "You're the absolute worst, you know that? Oh, Jodie, I'm so sorry. But why? What were you thinking, getting mixed up with this thing?"

"She lied," he stammered. "All I wanted to do was die, and there I was, staring down forever inside of her." A thin trickle of blood seeped out the corner of his mouth. "She wasn't there. None of them were."

"Who?"

"Carrie. Alison. My Jaelynn. I want to see my baby again." He coughed, and blood ran down his chin.

Min wiped it away with her hand and helped ease her brother back against the stone lip of the pool.

"Jaelynn's gone to be with the angels, dumbass. Her mama too. What made you think you were going to find them inside some bloodsucking bitch living in a watering hole?"

Min looked down into the abyss at the center of the pool. The bones were settling into place, or maybe they were rearranging themselves, taking on a new shape. Her heart skipped a beat, but Jodie clutched her hand, squeezing it even as she felt him slipping away.

"You pegged it. I'm a dumbass." He smiled, his teeth red with blood. Jodie winced and faltered when a spasm wracked his body. Slowly, he raised a bloody palm to her cheek and touched her ragged lip tenderly. "I'm so sorry. I know what she's done to you. I never meant...I never would have done something li—"

Jodie stopped. His eyes widened. He pulled his hand away from his sister's face and stared at the blood he had left behind on her torn skin.

"The blood." His teeth began to chatter. "I'm bleeding. It's...It's in the blood. She's—"

Min hushed him. "It's all right. It's gonna be all right." She pushed a strand of hair away from his eyes and smiled. Jodie's blood had formed a pool around her where she sat. "We don't have to be afraid anymore. We don't have to be alone. Neither of us do, ever again."

A strange light came into Jodie's eyes. He nodded. "I know why you did it. Take care of Benji. You keep him safe now."

"Like he was my own."

"You'd 'a been a great mama, Min."

"I think I will be."

Min lingered there, in the glow of the blue water, while the last of her brother's life flowed out of him. She waited to see if she would feel it—a loss deep inside, the breaking or a severing of bonds people said twins sometimes felt when one of them died.

Sure enough, in the silence of the cave, she felt something, but it was not Jodie.

CHAPTER

FORTY-ONE

Olivia stood like a sentinel on the front porch of the Burden cabin, scanning the woods for any sign of Min. It had been hours since the flies had driven her from the banks of the stream, and she was unsure what her next move should be.

The nurse had brought Benji home, and Olivia had tucked him into the bed at the back of the cabin, but there had been no sign of his great-aunt or even his grandfather. Min had been alive when Olivia last saw her, but hope drained fast while the clock in the little cabin ticked away the minutes and dawn grew nearer.

She was about to give up, trying to decide whether to leave the boy or take him with, when she saw movement on the side of the road. Gravel crunched underfoot. Someone was coming up the drive.

"Min! Is that you? Thank God!" Olivia started toward the steps but stopped short.

The thing walking out of the woods was not Min despite how closely it resembled her and the fact that it wore her clothes. This version of Minerva Burden was pale, with spider-long arms and legs, and it teetered awkwardly, like a child first learning to walk, while it climbed the drive to Olivia.

Every impulse in Olivia's body cried out for her to run, but her legs wouldn't work. She stumbled back to the cabin and braced herself in the splintery doorway.

"I am—" the creature began.

"I know what you are." Olivia wheezed. Her heart was beating too fast to catch her breath.

The porch light struck the creature's face. Its host's bone structure remained, but its skin and musculature was as unmoving as stone, unreadable and impossibly smooth, with no bruises, blemishes, or wrinkles. The imposter didn't appear young so much as ageless, like something beyond the reach of time. It peered up at Olivia with white eyes, and it grinned, offering a smile too wide to belong to any human.

Olivia's knees buckled beneath her. No one should have a mouth that broad and leering. It stretched almost ear to ear, and Olivia could imagine it swallowing her whole.

"Stay away!" she screamed. "Leave us alone!"

"I can't do that. There is a boy inside, and I am his family—the only family he has left."

"You're not human." Olivia's voice was a whimper.

The creature's ghastly smile was gone as quickly as it had come. It charged up the steps until it was so close Olivia could smell the pungent, acrid odor wafting off its stolen flesh. From that minor distance, Olivia noticed how much taller this thing was than her friend—at least four or five inches.

"You're a parasite," she whispered. Olivia melted aside, allowing the creature to pass by her into the cabin. She might as well have tried to convince her body to stand against a charging rhino or raging tsunami.

Inside, Seph raised her pale face and sniffed the air like an animal. Thunder roared overhead, and the power flickered once, then went out. Olivia froze, drenched in darkness, and pressed motionless against the wall while the creature spoke, unseen.

"With this body, I will no longer be hidden. I will no longer be alone."

"That body isn't yours." Olivia moaned tearfully in the doorway.

Lightning flashed in the distance. Seph stood silhouetted against the windows near the couch—a beast of extended, spindly proportions.

"It is now. I am alive in every cell. I am in the muscle and in the bone. Each drop of blood that runs through these veins contains me now. This body is more alive than it ever was before because of me. I have made it more than it was."

Olivia searched the dark for another glimpse of the creature, but Seph's voice floated to her from all directions. The creature was moving around the room, exploring the small house.

"Your friend, Minerva, is a flicker now, a tiny glimmer in the dark, feeding off my strength. And so I ask, who is the *real* parasite?"

"Fuck you." A sob rose in Olivia's throat, and she slid down the wall into a fetal crouch. "Go to hell," she whimpered from the floor.

"This is the bargain your friend made."

The sky lit up once more, flooding the cabin with cold, white light. For a split-second, Olivia caught sight of the creature standing in the hallway, staring toward the room where Benji slept.

"Min is happy where she is, resting in the safety my power brings. She no longer feels fear. She has everything she wants, and soon, she will have more than she ever dared dream of."

"And what's that?" Olivia was almost too afraid to ask.

"Legacy. Family beyond counting, beyond measure. She has seen my vision, and she has chosen. She fought for this, *killed* for it. She and I will live forever. Together, we will be the mother of legions."

A beam of light appeared in the hall, and Benji emerged from the bedroom, carrying a small flashlight.

"Aunt Min?" He turned the light on the creature, following the length of her body, then finally aiming it at her belly.

Min's soiled T-shirt stretched taut over Seph's belly, which had grown as round as a full moon. Something inside squirmed, pressing outward against the tight flesh. Something was alive and clawing to get out.

Olivia felt sick. Bile rose from her stomach, burning the back of her throat, but the boy appeared calm and took the creature's hand, allowing her to lead him toward the door.

"Come with me, Benjamin Burden. Our family grows tonight."

"Don't go with her, Benji. Run!" Olivia hissed.

Benji didn't seem to hear, but the creature reached out and grabbed Olivia's arm, hoisting her easily from the floor and dragging her along with them out of the cabin.

"The time of birthing is at hand, and you will be witness, Olivia

Reynolds—you out of all mankind. It is an honor, even if you do not yet understand all it portends."

Seph moved quickly, pulling Olivia down the drive and into the woods. Olivia's feet skipped and skidded over the ground, like a record player's needle that wouldn't catch.

"I will be near the water when she comes, and when the time is right," the creature promised, "my child and I will reshape the world to our liking."

There was a reason God had separated man from the meat-eating dinosaurs of old by millions of years. It was the same reason some other god somewhere had tried to separate beings like Seph from humankind thousands of years ago.

"Nations and kings—all of mankind—will fall before my progeny," the creature declared when the mouth of the cave hovered into sight at the bottom of the hill.

Inside, the walls were red and pulsing, and the air was heavy with the creature's own metallic scent. Olivia thought she would faint and collapse but doubted the creature would notice. Seph had her practically suspended aloft by then, showing no sign of fatigue in her long arm.

Only when they reached the pool at the heart of the cave did Seph release Olivia, allowing her to drop to her knees on the ground. Seph reached out and brushed Olivia's cheek with her finger. Olivia flinched, detesting the feeling of the other woman's skin. No longer human-like, it was cold rubber. A shudder exploded up her spine.

She flinched again when the pains of labor hit Seph and the monster screamed. Like a thousand voices joined in agony, the sound reverberated around the cave. Olivia covered her ears and prayed it would stop.

Every fiber in her being told her to flee. The demon child was coming. Its mother was incapacitated. The cave opening was *right* there.

Benji knelt by her side, shaking his small dark head. "She'll find us," he whispered. "And she'll be angry."

Olivia closed her eyes. If the boy had read her mind, the creature might have as well. She was trapped, a hostage at this most auspicious moment. They were on the brink of something, the edge of something big. Olivia couldn't escape it any more than Min had been able to... or Jodie.

Like lambs beneath the axe when the Month of Slaughter began, their fates had been sealed.

EPILOGUE

You were. You are. You are yet to come. Time is like that for our kind.

Though I feel you, wriggling and eel-like in my bloody hands, you are still inside me, squirming in my borrowed womb. I carry you in my core, even while I hold you in my arms.

Which is the real you—the one within or the one without? Both, I think. You then and you now—the two have always been and will always be. I have held this moment in my mind and heart since I was nothing but the dust of a dying star.

I have loved you and worshipped you across time, my daughter. Always and forever marveling at your design and the pretty, deadly thing you are and will become.

Across the cave, the human called Olivia watches your arrival and sees you as you are in that moment, pure and untainted by earthly matter—no hybrid thing like me. She looks at you—your teeth, your claws, your eyes that burn with a cold sort of fire—and she envisions a world awash in death. Finally, she understands.

In you, my true likeness is revealed. I am chaos and creation. From me will flow a thousand births and countless deaths, and our kind will once more rule this plane.

With water from the pool where I was held, I wash the cave dust from your bleached, wrinkled skin.

"Behold our future," I say as I pass you to your brother.

He is small and weak, and he fears you already. He is wise to do so.

You are my dark dream, and you shall know me as I am and have been. For I am Minerva, the mother who bore you. And I am Joseph, the father who planted his seed. I am Seph, child of the old god, Ymir, born like you in the Month of Slaughter. I am your father's sister and your brother's mother. I am hulder, the Raw God's kin, hidden no longer, and you, my child, are the first of many.

As a small publisher collaborating with an indie horror author, we make an incredible team. But we wouldn't be able to do what we so love without you. Thank you for taking the time to read *Hidden Children*, by C. S. Magnuson.

It would mean the world to us if you would take a quick moment and leave a review on any book-purchasing platform, especially our direct website, so other readers might take a chance on us too.

Also, please check out other books written by C. S. Magnuson—which we've included the excerpts of in the next few pages—or published by Horrorsmith Publishing, which you'll find a list of following the excerpts.

And don't forget to subscribe to our newsletter for the latest horror community book news and grab your free copy of HORRORSMITH:The Magazine from our website: www.horrorsmithpublishing.com

ONE MOUNTAIN. ONE CURSE.
ONE CHANCE TO SAVE THEMSELVES.

DARK THINGS CRAWL OUT

C. S. MAGNUSON

If you're interested in more *Horror in the Ozarks*, check out this excerpt of *Dark Things Crawl Out*, by C. S. Magnuson.

Chapter One

Night had long since descended upon the Heights. Like a woolen mantle, it wrapped the wooded hills in cloistering darkness, muffling everything and imbuing the forest with deep loneliness. Inside a derelict cabin at the end of a rocky path, Walt Weber's rheumatic joints ached. He paced from one side of his shack to the other and back again, unable to rest.

It was late spring and warm, though the temperate night air did little to lessen the throbbing in the old man's knees. His determined stride became a limp, and his feet scuffed and dragged against the hard-packed clay floor, wearing a trough in the surface. Every so often, he would stop to throw open the door and listen from the threshold, and each time, he heard nothing. Silence lasting through the day had crept into the night, tearing at the old man's mind and setting his nerves aflame.

Something wasn't right.

He gazed up at Hellion Ridge, its series of sharp points rising like a spine above the valley. Walt crossed himself. His heart pumped faster, and his nerves sang with agitation. He stepped back inside, bolting the door.

The tiny shack was as unkempt and disorderly as the slag heaps from the mine at the top of the hill, but he knew exactly where to find what he was looking for. He swept aside the clutter gathering dust atop an old steamer trunk, flipped open the lid, and rifled through the contents to the very bottom, where his fingers brushed flaking leather and parchment.

Walt pulled an ancient book into the wavering light of his kerosine lantern and heaved himself onto his bed. The rusted frame squawked in protest beneath his weight, despite age and booze having whittled him down to nothing. His hand shook, tracing the embossed lettering on the front of the leatherbound tome.

He peeled back the soft cover to reveal the erratic scrawl of Father Helias, his earliest friend and teacher. Walt swallowed hard.

His mouth had gone dry, so he reached for the jar of whiskey he kept by his bedside, taking a stiff belt of the stuff before he was able to flip through the first few pages.

"*Ja*," he said with a decisive nod after scanning the text.

It was all there. Everything Helias, the mad monk, had shared with him. The signs. The omens. The cryptic warning: *In silence, she wakes. In silence, she takes.*

Walt cocked his head and listened again, hoping against hope something might chase away the disconcerting quiet hanging like a stubborn storm cloud over the town and its surrounding hills.

The mining town of Tiefer Spalt had been his home since he was a child, and its constant symphony of falling rock and thundering stone was as familiar as his own heartbeat. The crashing and pounding along with the blasts from explosives had become the percussive accompaniment to his life, and their sudden absence left him wracking his brain, trying to determine a cause.

If there had been a tunnel collapse, the alarms would have sounded—first those at the mine on Hellion Ridge and then the great bell in the needle-like steeple of St. Gertrude's. Walt had listened for their peals all day, but they remained as silent as the mine and the dark woods.

The old man closed Father Helias's book and slipped it carefully inside his worn shirt, where it would travel close to his heart. Fearing something yet unknown, Walt then looked for a weapon with which to arm himself. His father's rifle hung over the door, but the old thing was rusted beyond use and likely to explode and kill whoever was foolish enough to try to fire it. Walt should have kept it in better repair, just as he should have kept himself in better repair.

"*Es ist zu spat*," the old German said, taking comfort in the language of his mother and in a second stiff gulp of whiskey from his jar. "Too late for regret." He sighed and opened the door, stepping out into a disconcertingly quiet night.

Walt lost his breath before he reached the edge of his property and would have lost his courage too if not for a faint glow on the horizon telling him morning was near. The coming dawn fortified him almost as much as the whiskey he had drunk, and he hurried on. A few hundred yards beyond the cabin, he passed the graves of his father and mother and, a dozen yards beyond that, the stone marking Father Helias's final resting place. The last of the zealot priest's acolytes, Walt had buried the cleric there himself decades earlier.

Voices drifted through the dark, and relief coursed through the old man's aching body. Finally, a sound! A noise other than the pounding of his blood in his ears to let him know he was not alone on this Earth. He paused to listen, thinking at first it might be a rescue party on their way to the mine. No, there were men on the hillside certainly, but they were not moving toward the peak or the digging operation within.

Revenue agents was Walt's next guess. He watched the shadowy figures sweep up the mountainside and fan out—a dozen of them, maybe more—covering a wide swath of rocky terrain. The way they hollered as they made their way through the trees told Walt his second guess was wrong as well, though. Revenue agents set on raiding the local stills wouldn't have made such a racket and alerted their query to their presence.

No, this was a search party, Walt deduced. Someone was lost in the woods, and by the tenderness undercutting the urgency in the men's voices, Walt guessed it was a child. The men were trying not to frighten the poor thing into hiding, so they called out coaxingly, but their voices were hoarse, as though they had been shouting for some time.

A little lamb is lost in the dark. Walt shook his head.

It was a pity but had nothing to do with him. He had his own mission and so turned his back to the men and set off resolutely toward the peak. The voices of the searchers receded, and the sound of running water grew louder. Walt worked his way carefully over the fallen trees and rocky outcroppings. Just ahead, a stream gurgled and gushed, its current running like liquid laughter down the hillside.

It was the first bright sound Walt had heard all day, but in the lingering moonlight, something glowed white and ominous against its banks.

The old man slowed his pace, taking each new step with hesitation. From a short distance away, even with his failing eyesight, he knew what lay in front of him. It was the body of a young girl—the very child the men on the hillside sought, no doubt. By luck, or by misfortune, Walt had happened upon her first, and with his lantern held out in front of him, he bent low to inspect the child.

Her head was thrown back in a most unnatural fashion, her eyes rolled up inside her skull so only the whites were showing. Like Jesus on the cross hanging above the altar in St. Gertrude's, her arms were flung wide, but her ankles were neatly crossed. She wore a white nightgown which flapped softly, moved by a breeze lighter than the sigh escaping Walt's lips.

The girl did not appear to have drowned in the shallow stream. Her body and clothing were dry. Only her pale-gold hair touched the water, spilling into the brook where it swirled like fine lake weed in small eddies around the rocks. Walt knelt and touched his hand to the child's cheek. It was firm, not soft and tender as a child's flesh should be, and cold enough to make him recoil.

He knew this girl. She was Anabelle Keller, the only daughter of the owner of the mine on Hellion Ridge. Her father had used family money to purchase the operation only the year before and, in that time, had become exceedingly rich in his own right. Walt had heard the people of town whispering amongst themselves. They said the pace at which the young man's wealth grew was matched only by the speed at which his recklessness increased.

"He digs too fast," they whispered. "He digs too *deep*." They would cluck their tongues and wag their heads. "Careless," they hissed when they thought no one else was listening.

Was it that same recklessness then, that lack of care, which had resulted in the mine owner's daughter wandering far from home so late at night? Walt wondered this, staring at the child. Or was it something else? What would draw this precious gem, so coddled and cosseted, away from her comfortable bed and deep into the lonely woods on a moonless night?

Walt reached out to Anabelle once more. Though he didn't relish the thought of touching that cold skin again, he had to be sure of something. He brushed back the high-ruffled collar of the dead girl's nightgown and inspected the white flesh of her neck.

It was still dark, but the sky grew lighter every second, and as Walt squinted, he made out a small injury inches below the girl's ear. He pulled his hand back as though scalded and rocked onto his haunches, gazing numbly at the child.

Something moved in the brush on the far side of the creek.

Walt looked up and caught a flash of something white—white enough to rival the pallor of the corpse before him. The silence of the night seemed to amplify then, growing and pulsing around the old man until his ears buzzed and his head ached.

He clutched at Helias's book inside his shirt, filled with a growing certainty the eccentric old priest had spoken the truth. "In the dead they rest. From the rot they rise."

For one mad moment, the old man considered gathering the child up and carrying her back to his cabin. There he could consult the priest's other writings to see if anything could be done. But the voices of the men he had encountered earlier drew closer, and the foolishness of this thought became obvious.

Walt was no longer a young man, no longer strong and able. He would move slowly with such a burden. It was not likely he would make it back to the cabin unseen, and if he did, what then? How long would it be before the town's men, led by either the child's frantic father or her influential grandfather, began to search the houses? They'd start in the Heights, where the outliers and outlaws lived, and reach Walt's cabin before long.

No. It would be unwise to take the child back to his place or to be found there on the riverbank near her body.

Being foreign-born and never having learned to speak English without the strong accent of his birthland, Walt Weber was no favored son of Tiefer Spalt. His neighbors' opinions of him hovered on the blade of a knife, as likely to fall on the side of mistrust and disdain as that of acceptance and trust. They would turn on him and blame him for the Keller girl's death.

There was nothing he could do but lay a hand across the girl's face and press her staring eyes shut. "Be at peace, child. For God's sake and mine, be at peace."

With a final glance over his shoulder, he hurried away from the stream and the pale corpse lying in gruesome repose along the banks. Above him, at a distance, rose Hellion Ridge, but the old man had his answers and would not make a trip to the mine that night. He had seen what he needed to see, and the quiet that had fallen over the mountain like a shadow now felt like a harbinger, a warning of a deeper, more lasting silence to come.

"There! I see something. This way, by the water. I think it's the girl," a voice cried.

Walt Weber ducked low to avoid detection. Scurrying back home in the easing dark, his mind raced. He needed a plan. He needed an army. He needed a drink.

**Find out what evil has awoken in the small mining town
of Tiefer Spalt. Purchase your copy of
Dark Things Crawl Out today!**

A LIGHT ON THE BAYOU

AUTHOR OF DARK THINGS CRAWL OUT

C. S. MAGNUSON

Cypress Cove. I had gone years without thinking of it, spent decades shoving the memory of it down deep inside. Not deep enough, though, apparently.

As soon as I lay eyes on the place, recollection surges upward like noxious gas from decaying matter at the bottom of a shallow pond. I sit motionless in the driver's seat. Andrew swings open his car door, and a wave of humidity forces its way inside, obliterating any residual cool. He points at his glasses, which have fogged over, before pulling them off and wiping them on his T-shirt.

"Welcome to Texas. What are the odds this old place has air-conditioning?" he asks, ducking out of the car before I can answer.

Scrabbly bougainvillea creeps outward from an untended bed. Its thorny vines cast off scarlet tissue-paper petals which swirl about in low eddies over the gravel of the driveway. I open my own car door and step directly into the center of a crimson vortex, disrupting the spiral and sending the feather-light petals scattering in different directions.

My breath comes hard and quick. I stare down at a red petal stuck to my shoe like a scab. Something about it—the splash of red on white—makes my heart race.

Keep it together. You can do this.

My pulse throbs violently in my neck, but I shake the blossom off and grab my purse from the back seat, turning it upside down. Bottles of anti-depressants and anti-anxiety meds tumble onto my lap, but none of them are what I need right now. I packed a bottle of Oxycodone—one with someone else's name on it—in my suitcase, wrapped neatly in my underwear so Andrew wouldn't find it. Unfortunately, if I want the pills, I'll have to go inside and unpack.

"Shit."

I heave myself out of the vehicle, taking my time to stretch my legs and then my neck, all while keeping the tin-can rental car as a shield between me and the house. Andrew races to the porch. He has already grabbed our cases from the trunk and bounds up the steps two at a time, dropping the bags on the welcome mat.

"I can't see inside," he calls down, peering through the tall, front window like a peeping Tom. "The curtains are drawn."

I will myself to face the house, craning my head back to take in the full height of the structure. Though I'm taller than I was at twelve, the house on Cypress Cove still looms as large as it did the day I first laid eyes on it. Stern and stately, it sits like an angry idol on the hill overlooking the water. The rosy hue of the brick contrasts with the wild gardens and smothering woods shrouding the house in an unflinching emerald hue.

It was when I first encountered it as a child and is now a great red wound in a wash of green.

Despite the heat, I shiver. A breeze wraps itself around me, carrying on its back the scent of pond weed and rotting vegetation. It stirs the Spanish moss hanging from tree branches overhead. As a child, I hated that moss, the way it looked like gray hair. Tightly curled, brittle, and dry, it was dead woman's hair.

Mama's hair.

Reluctantly, I approach the stone path leading up to the house. The start of the walkway is marked by two wide brick pillars, each sunken at an odd angle, like the columns of a ruined Grecian temple. A bird screams overhead, and I look up, only to stumble over a row of flowering plants flanking the walkway in thick clumps. The crimson blooms possess strange, slender petals curved outward like spider's legs. They run all the way up the path and along the front of the porch. As far as I can see, they circle the entire house in a blood-red ring.

Ring around the rosies.

"Why do you suppose the ceiling out here is painted this awful color?" Andrew is reclining in a porch swing hanging from the wooden ceiling, which is a frothy blue. "It seems like an odd choice—baby blue. I would have gone with a nice gray or even black, for a modern touch."

"If you paint a porch ceiling blue, it looks like water," I explain, eyeing the azure tint. "It keeps the wasps from making nests. But because it's the South with a capital S, they don't call it baby blue, they call it *haint blue* and claim it keeps the ghosts away."

"Seriously?"

I offer up a weak grin that may have been closer to a sneer, then join Andrew on the porch. "I suppose I'm lucky my dad threw me out when he did. Otherwise, I might have grown up with people who go in for all that crap."

"Grown up with them? Hell, you might have been one of them."

My half-hearted smile vanishes. "I wasn't. I was never one of them."

My sudden ire surprises me as much as it does Andrew, whose eyes grow wide. Something about what he said rankles, but he raises his hands in mock surrender.

"Salty much? I think it's charming."

I shoot him a dark look before retrieving the key from under the welcome mat—exactly where Emma Lee Yarborough said it would be.

Moisture has caused the frame to swell, and the hinges creak when I push open the door. The piercing sound rivals the scream of the insects in the trees surrounding Cypress Cove, as well as the shriek inside my head.

My father's overwhelming presence hits me like a tidal wave. Inadvertently, I shrink back, expecting something more solid than bad memories and the smell of his aftershave to come rushing out at me. When nothing does, I close my eyes, take a deep, shuddering breath, and step over the threshold.

Back in Curtis Brightwood's house for the first time in what seems like an eternity, I draw the musty air through my nose and into my lungs, tasting it on my tongue. The smell of moldering plaster, oxidizing metal, and damp wood seep into my core like a spell. I feel the plushness of wool beneath my feet and know I am standing on a burgundy red rug, which lays over oak floors so dark they are almost black.

Pins and needles shoot through my brain as memories awaken. I could tour the house without taking a single step off that entryway rug, without even opening my eyes. It is as if someone began pulling the ropes to raise a veil-like scrim as soon as I drove past that old welcome sign partially hidden by grass and weeds. The town, the house—a hazy pall of half-memories and vague mirages slowly comes into focus.

Welcome back, Achelois. Welcome home. The house on Cypress Cove seems to breathe.

My lip curls disdainfully. That isn't my name anymore, and the last part is wrong too. I'm back, maybe, but not home. This was never home.

"I don't belong here," I mutter.

Andrew pokes his head out of the living room.

"Did you say something?"

"No."

The throbbing midmorning heat has not yet fought its way into the old house, and Andrew at least finds the place cool and inviting. He darts this way and that, taking in architecture he has only seen in books, while I remain motionless a few steps from the front door, doing my best to ignore his giddiness. I focus on a crystal vase of decaying chrysanthemums sitting on the entryway table.

A pocket full of posies.

"Look at the plaster molding," Andrew calls out from the dining room. "Cherubs, egg and dart motifs, acanthus wreaths…If you really hate our house in California as much as you always say you do, we can sell it and move here." He rejoins me in the entry, still gazing up at the ceilings.

"You know the story of the man who built his house upon the sand?" I finger the petals of one of a dozen wilted flowers. "That's what this place is. Heavy bricks piled together on land with the consistency of custard. It seems grand at first, but you notice the cracks eventually. It's a miracle it doesn't all tumble down on my father's head."

The petals come off in my hand, and I let them fall onto the table before grabbing my suitcase and toiletry bag from where Andrew has dropped them.

"It's not a miracle." Andrew thumps the wall with the meaty part of his fist while I lug the bags up the stairs. "It's good engineering and constant maintenance. Your dad must have taken care of the place."

"Then it's the only thing he *did* take care of," I call back, reaching the top of the stairs and turning toward a set of double doors leading to the master bedroom.

His bedroom.

The room where my father once slept is simple, with few personal effects. Sparsely decorated, apart from a collection of framed photographs on the walls and dresser, it might as well be a monk's chambers. The plain white linens and faint but lingering smell of jasmine make it easy to imagine it as little more than a room in a hotel or bed-and-breakfast, which is fine by me. I don't need to feel any closer to Curtis Brightwood than I already do.

After dropping the suitcase at the foot of the bed, I take my carry-on through to the adjacent bathroom and set it down on the marble countertop. A vanity mirror as old as the house itself runs the length of it. Oxidized where humidity has worked its way in behind the glass, it reflects a smokier, darker version of the bathroom and the bedroom beyond. The white counterpane quilt of the bed appears gray, and the filmy curtains in front of the tall windows are long wisps of smoke.

I pull open a drawer in the vanity cabinet and find a collection of pill bottles to rival my own. Scanning the labels, I wonder what Curtis Brightwood had been taking before he died. Did he have medication for heartburn? Tablets to help him sleep when he tossed and turned, pricked by a guilty conscience?

I hope so…but no such luck. It's mostly vitamins. Fish oil for Omega 3s. Iron tablets. Calcium. There is one small bottle of morphine in tablet form which, I won't lie, holds some interest for me.

I dig through more vitamins, but the last bottle I pick up contains Viagra, which conjures more ideas of my father than I can handle right now. Gross. I shove the pills, along with the rest of my father's bottles, to the back of the drawer to make room for my own medication—the stuff Andrew knows about, at least—a regiment of anti-anxiety meds he jokingly calls "the complete Ken Kesey combo." I'm unloading it from my carry-on when something moves in the bathroom mirror.

Over my shoulder in the reflection, something long and upright shifts behind the gauzy bedroom curtains. Dark and phantom-like, it sways to one side then the other. I freeze as whatever it is moves forward, pushing the curtain out before it. It floats into the center of bedroom.

I spin around, my heart pounding painfully in my chest, just as the curtain drops.

It settles back to the floor but, a second later, swells again, lifting to reveal the window behind it, open a crack. I exhale in relief. It's just a draft. No shadow in sight.

I tromp downstairs again and locate Andrew in the kitchen at the back of the house. He stands next to a massive butcherblock table, making goo-goo eyes at the accompanying chairs.

"They don't make furniture like this anymore," he says. "Solid." He's come down from the peak of his earlier architectural high, but his skin is still flushed, and his eyes sparkle while he surveys the kitchen. "What's the upstairs like?"

"Stuffy. Go check it out if you want."

He doesn't need a second invitation and hurries to the stairs, leaving me alone in the kitchen, which smells like hog fat and homemade bread. The aroma of a century's worth of meals has bled into the paint and leeched into the cabinets. As the sun comes through the window, warming the small space, the odor seeps out of the wood and plaster like olfactory ectoplasm. I need fresh air.

Andrew's heavy footsteps sound on the floor above my head, and I slink to the back door, unlocking the prehistoric slide bolt and slipping out of the kitchen. I bound over the flagstone terrace behind the house and hop down a couple of treacherous-looking steps, landing in a row of the same red flowering plants growing in front.

As I suspected, they completely circle the house, but the ground beyond the flower beds is boggy, and the backyard stinks of decomposing grass.

Wanting to see the cove, I pick up my pace around the side, tugging at the gaping waistband of my jeans, which slide low on my hips. I head toward the thick water of the bayou. Six months of self-pity since I got fired, along with a steady diet of opioids and not much else, have slimmed me down to a sliver.

Trees rise from both the emerald-colored swamp and the grass-covered ground, making it hard to tell the difference between the two. I find it necessary to move more cautiously as I draw close, taking careful steps to avoid a shoe full of slime. My hesitation befits the location, though. Everything is unhurried on the banks of the swamp. Here, the atmosphere is apathetic, and the current barely moves. Even the mosquitos' drone is slower—a torpid, dreamy hum.

A long, narrow dock splits the inlet closest to the house, and I step gingerly onto the first wooden slat. It sags dangerously beneath my weight, but I continue to the end of the pier, where the canopy of cypress boughs opens up and I can finally see a welcome sky. Already sick of green, I take in the blue of the atmosphere with relish before looking down once more.

On one of the metal pylons beside me, in paint cracked and raised like alligator skin, someone has carved something. I squat, surprised to recognize my own name on the chipped surface.

I'm Achelois. Who are you?

ALSO BY C. S. MAGNUSON

Dark Things Crawl Out
A Light on the Bayou

ALSO BY HORRORSMITH PUBLISHING

The Devil Came Down the Mountain
Still, Dark Places
What We Do in Secret
Lake of Secrets
Haint Blue
The Taste of Tiny Bones
Haunted Halls
Their Hearses
Three Garden Village
Hidden Children

ABOUT THE AUTHOR

C.S. Magnuson is a writer and avid reader of horror and gothic tales. A bit of a wanderer, she has lived in multiple countries and many states throughout the U.S. but currently makes her home in Kansas City with her husband, two kids, and a horde of large and unruly canines.

When she is not working on a novel, she writes scripts and produces films and PSA's for individuals and organizations she hopes will make the world a better place. Having grown up in the mountains of California in a town with one traffic light and zero street lamps, she escapes to dark and desolate hills whenever she can to float in murky lakes and find inspiration in the shadowy depths of ancient caves and woods.

More Titles from
HORRORSMITH PUBLISHING

LISTEN CLOSELY...
THE DEAD MIGHT SPEAK...

THE
DEVIL
CAME DOWN
THE
MOUNTAIN

CHRISTOPHER BOND

THE DEVIL CAME DOWN THE MOUNTAIN
BY CHRISTOPHER BOND

For almost a hundred years, locals have proclaimed a portion of the Uinta Mountains in Utah to be cursed. They call the area the Murmuring Caves, the site of the historic Yangguang Massacre, where distortions and reverberations beneath the earth's surface create something very akin to human voices.

And if you listen long enough...you might just hear the dead...

Josh Bridges, an experienced dark tourist, has finally convinced his three best friends to accompany him in search of the Murmuring Caves. But they only agreed because of the tragedy Josh just lived through, which seems to have broken him. They'd do anything for their friend...

Even descend into darkness...

But when they call out for help, what answers them might not be safe...

It might not even be alive.

Will Josh and his friends—Trey, Mandy, and Amber—make it down the mountain?

If these walls could talk...
they'd speak of death...

THEIR HEARSES

E.L. GILES

THEIR HEARSES
BY E.L. GILES

Years ago, John Berryman was responsible for the deaths of his two children and their nanny. But John Berryman was never seen or heard from again. He simply...vanished.

Now, decades later, someone has finally purchased John Berryman's rambling old house.

Marc Larose is no stranger to loss. He hopes to bring the decaying structure to its former glory, a warm place where his family can heal and begin anew, but if these walks could talk, they'd speed of death. Only, Marc isn't listening.

Something vengeful still lingers in the shadows of the old willow, and it has its eyes set on Marc. It isn't long before he is caught in the tangles of mystery, fear, and deceit, where forces beyond his control are vying for his very soul.

Will Marc figure out who...or what...is haunting his new home before he becomes its next victim?

AUTHOR OF WHAT WE DO IN SECRET
CHRISTINA GRAVES
STILL, DARK PLACES
A PSYCHOLOGICAL THRILLER NOVEL

STILL, DARK PLACES
BY CHRISTINA GRAVES

The Seven Sisters of Still Water. Missing but not forgotten. Memorialized in graveyard stone...

Nora Gray, true crime podcast host, is being called back to her hometown over a decade later by a desperate mother. Another daughter, gone. And Nora knows more than anyone realizes, more than even she remembers.

They call it Skull House, this home back in the woods, rundown, abandoned. And for as long as Nora can recall, the local kids have dared each other to climb the stairs to the top, to brave the ghost of Helaena Barker, who they say waits in the attic behind the door...

But Skull House hides more than tales of ghosts, and it clings tightly to its secrets. Nora is convinced it also holds the missing clues to the Seven Sisters' disappearances and why Nora herself woke up in a field near the house, covered in blood, all those years ago.

While Nora investigates the missing girls, will she be able to trust anyone around her? Will she even be able to trust herself?

YOUR BEDTIME
STORIES
WILL NEVER
BE THE SAME...

THE TASTE OF TINY BONES

VINCENT HESELWOOD

THE TASTE OF TINY BONES
BY VINCENT HESELWOOD

No one knows where he came from...He's what lingers in the shadows behind you when you turn off the lights and race up the stairs...The darkness beneath the bed that keeps your feet tucked tightly under the covers...The Bogeyman...

But Evie "Creepy" Mortenson has unknowingly found a way to make him something more than what he was, something much more vicious, something much more hungry...

A simple blog post causes new nightmares to start, new fears that give him new life, and now, something is very, very wrong.

She's lost control of the monster she created, and children are starting to die.

Will she and Detective Ezra Dean find a way to stop him before he goes viral?

You thought you were afraid of the Boogeyman before...Just wait...

Children were
never supposed
to go inside...
HAUNTED
HALLS
W. A. ROBERTS

HAUNTED HALLS
BY W. A. ROBERTS

It's every mother's worst fear: Kasey's young son, Max, has gone missing. Except, Kasey is convinced he never left the house...

Under the scrutiny of local law enforcement in a town focused on her past, Kasey must navigate the hidden passageways of her home with a boyfriend she no longer knows if she can trust and a neighbor keeping something from Kasey she desperately needs to remember.

Will Kasey discover the neighborhood's secrets before it's too late and her son is lost to the house forever?

FROM THE AUTHOR OF HALLOWS EVE
WILLIAM OSWALD
HAINT
BLUE
What do you do if the Boo Hag is already inside?

HAINT BLUE
BY WILLIAM OSWALD

When their father commits suicide, Louis Lattimore and his sister, Ruby, are forced to move across the country at the behest of their mother, to a secret family estate tucked away among the sea islands of South Carolina.

Louis is soon befriended by his two new neighbors and learns his new home is nothing like his old one in upstate New York. But it's not just culture shock Louis is wrestling. The locals seem convinced the family mansion is haunted.

According to the local Gullah people, the manor is possessed by an insatiable spirit dubbed the Boo-hag. At the insistence of his new friends, Louis reluctantly seeks help from Auntie Caroline, an elderly member of the Gullah community revered to an almost supernatural status, and with good reason.

Is she the only person who can help save Louis and Ruby from the Boo-hag?

AUTHOR OF DARKNESS THERE BUT SOMETHING MORE
CASSANDRA O'SULLIVAN SACHAR
LAKE OF SECRETS

LAKE OF SECRETS
BY CASSANDRA O'SULLIVAN SACHAR

*Seventeen-year-old Callie Quinn's vacation is off to a terrible start. Her parents have forced her to spend the summer before her s
enior year of high school with an elderly aunt in Deerville, Pennsylvania, where there's nothing to do but watch old Westerns on TV and read the classics.*

But soon, a mystery catches Callie's attention: the drowning suicide of a pregnant teen during the 1940s. Haunted by dreams of the girl, it doesn't take much digging before Callie realizes that the story isn't what it appears to be. Why would a teen bent on suicide make a blanket for a baby who wouldn't survive?

For help, she turns to her only friend in Deerville, another outsider named Brian. Little by little, he and Callie get closer to the mystery of the girl's death, following a path that leads them deep into the prejudices of the 1940s. They also become closer with each other.

As Callie begins to open up about her past to Brian, she is forced to face hard truths—not only about a murderer who has been hiding in plain sight, but also the turbulent personal events that led to Callie's exile to Deerville in the first place.

HUSHED HORROR SERIES BOOK ONE
THE STILL
BELLA DEAN JOYNER

THE STILL
BY BELLA DEAN JOYNER

Lana Wellington and Derek Armary individually find themselves seeking fresh starts in Edelleen, Colorado, located along the calm banks of the South Platte River. But within the shadows of the town's historic mill, something evil stirs, something vengeful.

When the first dead body is discovered in the woods, followed by a second, Sheriff Curtis Haines believes he's on the trail of a serial killer. But by the time his own deputies begin to report sightings of a strange, robed figure, Haines remembers rumors of a decades-old murder and wonders if something more supernatural has fallen upon Edelleen.

With a failing marriage and small-town politics hampering his efforts, Haines leans heavily on the rest of the force and the citizens to find answers about what happened at the old mill all those years ago.

The creature crawling from the stagnant waters near the old mill has set its sights on Lana and Derek, who now must help Haines figure out who or what is responsible for calling it forth into Edelleen, and why.

But will they die trying?

A. A. PFAU

CREPUSCULAR

Don't trust
anybody...

CREPUSCULAR
BY A. A. PFAU

Thirteen-year-old Dylan Fisher and his classmates are returning to their sleepy coastal town after a week-long camp and an abnormal summer storm.

But before they even make it back into town, something stops them in the road.

Something hungry...

Knowing the bus is no longer safe, the teens attempt to make it back into town on foot, only to find everything deserted. Their loved ones are gone.

Or are they?

Don't trust anybody...

LUXURY APARTMENTS WORTH DYING OVER

THREE GARDEN
VILLAGE
LANCE REEDINGER

THREE GARDEN VILLAGE
BY LANCE REEDINGER

Three Garden Village. Luxury apartments, all the amenities, all the style. But the residents are leaving in body bags...

Zoe and the other employees at The Garden suspect something sinister is stalking the property, but local law enforcement and the complex's upper management simply attempt to explain the deaths away.

When the blood starts flowing over the once serene property, will anyone make it out alive?

Better lock your doors...